COACH "CATFISH" SMITH
AND HIS BOYS

Also by Glen Onley,
published by Sunstone Press

BEYOND CONTENTMENT

DISCOVER TREE

SUNSET

COACH "CATFISH" SMITH
AND HIS BOYS

A Novel Based on the Life of Coach Milburn "Catfish" Smith

by
Glen Onley

SUNSTONE
PRESS

SANTA FE

Cover art by Philip Tripp

Sunstone books may be purchased for educational, business, or sales
promotional use. For information please write: Special Markets Department,
Sunstone Press, P.O. Box 2321, Santa Fe, New Mexico 87504-2321.

Library of Congress Cataloging-in-Publication Data:

Onley, Glen, 1943–
   Coach "Catfish" Smith and his boys : the secret that drove him to
win / Glen Onley.
     p. cm.
   Includes index.
     ISBN 0-86534-424-8 (hardcover)
1. Smith, Milburn Albert—Fiction. 2. High school students—Fiction.
3. Football coaches—Fiction. 4. School sports—Fiction. 5. Teenage
boys—Fiction. 6. Texas—Fiction. I. Title.
PS3565.N65C63 2004
813'.6—dc22

               2004005337

Published in
SUNSTONE PRESS
POST OFFICE BOX 2321
SANTA FE, NM 87504-2321 / USA
(505) 988-4418 / *ORDERS ONLY* (800) 243-5644
FAX (505) 988-1025
WWW.SUNSTONEPRESS.COM

This story is dedicated to Coach "Catfish" Smith's former Mount Vernon, Texas players whose outstanding accomplishments, on and off the gridiron, inspired the writer to undertake this project. Especially, the writer seeks to pay tribute to a group of these men and their spouses who formed "Catfish Winners," an organization that honors their former coach by funding and awarding scholarships for deserving graduates of Mount Vernon High School. Through the year 2003, this organization has awarded forty-seven college scholarships.

FOREWORD

In the mid to late 1930s, with the nation still locked in the Great Depression, Waco and the Central Texas area got its main summer sports entertainment at the little playpen known as Katy Park. The old baseball park, which had been home to a Texas League franchise in the previous decade and to other Waco teams in other leagues for almost half a century, was located within a stone's throw of downtown Waco and was situated no more than 20 yards away from the Katy Railroad tracks. The main part of the grandstands ran alongside the first base line and on out toward right field. And the principal attraction at Katy Park in the good ol' summertime was the State Semi-Pro Baseball Tournament, which brought the best semi-pro teams to Waco to compete for the championship trophy, the scant money at stake, and the right to advance to the National Semi-Pro Tournament held annually in Wichita, Kansas.

To be a 10- or 12-year-old, to be all wrapped up in baseball, to get to go to Katy Park where the trains traveling on those nearby tracks often deafened the ears with their mighty warning blasts, to sit there and watch the best semi-pro baseball in the state played, ah, how close to heaven can a growing boy get?

And it was there that I first met Catfish Smith.

Understand, I didn't meet him in person. I watched him play, and I met him via the sports pages of the *Waco Tribune-Herald*, where sports editor Jinx Tucker almost always at tournament time gave plenty of space and ink to a tall catcher for the Mount Pleasant Cubs named Smith. Catfish Smith.

To be a player good enough to play in THE State Semi-Pro Baseball Tournament was compelling enough as far as I was concerned. And to have a nickname like Catfish, why, who could ask for anything more? As a youngster I was hooked.

Years later I finished high school at nearby La Vega and became a cub reporter at the *Tribune-Herald* even as I enrolled as a freshman at Baylor, and then I went off to World War II for three years. Then I came back home and got my college degree and eventually succeeded Jinx Tucker as sports editor of the *Trib* upon his death in December of 1953. And in 1959, when John Bridgers was named to replace Sam Boyd as Baylor's head football coach, lo and behold, in putting together his staff, Bridgers selected none other than Catfish Smith.

Yes, THE Catfish Smith.

He headed up Baylor's football recruiting and coached the freshman team and made his home on a street named Whipperwill. A Catfish on Whipperwill. I never did know if he picked out that street simply because of its name, but if he did, it wouldn't surprise me. Regardless, it was a combination you could hardly forget.

We always had a lot to talk about, Catfish and I, going back to old Katy Park and his baseball days there with the Mount Pleasant Cubs.

But even if there had been no Mount Pleasant Cubs in his background, we would have had plenty to talk about. Because Catfish was a talker.

"He had a wonderful sense of humor, and he was the best storyteller I've ever met," says J. R. Closs, himself a Baylor Bear going back to the late 1940s and later one of Catfish's closest friends both on and off the golf course.

Indeed, Catfish was a great storyteller and never at a loss for stories. At the end of the 1968 football season, Baylor decided to fire John Bridgers. He had been the Bears' head coach for 10 seasons, the team seemed to be losing ground, the alumni were unhappy, and since his contract had just run out, the decision was made not to renew it. A couple of days after that decision was announced, the city of Breckenridge opened the doors to a new attraction, the Texas High School Football Hall of Fame. One of Waco's greatest players, Boody Johnson, was among the first players to be enshrined. I was invited to attend the ceremony and say a few words about Boody, and I invited Catfish to make the drive to Breckenridge with me.

It was a very foggy evening and thus the drive to Breckenridge and back to Waco was a slow one. But Catfish had a fresh story for almost every mile. I remember it also was on that trip that he gave me at least three dozen reasons why John Bridgers should have been fired—and on the return trip to Waco he gave me fully as many reasons why Baylor should NOT have fired him.

That was Catfish, a man never at a loss for an opinion. But he also was a terrific coach who in his earlier years had been quite an athlete. But even more than that, he was a character. The *Readers*

Digest used to include in each issue a feature which carried the heading, "The Most Unforgettable Character I Ever Met." If I were going to compile a short list of the four or five most unforgettable characters I've ever met, Milburn Albert "Catfish" Smith would certainly be among them.

In 1979 Catfish Smith was enshrined in the Texas Sports Hall of Fame, that special Valhalla for the greatest sports heroes in this state's history, going back to the very first enshrinee, major league baseball's Tris Speaker, a native of Hubbard. I was a member of the selection committee that chose Catfish for induction; indeed, I made the motion that he be chosen, not because he was such an unforgettable character but because he belonged.

He was tall, lanky, outspoken, smart, athletic, and as quick witted as he could be. That he was an outstanding coach goes without saying. Indeed, the record says it all—a state basketball championship won at the tiny West Texas community of Carey which happened to be his very first coaching stop (and, mind you, that was in an era when all the high school basketball teams in Texas, regardless of classification, played to a single state championship); a super record in both football and basketball at Mount Vernon High School (59-8-3 record in football and 163-28 mark in basketball); a football winning streak at his alma mater of East Texas State that reached 29 games (it wasn't until Darrell Royal and his wishbone offense at the University of Texas won 30 games in a row that Smith's record in this state was broken); and a final three-year record of 30-2-1 at East Texas State.

Yes, the man could coach.

But he could do so much more—like coming up with the last word, and saying outrageous things, probably just to enjoy the shock value.

It was rather early in his married life, he once told me, that he and his wife, Dot, checked into a hotel in Wichita Falls so he could attend a coaching clinic that was taking place there. Some sort of PTA convention was also taking place in the city. One morning Catfish and Dot were riding down the hotel elevator, accompanied by five or six women who were there for the PTA convention. As the elevator neared the ground floor, Catfish said to Dot in a voice that everyone in the elevator had to hear: "I'll tell you one thing. We're either going to get married or we're going to quit coming to this hotel like this."

And then Catfish would laugh as he wound up the story: "You could just hear those eyeballs click."

Outrageous, yes. But he also liked to have the last word.

Shortly after his arrival at Baylor, the coaches were in a roundtable discussion about football strategy or tactics or some such, and the argument had become rather heated. When assistant coach Hayden Fry, fresh from a coaching stint at Odessa High School, insisted on his approach being the correct one, Catfish scornfully rebuked him.

"Hayden, as a coach you've never even won a precinct," he pointed out with a certain amount of emphasis.

Of course, Fry later became a head coach at SMU (a job Smith once turned down because, he later told me, athletic director Matty Bell was insisting he keep certain assistant coaches on his staff) and won a Southwest Conference championship, then went to North Texas and won gobs of games, and finally went to the University of Iowa and became a coaching icon in that state, putting together a coaching career that resulted in his enshrinement in the College Football Hall of Fame.

But he hadn't done all that winning when he took his place on Bridgers' staff at Baylor. In Catfish's eyes it probably wouldn't have mattered if he had.

Catfish also had the decisive word in a December incident I well recall. In 1961 a Baylor football team that was widely recognized before the season started as a strong Southwest Conference title contender rather quickly became a victim of key injuries and finished with only a 5-5 record. But that team featured such top-flight players as Ronnie Bull, Ronnie Goodwin, Ronnie Stanley, Herby Adkins, Bobby Ply and a third-string quarterback named Don Trull (two years later, Trull would lead the nation in passing and make first-team All-America), and the selection committee of a new bowl making its inaugural appearance on the football scene decided to invite the Baylor Bears to play in its game. That bowl was the Gotham Bowl in New York City. Baylor's opponent was Utah State, a team armed with the likes of future NFL great Merlin Olsen.

Baylor won the game, 24-9, in a contest played in freezing conditions at the old Polo Grounds. But the incident to which I referred occurred the previous evening. About a half dozen members of the official Baylor party were walking to a New York restaurant a few blocks from the team's headquarters hotel. Suddenly from the opposite side of the street came an old bum, approaching us to ask for a handout.

He never reached us. Catfish met him out in the street and waved him off with these words: "Man, get out of here. Can't you see I'm working this side of the street?"

He definitely knew how to make the most of a situation, especially when the odds were stacked against him. One season when he was coaching the Baylor freshmen, who were known as the Cubs (in that era, freshmen were ineligible to play on the varsity), he found himself with a team lacking in most of the talents that made for a good football team. Baylor's recruiting harvest the previous February had been rated mediocre at best. And the schedule called for the Cubs to open their season against the Texas Shorthorns, who were as long on pedigree as the Cubs were short. Darrell Royal's recruiters had just monopolized the blue-chippers at recruiting time. The Shorthorns, of course, were expected to overwhelm the Cubs.

"It will be the cow chips against the blue chips," Catfish wailed. And then his "cow chips" went out and won the game.

Another time, another place, another situation: late in the Bridgers' era, with Baylor's football fortunes in a deep decline, Catfish by then had become Baylor's chief fundraiser for athletics. It was a tough job. Old grads with money hated to see him coming. They would dodge him if they could. But Catfish knew how to foil them. He would take with him a young assistant, and as they approached the office of their target, Catfish would give instructions: "I'll go to the front door, and you go around back. That way, you'll catch him when he tries to duck out on us."

He was a hard man to duck out on, and as best I can remember, even in those grim years for the Bears, Catfish kept breaking the record for money raised annually for athletics. He did it with perseverance and determination, of which he had a full supply. He proved that in 1983. In April of that year he suffered a stroke, which left an arm and a leg paralyzed on his left side. At the hospital, the attending physician told his son, Jimmy, "He'll probably never use that left arm again."

Jimmy refused to accept the official word. "Oh, you don't know my daddy," he replied. "He's a competitor."

He was all of that, all right. He was squeezing a rubber ball with his left hand before he left the hospital, and it wasn't too long before he was back on the golf course, telling stories and making people laugh. He was truly an American Original, and on the following pages author Glen Onley will leave you convinced.

—Dave Campbell, Editor and Founder of *Texas Football*

PREFACE

This story is based on the lives of Coach "Catfish" Smith and "his boys," those young men who played football and basketball under his mentorship. Though the events and characters are based on real people and actual happenings, the author has through necessity created dialogue and detailed action for the sake of story flow and completeness. In doing so, the author has diligently strived for consistency with his knowledge of the personalities and events involved.

The characters and events in the story are based on information from many sources, including the Mount Vernon *Optic-Herald*, school yearbooks, *The Tiger's Tale*, various historical records, personal letters, and extensive interviews. Additional sources that might be of interest to readers are *A Walk Through Mt. Vernon* by B. F. Hicks and *Reflective Rays* by Ray Loyd Johnson.

In the story, the author has endeavored to capture the spirit and character of Milburn Albert "Catfish" Smith, his love for his players, his dedication to excellence, his driving desire to win, and through it all, his eternal hope to prepare "his boys" for the challenges of life, especially during the tumultuous times of World War II.

As you meet this unique and colorful man through the pages of this book, I believe you will agree that his story, and that of his players, must be told.

—Glen Onley
Greenville, Texas
April, 2004

ACKNOWLEDGEMENTS

Those who have contributed to the writing of this story are too many to list here; however, the efforts and assistance of some must be herein recognized.

The Franklin County Historical Association made available to the author microfilm copies of all available issues of the 1943-1950 *Optic-Herald*, as well as a workspace for reviewing the newspapers. B. F. Hicks and Pam Thompson were instrumental in providing access to this invaluable resource, while Jean Smith provided assistance and encouragement throughout the months the author scanned and extracted information from the news stories.

The Franklin County Public Library assisted in the discovery of pertinent documents and provided a workspace, while library employees Sue Stevens and Martha Slaughter, along with Glen Slaughter, loaned 1947 and 1950 yearbooks to the author.

Charles Lowry, head of the "Catfish Winners" organization and former player, provided pictures, personal documents, and insightful comments regarding the coach, players, and the town. Charles, a member of the 1947-48 "team of destiny," read and critiqued a major portion of the manuscript and, with his wife Peggy, provided unfailing support and encouragement throughout the process.

Herb Zimmerman, another member of that 1947-48 team, as well as my high school football coach, shared his experiences and memories based on an intimate relationship with Catfish. During his own coaching days, Herb often consulted his former mentor, and later coached with him at Baylor University. His comments after reading much of the manuscript were especially helpful.

H. B. Zimmerman, older brother of Herb, shared his experiences as a communications specialist deployed in the war against Japan, first at Bougainville and then as a member of the invasion force at Cebu. A much-decorated soldier, his memories, descriptions, and emotions radiate with authenticity and realism as only a participant's could.

14

Glenn Pierce, quarterback of the undefeated 1944 football team and guard on the 1945 State Finalist basketball squad, spent hours on the phone with the author, days reading the early chapters of the manuscript, and volunteered both his memories and his 1944-45 yearbook. Through the experience, the author gained not only invaluable insight, but also a treasured friend.

Maurice "Bud" Campbell, an All-State guard on the 1948 State Championship basketball team, provided personal records and copies of *Austin Statesman* articles covering the state tournament in Austin. Additionally, Bud shared memories and the unique perspective of a player who transferred to Mount Vernon High School, hoping for the opportunity to play on a championship team.

Dewey, Dale, and Johnny Moore provided the unique view of three brothers, all outstanding athletes, whose playing days spanned most of Catfish's years at Mount Vernon. Martha Moore, wife of Dewey, shared her unique view as a fan, student, band member, and majorette.

Gerald Skidmore, a two-sport athlete, not only lent his player perspective, but also a journalistic touch as creator and editor, along with Mildred Scheirman, of the high school newspaper, *The Tiger's Tale*. Written by students and copies provided by Gerald, Martha Moore, and Charles Lowry, this publication yielded an insider's view of school activities and events. Additionally, Gerald read the manuscript and shared thoughtful suggestions.

Gayle Tinsley, All-District guard on the 1947 undefeated football team, shared his football experiences, along with his recollection of a one-of-a-kind track event, the school's disciplinary process, and a view of family life beyond sports and school.

Dudley Miller, tri-captain of the 1950 squad, shared his scrapbook, stories, and described his role in stepping in to replace the injured starting center at a crucial juncture in the 1947 team's run for an undefeated Regional Championship.

Billy Ingram, reserve basketball player on the 1945 State Finalist team, provided team pictures with names and descriptions, and the distinctive viewpoint of a support-role player.

And I must thank Jimmy Smith, Catfish's son, and Nell Smith, the coach's wife, for their support and enthusiasm for the recording of this story. In addition to their encouragement they shared poignant stories that only family members could.

Last, I must thank all those contributors not named above, but who collectively added in a substantial way. Also, I must express appreciation to my wife Phyllis and to John and Debbie Boose, who read and edited the manuscript, offering insightful suggestions.

Without those listed above, there would be no story, and without the sharing of their memories, documents, pictures, and sentiments, there would be no book. So, with enormous gratitude, I acknowledge the contributions of each and every one of them.

1

May 10, 1943

"Get the patient off that stretcher and onto a gurney, pronto," the doctor barked as he hurried across the emergency room, his open white smock billowing behind him. "Nurse, bring a blood-pressure cuff."

Two hospital aides grabbed a gurney pushed against the wall and then headed toward the two army medics and a pair of airmen holding a green canvas stretcher sagging beneath the weight of one of their comrades.

"What have we got here?" the doctor asked sharply, grabbing the cuff from the nurse and checking the patient's pulse.

"He passed out at about twenty thousand feet," replied an army airman, staring down at his unconscious friend whose feet dangled over the end of the stretcher. "He's an airplane mechanic," the bomber pilot continued as the doctor strapped on the blood-pressure cuff. "Makes test flights with us when we're having a problem or checking out repairs. Flying has never bothered him before."

"Did you notice anything unusual before he lost consciousness?" the doctor asked, pumping the cuff. "Did he say anything?"

"Looked a little pale when he boarded this morning," the second airman said. "He usually bounces around like a lopsided ball, kiddin' everybody, and cuttin' up. Not this morning."

"Did he complain about feeling sick?" the doctor asked with a steady eye on the blood pressure meter.

"No. We were all busy when I heard a noise, turned, and saw him double over and hit the deck," the airman replied.

"Did he hit his head when he fell?" the doctor asked, scanning for marks along the patient's hairline and then shining a light beam into his right eye.

"Don't know for sure, but I think he was out when he fell."

"Notice anything else, anything unusual?" the doctor asked crisply.

"Back at the barracks, I've noticed him holding his hand against his stomach, and sorta hunching over," the pilot replied. "I think he has lots of stomachaches."

"And he drinks milk all the time," the second airman added.

"Nurse," the doctor said, "get one hundred twenty milligrams of sodium Phenobarbital into him. Then type his blood and prepare him for a slow-drip transfusion."

"What's the matter with him, Doc?" the pilot asked, frowning.

"I think this boy . . ." the doctor said, and then glanced down at the name patch sewn on the breast of the blue jumpsuit. "Milburn Smith has a bleeding ulcer."

"The tag says Milburn," the pilot explained, "but we all call him 'Catfish.'"

"Doc, can you fix him up?" the second airman asked.

"We'll try. He's lost some blood, maybe enough to produce unconsciousness. Also, perforated ulcers bring on severe pain and often induce shock," the doctor explained.

"Perforated ulcers?" the airman questioned.

"That's when an ulcer has progressed to the point where it has eaten a hole through the lining of the stomach," the doctor replied.

For a moment the airmen hesitated as if their minds were somehow suspended, their jaws slack and eyes locked.

"What'll you do to fix that?" the pilot finally asked.

"We'll stop the bleeding, get some antacid into his stomach, and try to slow down the production of otherwise normal gastric acids that irritate ulcers. We might have to operate. In any case, I expect he'll come around," the doctor said, motioning the aides to wheel the patient to a nearby examination room. "You boys stop back by the nurse's desk and take care of the paperwork for him, then you're free to go."

"Can't you wake him up, Doc?" the pilot asked, his eyes following his comrade. "I hate to leave him while he's laid out like he's . . ."

"I could, but he's in no danger right now," the doctor replied. "Besides, if you knew how bad a perforated ulcer hurts, you'd know he's a lot more comfortable passed out."

"Doc, don't let anything happen to him," the airman said. "He's the most important guy on our team."

"I'm sure the Air Corps has other good mechanics who can fill in until we can get this one patched up," the doctor said, forcing a smile.

"Not that team, Doc. Catfish is the best player on our basketball team. Why, sometimes he scores more points than all the opposing players put together."

"You'll have to get by without him for a while, boys. Quite a while, I expect."

Slowly the airmen headed for the nurse's desk, glancing back as two medical aides at McCaw General in Walla Walla, Washington, disappeared with their friend.

* * *

Catfish raised his head from the pillow and managed a weak salute as the uniformed man, the medical corps commanding officer, crossed the hospital room to his bedside.

"At ease," the colonel said. "I'm Dr. Miller."

"Nice to meet you, sir," Catfish replied. "Hope you've come to get me out of here, sir. I don't know what the hospital doctor told you, but I'm ready to get back to work."

"Let's talk about that," Colonel A. C. Miller said, stuffing his hands in his pockets.

"Oh, I'm plenty ready," Catfish assured him. "Two weeks in this place is like an eternity. I've got to get back to work."

"You're getting out, all right," Dr. Miller said in a tone that indicated there was more. "They've done about all they can for you here. The rest is up to you."

"I know," Catfish said, nodding his head, "that bland diet, sir. Maybe you can write something for me, spelling out the chow the Army's gotta feed me. Be sure and include . . ."

"Milburn," the colonel interrupted, pulling some papers from the inside pocket of his coat, "the military won't be feeding you much longer."

Catfish pushed upright in the bed, grimacing with the effort and his eyes wide, as though he were staring at a ghost.

"That's what I'm here to tell you," Dr. Miller continued. "I've prepared a medical discharge for you."

"But sir," Catfish said. "I've been in less than a year. The war, sir; it's not near over."

"For you, it is," the colonel replied, "at least as a member of the Army Air Forces."

"Sir," Catfish said, working his long legs over the side of the bed and pushing his weakened body upright, "I'm an airplane mechanic, a mighty good one. Those boys flying our bombers depend on me. I can't let them down, sir."

"You almost did exactly that," Dr. Miller said, "when you passed out up there. Can't you see that you're a sick man? Now, let's talk about your health."

"I'm a little weak, sir, but I'll get my strength back once I'm on my feet again. I'll eat . . ."

"Milburn," the doctor said, pushing an open right palm at Catfish like a stop sign, "sit down."

Catfish hesitated, his eyes wide and defiant, but his body lacked the strength to respond to his fiery spirit. Slowly, he slumped down on the side of the bed.

"I know you feel better right now," the doctor continued, "but those ulcers are still there in your stomach. Yes, the bleeding has stopped for now, but that ulcer could rupture again, and you might not be so lucky next time. It's a problem you'll likely have, off and on, the rest of your life. And, it'll be a short life if you don't eat right and take care of yourself."

"Sir, our boys, fighting the Germans in Europe and the Japanese in the Far Pacific, are dying every day. My chances, sir, fighting ulcers, are better than theirs."

"Milburn, in your condition, it's likely you'd never live long enough to face the enemy. Besides, it's done, the decision and the paperwork," Colonel Miller said, then released a deep sigh. "Now you sign these forms and drop by my office Monday morning about nine."

"Sir," Catfish protested, rising to his feet again.

"Private, that's an order," the colonel said sharply, pulling out a pen and slapping it down on the papers spread on the tray table beside the bed.

Slump-shouldered, Catfish took the pen, searched for the X and scribbled his name. Colonel Miller, having gathered up the pen and papers, headed for the door where he stopped and half turned toward Catfish.

"The attending physician noticed a scar on your abdomen from a prior incision," Miller said. "You knew you had ulcers when you enlisted. How did you pass the physical?"

"Had my appendix removed a couple years back," Catfish said, looking down.

"Yeah, and that scar is low on the right side," the colonel replied. "I'm talking about one higher on the left side."

"Gall bladder."

"Maybe you talked some doctor into saying that, but you've had a prior ulcer operation, right?"

"Worley Hospital in Pampa," Catfish said, nodding. "Took three doctors before I found one who'd sign off on my physical."

"I'm sorry, young man," Miller said, looking into the watery eyes of the tall airman. "I truly am."

*   *   *

"Specialist Milburn Albert Smith, ma'am," the towering Army airman said to the secretary at the desk. "Upon his order, I'm here to see Colonel Miller."

"I'll show you in," the thin, gray-haired woman said.

Inside, Catfish snapped to attention. "Specialist Milburn . . ."

"Have a seat, young man," Dr. Miller said, motioning to an army-issue, straight-back chair.

"With your permission, I'd rather stand, sir," the airman said, his face grim. "Will this take long, sir?"

With shoulders sagging, the doctor rose from his chair, picked up papers from his desk, and glanced out the window.

"You've got time, so relax and have a seat," Miller repeated with his tone softening. He slipped on his glasses. "I've done some checking."

"Yes, sir," Catfish replied, remaining upright and staring straight ahead with his gaze fixed on a calendar hanging on the plaster wall behind the desk. His eyes focused on Monday, May 24. Eighteen more days, he thought, and I would've made it a full year.

"You have an interesting past," the colonel said, ambling toward the window, and then turned and looked back. "You coached down in Texas, I believe."

Catfish did not respond.

"I'm told your basketball team captured fourth place in the state tournament your first year of coaching, then the state championship in your second," the colonel continued. "Not many coaches accomplish that in a lifetime. But the most remarkable thing about it, I am told, is that you did it competing against the largest schools in the state, Dallas, Fort Worth, Houston, while your school in Carey was one of the smallest."

The colonel looked up from the paper, eyeing the tall, lean airman, who stood rigidly, his eyes locked on the calendar.

"Milburn, I'm fascinated by this. A school administrator down there told me that your team was just a bunch of boys you rounded up off area farms. Son, how did you win over schools like Fort Worth Poly, and Crozier Tech?"

"Those Carey boys were hard workers, sir, and they were talented. I just polished them a little, here and there."

"How old were you at the time?"

"Twenty-three, sir."

"That young," the doctor said, and then paused. "And what inspired you to get into coaching?"

"General Robert Neyland, sir."

"You know the general?"

"No, sir, but my father does. Out of college, I wanted to play basketball for the Henrys of Wichita, Kansas, but when those Carey folks called in the summer of 1935, my father suggested that I call General Neyland. He was the football coach at the University of Tennessee at the time."

"What did the general say that convinced you?" the colonel asked, smiling.

"He said I should give it a try, if I had the courage to properly discipline my players, sir. He stressed that that meant every player on the team, including my best ones, no exceptions. And, sir, he said, 'Demand excellence in everything.' I took his advice."

"That would be General Neyland, all right," the colonel said. "I guess about everybody has heard about his seven maxims of football, but it's discipline and excellence, over and over like a drum beat, that define the general."

"Sir, would you please reconsider my discharge? The Army's spent a lot training me. And my record, sir; I think you will find . . ."

"Look, Milburn, there are some who would be delighted to get a medical discharge, so I admire your desire to continue your duties in the AAF. However, I think you can help your country in another way.

"Obviously, you have a special talent for leading young men, young athletes. For example, I contacted C. W. Brown, your school superintendent at Carey, and he said, 'Catfish worked those boys like a drill sergeant, and yet those young men would've followed him right over the edge of the Grand Canyon.'

"The armed services need leaders who follow Neyland's philosophy of discipline and excellence, men who take responsibility and respect leadership. We need young men who have conditioned their bodies and minds to endure hardships and to take challenges, always refusing to give up."

The colonel pushed away from the windowsill and walked over to Catfish.

"Milburn, we need you back in Texas developing future soldiers the General Neyland way. Hopefully, this war will be over soon, but until it is, we need you preparing young men to do their part."

The colonel grabbed a folder from his desk and shoved it toward Catfish who grasped it without varying his stare.

"Is that all, sir?"

"Good luck, Coach," the doctor replied, extending his hand.

Taking a step forward, Catfish shook the colonel's hand, then spun on his heels and left the office. The secretary glanced up as he passed, noticed his momentary hesitation, and acknowledged his slight nod toward her. She also saw the watery shine in his eyes.

2

May 28, 1943

The Cotton Belt train's shrill whistle screamed into late Friday morning's lazy warmth. Milburn "Catfish" Smith peered out the window at the flat-board sign that read, "WINFIELD." Slowly the clattering iron giant screeched to a stop, steam spewing from its brake system and steel boxcar connectors clanging in chain reaction. The tall airman-turned-civilian stood, grabbed his only bag, and headed for the exit.

There on the wooden depot platform stood his father, Sam, with two hundred fifty pounds of brawn evenly distributed over a six-foot-five-inch frame. The younger Smith had thought long about what he would say to this man he adored, an ex-sheriff of Titus County. His father had no time for a quitter, and right then the son felt like the worst possible kind.

With bag in hand, Catfish walked briskly toward the weathered building sitting just north of the tracks. Sam removed his hat and extended a hand. At six-foot-four, the son still felt like a little boy beside his father.

"How are you feeling, Milburn?" Sam asked.

"Fine, just fine, Dad."

"That's good. We've been worried, especially your mother. She's waiting inside."

They stepped through the open door, and immediately the graying woman spotted her son. Rising from the bench, she hurried toward him, arms open, tears trickling down her face.

"Milburn, Milburn," she called out. "I'm so glad you're home. How are you? Let me look at you." Holding her son at arm's length, she looked him over. "Why, you've lost weight, but we'll take care of that soon enough."

"I'm fine, Mom, but the doctor has me on this diet. He says . . ."

"Oh, don't worry yourself about that. I know how to feed my boy," his mother replied, hugging him again.

The train chugged away as they settled into the car and headed north on Cleveland Street, his mother sitting quietly in the passenger seat. Sam glanced into the rearview mirror, catching a glimpse of his somber son in the backseat, wistfully watching the cottage-like homes slip by.

"Is it a furlough, son?" the father asked.

Catfish took a deep breath, exhaling slowly. "Dad I'm out of the Army. I won't be going back."

There was a long, uncomfortable silence.

"They discharged me, Dad. This doctor, Colonel Miller, says I'm not physically fit to serve."

"Why, a little sickness don't keep a man out of the Army, son. In no time, you'll be fit again. Didn't you tell him you're an athlete, have been all your life?"

"That doesn't matter, Dad. I passed out while on duty, while in flight. Colonel Miller says if that should happen again, it could jeopardize an entire bomber crew, the plane, and the mission."

"Well, this war isn't over by a long shot. When you're better, we'll get another opinion. I expect they'll take you back."

"On the discharge papers, it says I'm not eligible for reenlistment. Dad, they won't accept me back."

Sam turned one block east, and after a lengthy silence, he asked what his son planned to do.

"I don't know," Catfish replied. "Colonel Miller suggested I get back into coaching, but I just can't get enthused about that. I'm a trained airplane mechanic. Maybe I can find work in that field."

"Milburn, the closest we come to an airplane in these parts is when one occasionally flies over."

"But it's not far to Dallas, and I know some fellows at the airfield at Wichita Falls. As soon as I get back to full strength, I'll do some checking."

Weeks passed and Catfish hardly got out of sight of the house. Then one day he rummaged through a closet until he came up with an old deflated basketball, headed south to the old home place, and pitched the ball through a hoop his father had long ago strapped to a huge oak just west of the house. When Milburn had been a youngster attending the Winfield school, his father had attached a barrel ring to the old tree, and Catfish, owning no basketball back then, had made do with an empty can.

Tiring of shooting hoops, he sat down on an old stump, the tree having long since been cut down for firewood. Looking at the old house and its surroundings, his mind wandered back to his youthful years when it seemed everything had gone so well for him.

*　　*　　*

Inspired by a local amateur basketball team, the Doris Candy Kids, Milburn had developed a love for basketball at an early age. With local fans packing the gymnasium for every contest, young Milburn had joined those at courtside with his eyes alert and his competitive spirit soaring.

Energetic, athletic, and taller than his classmates, Milburn then tried out for the local school team and instantly became its star player. When his father was elected sheriff of Titus County in November of 1928, the family moved to Mount Pleasant, the county seat, where living quarters were provided on the first floor of the jail, but Milburn stayed with friends in Winfield to complete that school year. Then in the fall of 1929 he attended Mount Pleasant High School where they had a football team. Instantly, he loved the game and found that as a pass receiver his basketball skills came in handy. His teammates quickly learned that Milburn not only had good hands, but he was tough, physically and mentally. The fall of 1930 found him enrolling at East Texas State Teachers College in Commerce, and that is where he got the nickname that was to become synonymous with his success in athletics.

"Young man," a Dallas sportswriter asked seventeen-year-old Milburn Albert Smith, a raw recruit on the college football team, "you gonna be another 'Catfish' Smith?"

Milburn had heard about a distant cousin, Vernon Smith, who was an All-American end at the University of Georgia and had picked up the unusual nickname.

"By the time I'm finished here, I'll make Cousin 'Catfish' look like a tadpole," the brash freshman replied.

Those who heard the cocky remark got a good laugh, but no one thought much more about it. However, four years later no one knew him as Milburn, but all one had to do around campus was mention "Catfish," and everyone knew who was being referenced. He had earned four letters in both football and basketball, had been twice selected All-Lone Star Conference in both sports and named to several Little All-America teams in basketball. "Catfish" stories abounded throughout the school and conference.

Then after graduation, while fishing at his brother Alfred's camp on Caddo Lake, he received a phone call from C. W. Brown, school Superintendent at Carey, Texas. Catfish had never heard of the place, but he soon learned that Carey was a tiny West Texas town just west of Childress, surrounded by a farming community of maybe a couple hundred people. Catfish had not intended to coach, but C. W. and his wife Silvia Boze, who had been a great college basketball player at East Texas State in 1924 to 1926, were a couple of Milburn's old college schoolmates, and he could not offhandedly turn them down.

Catfish then called General Neyland, coach at the University of Tennessee, and the ensuing conversation and advice would stick with and guide young Milburn throughout his coaching career.

Still undecided, Catfish had made the trip west to Carey where he visited with his friends, including Raymond Mattingly, a Winfield native coaching at nearby Bowie. After spending two days among the area's hard-working people, Catfish was thoroughly impressed. Also, maybe the challenge was just what he needed at the time. "Carey has never won anything," Superintendent Brown explained. The entire school system had less than a hundred students and no football team. Then came the clincher.

"We don't really have a gymnasium," Brown explained, with a nervous laugh. "But we've put up a couple of baskets on the stage in the auditorium."

Regardless, Catfish signed the contract so eagerly pushed in front of him.

Early that first season, 1936, his Cardinal basketball team played a tournament in Tell, where they won a couple of contests and found themselves in the championship game. They lost, but the players showed little disappointment. In the dressing room they were congratulating each other on their second-place finish when their coach walked in, the runner-up trophy clenched in his hand. When the players saw his grim face, their chatter hushed like a spigot slammed shut.

Catfish suddenly hurled the sparkling trophy against the cinder-block wall, shattering it into tiny pieces. Then for a moment that must have seemed like an eternity to his terrified players, he glared at them.

"I'm not starting our trophy case with a loser's trophy," he growled.

"Anybody can come in second. It takes a champion to win, and if you're not committed to becoming a champion, not willing to pay the price it takes to be a champion, then get out of this room right now."

No one moved.

"Okay, then get ready to work harder than you've ever worked in your entire life," he warned them. "The next tournament we play in, we're not leaving until they give us the championship trophy."

That team then went on a twenty-six-game winning streak and closed that remarkable season with forty wins against only eight losses. One of those victories was in the state tournament in Austin over a Crozier Tech team coached by the famous Doc Hayes, later to be the basketball mentor at Southern Methodist University. Those 1936 Carey Cardinals proved to be the fourth best team in the state, losing the semifinal contest to Cushing.

Later, when questioned about the trophy-smashing incident, the coach explained that he was not upset over the loss. "But those boys were happy with second place, and I'll never coach a team that's satisfied with anything less than winning."

Then in 1937, with Middleton, Foust, Redwine, Hunt, and Gresham forming the nucleus of his team, Catfish had led his Carey Cardinals to a 50-2 season and the state championship, defeating teams from Dublin, Fort Worth Poly, and then Gober in the finals, 26-18. Twenty-three-year-old Catfish Smith and his squad of country boys returned to Carey and added the Texas Schoolboy Basketball State Championship trophy to their fast-growing collection.

*   *   *

From those lofty heights, Catfish now sat on an old oak stump in Winfield, Texas, feeling rejected by his country's military from doing his part in its struggle to prevail in the greatest conflict in the history of the modern world, against the most fearsome enemies imaginable. His life was a shambles, and he had no idea how to put it back together.

3

June 20, 1943

On a Sunday afternoon, Catfish eased out the door of the Smith home and ambled across the covered porch that spanned the front of the rambling house and wrapped around the south side. With the sun flush on his face, he sat down on the outer edge with his long legs dangling over the side, slowly swinging forward and back. His strength had returned, and he was bored.

Spotting a shiny can a passerby had thrown on the side of the road, he slipped down and headed for it. He had only taken three steps when the toe of his right shoe struck a rock, ripping it free from the hot sand. Picking up the rusty-red stone, he eyed the can, which sparkled like a silver treasure in the sunlight. Assuming a pitcher's stance, he stepped forward with his left foot, arched his back, and hurled the stone. When it hit, the can jumped five feet into the air, then crashed onto the gravel-sprinkled road, spinning like a windmill blade in a storm.

"Good shot," someone called out from behind.

Turning, Catfish spotted his father standing on the porch, the crown of his straw hat within an inch of the overhanging roof. He was smiling.

A grown man caught playing a kid's game, an embarrassed Catfish stepped onto the road, picked up the can, and sauntered back toward the house.

"You ought to go down to the ball field and join in the baseball game," Sam said, motioning toward the open lot behind the school that sat a hundred fifty yards south of the house. "That Attaway boy, what's his name?"

"Eldon," Catfish said, turning away from the ball diamond.

"Yeah, well I saw him the other day up at the feed store. He asked about you. Said they play a little ball most every Sunday afternoon.

Sometimes they have a team over from Mount Vernon, Farmers Academy, or Hopewell. They'd like to have you join them."

"I reckon not," Catfish said, eying the dent in the can. "I don't even know where my ball glove is anymore."

"I do," Sam said, pulling it from behind his back and tossing it to his son.

Catfish reflexively dropped the can and caught the glove, and then shook his head. Slowly, he made his way over and took a seat on the edge of the porch, staring down at the old mitt.

"Ashamed, aren't you," his father said. "Worried that somebody'll think you're a slacker, that you somehow weaseled your way out of the Army."

"You hear somebody say that?" Catfish asked, springing to his feet, his eyes wide and glaring.

"No, Milburn. And neither will you," his father said, stepping down off the porch and facing his son. "Folks around here know you. They're your friends, and it's time you started acting like you've got nothing to be ashamed of. It's time you returned their friendship."

His father turned, climbed the steps, and disappeared inside.

For a moment, Catfish stood there, staring at the old screen door and into the darkness beyond. Then he headed toward the ball diamond, his pace slow and his demeanor lackadaisical.

As he approached the field, a game was in progress. A few spectators sat on the fenders of their old black Fords and Chevys parked well behind the chicken-wire backstop. Catfish hung back near a triangle of oaks, undecided. Slowly he scanned the faces. There was Eldon Attaway, Doyle Whitt, Frank Stinson, and Harvey Banks, once classmates but young men now. And Mabel Killingsworth stood leaning against a big elm that shaded a trio of cars, her once-girlish figure now filled out. Recalling a school picture where she had stood profiled, her chin turned to her left shoulder and her hand propped on her hip, he wondered if she was married. Probably, he guessed. Another woman sat in the passenger side of a black Ford, the door open and her legs dangling free. Mildred Black, Catfish thought.

Watching the game, he quickly saw that the Winfield boys were on the short end of the score, and unlikely to make a comeback. He thought he recognized one of the opposing players as a fellow from Monticello. Catfish slowly eased over toward the third base side of the field.

"Milburn," Attaway called out from second base. "Come take my place."

"Either call timeout or play ball," the umpire yelled from behind home plate.

"Substitution," Troy Steward hollered as he left the pitcher's circle. "Milburn, come chunk this thing for a while. You bat third when you get these guys out."

Catching the ball tossed to him, Catfish felt awkward making his way to the wobbly board that served as the pitching rubber. There was no mound, just a rough dirt area where the grass had been worn away. Regardless, Catfish's height and long arms made for a considerable pitching advantage.

After Catfish had completed three warm-up tosses, the hitter stepped into the batter's box. From watching earlier, Catfish knew there were no outs. Toeing the board, he rotated the ball in his hand, feeling the frayed seams, and checked the bases. Runners eased away from both second and third. If I walk this first one, he thought, at least it won't force in a run.

He chose to take a full windup since the only base that could be stolen was home, and that's where he was throwing the ball. He rocked and fired, releasing the ball from about two and a half feet above his head.

"Ball three!" the umpire yelled, as the batter hit the dirt, avoiding a high inside fastball.

"Any strikes on him?" Catfish questioned, realizing he had not asked for the count on the batter.

The umpire shook his head.

Eyeing Catfish, the hitter brushed at dust on his pants and eased back in the batter's box. If it had been properly marked, his front foot would have been outside the chalk line, headed in the direction of the third-base-side dugout.

Catfish rocked again, and let it go.

Pop! Dust flew from the catcher's mitt.

"Strike one!" the ump bellowed, shooting his right hand into the air.

That felt good, Catfish thought. This batter's not going to swing, so I'm just going to throw another one right down the pike.

"Strike two!" the umpire called.

The batter stepped out and met his coach who put his arm around the fellow's shoulders and whispered something. The hitter nodded, took a practice swing, and stepped back in the box.

On the next pitch, the batter squared to bunt, but the pitch was too low and fast for him to get his bat on the ball.

"Ball four!" the umpire called out.

"Wait a minute," Catfish hollered, striding toward home plate. "He tried to bunt the ball. That's strike three."

"The pitch was too low," the umpire yelled back.

Catfish turned toward the umpire who was calling bases. "Tell him. The batter tried to hit the ball. That's a strike, no matter if the pitch was low."

The base umpire nodded his agreement. After some hesitation, the umpire behind the plate yelled, "Batter's out. Next hitter, get in the box."

One out, Catfish thought. Somehow I've got to get two more without allowing a run.

A tall hefty fellow stepped into the box, taking a wide stance and crowding home plate. Scowling, he wagged his bat back and forth twice and then pointed the barrel end at Catfish.

Catfish guessed he was Monticello's slugger, and no doubt he had taken note of the fastballs thrown to the previous hitter. The big fellow would be wound as tight as a fiddle string.

Catfish took an exaggerated windup, rocked, and hurled the ball toward home plate. The hitter's eyes bulged as he took a wicked cut, well before the deceptively slow pitch arrived.

Then Catfish started the next pitch at the batter's head, causing him to lean back on his heels. When the ball broke across and down, the big slugger realized it was going to be a strike. Off balance, he made a weak swing and just tapped the ball back toward the pitcher's mound. Catfish grabbed it, checked the runner at third, and then tossed to first. Two outs.

For the next batter, Catfish reverted to his fastball and struck the fellow out on four pitches. He smiled as his fellow players congratulated him as they headed in for their turn at bat. Competing again felt good.

"I heard you played a little ball out in West Texas," Attaway said as they gathered at the edge of the backstop.

"I played for Pampa in the West Texas and New Mexico league," Catfish replied. "But I didn't pitch. Catcher has always been my best position."

"Stiff competition out there?"

"They've got some ballplayers out west, and most of the fields are open, no fence to knock the ball over. I learned to hit line drives and run the bases."

"How come you to quit?"

Catfish hesitated. "I ended up in Worley Hospital."

"Ulcers again?"

"Yeah, and I'd had my appendix removed a short time earlier. Seems like I've spent most of my life in hospitals."

"That why you came home and coached basketball before you went off to the Army?"

"Came back to get well," Catfish replied. "But when Coach Fox left at mid-year, I agreed to help out."

"Yeah, and Winfield didn't lose a game after you started coaching," Attaway said, patting Catfish on the back.

"We're sure glad to have you around, Milburn," another said. "Maybe you'll stay this time."

Catfish smiled weakly. "Thanks."

With a screaming line drive over the pitcher's head, he drove in a run, but the inning ended with him stranded on third base.

Back on the mound, he shut down Monticello's scoring and got another hit that helped close the gap in the score, but Winfield still came up two runs short.

As players were gathering up their gloves and bats, and the locals were congratulating the victorious visitors and heading for their cars, Catfish spotted an old friend over by the same trio of trees he had stood under.

"Hello, Charley," Catfish said, hurrying over and extending his hand. Charley Grady was a black man he had grown up with out on the southern edge of town.

"Milburn, it's been a long time," Charley replied, smiling broadly.

"What're you doing now?" Catfish asked.

"Mechanic," Charley replied. "I spent so much time workin' on old cars when we were kids, it just comes natural."

"How about that," Catfish said. "I'm a bit of a mechanic myself. Worked on Uncle Sam's airplanes."

"I'd be scared to death to be around one of those things. I expect a man would have to climb up on something just to reach the motor."

"Scaffolds," Catfish said. "They use these contraptions with wheels so you just roll them around."

"You'd never get me up on somethin' like that. I like fixin' things, but with my feet on the ground or crawled up under an old car."

"Charley, you were always a good hand with tools, especially working on cars, but to get ahead you need to open your own garage."

Charley laughed. "Milburn, I don't have no money."

"Why, the bank would loan it to you. Everybody around here would bring their old broken-down cars to you, and you'd get that loan paid back in no time at all."

"Milburn, no bank man is gonna loan me that much money."

"How much do you need?"

"Oh, I don't know. I've never planned on such a thing."

"Well, think about it," Catfish said.

Together they walked along the road that went south across the railroad tracks, recalling childhood pranks and Charley catching up on Catfish's travels. They split ways just south of town, Charley going east and Catfish continuing south.

Following a country road, Catfish came to the old Smith estate, long since sold. He swung his long legs over the three-wire fence and headed for a grove of trees. Past the line of oaks, he climbed a mound and stood on its flat top, gazing southward toward a densely treed lowland split by a creek a mile to the south. With the sun sinking below the western horizon, a blue haze hung over the treetops, painting a picture of a more primitive time. Taking in the solitude, he eased to the ground and sat cross-legged.

As a small boy he had played for hours on the old Indian mound, imagining what it and its people must have been like a century earlier. For him it became a private place, one for hours of undisturbed thought, and now he needed to think more clearly than ever.

The competition of the game had renewed his fighting spirit, and the encouragement of his friends had rekindled a fire that disappointment and physical ailment had reduced to dormant coals. He had always been miserable on the sidelines. The world was like a raging river, and he had to jump in and help tame the torrent or drown trying. Determined, he stood and headed home in the cool of dusk, a plan formulated.

The next morning, Catfish sat down and wrote a letter to Lieutenant A. J. Shields, supervisor of airplane mechanics at Sheppard Air Field in Wichita Falls, Texas. He requested his friend's aid in getting back into the service of the AAF.

After mailing the letter, Catfish searched the streets of Winfield until he located an old vacant automobile garage. He found the owner next door, got him to open it up, and looked inside.

"Whose equipment?" Catfish asked, seeing a toolbox full of wrenches, oil-stained fender pads, a couple of greasy jacks, and rusty ramp stands.

"My grandfather's stuff," the man said.

"That old stove still work?"

"I don't see why not," the man replied. "In fact, I fired it up last winter while I worked on my old pickup in here."

Catfish haggled out a price, including all the equipment.

"Now, show me the boundaries of the lot," Catfish said as they went back outside.

Satisfied that the old garage would be adequate, Catfish climbed into his faded green Pontiac and headed for Mount Pleasant. He knew a banker over there, and between his college years and that state championship at Carey, people had come to know him.

Late that afternoon, Catfish dropped by Charley Grady's house.

"Hello, Milburn," his friend greeted him, stepping out onto the old weathered front porch.

"Charley, do you think you could get off work for half an hour tomorrow?" Catfish asked.

"Right around lunchtime, I might. What for?"

"There's a banker at the First National in Mount Pleasant who's expecting you."

Charley stood open-mouthed, staring at his tall childhood friend.

"And I've located a garage, too," Catfish continued. "It's up town, a block from the railroad tracks. Good location and all the tools and equipment you'll need. I'll be your first customer. That old Pontiac needs a set of sparkplugs, a good greasing, and no telling what else."

"Milburn, I can't do this," Charley protested. "I don't know about loans and buying garages. I live on cash money. I've never been in a bank in my life."

"I'll go with you," Catfish said, patting his friend on the shoulder. "I'll meet you at the bank at noon tomorrow."

Charley Grady stood speechless as Catfish jumped off the porch and cranked up the Pontiac. Wheeling around and heading for the road, Catfish's long left arm shot out the window and waved through a churning cloud of dust.

A week later, Charley and Catfish spent a day cleaning up and arranging the equipment in the old garage. Then Catfish pulled his

Pontiac in. Before Charley had finished that job, Catfish had flagged down two other customers.

Every day for over a month Catfish checked on his friend while making his way to the post office to check box 115. Finally, on Thursday, July 29, there was a letter addressed to Mr. Milburn A. Smith, Winfield, Texas. Dated the prior Saturday, the return address was War Department, Army Air Forces Technical School, Sheppard Field.

Hurriedly, Catfish shook the contents to one end of the envelope and tore off the other. Sliding the contents out, he found the letter he had been waiting for.

Dear Mr. Smith:

You are hereby tendered an indefinite War Service Appointment as Jr. Instructor, CAF-5, $2000 p/a. Please report for duty at this office at the earliest practicable date.

Catfish shoved his arms in the air and let out a whoop. Then he read on.

Before resigning any position you now hold, you should make certain that you have no physical defect which would disqualify you for this position.

He read no farther. Slowly, he unfolded the enclosure, a Certificate of Medical Examination. Immediately his eyes scanned down to item five, Gastro-intestinal problems. He flipped the form over. *Example of Gastro-intestinal problems: Ulcers, inflammations, etc.*

The form had not changed since June 11, 1942, when he had enlisted in the Army Air Forces and had neglected to identify his condition.

A Joe Louis fist pounded into his stomach could not have hurt worse. His hope of active participation in the war effort, which he had secretly sheltered and kept aflame, was now snuffed out forever.

4

July 30, 1943

Blocked from re-entering the war effort, Catfish's recently rekindled spirit was snuffed out like a forest fire caught in a monsoon. He moped around through the weekend, avoiding people when possible.

Then late in the morning of August 2, he headed north along a hot, dusty country road, seeking solitude to consider the gulf that separated him from the future he craved. With the family dog trailing along, he turned east into the welcomed shade of a dense forest and followed a spring-fed creek that crossed the road at the bottom of a long hill. Hidden away in hundreds of acres of oaks, elms, and sweetgums, he came to a clear, cool pool of water nestled in a sandy bend of the stream. After hesitating a moment in the suffocating August heat, he stripped and waded into the refreshing water. Feeling youthful again, his thoughts drifted to his college basketball days. With his path into the war blocked, maybe he could still catch on with the Wichita Henrys or some similar team. The cool water and energizing memories lifted his spirits, and after drying in a patch of sun that penetrated the leafy umbrella above him, he dressed and headed home with a bounce in his step.

After crossing the road, he climbed the hill to the house and noticed a new model car parked in the driveway, one he did not recognize. As he headed for the front yard, he spotted a man sitting in a straight-back chair on the south porch, propped back against the wall. His father occupied a high-back, wood-slat rocker alongside the visitor, both at the east end of the porch, just beyond the mid-afternoon sun's reach. Though something about the guest, the shape of his head, his hairstyle, or maybe his general build, was familiar to Catfish, the man's name remained elusive. His dark business suit, with the coat draped across his lap, contrasted sharply with Sam's striped overalls.

Catfish hesitated at the edge of the yard, studying the situation as the two men talked casually, as old friends might. The man's apparent success immediately renewed the young man's sense of failure. After a few moments, with his head down, Catfish angled nonchalantly toward the porch, hoping to avoid notice.

"Son," his father called out, "Come over here."

With a deep sigh, the thin young man veered right and headed for the side porch. Glancing up, he recognized Millard Fleming, the head of Winfield's school district during Catfish's childhood days.

"Hello," the visitor said, rocking forward and meeting Catfish at the top of the steps, "it's great seeing you again."

Millard Fleming did not wait long to get to the point of his visit.

"Milburn, I'm now superintendent of Mount Vernon schools, and our coach just resigned to take the head job over at Highland Park in Dallas. I think you know the gentleman, Herman Morgan."

Catfish nodded. Herman "Sleepy" Morgan, an outstanding halfback from Sulphur Springs, had been Catfish's roommate and best friend during his freshman year of college. Also, Morgan had coached the Mount Vernon football team to an undefeated season in 1938. Coach Bob Killingsworth, another of Catfish's college teammates, had replaced Morgan, but Sleepy had returned that summer and tentatively agreed to mentor the Tigers for the fall of 1943. Then the Highland Park Scots had made Morgan a better offer.

"Well, that rascal's left me in a bind," Fleming continued. "Here it is August, less than a month before the football team is scheduled to begin practice, and I don't have a coach. I was hoping you'd come help us out for a few months."

Hesitating, Catfish glanced over at the school and the baseball field beyond. He liked Millard Fleming. In addition to serving as Winfield school principal, the man had once coached the local basketball team, and Catfish considered him one of the best. A native of Titus County, Fleming had coached the Stonewall basketball team to its first Interscholastic League State Tournament in 1921. In eighteen years of coaching the sport, Fleming had taken his teams to fourteen county championships, four district titles, and two bi-district crowns. His knowledge and love of the game were legendary throughout the area.

"Could I think about it a while?" Catfish asked.

"There's not much time," Fleming responded, loosening his collar. "As you can appreciate, I've got to line up a coach, pronto."

"Son," Sam intervened, "you really ought to give this offer serious consideration. You love athletics, and you've been a successful player and coach. The boys will look up to you, and I know you wouldn't want them to lose a season due to having no leader."

"Will you need me to teach, too?" Catfish asked.

"Yes, Morgan leaves us short in that area, also. Can you handle a history class?"

"I did out at Carey. I reckon I can again."

"Good," the superintendent said, grasping Catfish's shoulder in his meaty hand. "How about you ride over to the school with me now, and take a look at the facilities. I'll have you back in time for supper."

After Catfish changed clothes, they drove into Mount Vernon along South Holbrook Street. When they passed Majors Street, the superintendent pointed ahead to the left.

"The new high school," he said. "It's just two years old."

"Does it have a gymnasium?" Catfish asked, recalling the makeshift one at Carey.

"Sure does," Fleming replied with a chuckle. "Right in the heart of the building. It's got built-in bleachers on the east side and dressing rooms above the stage on the west side, with showers under the east stands."

As they pulled up in front of the wide brick building, Catfish eyed the long, narrow parking area with its two sets of stairs, each with five concrete steps, balanced north and south. They rose from street level to wide walkways that led to twin entrances. Three sets of twenty-pane windows lighted classrooms along the two side wings. Smaller, twelve-paned ones filled the middle section where the administrative offices were. All had lower inserts that pushed out at the bottom, letting cooler air in while keeping rain out. A second level crowned the center of the building, most of it enclosing the high, lighted ceiling above the basketball court.

As Catfish and Fleming stepped inside the double doors on the right, they entered a spacious hallway that extended westward to a north exit at the far end of the building and where it intersected a long wing that formed the school's backside. That wing housed a large study hall, a library, and classrooms. Another hallway ran the length of the south side of the building with similar exits attached to each end. A narrower walkway ran north and south along the administrative offices and beneath the bleachers, connecting the two long east-west hallways. It was there, right across from the administrative offices, that Catfish stopped in front of the elaborate trophy case.

"Whew!" Catfish whistled. "A regional basketball championship just last year."

"That's right," Fleming said proudly. "Last spring our boys defeated Plano, forty-one to twenty-four, in the finals."

"Got any of those players coming back?"

"We lost a few good ones to graduation, Wayne Pierce, Sammie Burton, and Leonard Rollings, but we've got some experience returning, too. I'd say a good basketball man could take Harry Pugh, Glenn Pierce, J. C. Cannaday, Lollis Loyd, and Charles Hogan and win, maybe even go to the state tournament."

"That nineteen thirty-eight Regional Championship trophy," Catfish said, pointing at an engraved football with a team picture propped up behind. "It says that team was undefeated and whipped Royse City forty to thirteen in the championship game. That must have been about the best team ever."

"That's right. In twelve games those boys scored four hundred and eighty-one points while allowing only forty-five."

"That's forty points a game of offense," Catfish said. "Who made that team go?"

"Number eighty-eight, Bo Campbell, an outstanding running back and kicker," Fleming replied, pointing at the picture, "and number seventy-seven, Skinny Davis, who went on to captain a fine Southern Methodist University team. And I ought to add number ninety, Glyn Jones, to that list. He was selected to play in the Texas State Schoolboy All-Star game."

"What did last fall's bunch do?"

"Five and two," Fleming said. "Only one bad loss."

"All losses are bad, but tell me about the worst one."

"Got skunked by Gilmer, twenty-seven to nothing. These are war years, Milburn, and it's a bit of a struggle to maintain a team. You should take a look at this fall's schedule and see if you want to make any changes."

"Is Gilmer on it?"

"No."

"Who can I call to set up a game with them?"

"I have a name back in the office," Fleming said, cutting his eyes over at his prospective coach. "They'll be tough again. Sure you want to play them?"

"How else can I know if we're getting better?" Catfish replied. "Who else beat us?"

"Pittsburg. They're on this year's schedule."

"What about Mount Pleasant?"

"Yeah, they're there, and they'll be rugged, too."

"A natural rivalry," Catfish said. "Only twelve miles away, a bigger school, and my alma mater. Playing them year-in and year-out will make us a better team."

After taking a lingering look at the gymnasium with its shiny hardwood floor, white wooden backboards, and elevated bleachers, Catfish and the superintendent locked up and headed back to the car.

"Milburn, I'd like to take you on up town and let you meet a few people, if you've got the time. Folks in this town like to get to know their coaches."

Heading up Holbrook Street, Fleming pulled in at the Chevrolet dealership on the left.

"Owner's name is Dave Bolger, a fine young man. He's also the chairman of our Infantile Paralysis Foundation. His brother, Rufus, has just been named Grade School Principal. He'll be replacing Jack Henry, a fine man who's joined the service."

After introductions and a look around the dealership, Bolger switched the subject to his most pressing project.

"A young man named Clarence Williams, who lived just four miles south of town, recently died of poliomyelitis, the most dreaded disease in Franklin County," Bolger said. "He was our first polio-related death. Mayor Tom McDonough and I have been encouraging our citizens to clean up every spot in the county, any place that might encourage the breeding of flies and other such insects. The coach in this town is always an influential person. I hope we can count on your help."

"Yes, sir, you can," Catfish said, though the coaching job was not yet finalized.

"Coach," the car dealer said as they headed for the door. "You need anything, just let me know. We support our kids in this town."

Back in the car, Catfish reached over and put his hand on the steering wheel.

"Before we go any farther, I think we'd better settle something," he said. "If you're offering me the job, I'm willing to give it a try."

"I'm offering," the superintendent said, smiling and extending his hand. "The school board will have to okay anything beyond the football season, but if you win a few games, I expect the job is yours for keeps."

With that settled, the superintendent drove north to the intersection with East Main Street.

"This is our medical center," Fleming said. "Across the street there is Crutcher Hospital. Just to the left on the southeast corner of the square is Rutherford Drug Store. If you need a good physician, Dr. Eddie Chandler has his office in the back. That side entrance is his. Catty-cornered are a couple more drugstores, Mercer's and Crescent's.

"Now, the building just east of the hospital is the Miller Hotel. It's seen some years, but it used to be the Palmer House, a colonial style, first-class boarding establishment. Milburn, I don't know what you might prefer for living quarters, but I want to encourage you to move to town. Folks here like their coaches to be an integral part of the community. Since you're single, you might want to check with the Millers or with Bill Campbell down at Hasty Courts."

"Thanks for the tip," Catfish replied. "Do they provide meals?"

"Yes, and their rates are quite good," Fleming replied. "Also, you might want to mention that you're the new coach. Both establishments are very supportive of athletics."

"If I can afford it, I'd sure like to live here in town," Catfish said.

The superintendent chuckled, then continued. "Now, if you'll look there adjacent to Dr. Chandler's office, you'll see the local newspaper, the *Optic-Herald*. Let's stop by and let you get acquainted."

Inside, the superintendent introduced Catfish as the new coach and athletic director, the first Catfish had heard of the latter title.

"Can we print the story in Friday's paper?" the owner and editor, Charles Devall, asked.

"You sure can. I've already cleared it with the school board," Fleming responded.

"Coach Smith, maybe you could give me a little background," Devall said, grabbing paper and pencil.

"There's not much," Catfish said. "I grew up down the road at Winfield, graduated from Mount Pleasant High School, and got my degree from East Texas State Teachers College in Commerce. I played a little ball in college, and then I coached basketball at Carey, Texas for two years, at Borger for four years, and then helped out at Winfield in the spring of nineteen forty-two. Recently, I was in the Army Air Forces."

"This town's partial to football," the newsman said. "What's your experience with football?"

"Milburn is being a little modest," Superintendent Fleming said, intervening. "In addition to basketball, he coached football at Borger and was twice an All-Lone Star Conference end in college." Fleming went on to summarize Catfish's two-sport playing days as well as his coaching years. "But the highlight of his coaching career has to be the two state playoff teams at Carey, the second one winning the schoolboy basketball championship of Texas. I believe his two-year record there was ninety wins against only ten losses."

The newsman looked up from his scribbling. "Did you say Texas State Basketball Championship, Superintendent?"

"I did, along with other tournament, district, and regional championships."

"No world championship?" the newsman asked, peering over the top of his spectacles and smiling.

Catfish shook his head. "If we'd played for it, I expect we'd have won it."

"Well," Devall said, rising, "it's a pleasure meeting you, Coach Smith, and welcome to our fine town. I'm sure we'll be talking again."

Back in the car, Fleming turned right at the southeast corner of the square, an elevated rectangular plaza with tall trees dotting the perimeter and perpendicular walkways crisscrossing its interior.

"The courthouse used to be on the plaza," Fleming said, and then pointed northwest. "But in nineteen twelve, they tore it down and built the one you see over there. The square used to have three public wells on it, and in those days, early every morning, businessmen flocked to them to get their daily supply before the water got low and stirred up. It's still a popular gathering place for country people coming to town on Saturdays, for viewing parades, and for public celebrations. You win a championship, and we'll get you and your boys up there, and the whole town will turn out to congratulate you."

Just north of Rutherford Drug Store, the superintendent pointed out The Lady's Shop, and then the Joy Theatre, Brown's Grocery, and Inman's Cleaners & Tailor Shop, all on the east side of the plaza. Turning west they passed the stately courthouse, then angled south along the west side of the square where M. L. Edwards Hardware and the post office were. The superintendent noted the First National Bank off the plaza's southwest corner, a two-story, red brick building with two large white columns. Continuing along the south side of the square, Catfish spotted L&M Grocery Store, Lewis Dry Goods, Crescent Drug Store, Parchman & Meredith, Mercer's Drug Store, The Lone Star Shop, and then diagonally across Houston Street, the long storefront of Lowry's Hardware & Furniture.

They turned right, passing Ramsay's feed store, then worked their way west past a two-story building that housed the city hall above the fire station. Cutting back north to Main, the superintendent headed west, passing a couple of service stations, then Hasty Courts, Miller's Cafe to the south, and Tinsley's Grocery to the north. A little farther west of downtown, they turned left onto Oak Street and weaved their way around to the football field, set off the street a couple hundred yards and enclosed by a fence. Wooden bleachers stood on the west side with an open-roofed press box perched at the top. They got out and walked onto the field.

"Good grass," Catfish commented. "We didn't have much grass on those fields in West Texas."

"Milburn," Fleming said, admiring the gridiron, "I think you should get with that fellow at the paper and announce when you want the football boys to report to practice. Rules don't allow it before September first."

"I'll do that, once I get the schedule set," Catfish said. "I'll come up to the school tomorrow and maybe we can make a few phone calls."

They then climbed back into the car and headed for Winfield.

The next morning Catfish was up early, dressed in his best clothes, and headed for Mount Vernon, where he found Superintendent Fleming in his office. Within a couple of hours they had the 1943 football schedule worked out, though Catfish was unhappy with having no September games. He would begin fall practices on September 1, while school would open twelve days later, and the first game was scheduled for seventeen days after that.

October 1	Clarksville	Home
October 8	Winnsboro	Away
October 15	Mount Pleasant	Away
October 22	Pittsburg	Home
October 29	Gilmer	Home
November 5	Talco	Away

The coach tried to schedule September opponents, even scrimmage games, but all the schools in the area had full calendars. Though Catfish would have preferred a contest to evaluate his players under game conditions and to break the monotony of practice, an open month was not all bad. It would provide time to get to know his players, evaluate their talents, and to teach them the new T-formation, replacing the single wing offense they were accustomed to. The greatest challenge would be getting a quarterback who could reliably take the snap from center, operate with his back to the line of scrimmage, and avoid fumbles when handing-off the ball to his running backs.

A little after lunch, Catfish took a copy of the schedule to the *Optic-Herald*, along with a handwritten note inviting all boys interested in playing football that season to be at the practice field at three o'clock the afternoon of September 1. While there, Devall introduced Catfish to L. D. Lowry, Jr., who had just handed the editor a typed message explaining that Franklin County's quota for the third War Bond Drive was $208,700.

"Wow! That's a lot of money!" Catfish said when the Chairman of the War Bond Drive explained the note. "How much for the citizens of Mount Vernon?"

"The city has the highest concentration of wealth in the county, so the goal for us town folks is ninety thousand dollars. There's some oil down around New Hope, so their quota is ten thousand five hundred."

"I want to do my part, so how do I go about buying war bonds?"

"Drop by the post office, and they'll be glad to help you," Lowry replied. "And Coach, if I can help you in any way, just let me know."

Catfish then made his way around the square and parked in front of M. L. Edwards Store. He slipped into the post office next door, a building once occupied by the Merchants & Planters National Bank, and asked about war bonds. The Postmaster, W. L. Nelson, invited him back to his office where Catfish made his purchase.

"Do you have a post office box, young man?" Nelson asked.

"No, sir, but I expect I'd better get one."

Within minutes, Catfish had been assigned box number 171.

Back at the school, Millard Fleming handed Catfish the teacher's version of the world history book and walked him to his classroom, the number fourteen tacked above the doorway. It formed a block-like section stuck onto the south end of the back wing, adjacent to an exit.

"Mr. Fleming," Catfish said, standing at the front of the room, "I'd like to set aside one day of the week, say Friday, for my students to discuss current events, especially the war. Most families are impacted in some way, and though it's a scary subject, I think it's better for them to know what's going on."

"Milburn, I think that's an excellent idea."

That afternoon Catfish dropped by the *Optic-Herald* office and explained his plan.

"Would you be willing to donate a few copies of the paper each Friday for my students?" he asked the editor.

"Sure. Just drop by on your way to school and pick them up," Devall replied.

Catfish then drove to Hasty Courts.

"I'm the new coach . . ."

"Why, I know who you are!" the woman said, interrupting. "Everybody knows about you and your basketball state championship. We're pleased as punch to have you here to take our boys to Austin and win one for Mount Vernon."

"Well, ma'am, I can't promise that, but I pledge to give it my best shot," Catfish replied. "What I'm here for . . ."

"A room," the matronly woman said, cutting him off again. "And I've got just the one for you. Mind you, we don't have many vacancies, but when this really nice one became available yesterday, I made up my mind to hold it for you."

"How'd you know . . ."

"Oh, phooey," she said, pretending embarrassment. "When Superintendent Fleming dropped by, the first thing I asked was, 'Is he married?' Plenty old, you are, and a nice-lookin' fellow. I expect some little gal will latch on to you soon enough, but so long as you're bach'ing it, I'd consider it a privilege to see after you."

"Thank you, ma'am," Catfish replied, wondering what other maneuvering Superintendent Fleming had done. "But I don't know if I can afford one of your rooms on a coach's salary."

"How does twelve dollars a week sound to you, includin' meals, laundry, and sweepin' your floor?"

"Well, ma'am," Catfish replied, stammering.

"Okay, I'll cut it to nine, but that's as low as I can go."

"I can afford that, I'm sure. Fact is, I was expecting . . ."

"It's a special rate, since you're our coach," she said winking. "So don't you go blabbin' to folks, not even to Mr. Campbell."

She led Catfish to the corner room that looked out over West Main Street. It was roomy, had well-placed windows to let in a breeze, a butane space heater, a large light bulb hanging from a high ceiling in the center of the room, and a good sturdy bed. The wooden floor was solid and had a good-sized rug covering the open area. He was not crazy about the wallpaper pattern, long-stem red and pink roses, but

46

he figured in the dark of night he wouldn't care whether the walls were covered with flowers or footballs.

"I'll take it," Catfish said promptly. "Pay in advance?"

"That's customary," the attendant said, extending her hand. "And here's your key. It's only a skeleton key, so if you lose it, any of our others will work. I'll check on your room every day and sweep and straighten up when it needs it, but that's no excuse for you to be sloppy."

Catfish exchanged nine dollars for the long-handled key and assured the woman that he was accustomed to cleaning up after himself.

The new coach spent the next couple of weeks sorting through football and basketball equipment. He was pleasantly surprised with the uniforms and general status of the facilities. He found shoes to be his number one concern and promptly headed for the superintendent's office.

"Sir," he said to Milliard Fleming, "how would I go about purchasing some football shoes for the boys?"

"I'm afraid we have very little sports budget, Milburn. Finances are quite slim with the war going on, so we ask the boys to provide their own."

"I understand," Catfish replied, turning to leave. "I'll think of something."

While coaching at Carey, Catfish had found that country boys generally had good work habits, and often the most incentive to excel in sports, their only avenue to college. In addition, many of them were accustomed to hard work and had the muscles and brute strength to prove it. However, most farm boys would not have the money to purchase a pair of football shoes.

Walking out to his old Pontiac, a plan developed in his mind as he recalled the names of men who had offered to help if he needed something. He decided to test them.

"Mr. Lowry," the coach said, having stopped by his huge store, "I hate to bother you with this, but the football boys will be showing up for practice in a few days and the shoes we have are about shot. I don't have a budget that allows me to purchase any, and I wonder if you have an idea how I might solve this problem."

"Coach, how many pairs do you need?"

"I think we could get by with a dozen."

"You walk over there to Parchman and Meredith's and tell Jeff to order what you need. Tell him I'm good for the cost."

"I can't thank you enough, Mr. Lowry. I plan to work these boys hard, and I expect they'll handle it better with some comfortable shoes."

Jeff Meredith did not hesitate. "Take a look at this catalog, Coach, and select the style you need."

When Catfish had made his choice, Mr. Meredith began filling out the order.

"What about sizes?" Catfish asked.

"I know these boys," he said. "I've measured their feet before, but I'll allow a little for growth. Later, if you find you need some odd sizes, just drop back by. I'll get them for you."

Catfish walked out thinking that with support like this, he had better field a winner.

5

September 1, 1943

On Wednesday afternoon Catfish arrived an hour early at the field house and busied himself to calm his nerves while waiting to meet his football players at three o'clock. Running out of things to do, he stepped outside and paced beneath the sprawling limbs of a large oak that shaded the entrance. About half past two the first player showed up, a five-foot-nine, sturdily built young man with a buzz haircut and a quick smile.

"Coach Smith," Catfish said, introducing himself.

"Robby Campbell, sir," the youngster said enthusiastically.

"What position did you play last year?"

"I didn't play," Campbell explained. "I broke my ankle my freshman year and laid out last season."

Catfish sized the boy up. He's got the build of a halfback, the coach thought, if he's got some speed, but having no experience at the high school level, the boy most likely would fill a backup role.

About then, a group of three players walked up. They introduced themselves as James Caudle, Charles Shurtleff, and Dan Cargile. Like Campbell, Caudle was the size of a back, but had a tough-kid look about him, one with muscles. At six-foot-two, Cargile had the raw-boned look of a boy used to shoving things out of the way rather than stepping around them, while Shurtleff was a six-footer with muscular arms and legs, a thick chest, and good looks. But there was something more about Shurtleff that captured the coach's attention. He moved with the ease of a cat, while his eyes sparkled with eagerness and confidence.

The next group to arrive included Harry Jack Pugh, a strapping six-foot-two athlete with ample meat on his bones. If he's got good hands and some speed, Catfish thought, we'll toss a few passes to him. He'll be a bear for some defensive back to bring down.

Following along with Pugh were two youngsters, one named Jerry Yokum and the other Tom Irby, both with lean, compact bodies and small, quick-looking feet.

Catfish's two biggest concerns, quarterback and center, the keys to success in running a T-formation, had not shown up. He began asking questions.

"Can any of you boys play quarterback?"

No one volunteered.

"What about center, snapping the ball to a T-formation quarterback?"

The coach got nothing but blank stares until Shurtleff finally pointed toward a couple of boys approaching along a worn footpath.

"Coach, here comes your quarterback."

After a quick look, Catfish eliminated the larger of the two. That left the one with fair skin, wavy hair, and a little-boy smile, definitely not the coach's image of a quarterback.

"Joe Clark," the husky one said. "And this is Glenn Pierce."

"Son, they say you're a quarterback," Catfish said to Pierce.

"I'll give it a try," the boy said, glancing at his teammates.

"What grade are you in?"

"Tenth."

"Do you have any experience at the position?"

"Last year I was backup to my brother, Wayne. He was great running the single-wing. He could run or pass, and handled the ball on most every down. He taught me a lot."

"Your brother," Catfish said, "where is he?"

"Graduated, sir."

"How old is he?"

"He'll be eighteen on October ninth."

"He's eligible to play another year. Think he'd be interested?"

"I don't think so, Coach. He'll be joining the Navy right after his birthday."

"Okay, have a seat here in the shade, boys," Catfish said as a few others straggled up.

"I'm Coach Smith," he said to the group. "Now, I don't know all your names, but I will soon enough.

"First, how many of you played football last year?"

Only six boys raised their hands.

"Okay, let's talk about teamwork and team spirit, because those are the most important factors in our success. While you're an individual and will have individual assignments, it's the team that counts most. We'll win as a team, or lose as a team. If you score three touchdowns but the team loses, you just had a bad day. If you block your man but the ball carrier is tackled short of a first down, it was a bad play. Everything is measured and valued based on team success.

"Now, let's talk rules. No drinking, no smoking, no soda pop, no candy, and no ice cream. School nights, you'll be home by nine o'clock, you'll make your grades, and you'll conduct yourself in a way that'll make your classmates, your teammates, and your parents proud. If you break the rules, you turn in your uniform. I don't care who you are, or how good you think you are. There'll be no exceptions.

"Boys, championships are earned. Nobody's gonna give it to you. We're gonna work hard, maybe harder than you've ever worked. We won't lose a single game because we aren't in shape to play hard from the first whistle to the final gun. You'll give the same effort no matter if we're ahead or behind. Championships are won by champions, and nobody is born a champion; you earn that status by working harder, longer, and by never, ever giving up.

"Are there any questions?"

In dazed silence, no one even moved.

"Then put on your uniforms and gather back here in five minutes."

As the boys filed into the dressing room, mumbling to each other, some cutting their eyes back toward their new coach, Millard Fleming walked up.

"What do you think?" the superintendent asked.

"As best I can tell, I have only a half dozen players with any experience, and they're from a single-wing offense. To run the T-formation, I've got to have a good ball handler and a reliable center. I'm not sure I've got either."

"Take a close look at Pierce. He's sharp, like his brother. He'll learn fast, and he's an athlete, no matter the sport."

"His brother, Wayne," Catfish said, "Was he a good ball-handler?"

"He sure was!" Fleming replied. "And a great basketball player."

"Mr. Fleming, I've got to have a good quarterback. Wayne is only seventeen. Maybe we could convince him to come back for another year."

"Won't work, Milburn. This past summer Wayne attended college down at Texas A&M. He's no longer eligible for high school athletics."

"I guess I'll give this younger Pierce a shot," Catfish said, rolling his eyes. "That leaves me needing a center, one that can get the ball to the quarterback with a quick snap motion, not a between-the-legs pass. That exchange starts everything."

"How come you want to use the T-formation? Nobody around here knows anything about it."

"That's reason enough," Catfish replied. "Folks may have trouble defending what they've never seen. The other is it allows things to happen quickly, with options."

"Who'll carry the ball?"

"Running backs, not the quarterback. The quarterback does lots of faking one way, then handing off of the ball the other way, and I'd like him to chunk a few passes."

"But if you fake two backs to the right, then give the ball to another heading left, there's no lead blocker for the ball carrier."

"That's right. Lead blockers pull the defense to the ball carrier like steel to a magnet. For short yardage, that's okay. Likewise, a decoy running back lures the defense to him, thus doing more to free the ball carrier than a lead blocker. Faking, misdirection, and quick dive plays replace the brute force of the single-wing. You'll see T-formation halfbacks break through the line on a counter play and gain ten yards before the defense can figure out what happened."

"I hope you're right, Milburn," the superintendent said.

"It'll work, but it all starts with the quarterback. I've got to have a good one."

"I think you'll find that young Pierce can do the job," Fleming said. "On Wednesday before the Mount Pleasant game last year, his brother hopped on the running board of the local fire truck when it started a run. Reaching the scene, Wayne leaped off and turned an ankle, so Glenn played in his place. He wasn't spectacular, but he played steady, error-free ball, and we won seven to nothing."

At that moment, the boys spilled out of the dressing room, and Catfish took a long look at his quarterback prospect.

"At least he looks larger with his uniform on," the coach mumbled, and then led his players to the football field as the superintendent drove away.

After lining the boys up on the goal line, Catfish trotted down to the fifty-yard stripe. As agreed, when he dropped his raised arm, the boys raced ahead. Pierce was not the fastest, but through determined effort, he led most of the race. Irby and Yokum slipped by him near the end. Another pleasant surprise was big Harry Jack Pugh who finished with Pierce and was gaining on those ahead of them. Another twenty yards, and he'd have caught them, the coach guessed.

"Trot back, and when I signal, race to me again," the coach instructed.

This time, he extended the distance to sixty-five yards.

As he expected, Pugh came even closer to winning, pushing Irby while Pierce came in third. The surprise was Charles Shurtleff. His competitive spirit kept him bunched with the leaders, and Caudle was right there, too. Yokum finished with Shurtleff, but the coach was convinced he was coasting.

"Yokum, you think you could play halfback?" Catfish asked.

"I sure do, Coach," the boy replied with a big grin.

"Okay. But if you don't finish in the top two this time, I'm gonna move you to the line. Would you like to play guard?"

"No, sir."

"Then lead this bunch of donkeys back down there, and let's see if you're gonna be a halfback or a guard."

The next fifty-yard sprint confirmed the coach's suspicions. Jerry Yokum just needed a little extra motivation.

"Okay," Catfish said, pointing at the fastest player on the team, "you get a shot at playing halfback. But the first time you give me a half-hearted run, I'll tear that uniform off your back and give it to some pinochle kid who doesn't have half your ability, but who'd fight a grizzly bear for the chance to run with a football under his arm.

"Now, while you boys are catching your breath, drop down and do twenty pushups. It takes more than speed to win football games."

While his players strained lowering and raising their torsos in the September heat, Catfish moved slowly among them.

"If there's no dirt on the tip of your nose, you're not dropping down far enough. I'm checking right now, and a clean nose will get you ten more pushups."

Twenty-five sweat-tipped snouts hit the dust, where dirt and moisture mixed to form tiny mud cakes. Catfish stared off toward the distant trees to hide his laughter.

"Okay, on your feet and form two lines, one to my left and the other to my right. Nothing is more basic in this game than blocking and tackling, and I don't mean grabbing at some runner's shoelaces. By tackling I mean sticking your shoulder into the runner's gut, lifting him off his feet, driving him backwards, and planting him on his backside. Anybody think they can demonstrate that?"

Shurtleff raised his hand.

"Shurtleff, move to the front of the line," the coach said, picking up an old football. "Halfback Yokum, come up here."

Catfish motioned Yokum to the front of the line opposite Shurtleff, and then turned to Robby Campbell.

"Burr, come up here and block for Wing-foot."

With Shurtleff and Campbell squared off in front of Catfish, one in a defensive lineman's stance and the other in an offensive set, the coach positioned Yokum about five yards behind his blocker.

"When I call out 'hut', the action starts," Catfish explained. "Shurtleff, your goal is to shuck that blocker and demonstrate the perfect tackle, using Mr. Yokum as a tackling dummy. Burr will try to prevent that, but I'm counting on you, Mr. Defense. And our halfback deluxe is going to catch the ball, run straight ahead, no dodging or sidestepping, and run smack over you, Mr. Shurtleff."

The three participants got into position, their sweaty faces grim and their eyes steady. The two lines of boys leaned to one side or the other and craned their necks to watch the collision that was about to occur, the first serious contact in front of their new coach.

"Hut!" Catfish called out and tossed the ball to Yokum.

Shurtleff plowed ahead, grabbed the smaller blocker by the shoulder pads, and shoved him aside. Yokum leaned forward with his head lowered like a battering ram and charged toward the tackler with all the power he could muster. Shurtleff gathered his feet under him, crouched low with his weight distributed on the balls of his feet, and then lunged forward as the runner crashed into him. The tackler's right shoulder slid beneath Yokum's lowered head, pounding into the runner's abdomen. Shurtleff straightened his back and kept his legs churning, lifting the runner's feet off the ground to flail powerlessly in the air. Then Shurtleff drove him backward and slammed him against the parched summer earth.

"I hope somebody got a picture of that!" Catfish shouted, rushing toward the two players. "Yes, sir, Mr. Shurtleff, I'd sure like to have a picture of that tackle."

The coach eased over, helped the startled Yokum to his feet, and then pulled him aside. "Wing-foot," the coach said, lowering his voice, "even a scat back sometimes has to lower his shoulder and take on a tackler. Now, I'm going to give you another chance, and I suggest you tuck that ball under your left arm, keep your head up, lower your right shoulder, and swing your forearm into the tackler's chest. You've got to meet force with force."

Catfish gave the same trio time to reset. He glanced at Yokum and caught a glimpse of tears in his eyes, but the lad's heat-flushed face was set hard.

"Hut!" the coach barked as he pitched the football to the runner.

Again Shurtleff shucked the smaller blocker and readied himself for a repeat performance. Yokum charged ahead like a wild bull, and when he reached the tackler, he dropped his right shoulder and swung his forearm up from knee level like a boxer delivering his best uppercut. The ball popped free from the runner's left arm, but Wing-foot paid no heed. The force of the forearm popped Shurtleff's head back, stunning him, took away his leverage, and broke his initial grip. Momentarily Yokum hesitated, but then he bellowed a guttural sound and with his legs pumping like two pistons, drove forward. The tackler tried to hold on, but peeled off to his right and fell to the dirt. Free, Yokum sprinted forward about five yards, and then turned and glanced back.

Catfish wore a smile that would have done a big-mouthed bass proud.

"Yes, I'd like a picture of that, too!" Catfish said. "But Yokum, you've got to hold on to the ball.

"If you aspiring backs will run like Mr. Yokum just did, and you defensive men will tackle like Mr. Shurtleff demonstrated a few minutes ago," Catfish said, reaching his hand down to Shurtleff, "we'll have the toughest, hardest-hitting football team in the state."

The boys whooped and back-clapped while Yokum and Shurtleff eyed each other with newly found respect.

The blocking and tackling drill continued for most of an hour, the coach requiring every weak effort to be repeated until he was satisfied the player had done his best.

"Now, let's line up and do a little running, boys," the coach said, and then demanded silence when he heard grumbling.

"I know you're tired, but just imagine we're playing Winnsboro. It's the fourth quarter, the clock is ticking down, the score is tied, and you've just broken loose with the ball at midfield. Are we going to lose the championship because you're too tired to run fifty yards at the end of a hard-fought game?"

The players, weary and battered, lined up on the goal line while the coach positioned himself at midfield. Catfish raised his right hand, hesitated, and then dropped it like so much dead weight. The boys took off, elbowing each other, fighting for advantage. After a little jockeying, Yokum, Irby, and Caudle eased ahead of the pack. With their faces twisted, their eyes squinted almost shut, and sweat pouring from every pore, they pumped their arms and legs more with willpower than with the waning strength in their exhausted bodies. Yokum beat Irby by half a step with Caudle fading a little at the end, and the rest following, shoulder pads flapping and faces contorted. At the last second, big, tall Harry Jack Pugh dove forward across the finish line ahead of Pierce and Caudle.

"Some of you scored that winning touchdown," Catfish said, "but others failed. Yokum, Pierce, Irby, Caudle, and Pugh, you're finished for the day. I feel certain the rest of you want a second chance to lead your team to victory, so go line up again."

They did, and they gave it their best effort. Some barely finished, stumbling across the imaginary goal line and then collapsing to the ground, their chests heaving for air.

"That's all, boys," Catfish said and had turned toward the dressing room when he noticed a gray-haired black man who stood along the sideline watching.

"Hello, Coach," the man said, catching up with the long-legged Catfish. "I'm Bob Suggs, a big fan of Mount Vernon sports."

"Glad to meet you, Mr. Suggs," Catfish replied, not slowing down.

"Coach, where's Clarence Crowston?" the shorter man asked, hurrying to keep up.

"Who?" Catfish stopped and turned to face Suggs.

"Crowston. He's a hoss of a runner, Coach," the elderly man said. "And it looks like you could use him."

"Where do I find this Crowston boy?" Catfish asked, recalling that Superintendent Fleming had mentioned the name as a basketball player.

"Up north of town, I think," Suggs replied, then pointed to a man who had been watching from the shade of the stands. "Maybe Mr. Newsom knows."

Catfish thanked Suggs and headed for the other man.

"Mr. Newsom?" Catfish asked.

"Curly Newsom," the man replied, extending his hand.

"I'm Coach Smith, and that fellow over there said you'd know how I could locate a boy named Crowston."

"He's a farm boy. Lives up around Hagansport," Newsom said, and then gave directions.

Together they walked down to the field house where Newsom headed for his car and Catfish veered toward the dressing room. Hesitating at the doorway, the coach overheard his players having a heated discussion.

"We never ran one play," somebody complained. "It was just run, run, tackle, tackle, and block, block. Clarksville will come in here, and we won't even know how to line up."

"I ain't coming back," another growled. "This ain't football. He's a madman taking out his insanity on us."

Willing to let them vent their frustration without challenge, Catfish stopped, and as he turned away, he heard an angry voice.

"You ever won a state championship?"

"No, and neither have you," one of the boys replied.

"That's right, but he has," said Shurtleff, jerking his thumb in the coach's general direction. "I think I'll hang around and see how it's done."

6

September 2, 1943

The next morning Catfish drove his old green Pontiac past the plaza and headed north on highway thirty-seven. Following Curly Newsom's instructions, he found the Crowston farmhouse in the Hagansport community.

"Good morning, Mrs. Crowston," he said at the door. "I'm Milburn Smith, coach at Mount Vernon. I apologize for interrupting, but I'd like to talk to your son, Clarence."

"He's with his father," the woman said, motioning toward the backyard.

"Thank you, ma'am. I'll just ease around there and have a word with your boy."

Catfish found Clarence underneath a faded black 1939 Ford car with the driver's side propped up with a stack of boards supporting the frame. The boy's father was stretched out beside him as the two disassembled a worn-out clutch.

"Clarence, could I speak to you for a minute?" Catfish asked, kneeling down and peering at the pair of shade-tree mechanics. "I'm Catfish Smith, coach at Mount Vernon."

The kid crawled out and looked up from a handsome face. His badly worn knit shirt clung to his sweaty back, chest, and shoulders, outlining an upper torso of bulging, hard muscles. As the boy stood, his taut thighs looked like they would burst open the old blue jeans he wore. At six feet and one hundred seventy-five pounds, he looked stronger than anybody in the prior day's practice. If this kid can run, Catfish thought, tackling him has got to be like bulldogging a rhino, plenty to grab but impossible to throw.

When the coach extended his hand, the boy hesitated, glancing down at his grimy palms.

"Clarence, I hear you're a fine football player," Catfish said, ignoring the grease and dirt. "We had our first practice yesterday, and I was quite pleased with the boys' efforts. I can see the makings of a strong football team, one that just might win a district title. How'd you like to be on a championship team?"

"Coach, I'd like that, but once school starts up, I'd have no way to get home after practice. The buses would be gone by then, and I'd have to walk. When the days get shorter, it'd be dark before I could get out here."

"I understand, son," Catfish said, glancing at the broken-down car. "But is there anything else that would keep you from playing football?"

"I reckon not, Coach, if those teachers won't kick me out of school."

"Good," Catfish said, smiling. "Now, if I drive you home every day after practice and on Saturday mornings after games, would you agree to play for me?"

"Sure, if Ma and Pa say it's okay."

"How about it, Mr. Crowston?" the coach asked, peering underneath the propped-up car.

The boy's father crawled out and slowly pushed to his feet, a solidly built man.

"You sayin' you'd get him home in time to do his chores every day?" Clarence's father asked, wiping his massive hands on the legs of his overalls.

Catfish hesitated, as if considering the consequences of breaking a promise made to this plow horse of a farmer.

"I'll get him here, and help with his work, if necessary," Catfish replied. "I think your boy's got the potential of being an outstanding player, and I'll do whatever it takes to ensure he has every opportunity."

"I sure can't be runnin' to town to fetch him," the man said, glancing around at the old Ford. "Now son, you'd better get your ma's word on it before you go gettin' your hopes up."

After Clarence had wiped his hands on an old rag, he and Catfish headed for the house.

"Hold up a minute, son," Mr. Crowston said. "Help me get this car off these blocks."

Catfish watched as the boy joined his father beside the Ford. Bending his legs and bowing his back, Clarence slipped his hands under the car frame below the driver's door while his father did the same beneath the passenger door. The father glanced at his son, nodded his head, and the two lifted the side of the car a few inches off the stack of boards.

"Coach, could you slip those blocks out for us?" the man asked, his voice husky with strain.

Amazed at their display of strength, Catfish dropped to his knees and knocked over the two stacks of boards, eased back, and watched while Clarence and his father lowered the car to the ground.

The three then walked around and slipped through the front door where Catfish explained his plan to the boy's mother. After the coach had repeated the explanation three times, it was all settled.

"Hold on there, Coach," Mr. Crowston said as Catfish and Clarence headed for the Pontiac. "I reckon I can do the afternoon chores this fall. No use you wearin' out your car haulin' my boy 'tween here and town."

"Thanks, sir," Catfish said. "I'll find a good place for him to stay in town, and check on him every night."

Satisfied, Mrs. Crowston packed the boys clothes into a cardboard suitcase and sent him off alongside the coach with the understanding that Catfish would watch out for him, "like he was your own."

It did not take long for the coach to convince the superintendent to hire Clarence as a school janitor to sweep floors and empty trashcans each day after practice. With income enough for Clarence's room and board assured, the coach then explained his problem to Mrs. Bessie at the Miller Hotel.

"Everything is all set, Mrs. Miller, if I can find him a place to stay here in town. But it's got to be where I can keep an eye out for him, and with somebody who'll feed him properly."

With a nod and a smile from Mrs. Miller, a deal was struck.

About two o'clock that afternoon, Clarence showed up at the coach's door, and they turned the green Pontiac toward the football field. Recalling the grumbling at the end of yesterday's practice, Catfish was concerned that only half the boys would show up. But that worry was overshadowed by the prospect of seeing this Samson-like farm boy run with a football. Though Catfish was tempted to immediately put a uniform on Clarence and have him sprint up and down the field, he settled for playing catch with his new prospect until the other players arrived. Not only could Crowston catch the ball with ease, but when the coach overthrew or missed to one side or the other, Clarence always managed to leap and corral the ball, displaying the agility and quickness of a cougar.

Gradually the boys drifted in, sore, tired, and lacking the enthusiasm they had arrived with twenty-four hours before. As their numbers grew, Catfish's concern over defectors melted away as all the players of significance filed in, dressed, and made their way onto the field.

Any question about Crowston's speed got answered on the initial fifty-yard sprint. Yokum, pumping his arms, grimacing, and giving it his all, was the closest behind Clarence, yet trailed the farm boy by five yards. Well before Crowston reached the finish line, the coach was wishing for another picture, one with his newest prospect framed squarely in the lens while gliding down the field like a gazelle. The boy's face was relaxed, as were his hands and fingers, and the only movement of his head was forward. All motion of his arms, shoulders, legs, and his feet was perfectly synchronized and so effortless that it appeared he could run forever.

Immediately Catfish thought of Bob Suggs, the man who had told him about Crowston. Spotting Suggs sitting high in the stands, the coach waved, prompting the avid fan to return the greeting, white teeth gleaming.

The players were grateful when Catfish cut short the sprint session, regardless of the reason. Crowston had passed the first test, but running across an open field like a deer is one thing, while slamming helmet-to-helmet into opposition like a bull ram is quite another. The coach could not wait to find out which he had.

"Form two lines, and let's do a little head-on tackling," Catfish said.

A brutal drill, it pitted three boys, a runner, a blocker, and a tackler, against each other in vicious combat, while the others looked on and waited their turn. The coach considered Shurtleff his best tackler, and he wasted no time getting him lined up against a weak blocker with Crowston the ball carrier.

"Hut!" hollered the coach as he tossed the football to the fleet farm boy.

Shurtleff shoved the blocker aside like he was a cardboard cutout, and took aim on the ball carrier. When Clarence reached the tackler, he juked a half step to his left and then darted past Shurtleff to the right. The ace tackler managed to stretch out his left hand and only slightly brush it against the runner's left leg.

Crowston not only had speed, but he showed cat-like agility with an instinct for using both to avoid a tackler.

"Okay, let's do that again," Catfish said, smiling inside, "but this time, Clarence, I don't want you dodging the tackler. There'll be times when the only way to get the three yards we need is for you to lower your shoulder and go straight ahead. Let's see if you can get those yards the hard way."

Again Shurtleff heaved the blocker aside and leaned forward, ready to attack. The pop must have been audible for three blocks when these two young rams collided. It might have been a standoff except for the runner's forward momentum. To Shurtleff's credit, he hung on and eventually penned Clarence's heels together and brought him down, five yards later. For the remainder of the drill, Crowston substituted for every runner who appeared overmatched by a tackler. If Catfish's defensive players could learn to tackle Clarence, the coach believed, they would be capable of bringing down the toughest of opposing ball carriers.

"Anybody here think they can stop Swede for no gain?" Catfish asked. While cycling each player through the drill three times, he had begun referring to Clarence as "Swede."

All eyes switched to the farm boy, a fair-complexioned blond, as if he were a seven-foot Viking. When no one stepped forward, the coach muttered something about not having to kick anybody off the team for lack of intelligence.

The coach then proceeded to put his troops through a grueling workout that consisted of drill after drill, leaving his players wondering if their mentor knew a single football play. Catfish talked constantly, sometimes yelling at a player he thought was not giving one hundred percent effort. But he was just as quick to wrap his arms around a boy's sagging shoulders and praise him for getting it right. The theme that ran through everything the coach said was, "To be a champion, you have to work harder and longer than everybody else. If you don't want to pay the price, check it in now, because it's only going to get rougher and tougher."

Another trait soon noticed by his players was Catfish's fondness for the underdog. Repeatedly he would ease over beside one of his smaller players, drape an arm across his shoulders, and with a twinkle in his eye, say, "It's not the size of the dog in the fight, son, but the size of the fight in the dog."

Often he would follow this trite saying with a demonstration of how to gain leverage, how to surprise an adversary, and how to overcome a lack of heft with quickness and wits. Without pads, Catfish would line up as a blocker or tackler and show his charges how to gain advantage with a forearm shiver, or how to grab the opposing blocker and yank him forward while slipping past him, or demonstrate how to cut the feet out from under a larger defender with a rolling body block. "Hit 'im before he can hit you, and hit 'im hard when he's most vulnerable," he would instruct them. After a failed attempt by one of his smaller players, the coach would bend down and whisper advice through his leather ear-hole, pat him on the head, and then sic him on some boy half again his size. By the end of practice, he had Robby Campbell blocking like he was six inches taller and thirty pounds heavier, and every small player on the team sported a bulldog attitude.

After practice on Friday afternoon, Catfish gathered his boys under the old oak tree in front of the field house. After three days of intense practice in early September's caldron, the players were looking forward to staying out a little later that night, maybe having a milkshake with a girlfriend at their favorite cafe, and two days without wind-sprints or that bone-rattling blocking and tackling drill.

"Boys," the coach began, "we've had three good practices, and I like what I've seen. We may not have the talent of some teams on our schedule, but you've got more fighting spirit than any group I've ever seen. And I'd rather lose with a bunch of boys like you than win with a truckload of talented hotshots."

He hesitated, scanning every sweaty, dirty face peering up at him from the late afternoon shade.

"And I promise you," he continued, his eyes narrowing and hard-lined ridges rippling the length of his clenched jaws, "I don't like to lose, not ever!"

Again, he eyed his players, letting his words, along with a fierce determination emblazoned on his face, work on their minds.

"In the past," he continued, "you boys have run a single-wing offense. That's all you know. But we're going to operate from the T-formation this year. So far, we've just worked on fundamentals, but starting Monday, we'll have two practices a day. At nine each morning, we'll practice the new offense, then at three in the afternoon, we'll continue our work on fundamentals. Tomorrow morning at nine, we'll begin the transformation to the new offense, so you boys be in bed by nine tonight. Pierce, you and Clark get here thirty minutes early. Now, you're free to go."

For a moment, the boys were immobilized by what they had heard. Their new coach, already the toughest taskmaster they had known, had just taken his brutality to a new level. Some were not sure they could handle it, emotionally or physically, but slowly, they pushed up from the ground and filed quietly into the dressing room.

After showering and dressing, Shurtleff, Cargile, and Pierce walked up West Main to the plaza. Ambling along the storefronts on the south side, they turned in at Mercer's Drug Store, a favorite hangout for school kids and for regular Saturday morning rehashing of Friday night's games. The boys slipped onto three tall stools fronting the long, narrow counter and sat quietly.

"What'll it be for you boys?" Fred Mercer asked, studying them from behind the counter.

When they did not answer right away, he continued. "How about milkshakes? You boys look like you could use some energy."

They shook their heads in unison. "Against the rules," Cargile volunteered.

"That new coach, I suppose," the druggist guessed.

"Yeah," Pierce said. "We can't eat anything good."

"How about hamburgers?" Mercer asked. "On the house."

The boys nodded, smiling for the first time in three days.

By the time the trio had devoured their free burgers, they were horsing around and laughing at practice incidents that had seemed almost tragic earlier.

"Coach Smith is long and lean, like a snake," Cargile said to Mercer.

"Yeah, like a West Texas rattler," Pierce agreed, "but meaner."

"If he comes in here," Shurtleff said, picking up a topless saltshaker filled with toothpicks, "hide these things. He'd eat every last one of them as an appetizer."

"Yeah, better put out some galvanized nails for him," Cargile said, laughing.

"He must be one tough son-of-a-gun," Mercer said with a low whistle.

"He's tough, all right," Pierce said. "I bet his hide is as tough as that mesh outfit that Sir Galahad wore, that wiry stuff that a sword wouldn't cut."

The other two frowned at their quarterback.

"Sir who?" Cargile asked.

"Oh, never mind," Pierce said, glancing from one empty face to the other. "We'd better get on home before Coach has us running laps for breaking curfew."

64

As they got up to leave, Pierce noticed a girl enter from the back room, and hesitated.

"See you tomorrow," he said offhandedly to Cargile and Pugh as they glanced back from the doorway.

"Could I help you?" the girl asked as Pierce eased back onto the stool.

"Coach Smith says everything is off limits," he replied. "I'm Glenn Pierce. I don't think I've seen you around before."

"Gwendolyne Orren," she said. "I live in Saltillo where my father works for Gulf Oil, but I'll be attending school here this year."

"How'll you get back and forth?"

"I'm staying with the Clintons. Mrs. Argeree lets me use a room through the week. They're right across the street from the school."

"Looks like you're getting ready to leave," Pierce said, sliding off the stool. "If you're heading home, I'd like to walk along with you. I live on Rutherford, a couple of blocks farther south."

Glenn had been immediately struck by Gwendolyne's easy smile, curly hair, and pretty face, and kept glancing over at her as they walked along Main toward Holbrook.

"If you get sick," he said, struggling for a subject, "there's the hospital. Of course, it's not a very fancy one. Last year I got sick with strep throat and ran a high fever. They tried about everything, thinking I had diphtheria, but my fever just shot on up. Finally, Dr. Chandler gave me sulfa drugs, and I got over it."

"He must be a good doctor."

"Practically a neighbor," Pierce said. "He lives on South Kaufman. I used to mow his lawn, and his neighbors'."

They turned south on Holbrook Street, and ambled along to the Cottonbelt railroad, where Pierce hesitated between the rails.

"I work down at the ice house, when they need a little help," he said, pointing west to a building just north of the tracks.

By the time they reached the Clinton's home, Glenn knew he wanted to see Gwendolyne again.

"Will you be at Mercer's tomorrow?" he asked.

"No, my father will come get me tonight and bring me back early Monday morning."

"Okay if I drop by and walk you home again Monday afternoon?"

"Sure," she replied, flashing an easy smile.

When the main body of the squad arrived Saturday morning, the new coach had already spent half an hour working with Pierce and

Clark on the center-to-quarterback snap, the most frequent and critical ball exchange in the playbook. While Catfish worked this duo, the other players pulled their dirty, sweat-stained jerseys over their shoulder pads, slipped into shorts instead of their padded pants, and laced up their new cleated shoes. Joining the quarterback and center, they got their first lesson in the T-formation.

From a clipboard, Catfish showed them the first play, a simple halfback dive. At the top of the page it read, "23-Dive." Its mirror image, "44-Dive," was drawn on the backside of the page.

"To understand the play scheme," the coach said, "you have to know the numbering system. The first digit refers to the ball carrier. The quarterback is the 1-back; left half is the 2-back; right half is the 4-back; and the fullback is the 3-back. Now, the gaps between the linemen are numbered, odd numbers to the left side, even to the right, starting with the gap between the center and guard and moving out. So, to the left is the 1-gap, 3-gap, 5-gap, and out wide is the 7-gap, and to the right is the 2-gap, 4-gap, 6-gap, and 8-gap. 0-gap is right up the gut, behind the center. Now, on 23-dive, who carries the ball?"

"Left half," Pierce said.

"And where does he run with it?"

"Between the left guard and tackle," Shurtleff answered.

"That's right. Everybody got that?"

The boys all nodded. It seemed pretty simple, given time to think about it.

Then the coach lined them up, spacing the linemen a foot apart. He positioned Pierce at quarterback directly behind the center, and the fullback, Crowston, three steps behind him. The left half, Irby, was set to the fullback's left, and the right half, Yokum, to his right.

"Let's walk through this," Catfish said. "Linemen, there's no defense, so when the ball is snapped, just jog straight ahead for five yards."

Pierce barked, "Down, set, hut one!"

Clark slapped the ball up to the quarterback's hands. Pierce took it, quickly turned to his left and stuck the ball into Tom Irby's gut as the halfback trotted straight ahead, splitting the space between the slow-moving guard and tackle.

"Excellent, Pierce," Catfish said, clapping. "Irby, be sure and get your right arm up, elbow high, and your left arm cradled down below, so the quarterback can slip the ball between them. A lazy right elbow will cause a fumble every time."

They did the same thing on the other side, 44-dive. Then the coach had them run the play at full speed, still without a defense. When they were running the twin plays smoothly, he added defensive players, but the hitting was only half-speed.

The coach then turned to the linemen.

"A foot-wide gap may seem too much to you, but there's a reason," he said. "First, we know the snap count, and we're gonna be faster off the ball than our opponents. Second, the wide spaces will invite the defense to slip into the gaps, and that will just give us better blocking angles."

Next, Catfish showed the linemen how to perform straight-ahead blocking, each lineman responsible for the opposing player in front of him.

"Remember, you know the snap count, so shoot out there that split second before the defense sees the ball move, and get your head on the side opposite the way you want to drive the defensive man. Knock him down if you can, but the main thing is to keep him shielded from the ball carrier."

He had them run the two basic plays while he concentrated on the guard and tackle, making sure they positioned themselves correctly and walled their defensive counterparts away, forming an open lane for the ball carrier.

"On dive plays, there's no time to do anything fancy, so you'll block straight ahead. It's basic, power football, and you linemen will determine if we succeed or fail."

Then he taught them two more companion plays, 45- and 26-slant. On 45-slant, the left-side linemen angle blocked to their right, and the off-side guard, the right guard, pulled down the line to his left to help the left halfback double-team block the defensive tackle. With that scheme understood, he taught an alternative. With straight-ahead blocking, the left end and tackle would double-team the defensive man in front of the tackle, while the left halfback blocked the defensive end. The blocking scheme used, the coach explained, would depend on the defensive alignment.

While the blockers made a lane for the runner, the quarterback would spin clockwise, fake a handoff to the fullback through the 2-gap, and then give the ball to the right halfback through the 5-gap.

"The fake to the fullback will pull the linebackers to the middle so when the ball carrier breaks through the line of scrimmage off left tackle, he'll have room to run," Catfish explained.

67

The first attempt failed. When Pierce stuck the ball in the fullback's cradled arms, then tried to pull it out, the ball tumbled to the ground, but Pierce and Crowston quickly came up with a solution.

"Swede," the quarterback said, "don't clamp down on the ball when it's a fake. I'll slide my hands toward the far end of the ball to protect it from accidentally getting knocked loose." Then he turned to the halfback. "I'll pull my hands to the near end of the ball when I'm giving it to you, so clamp down on it, and I'll slip my hands out."

After a few practices using that technique, the fakes and handoffs went smoothly.

For two hours they ran these four basic plays, then Catfish lined the boys up for wind-sprints. He again went through the motivational scenario of the game-winning run with the district championship on the line, focusing on the second tier of runners rather than the leaders.

As the boys left practice, Catfish was in an unusually good humor. The exchange between center and quarterback had gone well, and Pierce had proven to be a quick learner, sure-footed, and adept, even sneaky, in handling the ball. The two halfbacks showed quickness, requiring only a slight opening to pick up five yards. And his best offensive weapon, Catfish believed, was yet to be unleashed.

7

September 10, 1943

On Friday before the start of classes on September 13, Superintendent Fleming called all his teachers together in the high school gymnasium. The elementary school included the first eight grades; high school consisted of ninth through eleventh. To encourage mingling among the staff, tables with snacks, coffee, soft drinks, and punch were arranged at one end, while four large round tables with chairs stood in the center of the shiny hardwood floor.

Catfish arrived early and dropped by the superintendent's office where he got his nametag, a list that identified teachers to grades and subjects, and the most recent yearbook. The coach took these to his classroom, pulled the door closed, and studied the list.

High School

Principal:	Paul G. Arthur
Agriculture:	W. G. "Hoot" Gibson
Homemaking:	Miss Viola Gillespie
Spanish:	Miss Irene Binnion
Science:	Mrs. Irene St. Clair
English:	Miss Erlena McBrayer
History:	Mrs. Mary Grace Arthur
Coach/History:	Milburn Smith
Business:	Miss Marion Holcombe
Math:	Kemper Zercher

Grade School

Principal:	Rufus Bolger
1st grade:	Miss Beth Cargile
2nd grade:	Miss Mary Lou Stringer
3rd grade:	Mrs. Evelyn Newsom
4th grade:	Mrs. Ruby Jo Jones
5th grade:	Mrs. Laura Garner
6th grade:	Miss Virginia Grace Adams
7th grade:	Miss Gertrude Smith
8th grade:	Miss Faye Chessire

If Catfish's boys were to have trouble with schoolwork, he guessed English, math and science were the most likely subjects. He underlined the names of Erlena McBrayer, Kemper Zercher, and Irene St. Clair, and since he had not yet met the high school principal, he circled Paul Arthur's name as well. Using the yearbook, he matched names to faces for the returning teachers, all new to him except Irene Binnion whom he had known from their college days in Commerce and from 1942 when both had taught at Winfield.

With a kaleidoscope of pictures and names spinning in his head, the coach then made his way down the hall and entered the gymnasium through the south doorway. The teachers were gathered in three bunches near the far end, so Catfish ambled along the west wall unnoticed until he reached the small group gathered around Superintendent Fleming in front of the stage.

After Catfish had met the two principals and Hoot Gibson, Fleming took the coach around and introduced him to the other high school teachers. Irene Binnion smiled and waved as Catfish walked up.

"Coach Smith, I'm curious," she said after introductions. "Have you settled down any?"

"Yes, ma'am," he replied. "Considerably."

"I remember the time we were all assembled in the auditorium at East Texas State," she said, intentionally drawing the attention of the surrounding teachers. "We were listening to a visiting speaker, some celebrity invited by President Whitley. Suddenly, the speaker goes silent, his eyes fixed on something rolling down the wide center aisle, which started at the big double doors in back and sloped right down to the foot of the podium. Well, I was seated along that aisle, so I saw it right away, but others stood and craned their necks. Some even got up and walked over so they could see. It was a full roll of toilet paper tumbling along, leaving a narrow, white path right back to those double doors. The students all got a big laugh out of it, but President Whitley wanted to boot you out of school right then and there, Milburn."

Catfish, towering over the other teachers, shifted from left foot to right and back again while his face grew warm and flushed.

"That fellow was one of the dullest speakers I've ever heard," he said, "and I thought the place needed livening up a bit."

When the laughter settled, Miss Binnion continued.

"And what about that fall when you showed up on campus in the back seat of an old black Ford chauffeured by your friend Charley Grady? I heard you pulled up in front of President Whitley's home, stepped out wearing a stovepipe hat and black tails, and knocked on the front door."

"It'll make perfect sense to you when I explain," Catfish said. "It was the start of my sophomore year, and throughout the previous term, President Whitley had treated me like I was some country bumpkin. He didn't want me in his school, so I thought I'd just show him I could put on airs with the best of them."

Now, thoroughly introduced to the teachers of Mount Vernon High, Milburn Smith, new athletic director, coach, and world history teacher, milled among the group for maybe half an hour before he sought out the English teacher.

"Miss McBrayer, I'm sure some of my football players will be in your class, and I want to make sure they do their assignments. If one starts goofing off, just let me know."

"Coach Smith, I don't anticipate a problem, but I'll be in touch if there's one I can't handle."

Catfish then spotted the science teacher who was visiting with the math instructor.

"Just the two I've been looking for," Catfish said, joining them.

"I'm Irene St. Clair," the woman said, "and this is Kemper Zercher, my brother."

"It's a pleasure meeting you," Catfish said, shaking Kemper's hand. "I want both of you to know that I expect my boys to get their assignments and behave in class. So, if one of them gives you trouble, just contact me, and I'll take care of the problem."

"I appreciate that, Coach," Mrs. St. Clair said, "but tell me something. How would you motivate a student that we teachers can't?"

"Ma'am," he replied, "teachers usually explain to a student how learning his lessons will give him a happier future, while I show him how it'll make his life considerably more pleasant right now."

Mrs. St. Clair stood, hands on hips, shaking her head while her brother enjoyed a good laugh.

After visiting another twenty minutes, Catfish eased out and headed home where he drew up more plays to be taught to his boys the following morning.

From the first day, the coach drilled his boys in the basics of the game. He demonstrated, coaxed, berated, and cajoled his boys until they began to show real promise. Though young, he knew he had a few special players such as Charles Shurtleff, Glenn Pierce, Harry Jack Pugh, Dan Cargile, and that dynamite blond fullback. Others, like Jimmy Pierce, Joe Clark, Tom Irby, Jerry Yokum, and James Caudle, were consistent, steady players, while hard-working young Robby Campbell proved to be a coach's delight. Catfish had others who were not especially talented, but who had shown heart and toughness, especially the smaller ones to whom he had given so much attention and encouragement.

After practice one afternoon, with Glenn Pierce headed for Mercer's to see Gwendolyne, Dan Cargile and Harry Jack Pugh hung around and helped Olan Ray Brewer gather up footballs.

"We'll finish up here," the coach said, noticing the two. "You boys shower and get on home."

"Coach," Harry Jack said, "we're country boys, and sometimes it's mighty hard to get a ride home after practice. We thought maybe you could arrange a room for us at the hotel, like you did for Swede."

For a moment, Catfish eyed the two.

"You boys realize you'll have to work for your keep, don't you?"

"Yes, sir."

"And you know I'll be watching you like a hawk. You mess up just once, and you'll be thumbing rides again."

"We won't cause you any trouble, Coach."

Catfish soon had jobs at the school for the pair, and they shared a room at the hotel. At nine o'clock their very first night there, Mrs. Miller knocked on their door.

"Yes, ma'am?" Cargile said, peeking out.

"Phone call for you two," she explained.

The boys followed her to the telephone, and Cargile took the handset.

"Hello," he said tentatively.

72

"You boys got your homework done?" Catfish asked.

"Yes, sir."

"Then why is the light on in your room?"

"Just getting ready to switch it off, Coach."

"If it's not out in five minutes, I'm coming over there and taking the light bulb."

"Yes, sir."

Walking back to their room, Harry Jack glanced over at Cargile. "How'd he know our light was on?"

"He probably sneaked around and looked through our window," Cargile replied.

"You think he checks on all the players like that?"

"I don't know, but switch that light off right now," Cargile said as they entered the room and then headed over to look out the window.

The next day when they explained about the call, they learned that Catfish had been checking on several other players, too.

"I'd just got home three nights ago and stepped onto the porch when I heard the phone ringing," Shurtleff told them. "I might near ripped the door off its hinges getting inside before my mother could answer it."

"What do you think he'd do if you weren't there?" Pugh asked.

"I don't know, but I'm downright certain I wouldn't enjoy it."

*   *   *

The first day of class, Catfish explained to his students his plan for discussing current events each Friday.

"I don't care how you keep up with the news, but you're expected to come to class ready to discuss some recent event of significance. For anyone who doesn't have access to a newspaper, I'll have a few copies of the local paper here on the corner of my desk."

The first Friday Catfish was anxious to learn what his students thought was newsworthy. After handing out the newspapers to a few, who obviously were not prepared, he asked for a volunteer to introduce their chosen subject.

"The Tidewater Drilling Company has found oil on the Gilbert place near South Franklin," a boy mentioned. "My dad said that was important."

"I agree," Catfish said. "But tell us why it's significant."

"Well, cars and trucks use oil, and so do tractors and things like that."

"Yes, and it'll be good for the local economy, as well," Catfish said. "But the demand for oil products is especially high right now. Can anyone tell me why?"

"The war," a girl said. "That's why we have rationing of everything."

"That's right," Catfish replied, pleased with the answer. "Now, someone tell us about the war. Who's fighting?"

"We're fighting the Japanese," a boy replied. "They bombed our ships in Pearl Harbor, and now we've got to whip them good."

"Why did they attack us?" Catfish asked.

"Because we won't let them have our scrap iron and stuff like that," a boy replied. "Last year I helped gather up all the old rusty iron around our place and haul it up to the town square. Everybody did. They loaded it on a train and gave it to our army."

"The embargo," Catfish agreed. "But maybe there's another reason. Who else is involved in the war?"

"Hitler," a girl replied. "It's horrible how he's slaughtering people in Europe."

"Of course it is," Catfish said. "But this war is called a world war. Why?"

"Because so many people are fighting," a boy replied. "England and France are fighting the Nazis, too."

"That's right," Catfish said. "The war started September 1, 1939, when Germany invaded Poland. Two days later, both England and France declared war on Germany, and the conflict spread quickly. Those aligned with Hitler are called the Axis powers and those aligned with England and us are known as the Allies. It's called a world war because forty-three nations are involved in the conflict, though the Axis is generally thought of as Germany, Italy, and Japan, while the Allies are considered to be the United States, Great Britain, France, and Russia. And the war is being fought throughout major portions of the world: Europe, Africa, Asia, and the major oceans.

"Earlier, I mentioned there might be a second reason that Japan attacked us, other than the embargo and freezing of their funds in our banks. Though the Lend-Lease Act allowed us to provide war materials, food, and clothing to our friends in Western Europe, we were not directly involved in the war, and Germany, Japan's ally, wanted to make sure it stayed that way. Striking us in Hawaii and pulling us into a war in the Pacific, these two believed, would cripple our navy so we could not effectively oppose Japan's expansion plans in Asia and might keep us out of the European conflict.

"Now, let's get back to more current events. Do you think their ploy has worked?"

"No," a boy replied. "I think we're gonna storm Europe and hang Hitler."

"That's right," another spoke up sharply. "Italy gave up only five days after we invaded them, and by the time we get through with the Germans, they'll be begging to surrender."

"You're right about Italy. They surrendered September eighth, about a month ago. Earlier in the summer, their leader, Mussolini, was stripped from power and imprisoned by his own people.

"But when we invade Germany, do you think it will be easy? Remember, they have devised a new technique of waging war, *blitzkrieg*, that has helped them defeat most of Western Europe, including France and its impenetrable Maginot Line, in less than a year."

"We'll whip them Nazis, and when I graduate, I'm gonna volunteer to go help do it."

"Son, I appreciate your patriotism, and the fact that you and so many of today's students will be soldiers in the near future is one reason it's so important that we know what's going on in the world."

A girl raised her hand, and Catfish nodded at her.

"Ensign James Musick Drummond from Hopewell, a friend of my family, just married Ann Watson from Lone Oak. He recently received his air wings at the naval base in Corpus Christi, and now he'll be going off to war. I think it's a shame that so many boys have to go fight and maybe die in a few months, leaving so many young widows behind."

"War is terrible," Catfish replied. "But evil men like Hitler have to be stopped, and we can't depend on someone else to do the job. I admire your friend for doing his part. I would consider it a privilege to do the same. We will hope and pray he returns safely to his wife.

"That'll be all for today. You may use the remaining ten minutes to study or read the paper."

*   *   *

By the first of October, Catfish's twenty-three football players were weary of practicing and tired of beating up each other. They wanted a real opponent to turn all their fury against, and they were anxious to display the skills they had worked so hard to develop. Their eagerness to test themselves, to garner that first win, was matched by that of their coach.

At nine o'clock the morning of the first game, the student body assembled in the high school gymnasium, filling the stands on the east side. On the elevated stage across the gym floor, Catfish and his players sat in three rows of folding chairs behind the podium from which Superintendent Fleming spoke. After being introduced, Principal Arthur called the names of the new teachers, having them stand, the last being the world history teacher and coach.

Catfish stepped up to the podium, towering over it. From the gym floor below, the cheerleaders stared up at him as if he were a giraffe peering down on them. From the bleachers across the way, the student body became still, quiet, attentive.

"I'm proud to be coach of the Mount Vernon Tigers," he began, and then waited momentarily for the sporadic applause to fade.

"This school has a proud tradition. Its teams, football and basketball, are considered the standard in this part of Texas. Only last year our basketball team went to the state tournament in Austin. A few years back, our undefeated football team won district, bi-district, and then the regional championship. They have shown us the way."

This time, the coach waited while applause throughout the student body rattled the windows. At the first sign of the roar weakening, Catfish raised and lowered his large open hands, hushing and reseating the crowd.

"Now we enter a new era. The accomplishments of the great Tiger teams of the past will only stir our opponents to play their best against us. So week after week, we have to prove to them, to you, to this community, that we are worthy of wearing that purple and white uniform, worthy of representing you."

He hesitated, his face becoming solemn as he leaned forward, his left hand gripping the ridged side of the podium and his right extended toward the student body, his long index finger pointing at the silent audience.

"Right here and now, I promise you that these boys behind me will rise to the occasion. They will show that great Tiger fighting spirit every minute, every second, of every game, and they will make you proud!"

The place erupted, students jumping to their feet, clapping and hollering, and a few boys split the air with shrill whistles. The superintendent, principal, and teachers uncrossed their legs and joined

76

in. The players' faces beamed as chill bumps popped up on their arms and the hair on the back of their necks bristled.

When the cheering subsided, Catfish introduced each player by name, preceded by their number stitched in purple on the white football jerseys pulled over their street shirts. The students and faculty applauded each player, with the noise level dipping only momentarily as the coach called the next athlete.

When it was over, Principal Arthur brought the pep rally to a close, sending the students to their next class. Millard Fleming stepped over to Catfish.

"I've never seen it done better," he said, a wide smile gapping his face. "If those boys could step on that field right now, they'd beat the tar out Clarksville."

For the coach and his boys, the following hours seemed like days. Finally, school let out and most of the boys ambled up town and hung around in the local cafes and the popular Mercer's Drug Store until time to head for the field house. Then time really dragged while they sat around on hard benches or stretched out on the cool concrete floor.

After a while they could hear cars arriving, then the familiar grinding gears of a school bus. The cacophony of horn blows, symbol clangs, and drumbeats indicated the bus had delivered the school band.

Then another bus pulled up and stopped in front of the field house.

"They're here," Caudle said, rising to his feet as if he were going out to challenge them.

The other Mount Vernon players sat up, listening. Catfish stopped taping Glenn Pierce's left ankle long enough to scan the boys' tense faces. The gray cinderblock wall dividing the field house effectively separated the two teams, but it reached only as high as the paper-thin ceiling. Voices from the visitors' side pierced the covering and bounced down to the Tigers' side.

"When did we last play these guys?" someone from the Clarksville team asked.

"Three years ago, I think," someone answered.

"Who won?"

"We did, twenty to a big, fat goose egg."

"They any good this year?"

"The last few seasons they've lost more than they've won, and Gilmer whipped them twenty-seven to nothing last year. Then Pittsburg sent them home with their tails tucked between their legs, too."

"But they've got a new coach."

"I heard he got kicked out of the Army."

"Maybe so, but he won a state championship someplace out in West Texas."

"That was basketball in a little two-bit town that didn't even have a football team."

"Boys," Catfish said, his eyes flashing from one of his players to the next, "put on those uniforms."

His boys had been waiting for hours to hear that.

The racket of flopping pads and cleats on concrete muted the voices from the other side. Then, in their white uniforms with purple numbers, Catfish's first Mount Vernon team filed out and followed him toward the gridiron.

They took their time warming up, stretching, going through several muscle-loosening drills, and then ran a few basic plays against an imaginary defense. When the Clarksville team sprinted onto the field, some of the Mount Vernon boys gawked at the visitors.

"Get back to what you were doing," Catfish barked. "You'll get a good look at them soon enough."

A game is not like practice. Some players look great in scrimmage, but freeze up or become muddle-headed when shoved into the spotlight of a real contest. With six players on the starting team who had never played in a football game, Catfish had the jitters, too. After a month of practices, two per day for three weeks, his boys had learned their assignments, absorbed the fundamentals of blocking and tackling, and had honed their skills. But how would they perform during a game?

Knowing that the initial play of a game can set the tone for several minutes, Catfish was ready, whether his team kicked or received. He had drilled his team on the kicking game until the boys were sick of it.

Mount Vernon won the coin toss and elected to receive the kickoff because Catfish believed he had a superior trio of kick-return men in Yokum, Glenn Pierce, and Swede. Pierce was a sure-handed, smart runner, and in a critical situation he could be used for a reverse or an across-field pass. As for Yokum, he had wings for feet. Just a little opening was all he needed. But Catfish preferred that his blond fullback return the ball because he could outrun most everybody, or he could run over a tackler if the need arose. Given an open field, he became a gazelle in a tiger's body.

The end-over-end kick went to Yokum. He veered toward the middle of the field, spotted Crowston and Pierce leading the way, and tucked in behind them. Finally, two Clarksville boys tripped Yokum up just short of the fifty-yard line. It was the kind of start Catfish had hoped for.

The coach had already given the first three plays to his quarterback. Yokum on a dive behind right tackle, big Dan Cargile, then Irby on a slant to the right side, both setting up the third play, a counter to Crowston behind left guard, Charles Shurtleff.

Yokum picked up four yards. Irby then got five more, leaving third and one yard needed for a first down. With the defense set to stop another run to the right, Pierce faked the dive play to Yokum, then spun and handed the ball to Swede who, after one step to the right, countered to the left of center. Shurtleff had driven his man to the inside, while Jimmy Pierce shielded his man to the outside, letting Crowston break through the line where a linebacker came at him, head on. The Swede did not juke or dodge, but lowered his shoulder, bowled the tackler onto his backside, and then veered to the outside. A defensive back made an effort about ten yards later, but he was no match for the powerful fullback. From there it was a footrace, and the Swede was not about to be caught. The scoreboard showed Mount Vernon six, Clarksville zero. Crowston added a point with a perfect kick out of the hold of his quarterback.

On the kickoff Mount Vernon stopped Clarksville on their twenty-seven yard line, and Catfish anxiously watched his defense go to work. Due to the new offensive formation and strong emphasis on fundamentals, he was less confident of his defense. But his boys were excited and swarmed the opposition to a minus two yards in three running attempts.

Mount Vernon received the punt and started their second offensive effort from their forty-yard line. They ate up yardage in chunks, ending the drive with a fifteen-yard sprint up the middle by Swede.

At halftime, the score was Mount Vernon nineteen and Clarksville zero. Catfish started the second half with backup players, those undersized bulldogs he had spent so much time developing. Though unable to score, they scared Clarksville a couple of times, while giving up no points. With no second-half scoring, the game ended 19-0. The Mount Vernon dressing room was bedlam until Catfish asked for quiet.

"Boys, the hard work paid off tonight. I want to be the first to congratulate you."

The players roared until their coach hushed them.

"Now, forget about this one. It's done. I don't want to hear one more word about tonight's game. If you fall in love with this week's victory, you'll get a broken heart with next week's loss.

"Now listen up. Next week we play Winnsboro. We go to their field. You can bet they'll have blood in their eyes and fire in their bellies. So, right now we start preparing for the Red Raiders. I'll see you Monday at practice."

Saturday morning Catfish called Glenn Pierce. "How'd you like to do a little fishing?"

"Sure, Coach Smith," his quarterback replied, surprise in his voice.

Catfish drove over to the hilltop on Rutherford Street and picked up Pierce.

"Where do you fish?" the boy asked, settling into the seat.

"A little private pond in Winfield," the coach replied.

Along the way, Catfish talked about everything other than football. Pierce had never seen his coach so relaxed, so at ease. It occurred to him that this might be how Catfish escaped the pressure of coaching.

The coach turned right at Winfield, climbed a short hill, and pulled into a lengthy drive. Soon Catfish had pulled out his fishing equipment, and they struck out down the slope to a small pond northwest of the house.

After fishing a while and catching a few bass, which they threw back, Catfish turned to his quarterback.

"What do you think about Winnsboro?" he asked.

"We can beat 'em," Pierce replied.

"We've got to win this one," the coach said firmly. "Winning and losing are habit forming, like most anything else. You win three or four games, and you expect to win the next one, and the one after that. Same thing if you lose."

"Yes, sir."

"Are the boys excited about the game?"

"I think so," Pierce replied.

"We've got to make sure. Isn't your brother's birthday coming up soon?"

"Next Saturday," Pierce said, wondering at the question.

Soon they reeled in their lines and headed up the hill. At the car, Catfish pitched his fishing equipment inside then motioned Pierce to follow him to the door of the adjacent house.

Sam Smith stepped through the doorway as they reached the porch.

"My father," Catfish said to his quarterback. "Dad, this is Glenn Pierce."

Pierce's hand disappeared inside Sam's, as Catfish called to his mother, Ida. After a short visit, the coach said his goodbyes, and he and Pierce drove back to Mount Vernon, never mentioning football.

Catfish worked his boys long and hard the next week. His primary concern was player overconfidence, so all week he built the Winnsboro players up to be supermen, while convincing his boys that they were the underdogs. Based on Assistant Acie Cannaday's scouting report, Catfish put in a few new plays for the Red Raiders, which also served the purpose of keeping his players from becoming complacent and bored by repetition. While practicing the new plays, he introduced his players to a saying they would hear throughout the season.

"Run it right, or run it all night," he would bellow when his players struggled to learn their new assignments.

Thursday after practice, Catfish was helping the manager gather up footballs when Bob Suggs came over.

"You going to the game tomorrow night?" Catfish asked, having seen the man at every practice.

"Oh, I'd sure like to," Suggs replied, "but, Coach, I don't have no way."

"Well, how about riding on the bus with me and the team?"

The man hesitated. "I don't know, Coach."

"Why not?"

"Some folks might not think it proper."

"Ah, you just be here at the field house tomorrow afternoon at five. If anybody's got a complaint, let them see me about it."

Then Friday morning came, and the coach was nervous, not because of a pep rally or a football game, but because he had something he knew he must say to his players, fellow teachers, administrators, and students. It would be the hardest thing he had ever attempted to do.

8

October 1, 1943

For a moment Catfish stood at the podium, scanning the expectant faces of the Mount Vernon student body assembled in the bleachers across the gym floor for the traditional Friday morning pep rally. Teachers, school-board members, business leaders, and other townspeople crowded the entrances and spilled onto the polished hardwood.

The team's impressive showing against Clarksville had fan expectations skyrocketing, but of greater concern to the coach was the swelled heads of his players.

"Tonight," Catfish said, "we travel to Winnsboro to play the Red Raiders, a tough football team. I expect they have more talent than we do. No doubt they have more size. We slipped by them last year, but that'll just make them more determined to win this time. So, we need all you students and your parents to show up down there to support these boys behind me. They're in for the fight of their lives."

He then paused, letting his remarks sink in. Slowly, frown wrinkles gathered between Catfish's eyes, and he gripped the edges of the podium as if for support.

"Now, I want to talk about something more important than a football game, more important than winning a district championship."

His throat tightened, and he hesitated for a moment.

"There's a war being fought by young men not much older than these boys behind me. Some students who were here with you last year, friends, brothers, cousins, acquaintances, are now in Western Europe or in the Far Pacific, risking their lives for the freedoms we enjoy every day. Our quarterback has a brother, Wayne Pierce, who was sitting up here on this stage last year, just like Glenn is now. But he's answered a higher calling. Tomorrow, October ninth, he reaches his eighteenth birthday, and he will enlist in the Navy. Well, tonight we're gonna play this game for Wayne Pierce, and for all the Mount Vernon boys who are serving their country. Especially, we'll remember those who have already paid the ultimate price."

Catfish gripped the podium in silence as his face clouded. He looked down, shuffled his feet, and then raised his watery eyes to the crowd.

"As soon as possible after Pearl Harbor, I enlisted in the Army Air Corps. I wanted to do my part," he said, glancing down. "But I passed out in a bomber plane at twenty thousand feet. I had bleeding ulcers, so the Army doctor wouldn't let me stay. But I promise you, if they would take me back, I'd reenlist today."

He looked down again, trying to corral his emotions.

"So I'm coaching now, trying to develop these young men to be strong, physically and mentally. It may not be much, but it's my way of contributing.

"On the gridiron, a mistake penalizes your team. Over there, it can cost a life. Tonight, we can call timeout if we get tired or confused. Over there, there are no timeouts. Here, we practice all week to be ready for the contest on Friday night. Over there, the contest is all day every day. Tonight, I want my boys to show the steadfastness, the determined spirit of those young men fighting for their country, especially those who've been wounded while taking out the enemy or while saving a comrade.

"There's an award for such courage, such bravery. It's called the Purple Heart. Tonight, our team will play for something above and beyond winning a football game. Through our supreme efforts, we'll honor all Purple Heart recipients."

As Catfish turned and slowly left the stage, Millard Fleming jumped to his feet and started applauding. Then Paul Arthur joined him, followed by teachers, townspeople, and a teary-eyed student body.

*   *   *

Catfish arrived at the field house about four and began checking equipment, laying out the game uniforms, and seeing that the manager's kit had all the necessary items like tape, scissors, extra shoestrings, and chin straps. As five o'clock arrived, the boys began showing up. While loading the bus, Catfish kept an eye on the road and the streets beyond.

"Anybody seen Mr. Suggs?" he asked his players.

The boys shook their heads.

"Anybody know where he lives?"

"I think I do," James Caudle replied.

"Good," Catfish said as they loaded up. "You sit right behind the bus driver and give him directions to the house."

When the players were aboard Narvel Lawrence's white bus with "MOUNT VERNON TIGERS" stenciled in purple letters on the sides, Caudle pointed the way to Bob Suggs's home.

Catfish slipped out and knocked on the door of a small gray house.

A few minutes later, Bob stepped through the doorway, boarded the bus with a coat draped across his arm, and took a seat beside the coach.

Meanwhile, the players sat subdued, as they did throughout the thirty-minute drive to Winnsboro and then in the locker room while waiting for the game to start. It was as though they were on the eve of a battle.

The game started with the Red Raiders kicking the ball to the Tigers, and Irby returning it to the forty-yard line. On the first play Swede Crowston set the tone. He blasted through a hole to the left of his center, ran over a defensive player, and continued twenty-five yards until three of the opponents finally rode him to the turf. Harry Jack Pugh, Charles Shurtleff, Dan Cargile, James Caudle, Joe Clark, and Jimmy Pierce dominated the line of scrimmage, and the Tiger ball carriers only needed three plays to score.

Mount Vernon's emotional, swarming defense stifled the Winnsboro eleven while the purple-and-white offense scored four more touchdowns and two extra points. The score quickly ballooned to 32-6, Winnsboro's lone score coming when they blocked a Mount Vernon punt, sending the ball careening into the end zone where a Red Raider pounced on it.

Back in the dressing room, the boys refused to celebrate. Oh, they patted each other on the back, hugged, and pumped hands, but without their usual boisterous uproar. They displayed the same subdued mood on the bus ride back to Mount Vernon.

The following morning about breakfast time, Charles Devall from the *Optic-Herald* walked the few steps east from his office to the Miller Hotel where Catfish waited for the three boys housed there to finish their meal before driving them to their respective farms. Devall grabbed the opportunity to interview the coach.

"Quite a team you've got, Coach," the newspaperman said.

"All the boys played a great game," Catfish replied. "It's hard to beat a team with the spirit our boys showed last night. In all my years of coaching, I've never seen such grit and determination in a group of young men."

He hesitated a moment, a cup of coffee in his left hand, his elbows resting on the tabletop. "And another thing. I've never seen such loyal, enthusiastic sports fans as Mount Vernon has. They're our twelfth man."

While the reporter scribbled, Catfish stared out the window.

"I hope you'll write something else," he said. "Our manager, Olan Ray Brewer, doesn't get much attention, but we all appreciate him. He's our unsung hero."

*   *   *

Monday afternoon the team showed up for practice, and their subdued mood was gone. The acclaim lavished upon them over the weekend and at school had them laughing, pulling pranks, and generally enjoying themselves. With a strut in their walk and brashness in their voice, they left little doubt about their attitude. Their coach had seen it before.

As a player, Catfish had been confident, even cocky at times. On a few occasions he had exaggerated his self-assuredness to challenge himself, to push himself when he might not otherwise be highly motivated. Confidence follows on the heels of success, and he appreciated this in his players. Yet, with only two wins under their belts, he felt a need to temper their cocksureness.

Catfish immediately set out to get them focused on and respectful of Mount Pleasant, the opponent scheduled for Friday night. The boys willingly worked hard, though the coach gave them little choice, but all week they wore the air of victors.

After practice Thursday, Catfish was worried about his team and stopped by Mercer's Drug Store on his way home. Glenn Penn, a young soldier on furlough that the coach had come to know, came in and joined Catfish at his table.

"I guess you're riding high with two big wins right off the bat," Corporal Penn said.

"Too high, maybe," the coach replied.

"Ah, Catfish, you worry too much."

"Maybe so," he said, "but these boys from Mount Pleasant . . ."

"What's the matter?" Penn asked when Catfish stopped in mid-sentence and stared at the entrance.

"Who's that good-looking gal?" the coach asked.

The corporal glanced around and chuckled.

"Forget her," he said. "She's my sister."

"No, that pretty thing is no sister of yours."

"Sure she is!" Penn said, then turned his head and profiled his face. "Can't you see the resemblance?"

"None whatsoever."

"Dorothy Nell," Penn called to the woman. "Come over here a minute."

The young woman hesitated momentarily, and then walked over.

"Coach Smith doesn't believe you're my sister," the corporal said. "You tell him."

"I'm afraid he's right, Coach Smith," she said, extending her hand.

"Pleased to meet you," the coach replied, rising awkwardly. "And you can call me Catfish."

"It's nice meeting you, Coach Catfish," she replied, smiling, and then turned and walked away.

"See there!" Penn crowed. "Now look at me real close. See the likeness?"

Catfish slowly shifted his eyes from the retreating young woman to his friend seated across the table.

"Are you sure you're not adopted?" Catfish asked.

"Don't you think I'd know if I was an orphan?"

"Yeah, I guess you would," Catfish said, then smiled. "Because, nobody would have picked you."

Penn shook his head in pretended disgust.

"Tell me," Catfish said, "is she dating anybody?"

"Not much," Penn replied. "She had a steady boyfriend a few years back, a fellow named Lendon Davis. Everybody called him Skinny."

"What happened? I mean, why did she quit him?"

"He was a star player on Mount Vernon's 1938 championship team, but then he went off to Southern Methodist University and captained their football squad. Later, I heard he joined the Navy."

"How old is she?"

"Too young for you," Penn said, rising to his feet. "Guess I'd better walk her home. It's getting dark out, and there are wolves out there nearly as bad as the one in here."

"Me, a wolf?" Catfish protested, jumping to his feet. "Why, more likely I'm the trusty woodsman who'd save her."

"There's about as much truth to that as there is in the fairy tale itself, but come along anyway."

"I'll join you as far as the hotel," Catfish said, hurrying. "I need to check on my boys."

They rushed through the doorway and followed Dorothy Nell, who was headed east along Main Street. As they crossed Houston Street, often referred to as Smoky Row, they caught up with the young woman, Catfish to her left and her brother to her right, and three-abreast they proceeded to the intersection with Holbrook Street, where the Miller Hotel sat on the north side of Main.

"It's nice out tonight," Catfish said, glancing up at the purple sky. "I believe I'll just tag along with you, if that's okay."

They turned right on Holbrook and headed south until they reached Bolger's Motor Company where they crossed diagonally over to the Penn's home.

"It was a pleasure meeting you, Dorothy Nell," Catfish said, stopping. "And I hope to see you again soon."

"Wait just a minute," Glenn said as Catfish turned to walk away. "I want you to meet our parents. You'll see just how proud they are of their son."

The brother and sister headed for the door, and Catfish followed, muttering something about not mentioning the adoption thing.

When Glenn had called Frank and Lizzie Penn to the door, Catfish extended his hand. He declined their invitation to come inside for coffee, explaining that he had to get along to check on his players.

The coach then set a brisk pace up Holbrook to the hotel where his boys were gathered in Cargile's room studying for a test. Satisfied, Catfish stuffed his hands deep in his pockets and headed on home.

The next morning at school Assistant Coach Acie Cannaday stopped Catfish in the hallway and warned him that Mount Pleasant would be their greatest test so far.

"They're bigger and stronger than we are," the assistant explained, "and, they've got a team made up mostly of returning lettermen, so they don't make many mistakes."

The warning proved prophetic. The Tigers from Titus County dominated the line of scrimmage, boxed in Mount Vernon's ball carriers, and won 13-0. Mount Vernon's valiant effort at the end of the first half, running out of time with a first down on Mount Pleasant's three-yard line, provided little consolation for Catfish and his squad.

"Mount Pleasant just beat us," Catfish explained to Devall of the *Optic-Herald* the next morning. "I have no alibis to offer. We believe this game, hardly an hour long, taught us more about playing championship football than everything else we've learned to this point. We lost a hard-fought game, but that's history now.

"Next on our schedule is Pittsburg. We look forward to playing with more determination than ever, and I assure you we'll do our best to make the Pirates pay for last night's defeat.

"And let me add this. I'm as proud of these boys in defeat as in victory."

But something was bothering the coach. Bob Suggs had not made the trip to Mount Pleasant, the first game or practice the man had missed. So, Sunday afternoon Catfish paid a visit to Bob's home. The loyal fan was in bed fighting a fever.

"Mr. Suggs, you get well soon. I don't want you to miss another game," Catfish told him as he was leaving. "I think maybe you bring us good luck."

The man laughed weakly, and promised to be there for practices as soon as he was able.

"But I don't know about the Pittsburg game," Suggs told the coach.

"What do you mean?" Catfish asked.

"Some folks down there don't like my kind," Suggs explained.

"Your kind?"

"Jim Sowell, a shoeshine man over at Tom Newsome's barbershop, got roughed up down there a few years back. Some of those Pittsburg fellas grabbed him and took him out of town a ways. They stood him in a mud puddle and ran their horses at him. He got knocked down and stepped on a few times. Jim finally got away, but who knows about next time?"

"I promise nothing like that's gonna happen to you, Bob," Catfish said, grim-faced. "We haven't beaten the Pirates since nineteen thirty-nine, but if you'll go with us, we'll win this year."

Reluctantly, Bob agreed.

"Boys," Catfish explained at Monday afternoon's practice, "Mount Pleasant knocked us off that pinnacle we were perched on. In doing so, they showed us our weaknesses. We didn't block their defensive ends, and we allowed them to throw two touchdown passes on us. Now we know what we have to work on, where we've got to get better. If you want to be a champion, you have to pay the price, so let's get started right now."

Practices that week proved to be the toughest yet for Catfish's football team. With a determination his players had not previously seen, he drove them to correct deficiencies, but he also worked two new players into the lineup. Shurtleff was out with a cracked nose from the Mount Pleasant game, and Dan Cargile turned up ill on Wednesday. "Puny may be ready by Friday night," Catfish told his players, referring to Dan Cargile, "but we've got to be ready to play without him."

Catfish did not rely entirely on hard work. He had noticed that his quarterback could throw the ball with unusual accuracy. Further, he knew Harry Jack Pugh could catch a football, as could Yokum and Crowston. So he added pass plays, knowing that Pittsburg would be geared to stop the Tigers' familiar running game.

To make the pass play most effective, Catfish put a halfback in motion, the left half trotting toward the right sideline while staying parallel to the line of scrimmage. Then on the snap count, Yokum would cut upfield and drive the defensive back deep. Meanwhile, the right end, Pugh, would brush-block the defensive man in front of him and then slip out into the right-side flat, an area vacated by the defensive player chasing Yokum. Pierce would fake a handoff to Crowston up the middle, pulling the linebackers in, and then drop back five yards and throw to the open receiver. If his halfback was behind the defensive back, he could throw deep. If not, then Pugh would be open and become the target. The same play could be run with the right halfback and end to the left side.

Then on game day, just before the team went onto the field, Catfish revealed his last secret weapon.

"Boys, Mr. Suggs has been in bed with a high fever for a week," Catfish said. "But, he got out of his sickbed to be here with you tonight. And at considerable personal risk, he is here to support this team, so I'm dedicating this game to him. Now I know you boys won't let him down."

With Bob Suggs safely beside Catfish on the sidelines, the game got underway, and on the second offensive play of the game, after running Crowston into the middle of the line as expected, Pierce faked a handoff to the fullback, made the required five-yard drop behind the line of scrimmage, and lofted a spiral to Pugh in the right flat. That play took the ball to the opposition's twenty-five-yard line. After two running plays, which gained another first down at the twelve, Pierce again faked a handoff to Crowston, and tossed an easy aerial to Yokum for the score.

Catfish's defense then proved capable of throttling the Pirates' offense, so the coach rested on his seven-point lead and pounded away with runs into the line. Between Crowston and Yokum, the Tigers moved the ball, stopping themselves with a couple of penalties and a fumble.

The only push Pittsburg made toward the Tigers' goal line came early in the final period with the outcome still undecided. The Pirates hammered away until they reached Mount Vernon's fifteen-yard line. Catfish turned and saw his entire group of reserves, with tears in their eyes, pleading with their defensive teammates to stop their opponent. Their appeals must have been heard because repeatedly, Campbell, Pugh, Horne, and "Jolting Joe" Clark broke through the Pirates' forward wall and threw Pittsburg runners for losses, eventually taking over the ball on downs back on the twenty-five.

Then the Tiger offense put together a punishing, time-consuming, seventy-five-yard drive, culminating with Crowston knifing off right tackle on one of the most outstanding runs his coach had ever witnessed. Devall of the *Optic-Herald* counted six Pirate players who attempted to bring down the fifteen-year-old along his way to the end zone. "Some of those Pittsburg boys owe the Swede for a sightseeing tour they took on his back," the newsman would report in his paper. After missing the extra point, the score stood at 13-0. With only four minutes left in the contest and Mount Vernon's stingy defense on the field, the coaches and fans knew the outcome was decided.

Catfish kept Bob Suggs by his side as he made his way to the dressing room where the *Optic-Herald*'s Devall slipped inside and asked Catfish why, after early success throwing, he had not passed more often.

"I always favor the run," the coach replied, "but tonight I think we showed that our quarterback can complete the forward pass. I don't want my boys to start relying on the pass, but in the future, I expect we'll mix in more of those."

"Was Pierce the key to winning?" the newsman asked. "Or was Crowston?"

"This *team* won the game, not any one player," Catfish said. "Campbell and Horne had great games, and I think 'Jolting' Joe Clark has become the best center in the district. He and Jimmy Pierce made tackles all over the field tonight. But I especially want to mention another player. Big Dan Cargile lay in bed sick most of the week, but he pulled on his uniform and gave us his best effort of the year. That's what champions do. They step to the front when the challenge is the greatest.

"And let me mention the unsung heroes, the reserves on the bench. They not only work as hard in practice as the starters, but tonight they rallied their mates on the field when it looked like the Pirates were going to score and tie the ballgame." Catfish then slipped his long arm around the shoulders of Bob Suggs. "I want to point out that we dedicated this game to Mr. Suggs. He showed more courage than any of us, just being here."

Starting Monday afternoon Catfish reminded his team that Gilmer, their next opponent, had thrashed them 27-0 the prior season.

"This is the game we've been waiting for," he told his players, excitement in his voice. "Against the Buckeyes, we'll see how much we've improved. Right now everybody is saying Gilmer is the best. If you want to be champions, you've got to beat the best."

All week his voice rang with enthusiasm, his demeanor like that of a child anticipating Christmas morning. He added a few pass plays, one a toss to Dan Cargile on a tricky play where the right tackle became an eligible pass receiver. The boys sensed their coach's determination and eagerness to meet the challenge of one of the best teams around, and they were sky-high by game day.

The entire student body became caught up in a wave of school spirit. Miss Binnion decided a school song would help capture and propagate that spirit. She invited Gwendolyne Orren, Joyce Hill, June Godwin, Frances Cowan, Patsy Irby, and a few other female band members to drop by her room at the Merediths where she boarded. They put together the words and the melody, the band put it to music, and the student-body adopted it. Friday morning, November 12, it became the highlight of their pep rally.

TO OUR SCHOOL

Dear Mount Vernon High School,
We all love you!
We'll never fail you,
And we'll ever be true;
Loyal to our colors,
Purple and white -

Mount Vernon High School,
You're our delight.

Our wisdom and our knowledge,
We owe to you;
Through the many ages
You have never failed.
In sports and in our studies
You have reigned supreme,
Mount Vernon High School,
We're all for you!

The song was dedicated to "the 'Living Spirit' of Mount Vernon High School, that inimitable force that guides and inspires, from the tiniest tot enrolled in our school to those gallant lads who are representing us from the Rhine to the jungles of Saipan, to all who have been a part of our beloved school."

Even the weather, a cold wet day, could not dampen their excitement; however it did impact the Tigers' game plan. A heavy rain fell throughout most of the game, so Catfish abandoned the pass plays his team had diligently practiced.

After Gilmer recovered a Mount Vernon fumble on the Tigers' thirty-five-yard line, the Buckeyes bulldozed their way into the end zone, and then followed the score with a successful point-after.

Limited to the ground game, Mount Vernon pounded away with Crowston, but the Buckeye defense was ready for him. Though Swede gained substantial yardage, drive after drive fizzled and ultimately broke down.

Finally, in the fourth quarter the Tigers heard their band strike up their newly adopted school song. With the Buckeye defense focused on Crowston, Yokum broke an off-tackle play for thirty-five yards. The invigorated Tigers then jammed the ball into the end zone, bringing them within a point of the Buckeyes. A successful point-after would tie the game, but Yokum kicked the slippery ball wide left, leaving the Tigers trailing, 7-6.

Like two weary but determined rams, they battered each other, but neither team scored again.

Tired, soaked, and with heads steaming like boiling water on an ice-cold morning, the Tigers were sitting dejected on wooden benches in the dressing room when Catfish appeared in the doorway. After this, their second loss, the players braced themselves for a dressing down, but the coach surprised them.

"Boys, you played a quality team tonight. We didn't win, but we showed them that we are right there knocking," he said, rapping his knuckles on the door at his back. "Next time we meet, we'll tear that door down and barge right into the championship room. We won't rest until everybody recognizes us as the best team around. Now, lift those chins, look me in the eye, and make this promise. We won't lose again before we play the Buckeyes next year. Then we'll show them who's the best team in East Texas."

The room erupted with shouts of "Next year!" and "We'll be back!"

Meanwhile, editor Devall spoke with some of the Buckeye players. "Mount Vernon has a tough team," a Gilmer player was quoted as saying. "They'll knock you down, smile at you, help you up, then on the next play, they'll knock you down again. Talco, watch out!"

Most fans thought it was the other way around. Mount Vernon had never defeated Talco on the Trojans' field, but Catfish had a couple of ideas about how to change that.

"Boys," he said to his players just prior to the game, the season finale, "let's dedicate this game to the seniors, the last they'll ever play for the good old purple and white Tigers. It's the last contest that sticks with players through the years, so let's make it a good memory.

"As I told you last Friday after the Gilmer game, the losses are mine and the wins are yours. Now, go out there tonight and make this one of yours."

A norther chilled the night air, sending fans gathering around open fires and huddling under thick blankets. With cold but dry conditions, Catfish jumped on the opportunity to open up his offense and give the fans a taste of what they could expect the next fall.

On the first offensive possession, Swede was unstoppable and put the Tigers up 7-0. Then in the second quarter, Pierce threw a pass to Pugh for a thirty-five-yard touchdown. Not satisfied, at halftime Catfish told Pierce to throw the tackle-eligible aerial to Dan Cargile.

On the first play of the second half, Pugh, the lanky right end, lined up a couple of feet behind the line of scrimmage while Irby was set on the end of the line to the left. The defense did not notice the odd alignment. Pierce faked the dive play to the left, and then dropped back to pass. Meanwhile, Cargile, the tall, raw-boned tackle, had only lightly brushed the defensive man in front of him, thus letting immediate penetration into the backfield where Crowston shocked the defender with a teeth-rattling block. Pierce then flipped the ball out to Cargile who had drifted toward the right sideline, all alone. The big tackle then outran a surprised defense to the goal line, making the score 20-0.

From that point, Catfish substituted his backup players, rewarding them for a season of hard practice but limited game experience. Finally, Talco managed a touchdown against the reserves, finalizing the score at 20-7.

Catfish congratulated his players on a good season, and then warned them that a four and two record would not be acceptable the following year.

"We'll play more games," he told them, "and I'll schedule the best teams I can find. We can't call ourselves champions until we defeat the best. But starting Monday, we'll begin preparing for basketball. Before this season's over, we're going back to Austin, and we won't leave until folks down there know who we are!"

On the bus ride home, Catfish asked Bob Suggs if he liked basketball.

"If you're coaching, I'm sure I will," the man replied, smiling.

"Practice begins Monday afternoon. I expect you to be there."

As he had done with football, Catfish used the first basketball practice to assess the boys' skills. From football he knew Shurtleff, Pugh, Pierce, Crowston, and Caudle, but he quickly got to know Lollis Loyd, Charles Hogan, and J. C. Cannaday, three outstanding athletes. Added to this core of players was tall Robbie Knotts, along with J. C. Morgan, Billy Ingram, J. M. Connley, and Billy Stinson.

Monday, their first practice was spent working on fundamentals. For two hours Catfish drilled his players on dribbling, passing, setting screens, and rebounding. Another hour was spent on running and general conditioning. He ended practice by having the boys elect a captain for the team.

"A captain has to lead the team on the floor. As you know, once the game starts, I can't talk to you, so the captain has to make on-court adjustments, along with decisions that can determine the outcome of the game. Vote for a player you trust, one who puts his team first and who will give one hundred percent all the time."

Catfish left the gym while the players elected Glenn Pierce, a tenth grader, to lead them.

"Boys," Captain Pierce said, "if Coach were in here, he'd tell us to practice our free shots, shooting each one like you're in a tied game

94

with one second on the clock. When you've made ten in a row, head for the showers. Let's get to it."

Tuesday morning, November 16, Catfish started his first-period history lesson as usual, but then everything changed when a grim-faced Superintendent Fleming called the coach from his classroom, leaving a substitute teacher to take his place.

9

November 16, 1943

"Milburn," the superintendent said when they were alone in the hallway, "your brother Alfred just called. Your father died at home about an hour ago."

Stunned, Catfish stared at Fleming in disbelief. His sixty-nine-year-old father had seemed in good health upon his last visit, but the demands of a football season and teaching had prevented his checking on his parents in the past month.

"Did Alfred say what happened?" he finally asked.

"Your brother said Sam was up during the night with severe indigestion, but the doctor suspects a heart attack."

"He was a proud man, a fighter," Catfish said, turning toward the window. "If he had known what to do . . ."

"Some things you just can't fight," Fleming said, placing a hand on the coach's shoulder.

"I'd better get on out there," Catfish said. "I'm sure Mother is in no shape to deal with funeral arrangements."

"Take all the time you need," Fleming said. "I'll explain the situation to your boys this afternoon, and we'll keep them practicing until you get back."

"Thanks. I know this isn't easy for you, either," Catfish said, "and tell Mr. Suggs, too. He'll wonder why I'm not working with the team."

Driving to Winfield, Catfish was thankful that his parents had sold the farm and moved to town. In the coming months, his mother would be terribly lonely, and she would appreciate having neighbors and friends close by.

When Catfish reached his parents' home, several cars lined the east side of the street in front of the house. He turned onto the dirt drive and pulled up behind his brother's car. Chickens cackled from their coops behind the garage as he headed for the porch. The image of his father swaying back and forth in the old porch swing popped into his mind. Recently, Sam had often slipped out to the swing to enjoy the sun's warmth during the cool morning hours and the shade in the hot afternoons.

Stepping into the living room, Catfish spotted his brother Morris, along with two members of the Masonic Fraternity of Mount Pleasant. Catfish quickly made his way to his mother's side and looped his arms around her sagging shoulders.

"Why did the Good Lord take him, Milburn? Why?" she asked, sobbing. "How will I go on without my Sam?"

"We don't know why, Mother," Milburn said, struggling with his emotions. "We'll all miss him, but don't you worry about a thing. Us boys will take care of everything."

At noontime members of Winfield's First Baptist Church brought food for the family. A smorgasbord of dishes covered the large table in the dining room while neighbor women hurried back and forth from the kitchen, warming food, filling glasses, and gathering and washing plates and utensils. Throughout the afternoon, a steady stream of friends and well-wishers dropped by.

Sam T. Smith, a lifelong resident of the area had been among the founders of Winfield, twice Sheriff of Titus County, a carpenter and farmer, and an active member of the community. Everyone in town seemed to be his friend, as well as dozens of citizens from both Mount Vernon and Mount Pleasant.

Mid-afternoon Catfish caught his brother's elbow and ushered him into the main bedroom, where they discussed funeral plans. When the arrangements were settled, Catfish phoned them to Superintendent Fleming. The service was set for three o'clock Wednesday afternoon at the local First Baptist Church. Reverend John Whitt of Mount Vernon, a family friend, would lead the service, which would be followed by interment at the cemetery on the south edge of town.

The superintendent notified the *Optic-Herald* and then announced to the students and faculty that classes were cancelled for the afternoon of the funeral.

The news was especially disturbing to Glenn Pierce. Just weeks earlier he had met Catfish's father, an apparent pillar of strength and health. How could life so quickly abandon a person? With school dismissed, the young quarterback walked home, thoughtful and confused.

At the service Catfish sat beside his mother with his long arm draped around her slumped shoulders. Glancing back, he was pleased to see most of his fellow teachers seated behind Millard Fleming's family. Then the coach struggled to hold back tears when he spotted his players, dressed in their finest, filling three long pews. Even Clarence Crowston wore a freshly pressed dark suit, though the coach knew he did not own one. Joining the players was Bob Suggs, wearing a gray suit with a matching vest, white shirt and dark tie. School board members, businessmen, and his assistant coach all attended, some having to stand in the back and along the walls. And there, three rows back, sat Glenn and Dorothy Nell Penn.

Reverend Whitt then gave a brief review of Sam's life, his family, and his contribution to the community. At the close of the service, many mourners filed by the open casket at the front of the church, some stopping at the reserved section to express their sorrow and sympathy to the family. Then the pallbearers, H. S. Cody, Jr., Edmond Cody, Andrew Cody, Quince Roper, Lester Martin, Louis Black, and Millard Fleming, carried the closed casket to the waiting hearse.

At the cemetery, after most of the mourners had gone, Catfish kept a steadying arm around his mother as they lingered beside the mound of fresh dirt, which lay on the east slope of a hill that dominated the cemetery landscape. Slowly his mother moved away, stopping beside a small grave. Catfish followed, staring down at the tiny marker that bore the name of Minnie Smith, who had been born March 9, 1910 and had died May 31, 1911.

"Your sweet little sister," Ida said, sobbing softly. "Died the year before you were born."

"I wish I could have known her, Momma," he replied. "I wish you could have had her with you all these years. She'd know how to comfort you better than us boys."

With tears blurring his vision, Catfish raised his eyes and scanned the jagged rows of gray stone markers, many darkened by years of weather and mold. Would he be there one day? The military doctor's words came to him as if the colonel now stood beside him. "Your life will be a short one if you don't eat right and take care of yourself."

As Catfish surveyed the cemetery, he spotted Charley Grady standing alone, watching from beneath a canopy of sprawling limbs of an old oak. Leaving Alfred to tend to his mother, Catfish headed over and thanked his childhood friend for attending, though he guessed that Charley had avoided the church service.

"Milburn," his friend said with tears streaking down his face, "you've always been like a brother to me. And Mr. Sam, he was . . . a fine man and a good daddy."

The two hugged, and while dabbing a handkerchief at his eyes, Catfish led his childhood friend over to his mother and brothers. Charley struggled to express his feelings to the family, and again embraces sufficed where words failed.

As they headed for their cars, Catfish insisted that Charley come home with the family. "Our church friends brought more than we can eat," Catfish explained.

Memories, even laughter, dominated the family gathering around the table, so reminiscent of bygone days when Charley had often dined with the Smith family. Around almost daily, he had always helped with whatever was going on at the Smith farm, in the fields or meadows.

Somehow, having Charley with them again made Sam's absence less painful.

*   *   *

Catfish arrived at school early Friday morning and dropped by the superintendent's office to thank him for his kindness to the Smith family.

Millard Fleming handed him a newspaper clipping, Sam T. Smith's obituary.

"I know how you felt about Sam," Fleming said, "and I thought you might like to have this."

Fighting to control his emotions, Catfish nodded, folded the article, and stuffed it inside his wallet.

"For what success I've had, I owe my father," Catfish said. "He was a kind man, but he also demanded I do my best in every way. He insisted that I go to college, make my grades, and now I'm coaching here in Mount Vernon because of him."

"Milburn," the superintendent said, "I asked you to come help out a few months, but now I'd like to offer the job for the remainder of the school year."

"I'd like that. I'm sure that's what my Dad would want me to do," Catfish replied, the image of his football team at the funeral flashing into his mind. "Besides, I've taken a liking to the boys, and I believe we can have a fine basketball season."

"I'll speak to the school board," Fleming promised.

Heading for his classroom, Catfish met some of the football players and thanked each for attending the funeral. He gave a special thanks to Crowston, who seemed embarrassed when Catfish mentioned the suit.

"Borrowed it from Harry Jack," Crowston explained.

Later, Catfish saw Harry Jack Pugh and thanked him for his thoughtfulness. Pugh shook his head, his face twisted into a frown.

"What's wrong?" Catfish asked.

"I had to give that suit to Swede," Pugh said. "He returned it the day after the funeral, but I noticed the legs of the pants were about two inches too short. Swede had had them cut down to fit him."

Catfish could not help but laugh.

For four days the unexpected death of his father kept popping into Catfish's mind. Among the memories, spanning the spectrum of happiness and sadness and father-son conversations, Catfish always came back to the same burning question. Had he been a disappointment to his father?

Frustrated from wrestling with unanswerable questions, on Saturday morning he walked to the City Café, which was on the southeast corner of the square, and slipped inside. Glenn and Dorothy Nell spotted him as he entered and waved him over to their corner table.

Noticing the grim look on Catfish's face, Dorothy Nell expressed her sympathy at the loss of his father.

"Thanks," Catfish replied, his voice subdued. "My father was an inspiration to me. He insisted that I get a good education, though his was rather skimpy. Yet, he was successful at everything he ever did, whether farmer, carpenter, or sheriff. I wish I had done more to make him proud of me."

"But you've been successful, too," Glenn said. "You won that state championship out at Carey, and everybody says you'll do the same here."

"Why do you think you let him down?" Dorothy Nell asked.

"They kicked me out of the Army Air Corps," Catfish mumbled. "I don't think Dad ever understood that."

"What do you mean, they kicked you out?" Glenn asked.

"The Army doctor said I wasn't physically fit," Catfish explained. "Stomach ulcers."

"That's no disgrace," Dorothy Nell said, placing her hand on top of his. "You couldn't help it, and I'm sure your father understood that."

Catfish nodded, but throughout breakfast, in spite of Dorothy

Nell's repeated attempts to cheer him up, he would return to the subject of his father's death.

"Some people say those in Heaven can look down on us," Catfish said, pushing away from the table and getting to his feet. "Before I'm through, I'm gonna make my Dad proud."

"Sure you will," Dorothy Nell said, as she stood up beside him. "You'll be the best coach in all of Texas, and your father will be the happiest saint in all of Heaven."

For a moment, Catfish's eyes met hers, and then he smiled weakly, nodded and headed for the door.

Glenn paid their bill and then caught up with Catfish and Dorothy Nell who had stepped out onto the sidewalk, where a war bond sign stared at them from the side of Rutherford's building across the street.

"Did you read M. L. Edwards's comment in the paper?" Catfish asked. "Well, he says there's one million two hundred thousand dollars on deposit in the bank here, and we can't sit back, stockpiling our money, and not meet our obligation to the fighting soldiers. He points out that we here in Mount Vernon have never been bombed, but that Hitler and Tojo have cold-bloodedly attacked their neighbors, and if we don't support the war effort now, we could someday be facing their armies right here at our doorsteps."

"For some people," Glenn said, "times are hard. Even buying a war bond is more than they can afford."

"Yeah, but that money in the bank belongs to somebody, and I agree with Mr. Edwards. Some of it should be used to meet our quota for the bond drive."

Standing on the street corner, Catfish glanced toward the Joy Theatre.

"Dorothy Nell," he said, "how would you like to go see that Ginger Rogers and Cary Grant movie this evening?"

"Are you offering to take me?" she asked, smiling.

"I sure am," Catfish replied. "Okay if I pick you up at six?"

"I'd like that."

"What about me?" Glenn asked, pretending to be slighted.

"I don't think we need a chaperone," Catfish replied.

With a nod to Dorothy Nell, he headed for the post office where he purchased two war bonds.

*　　*　　*

With the car heater going full blast, Catfish pulled up in front of the Penn home. He stepped out into the bitter chill and hurried to the door. Dorothy Nell answered his knock and quickly slipped into her long coat, which completely covered her chocolate-colored, pleated skirt. Her curled brown hair fell to her shoulders, matching the tint of her eyes and the brown saddle strap across her otherwise white, lace-up oxford shoes. Her face was soft and clear, her smile natural and easy.

He angle-parked the old Pontiac in front of the theatre and purchased tickets while she rushed inside where they joined a dozen people sprinkled on either side of the center aisle that split two sections of seats. Dorothy Nell led the way and picked a place on the right-hand side, three rows behind the nearest patrons, and they settled in to watch *Once Upon a Honeymoon.*

About half an hour into the movie, Catfish reached over and took her hand in his. When she glanced up at him, he winked, and she leaned her shoulder against his.

When the movie was over, he drove her home and walked her to the door.

"Milburn, thank you," she said. "I enjoyed the evening."

"Maybe we'll do it again, soon."

A week later Superintendent Fleming showed up at basketball practice, climbed the six steps to the elevated stands, and took a seat beside Bob Suggs. They watched as Catfish taught Harry Jack Pugh, J. C. Cannaday, and Swede Crowston how to block the defender away from the goal when the opposition attempted a shot.

"When the ball goes up," the coach explained, backing roughly into Pugh, "move to the closest opposing player, turn your backside to him, keeping contact so you know when he tries to slip around you. Keep your hands up high, elbows out, and knees flexed so you can spring to the rebound. When the ball comes off the rim, leap to it. Don't move under it and jump. Jump to the ball. When you have it, pull it down two-handed and tuck it in against your chest with your elbows out like airplane wings. Then quickly look down court for one of the guards."

Catfish then moved out front to Lollis Loyd, a guard.

"Son, when that shot goes up, you break for center court, looking back for the ball. Pierce, you head down the sideline, angling toward the goal.

"Now, Pugh, when you get the ball, turn and throw it, using an overhead pass, to Loyd at mid-court. Then without dribbling, Loyd, you whip the ball to Pierce who should be within a dribble or two of the goal.

"Okay, get your positions and let's try it," Catfish said, then shot the ball toward the goal, intentionally missing to Pugh's side.

The big center blocked out the defender, leaped for the ball, and then sent it sailing to Lollis Loyd in the center circle, who immediately made a chest pass to Pierce approaching the far goal from the right side. The guard glided in for the layup.

"That's good!" Catfish shouted. "The key is making it happen quickly, before the defense can get back."

They then practiced against a live defense, subs who knew the plan and immediately disrupted the pass to center court. The coach called Pugh, Cannaday, Crowston and Loyd aside.

"Loyd, you've got to be aware of the opposing player, and vary your moves accordingly. Instead of going directly to center court, first move toward the sideline, then dart to the center circle when the inside boys grab the rebound. If the defensive player insists on defending the center circle, then we'll run the same thing but down the side of the court. You inside boys have to be alert and find Loyd. You can't just blindly throw the ball to where you think he'll be."

Soon they were executing the techniques eighty percent of the time, and Catfish told his players they could head for the showers after making ten consecutive free shots. While they practiced from the foul stripe, the coach walked over to the sideline and watched. Superintendent Fleming eased down out of the stands and joined him.

"The school board was glad to offer you a contract, Milburn," Fleming said, handing him a folded sheet of paper.

"You have a pen?" Catfish asked after scanning the document.

Catfish scribbled his name on the contract and handed it back to the superintendent, smiling and offering his hand.

Now the team was officially his, and he hoped his father was looking down approvingly.

*　　*　　*

For the first scrimmage game against Saltillo, the starting five players were Harry Jack Pugh as center, J. C. Cannaday and Swede Crowston as forwards, and Glenn Pierce and Lollis Loyd as guards. Charles Hogan was a capable backup guard, while Shurtleff could sub at forward, and Knotts at center.

Though the scoreboard was not used and the coaches were allowed unusual freedom to interrupt and instruct their players, the competition was intense. Above all else it gave the coaches a chance to see their boys under game-like conditions, and Catfish was both pleased and disturbed.

Giving an all-out effort, the Mount Vernon boys won, but under the pressure of competition, they forgot much of what their new coach had taught them, reverting to playground habits. To the coach's surprise, Crowston led the Tigers in scoring with twelve points.

The two teams played a rematch the following night, and again the Tigers prevailed, 16-13. Cannaday led with eight points, while Hogan had three, Pierce and Pugh two each, and Crowston only a single counter.

After a few more practices, they scrimmaged a good Blossom team and clearly were outplayed, but Catfish was not worried. The stiff competition was designed to measure his team before the games counted.

With school dismissed for the Christmas holidays, Catfish arranged a small tournament, inviting the best teams available on short notice. Though less than topnotch competition, they would provide the first test of his team under real game conditions, with officials, fans, and tracking of personal fouls. The boys must have found it to their liking, because they won all three games, including the championship contest on Saturday night.

Reaching home that evening, Catfish picked up the newspaper nestled against his door. Inside, he quickly scanned the front-page articles, and then turned to a full-page ad that caught his eye. "Let's Back the Attack" the headline read in big bold letters. War bonds, Series E in denominations from twenty-five dollars to a thousand, were available as part of the fourth War Loan. They could be purchased at seventy-five percent of their mature value, accruing interest at the rate of 2.9%, compounded semi-annually.

The lower portion of the page listed the local businesses sponsoring the ad, thirty-three of them. They included five grocery stores, four cafes, three drug stores, three feed stores, three clothing stores, a hardware and furniture business, a car dealership, an insurance company, the bank, a jewelry store, the theatre, a service station, and five individuals, counting the postmaster and county judge. Hardly a business in town had failed to contribute.

An accompanying article carried the heading of "The Soldier in the Foxhole." It described a boy in a muddy foxhole, dodging enemy bullets, himself without adequate supplies and equipment. The article then mentioned the difficulty in getting homefolks, safe in their homes and businesses, to buy war bonds to adequately supply the boy in the foxhole. Continuing, the article stated that the people of Mount Vernon had been spared inconvenience and physical suffering, so they should make sure the town reaches its goal of seventy-six thousand five hundred dollars, of which only thirty-two thousand had currently been contributed. "We owe it to the boy in the foxhole," the article concluded.

The following day, Catfish picked up the phone and called the War Loan chairman, L. D. Lowry, Jr.

"I saw the ad in the paper," Catfish said. "I'll get down to the post office and purchase additional bonds Monday, but is there anything more I can do?"

"Maybe there is," Lowry responded. "You've become quite a popular fellow around town. I think it would help if you could be available down around the plaza the next three Saturday mornings, just to greet people and encourage them to support the cause."

"I'll be there," Catfish said.

Meanwhile, now two weeks into January, the Tigers were headed into their district games, the ones that really counted. An article in the *Optic-Herald* highlighted Catfish's past accomplishments by pointing out that his greatest success had been on the hardwood where his teams had won two hundred ninety-eight games while losing only forty-two, an impressive eighty-eight-percent victory record.

In their first district contest, the Tigers tangled with their nearby rival, Mount Pleasant. Led by Captain Pierce, Mount Vernon overcame a four-point halftime deficit, and squeaked out a win, 25-24, with Hogan's nine points leading the way.

Three days later, January 17, Catfish's boys played Mount Pleasant in a return match. The visitors started fast, but Mount Vernon caught up and held the lead with one minute remaining in the contest. Mount Pleasant then grabbed a two-point advantage, 25-23, and appeared to have the game won, but Glenn Pierce made a bucket that tied the score with only seconds left. Then Cannaday stole the inbound pass and was fouled. He missed the first free shot, but sank the second, and Mount Vernon won again by a single point, 26-25. Cannaday's ten points led the Tigers.

The following Thursday, Catfish's team met Winnsboro in Mount Vernon in a breakout game for the Tigers. Cannaday fired in seventeen counters, and Catfish's quintet racked up forty points while allowing the Red Raiders only fourteen. The next night the Tigers put on an even bigger offensive show with a singeing of the Winfield Bearcats in which the Tigers poured in sixty-four points and allowed only twenty-five.

Monday night, the coach took his team to Winnsboro for a district rematch. Both teams struggled through the first half, as indicated by a pitiful 9-8 score, but the second half found the Tigers playing much improved on both ends of the court, scoring a dozen points while their tenacious defense shut out the Red Raiders. Scoring nine points, Harry Jack Pugh led his team to victory, 21-8.

Then on Friday night the Tigers played the Winfield Bearcats in a rematch. It proved lopsided to the tune of 51-9, with J. C. Cannaday leading Mount Vernon with eighteen points.

On Saturday morning, January 29, Catfish pulled on his coat and headed for the plaza. He stood on the south side in front of Crescent Drug Store, meeting people and explaining the importance of the War Bond Drive.

"We've only got until February fifteenth," he explained to several men, "and we still lack forty-three thousand dollars. We just can't let our fighting boys down. Almost everybody can buy a twenty-five dollar bond. It's only eighteen dollars and seventy-five cents."

Several nodded their agreement and headed for the post office.

The following week his basketball team defeated Leesburg by a score of 49-32, Harry Jack Pugh accounting for nineteen of the points and little Charles Hogan, a defensive standout, adding nine. That victory was followed by another over the Deport Bulldogs, 35-19, though the Tigers led by only one point at halftime, 14-13. Again Pugh showed good offensive ability with ten points, barely outshining McDowra of Deport who had nine.

The next Saturday morning, Catfish returned to the plaza. His basketball team's only loss had been an early-season, non-conference contest with Blossom, and local fans were eager to talk to their coach about an upcoming rematch, followed by the district championship tournament to be played in Mount Pleasant the following weekend.

"First, we have Blossom here next Thursday, and that'll be a good test of our squad as we head into the district tournament on Friday night. The best eight of fourteen district teams will compete for the title, so it'll be tough to win it all, but that's exactly what I intend us to do," he said to a group of fans.

After talking basketball to the growing gathering, he urged them to buy war bonds.

"We lack nine thousand dollars and have only four more days to reach our quota," he told the people. "It would be an embarrassment to our town to fail our soldiers. How could we ever face our returning boys, some disabled for life?"

"Coach, are you suggesting we spend our money on war bonds rather than on tickets to see your team play for the championship?" a fan asked, hurrahing the coach.

Catfish smiled as the group laughed, then his face turned solemn. "I'd forfeit our remaining games, if that's what it took to support our boys fighting the war."

Their laughter hushed as if instantly swept away by the sternness of his voice and the intensity in his eyes, and the group dispersed, many making their way toward the post office.

That afternoon Catfish called Dorothy Nell and invited her to go to the theatre with him. She accepted, and he suggested that he pick her up early enough to have dinner at Reeves' Cafe. The budding relationship was solidifying and had become a popular subject throughout the community. Some hoped for a wedding, selfishly thinking that the coach's marriage to this popular local girl might tie him to the town.

On Thursday night, Catfish's Tigers found the Blossom team to be as tough as it had been back in December, and came up short by a score of 31-21. Though the coach hated losing, he saw a silver lining in this defeat. His team had won several games by lopsided scores and had become a little overconfident, and he hoped the loss would show them that they still have a lot to prove along the journey to a championship.

Headlines in Friday's paper announced that Franklin County and Mount Vernon had exceeded their war bond quota by fifty-three percent. Chairman Lowry thanked everyone who had worked so diligently to make the drive a success, mentioning Mrs. G. W. Rutherford and her committees, along with Scoutmaster Rufus Bolger and his Boy Scouts. With a big smile and a handshake, Catfish thanked everyone he saw.

That night, February 18, his basketball team gave Tiger fans another reason to celebrate by winning their first game of the district tournament, outscoring Gilmer 28-15. The victory set his team up for a three o'clock Saturday game against Mount Pleasant, who had defeated Talco by a whopping 53-16 score.

Saturday morning, the coach called Dorothy Nell and asked if she would be at the semifinal game.

"I wouldn't miss it," she replied.

"I'd like to sit with you," he said, "but I'll be coaching my boys to win that district trophy."

"Well then, I guess I'd better plan to stay for the championship game," she replied.

"Sit right behind the bench," he suggested. "I think you bring us good luck. Besides, I want you where I can see you at a glance."

For the third time Mount Vernon defeated Mount Pleasant by one point, 22-21. Then Deport whipped Winnsboro 40-25 and thus advanced to meet Catfish's Tigers in the championship game to be played at eight o'clock.

After accepting congratulations from several Mount Vernon fans, Catfish stepped over to Glenn, Dorothy Nell, and their father, Frank Penn.

"There's a nice restaurant up at the north end of town. It's next to Gaddis Courts on the south side of highway sixty-seven," he said. "I'm taking the boys there, and I thought you might want to join us."

Superintendent Fleming and his son, Gene, families of several of the players, and Dorothy Nell and her father showed up at the restaurant about six o'clock. While the players waited for their meals, Catfish eased over and took a seat at the table with Dorothy Nell and Frank, Glenn having joined friends across the room.

"If you win tonight, when will your team play next?" she asked Catfish.

"As district champs, we'll qualify for the regional tournament in Commerce next weekend. Tomorrow the regional officials will announce the pairings of the qualifying teams."

"Coach, there's lots of talk about going to the state tournament. Do you think your team is good enough?" Frank asked.

"I don't know," Catfish replied. "We played good defense this afternoon, but we didn't shoot the ball very well. The competition at regional will be a lot tougher, but all season these boys have found a way to win. I never know who'll lead us in scoring, but there's good news in that. Pugh, Loyd, Pierce, and Cannaday are each capable of leading us on any given night, so our opponents can't gang up on one player and shut us down."

"What about Deport tonight?" Dorothy Nell asked.

"We've beaten them twice this year. Both games were really close

108

at halftime, fourteen to thirteen, I think. Then we've been able to shut them down in the second half. A kid named McDowra is their best shooter, and I plan to put Charles Hogan on him. That'll take one of our regulars out of the game, but if Hogan can hold McDowra to less than ten points, we'll win."

As Catfish said, he inserted Hogan in the game in place of Crowston.

"Son," Catfish told Hogan just before sending his team onto the court, "I want you to deny McDowra the ball. You stay with him wherever he goes. If he heads for the restroom, you be there to open the door."

Both teams appeared nervous early in the game, so the defenses dominated play. Since Mount Vernon had scored thirty and thirty-five points against Deport earlier in the season, the Bulldogs decided to slow down the game. A low-scoring contest gave them the best chance to win, they believed. With no shot clock to force them to shoot, they dribbled endlessly and passed the ball back and forth away from the goal, hoping to get the ball to McDowra, their best shooter. But as Hogan had been told to do, he frustrated McDowra, sticking to him like syrup on a pancake.

Meanwhile, Mount Vernon's outside shooting was off, and when the ball was passed inside to Pugh or Cannaday, Deport players swarmed the ball, fouling the Mount Vernon players rather than allowing a shot. Cannaday and Pugh were making about half of their free throws, and the score stayed close. When it was over, the Tigers had played their worst offensive game of the season, but had won another one-point squeaker, 12-11, qualifying them for the regional tournament in Commerce.

The following day, Catfish learned that his Tigers would be matched against a Plano team, one he knew little about. The game was set for three-fifteen the afternoon of February 26, a Saturday, in East Texas State's Whitley Gym, where ten years earlier Catfish had played and starred for four years. To him, it was home court.

10

February 21, 1944

A quick look at the trophy case Monday morning reminded Catfish that Mount Vernon had defeated the Plano Wildcats 41-24 in the finals of the regional tournament the previous year. The leaders of that Tiger team had been Leonard Rollings, Wayne Pierce, Lollis Loyd, and Sammie Burton. A few of Catfish's players, including Pugh, Glenn Pierce, and Cannaday, had been on that team, and they shared what they remembered; however, as the Tigers' team had changed, the Wildcats probably had as well. The coach decided to make a phone call to the basketball mentor at East Texas State, who closely followed high school teams in the area, always with an eye out for recruits.

"I saw them play Commerce for the district title," Coach Vinzant said. "They're big inside, but their leading scorer is McCallum, a guard. He gets help from Stinson, Alderson, and Howell. They're well coached by Bill Williams, but they're not a high-scoring team. In an earlier game that they lost to Commerce, they scored thirty-three points while giving up thirty-seven. Then in the championship contest, they again scored thirty-three but held Commerce to twenty."

By practice time that afternoon Catfish had his game plan mapped out. Plano's height would hamper Mount Vernon's inside shooting, so he focused on two options. First, he hoped to use his team's speed to beat their big men down court and get uncontested points. Instances when that failed, he would send his guards inside with the ball, collapsing the defense, and then pass the ball back out to open perimeter shooters.

The strategy worked, and Mount Vernon won 29-22. Little Charles Hogan not only shut down McCallum, but he also led the Tigers in scoring, catapulting Catfish's team into the regional championship game against a solid Quitman team that featured the Ingram boys, along with a tall center named Dick Gilbreath.

While Catfish's boys watched the next game, he found Dorothy Nell in the stands and asked her to take a walk with him. They crossed the campus to the main building, a large three-story brick structure shaped like a T, where he had attended classes for four years. From there they headed down by the football field and climbed ten rows up into the empty bleachers.

"Did I ever tell you about the time Coach Dough Rollins threatened to kill me?" he asked, looking out across the gridiron.

She shook her head, smiled, and looped her arm through his.

"Well, there was a minute and a half left in a fourteen-to-thirteen game against Sam Houston State in Huntsville. I'd just caught a touchdown pass to put us ahead and was feeling proud of myself. After our defense got the ball back, we just wanted to run out the clock, but our offense fizzled. Facing fourth down with less than two yards for a first, we lined up and kicked the ball away, giving the Bearcats one last chance to score and win the game. From my left end position, I ran down the field to tackle their punt-return guy when he caught the ball. About halfway there, this lout practically tackled me, but it just so happened that an official was right there. Well, I glanced up to protest, and the ref nodded that he had seen the illegal hold.

"Back on my feet, I saw the ball carrier slip through my teammates and head my way. I was the only one left to tackle him, but I just stood there, not making a move to stop him. In fact, as he breezed by me, I turned and waved bye to him.

"As the boy galloped toward the goal line, I eased over toward our sideline where Coach Rollins was steaming mad.

"'Get off the field!' he yelled at me. So I stepped over next to him.

"'Coach,' I said, 'it's not a touchdown. The play is gonna be called back. One of their guys practically tackled me, and the ref saw it.'

"Back then the referees didn't have flags to throw, so Coach Rollins didn't know about the penalty."

Dorothy Nell glanced up at him, shaking her head.

"Sure enough, the referees brought the ball back and penalized the other team, so I asked Coach Rollins if I could go back in the game," Catfish continued.

"He hesitated while staring at me like he hated me, then nodded.

"We won the game, and afterwards I caught up to Coach Rollins.

"'You're not still mad at me, are you?'

"He said, 'No, but when I saw you just stand there and let that boy score, I'd have shot you if I'd had a gun.' 'Coach,' I said, 'if not for that penalty, you know your Catfish would've got him.'"

"What would you do if one of your boys did something like that?" Dorothy Nell asked.

"I'd shoot him," Catfish replied, laughing. "Let's go get something to eat."

They borrowed her father's car, and drove downtown, leaving the car in the red-bricked parking area in the center of town.

"When I was in school here, I usually ate at the school cafeteria," he said, opening the door at Renfro's Cafe, "but when I could scrape up a few dollars, I'd come here to treat myself."

After a quick bite, they drove to Washington Street, stopping in front of a house with the address 1709 tacked on a gray porch post speckled with flecks of white paint.

"That's where I lived," Catfish explained. "Cost five dollars a month. Sometimes at the first of the month, I'd have to avoid the landlord for a week or so, waiting on a letter from Daddy with rent money."

Catfish sat quietly for a moment.

"His letters were always short," he continued. "He was sheriff, so he'd write me on Titus County stationery. The letterhead took up a fourth of the page with all the county office titles and occupants listed. The note might consist of three sentences, though you'd never see a comma or period. The last sentence usually said something like 'Be sure and get everything you can out of school,' or 'Be sure and do your best in school.' Then he'd sign it, 'from Dady Sam T Smith.' I guess nobody ever told him to use a double-d. I sure didn't."

Again, Catfish paused, staring through the windshield.

"I sure looked forward to those letters," he said, softly. "But there won't be any more."

"No," Dorothy Nell said, leaning over and kissing his cheek, "but I'll write to you sometime."

"If I were some place far off, like in the war," he asked, glancing over at her, "would you write me a love letter?"

"Sure, but don't you go anywhere far off, unless you take me with you."

Catfish smiled, cranked the car, and headed back to the gym.

Jim Goolsby, coach of the Quitman Bulldogs, had a talented quintet, and Catfish expected a hardnosed battle. He knew Goolsby from their mutual East Texas State playing days and admired his tenacity and competitiveness.

The championship game was close all the way, with Quitman usually ahead by a point or two. The frenzied ending was set up when Mount Vernon's Cannaday made a bucket, giving the Tigers a one-point lead, 30-29. With less than ten seconds on the clock, the Bulldogs had the ball out of bounds beneath the Mount Vernon goal and one last chance to win. Before the Quitman player, standing outside the line with the ball, could pass the ball to one of his teammates, Swede Crowston hollered at the Bulldog player while glancing at the referee.

"Hold it!" Swede bellowed, extending his hand toward the Quitman player like a stop sign. "Here, let me have the ball."

In one of the most bizarre plays ever, the Bulldog player handed the ball to Crowston who immediately took one dribble, stepped back, and dropped the ball through the hoop, giving Mount Vernon a three-point lead with four seconds to play. Quitman could not possibly score twice before the game-ending buzzer, so the improbable play assured the Tigers of the regional championship. Quitman protested the maneuver, claiming Crowston had called timeout, but the referee correctly explained that the alert Tiger had neither asked for a halt of play nor signaled a timeout with his hands. He had simply said, "Hold it!" to the opposing player.

Quitman took a desperate shot in the final seconds, but the ball bounded off the backboard harmlessly. The game was over, and the Tigers were headed for the state tournament in Austin.

The Regional All-Tournament Team, chosen by coaches from Mount Vernon, Quitman, Buckner, and Plano, consisted of Cannaday and Pugh of Mount Vernon, Dick Gilbreath of Quitman, Stinson of Plano, and Clark of Buckner.

On Sunday afternoon, Superintendent Fleming dropped by Catfish's room at the Hasty Courts. The coach was still beaming from the Regional Championship and the excitement of having a shot at winning the state title.

"I got a call a few minutes ago," Fleming explained. "You'll be playing Throckmorton on March ninth, a week from Thursday afternoon, in Gregory Gym at Austin."

"Do you know anything about the Throckmorton team?" Catfish asked.

"Only that they are very tall and quite good."

"Tall usually means slow of foot," Catfish said. "Unless I learn different, we're gonna try to run them out of the gym. Again, I'll play Hogan a lot and let him streak down court after every shot they attempt.

If they'll miss a few and we can grab some rebounds, we'll turn them into points for us."

Since the state tournament did not start until Thursday of the following week, Catfish gave his team a couple of days off to rest while he tried to learn more about Throckmorton, as well as the other teams that had qualified for the tournament.

On Friday he was back in his history class. The current event the students wanted to talk about was the state playoffs and Mount Vernon's chances of winning it all.

"Look," Catfish said, "the basketball team and winning a state championship are as important to me as they are to anyone, but there are other important things going on in the world. Can someone tell us what's happening in the war?"

"My daddy says we are getting ready to invade Germany," a girl said. "We've sent thousands of soldiers to England to get ready for it. He says it's a secret when and where we'll attack, but it's gonna happen soon."

"Who will lead the invasion?" Catfish asked.

"General Eisenhower," a boy replied.

"Do you think the Germans will be ready for us?"

"I think they're tired of fighting and being bombed constantly by our Flying Fortresses," a boy said. "They'll give up pretty quick."

"Students, we will win the war in Europe, but it won't be easy. The German military machine, the *Wehrmacht*, is still deadly. Like a sports champion, they're the best until somebody proves otherwise."

"Sir," a girl said, holding one of the newspapers. "In the paper it says Ensign James Musick Drummond from Hopewell was killed in a crash when his plane recently collided with another one. Also, it says Leonard Holmes has been missing in action in Italy since mid-January. Both went to school here just a few years ago."

While his stunned students sat hushed with their thoughts, Catfish glanced at the empty desk of the girl who, back in September, had told his class about Drummond, a family friend. She had been distressed that the recently married ensign had been ordered to war, leaving his young wife behind.

Remembering a former student whose recent experience had turned out more positively, Catfish hoped to balance the bad news.

"Do any of you remember H. B. Zimmerman, Herb's brother?" he asked.

Several hands went up.

114

"He's in the war on the other side of the world, down in the Solomon Islands. Sergeant Zimmerman is a communications specialist in the Regimental Headquarters Company of the Americal Division. Just a few weeks ago, he was awarded the Bronze Star for crawling up a mountain designated as Hill Two Sixty on Bougainville Island. While under heavy enemy fire and armed only with an army forty-five-caliber handgun, he strung telephone wire off a heavy spool, connecting the command post to the front line so the fighting men could direct mortar fire against a fortified machinegun nest. The Allies not only took that hill but also routed the Japanese who had held the island since nineteen forty-two."

"Where is Bougainville Island?" a student asked.

"North of Australia, at the upper end of a chain of islands called the Solomons. It's inhabited by Melanesians."

"Why do we care about all these islands? It's Japan we're fighting."

"We've got to capture key islands to protect Australia, our ally, and to set up airbases and supply depots within striking distance of Japan. Eventually, Sergeant Zimmerman and tens of thousands of our soldiers will have to invade the Japanese mainland, just as we now prepare to invade Western Europe and Germany."

"It looks like the war is going to last a long time," a solemn-faced boy said, undoubtedly thinking about his upcoming eighteenth birthday.

Catfish nodded, then allowed the students to study quietly the remainder of the class period. He tried to grade some papers, but his mind kept going back to the war, the planned invasion of Western Europe and the seemingly slow progress of the Allies toward Japan. These events and their unknown outcome created an emotional weight that made his goal of winning a state basketball championship fade almost into obscurity.

The team practiced Monday and Tuesday, focusing solely on running a fast-paced offense and making foul shots. With thoughts of the courage and sacrifice required for the impending invasions in both the European and Pacific warfronts on his mind, Catfish pushed his boys harder than usual, continually reminding them that a supreme effort would be required to defeat the top-level competition they would be facing.

"Remember," he told his players, "that your first opponent, Throckmorton, could very well be the best team in the tournament, the eventual champion. We've got to approach this game as if it were for the state title."

In spite of his repetitious warnings to his players, he confided in Superintendent Fleming that he was pleased with his team's progress and liked their chances of beating Throckmorton. "Sidney Lanier looks to be the best team in the tournament," he suggested.

"That's not surprising," Fleming replied. "They beat us out last year."

On Wednesday morning, March 8, the day prior to the first round of the state playoffs, Miss Viola Gillespie, the homemaking teacher, needed a block of ice for the department's icebox. She spotted Glenn Pierce in study hall and asked if he would get the ice for her. Using a borrowed pickup, Pierce drove to the icehouse where he sometimes worked, grabbed a set of tongs, and sank their sharp teeth into the sides of a twenty-five-pound ice block. He lifted the chunk and headed for the lowered tailgate of the truck. As he heaved the mass of ice into the bed of the pickup, he felt a sharp pain in his lower back. For a moment, he stood there immobile, hunched over slightly. Slowly, he eased himself onto the tailgate, hoping to relieve the pain. In a couple of minutes he felt better and returned the tongs to the icehouse dock, then walked gingerly over to the pickup.

Back at school, he eased into study hall and asked Swede Crowston to help him. Swede, teasing Pierce about being a weakling, reached into the bed of the truck, grabbed up the ice block like it was made of cork, and took off for the homemaking department.

"Slow down, Swede," Pierce said, grimacing.

"How you gonna play basketball tomorrow if you can't even walk without hurting?" Swede asked.

"I'll be better by then," Pierce replied, "so don't say anything about this, especially to Catfish."

They delivered the ice and slipped back into class.

Right after lunch, the team, along with Superintendent Fleming and Bob Suggs, loaded up and headed for Austin where they checked into a modest motel on the city's outskirts, a lesson Catfish learned after seeing his first Carey team awed by the plush and glitter of downtown.

As Pierce hoped, when he got up Thursday morning, his back felt better, and he participated in the team's light workout at a nearby high school court. With last-minute preparations complete, the team headed for Gregory Gym a little after noon, arriving well before game time.

When Catfish and his boys reached the entrance, an attendant stepped up and held out his arm like a lowered gate at a railroad crossing, halting the group.

"I'm Coach Smith," Catfish explained, "and these boys are the Mount Vernon Tigers. We're here to play in the state tournament."

"That's fine," the man said, and then nodded toward Bob Suggs, "but he can't go in."

"Mister," Catfish said, "What's your name?"

"Wilson," the attendant replied.

"Mr. Wilson," Catfish said through clenched teeth, "if Bob Suggs doesn't go in, then I don't go in and neither does my team. While Throckmorton is standing around waiting for us to show up, I'll be sitting in the office of the *Austin Statesman*, explaining how you refused to let us play for the state championship. Now, I don't know if you can imagine tomorrow's headlines, but I'll bet your boss can. Maybe you ought to check with him before you turn us away."

The attendant called over a helper and sent him running. Soon, the messenger returned and whispered in Wilson's ear.

"You can go in," the attendant muttered, and then cut his eyes at Bob Suggs, "but there's no place for him to sit."

"That won't be a problem, Mr. Wilson. He'll sit on the bench right beside me," Catfish replied, and then brushed past the man while motioning the others to follow.

The Throckmorton team was tall, as advertised, but Catfish had prepared his team. While loosening up prior to the game, Pierce realized his back had stiffened as a result of the earlier practice, and each shot attempt brought on excruciating pain. He would have to focus on defense and short passes and hope his condition would improve.

The Tigers played like a pack of demons from the opening gun, and that kept them in the contest. Pierce had to call timeout twice because of his back injury, but he managed to stay in the game, defend his man, and make some timely passes. Though they had to come from behind twice, they won, 30-28. Cannaday and Loyd led the team in scoring with eight each, making shots off timely passes from Glenn Pierce, but as soon as the final buzzer sounded, the team's captain dropped to his knees, clutching his back.

"What's wrong, son?" Catfish asked, rushing over.

"Hurt my back," the boy replied through clenched teeth.

"He sprained it yesterday, Coach," Swede said, "but he wouldn't let me tell you."

Catfish and Crowston helped Pierce to his feet and practically carried him into the dressing room.

Instantly, the coach began worrying. He realized his captain was now doubtful for the semifinals the next day against the defending state champions, Sidney Lanier of San Antonio, the team he rated as the best in the tournament. Lanier's earlier victory over El Campo by a convincing score of 38-21 just heightened the coach's fears.

All evening, Catfish fretted over how to attack the Lanier team led by Escobedo, an All-State guard for the past two seasons. The coach knew that most everyone expected the San Antonio team to win and to repeat as state champions. How could his little team beat them, especially without its captain?

All season the coach had felt fortunate to have six players capable of starting any game. In many situations, substituting Charles Hogan for Lollis Loyd or for Swede Crowston had been crucial to victory. But he needed Glenn Pierce in the game. He depended on the team captain to direct fellow players on the floor, to call timeouts when needed, and to adjust player assignments, things the rules prohibited the coach from doing during the contest. Pierce was his coach on the court.

The next morning Catfish gathered his team together at the hotel.

"How's the back?" he asked Pierce.

"Better," the captain replied, his body language saying different.

"Okay, boys," Catfish began, "are you glad to be here?"

His players roared.

"Me too," Catfish said, beaming enthusiasm and confidence that immediately melted any tightness in his players. "You've already shocked most folks who think they know a thing or two about basketball in this state, but we've got one more surprise for them."

Again the boys whooped and whistled.

"That's right," Catfish said, motioning them in close. "They beat Mount Vernon last year, and they think this time will be even easier. But, we've got a surprise for them. We're gonna whip the defending state champs this afternoon, and I'll tell you how we're going to do it.

"You boys remember how we won the district championship game? We played defense like Deport had never seen before. Little Charles Hogan here proved to all of us that he's capable of shutting down the best player on any team."

Catfish hesitated, his sparkling eyes scanning the faces of his players and then settling on Hogan with a wink.

"That's right, Charles. You're gonna guard Escobedo. They say he's the best offensive guard in the state. Well, when you shut him down, then I think that'll make you the best defensive guard in the state."

All his teammates reached a supporting hand to the smallest and quickest player on the team. "You can do it," several of them chirped.

"But that won't be enough to win," Catfish continued. "Every one of you has got to play just as hard as Hogan. You've got to press them every minute, every second, whether or not your assigned player has the ball. Do that, and they'll make mistakes, which we'll turn into points for us. We're gonna show these folks a new brand of basketball, a kind they won't soon forget."

That afternoon, Catfish and his small-town Mount Vernon Tigers shocked the basketball gurus of the state of Texas. Little Charles Hogan held the twice All-State Escobedo to three points, all on free throws. Hogan's teammates mimicked his fierce style of defense and held the defending state champions to seventeen points while scoring nineteen. Sportswriters, fans, and opposing coaches were saying it was the greatest upset in the history of Texas schoolboy basketball. For Catfish and his Tigers, it was no more than they expected of themselves.

The dramatic win propelled the Tigers into the state championship game the next day against the Nocona Indians. Catfish was back for another state championship trophy, and the number of fans who believed he could do it was growing.

11

March 11, 1944

With victories over two teams that the Texas sports world had not believed possible, the Tigers were feeling good about their chances of winning the championship game against Nocona.

Their coach's confidence was soaring for another reason. His team had grasped the techniques he had taught them, had made the adjustments he asked for, and was playing tough, sound basketball. Yet there was something beyond those basic confidence builders. His players had shown the ability to find a way to pull out ballgames at the end when one shot, one pass, or one turnover of the ball was the difference between victory and defeat. They expected to win, and at the championship level, Catfish knew that this one intangible element was often the deciding factor.

In the locker room just prior to going onto the court, Catfish's advice to his team was simple.

"Boys, I want to dedicate this game to the fans of Mount Vernon, to your fathers and mothers, your classmates, your school. Just go out there today and play your best. Do that, and you'll walk off the floor as champions, no matter the score."

The first quarter revealed two well coached, evenly matched teams, each playing good, solid basketball, and it ended with Nocona ahead, 8-6. Then in the second period, the Tigers' shooting went cold. They scored only two points, and trailed at halftime, 14-8.

In the dressing room Catfish scanned his boys' gaunt faces. This was their third game in as many days, each against a physically superior team. The Tigers' style of basketball, hard-nosed defense and fast-paced offense, had drained them of energy.

"Mr. Fleming," Catfish called to the superintendent, "these boys are dead tired. We've got to pump some energy into them, got to give them a fair shot at winning this game. If you could round up three or four Coca Colas and some sugar, I think we can rejuvenate these boys."

The superintendent headed for the door, and in moments he returned with five soft drinks and a handful of sugar packets from the concession stands. Catfish funneled some of the white crystals into the bottles, shook them up, and then watched his boys guzzle down the high-octane mixture.

The third period began as a continuation of the second, and soon it appeared the outcome was decided with the Indians leading 21-10. An eleven-point deficit, especially against a championship-level team, would be nearly impossible to overcome. But in the closing minutes of the period, the Coca Cola and sugar kicked in and triggered the Tigers into a frenzy of smothering defense and down-court dashes with stolen passes and loose balls, enabling them to close the gap to 26-20. Then in the final stanza, the Tiger fans got what they came for when Cannaday and Hogan went on a scoring spree. Repeatedly, Pierce slipped past his defender, dribbled for the goal, attracting a second defender, and then flipped the ball back out to an open Cannaday, Loyd, or Hogan who sank open shots. With less than a minute to play, the Tigers had pulled within one point, 29-28. Captain Glenn Pierce called timeout and gathered the players around him under Mount Vernon's goal.

"Look," he said, smiling at his teammates who were bent at the waist, heaving for breath, "this is exactly the situation we have handled all year. Those Nocona boys over there are scared to death right now. We're breathing down their necks, and they can feel the heat. Now, here's what we're going to do. They've got to inbound the ball, and we're going to guard everybody except the player passing in the ball. Don't let anybody break down court on you. Instead, force somebody to come back toward the passer to get the ball. Hogan, you're going to roam free about twelve feet in front of the passer, watching for one of their players to dart back for a short pass. When he does, you break into the passing lane and steal the ball. There's plenty of time for us to score."

It worked just like Pierce described it. When a Nocona guard raced back to take the inbound pass, Hogan saw him coming and dashed in to steal the ball. Frustrated, the Indian player then reached to slap the ball away and fouled Hogan.

Standing at the free throw line, Charles glanced up at the clock. Ten seconds left. One shot would tie the game, and if he could make both free throws, the Tigers would lead by one.

With the crowd gone silent, Hogan bounced the ball twice, took a deep breath, and shot. The ball swished through the net, and the Tiger fans erupted. As Hogan prepared to shoot the second free throw, the crowd again hushed. As before, Charles bounced the ball twice, inhaled deeply, and then exhaled slowly. His shot was smooth, but it was a little long and bounded off the back of the rim into the lane where an Indian player grabbed it. With the score tied, 29-29, Nocona had the ball and a chance for the last goal.

The Indians quickly moved the ball down court, but with time running out, they took a rushed shot and missed, leaving the final outcome to be decided in three minutes of overtime.

The Mount Vernon players huddled around their coach while Catfish scanned their faces and smiled. They were physically tired, but the coach could see the excitement and determination in their eyes.

"Just three more minutes of hard work," he said, "and you'll be state champions. Defense has brought you this far, and that's what will win it for you, so don't let up."

In the extra period, Mount Vernon's defense shut down Nocona while Cannaday made a free throw for the Tigers, and Captain Pierce sank a goal, giving Catfish's boys a three-point edge, 32-29. Mount Vernon fans were delirious. Then with a minute and three seconds remaining, a Nocona player forced Hogan out of bounds. Thinking the opposing player had fouled Hogan, the Tigers headed for the free throw stripe. An alert Nocona player realized the official had awarded the ball to his team, so he quickly grabbed the ball out of bounds and sailed it down court to his streaking teammate Eastus who made an uncontested layup, closing the gap to 32-31.

With a one-point lead and the ball, Catfish's boys headed up court, watching the clock steadily tick down. Teague, one of the Indians' most reliable players, managed to steal an errant pass and head back the other way. Hogan and Pierce cut off his path to the goal, but with thirty seconds left, Eastus heaved a long, near-impossible shot toward the rim. As they had been taught, the Tiger defenders sealed off the area around the goal, determined to get the rebound, but there was no rebound. The ball swished through the net, putting Nocona ahead, 33-32.

After inbounding the ball, the Tigers pushed it down court where they fired three shots, each one careening off the goal into the hands of a teammate. Then time ran out, and finally the Tigers had come up short in a one-point game.

122

Quickly, Catfish gathered his boys around him.

"Keep those heads up, boys. You played a great game, and like I told you earlier, you are leaving this court as champions in my book."

Later, in the dressing room, with his players sitting around in a daze, replaying the ending and finding it impossible to comprehend that they had missed three consecutive shots, any one of which would have won the game, Catfish eased to the center of the room and asked for their attention. With his players focused on him, sportswriters with pads and pens scattered about, and proud parents looking on, Catfish towered over the group as he waited for quiet.

"Today ends one of the most enjoyable seasons of my coaching career," he said. "I have never worked with boys who showed a greater desire to win. This group has led this coach, rather than their coach leading them. Through a grueling football schedule and a long basketball season, these boys have never once quit hustling, never once given up. Also, I want Mount Vernon and Franklin County fans to know that we have appreciated their fine support. I have never before seen such fan loyalty. And to you parents, I want to say that behind each of these players I have found a great mother and father, and that is the basic reason for our success. It has been an honor to work with these young men."

Catfish then hesitated, trying to blink his eyes clear. "I'm sorry I didn't do enough to take this team to first place, but I can honestly say I am prouder of these boys in defeat, than a lot of teams in victory."

It was a stirring end to a season that lacked only one basket capturing the Texas State Basketball Championship for the Tigers of Mount Vernon and their coach, Milburn "Catfish" Smith, whom Superintendent Fleming had hired back in August to "help out for a few months." The coach had reason to be proud. His 1944 Tigers had won twenty-eight games while losing only three, the state championship contest to Nocona and two non-conference games to Blossom, a squad that was runner-up to Prairie Lea for the Class B state championship.

Upon the team's arrival in Mount Vernon, the townsfolk welcomed their basketball champs home with a huge banner that stretched from the south side of the plaza to the storefronts across Main Street. "STATE FINALIST" was stenciled in purple letters on the white banner. The high school band, directed by Mrs. Vera Mitchell, lined the south side of the plaza. They played the school song while the "Faithful Five" twirled and tossed their batons in unison. The Five, dressed in their jodhpur-style uniforms, consisted of drum major, Joyce Hill, and majorettes June Godwin, Frances Cowan, Nell Newsome, and Gwendolyne Orren.

At the edge of the crowd stood a young sophomore, watching the Faithful Five's every move. How badly the petite cornet player wanted to be a majorette, but to have even a slight chance, she would have to prove to the band director that she was an accomplished twirler. Young Martha Hill did not even own one, and she had no money to overcome that deficiency. Her father owned Hill's Grocery on South Kaufman Street, but Mount Vernon had an abundance of grocery stores, none with a corner on the market. Determined, Martha had cut the handle off an old broom and improvised. Every chance she got, she studied the current twirlers every move, as she did now. The next day she would emulate them for hours, spinning and tossing her broomstick.

The fans that lined the plaza and storefronts spilled into the wide street and clamored for Catfish to address the crowd. Remembering Superintendent Fleming's promise back in August for just such a celebration, he climbed the concrete steps to the elevated plaza and praised his players and thanked the loyal fans of Mount Vernon and the surrounding countryside.

The Rotary Club then paid tribute to the team with a banquet at the First Methodist Church. That was followed by a dinner sponsored by Mrs. A. P. King, Mrs. Lester Martin, and Catfish's mother, Mrs. Ida Smith. After Catfish repeated his praises for the team and fans, T. H. Browning lauded the coach and players, as did G. W. Rutherford, L. D. Lowry, Jr., and Superintendent Fleming. An uninformed visitor would have thought Mount Vernon had won the state championship.

The most emotional occasion then came when the team was honored in the school auditorium before the student body, fans, teachers, and school administrators. Catfish recognized each player, announcing that Lollis Loyd and J. C. Cannaday had been selected to the Class A, All-State first team, the only school in the state to have two players so honored. And he praised Glenn Pierce, captain of the team, for his leadership. He pointed out the stellar play of Harry Jack Pugh, and his personal choice as an All-State defensive player, Charles Hogan.

When Catfish took a seat, Superintendent Fleming stepped to the podium.

"I have some good news, too, " he said, turning and smiling at the coach. He then pulled out a document, unfolded it and waved it before the crowd. "We've convinced our temporary coach to come back for another year."

The crowd chanted "Catfish, Catfish, Catfish . . ." until the coach returned to the podium.

"Thank you for your unfailing support," he said. "Without a doubt, Mount Vernon has the most enthusiastic and faithful fans in the state."

"Now," he continued, "basketball season is over, and in two weeks we'll begin spring football drills. We'll lose only two players to graduation from last fall's fine team, Lollis Loyd and James Pierce. With the fighting spirit these boys have shown, they will improve on last fall's record. In fact, I'll tell you fine folks right now, if Mount Vernon doesn't win the district title, you'll need to get yourselves a new coach."

After a few more minutes of celebrating, the students were dismissed to their classes.

During the two weeks before the beginning of football spring drills, Catfish spent most of his spare time helping the Red Cross War Fund reach and exceed its goal by $685. With his popularity at an all-time high, he encouraged Saturday's downtown crowds to contribute generously. Ultimately, the goal was surpassed because owners of some local businesses, the First National Bank, Rutherford Drug Store, Lowry's Hardware & Furniture, and Humble Oil Company, each contributed two hundred fifty dollars.

When Catfish was not promoting the cause of the Red Cross, he switched his attention to Dorothy Nell Penn. At the Ration Office where she worked, they threatened to put him on the payroll. Every Saturday night the couple had dinner together at one of the local eateries and then took in the movie, and every Sunday they sat side-by-side at the First Baptist Church and listened to Reverend Whitt's sermon.

"Dorothy Nell," Roy Smith said when she stepped inside Crescent Drug Store one day, "when are you and Catfish going to get married?"

"Not before he asks me," she replied, laughing.

"I can't imagine why he hasn't already proposed to you," the druggist said.

"Maybe he can't make up his mind if I'm the right girl for him," Dorothy Nell replied.

"Why, he's not interested in another girl. That boy worships the ground you walk on."

"That's true," Dorothy Nell said, "so long as I'm strolling across the football field."

They laughed, but Roy Smith's question was the same one being bantered about by all the locals. At twenty-three years of age, pretty Dorothy Nell was the darling of Mount Vernon and the target of every matchmaker around. She was often described as "the nicest, sweetest girl in town," and Catfish was the most eligible bachelor. With his flare and coaching success, he had taken the city by storm, but the days passed and time for spring football drills arrived with people still puzzled.

A couple of key players from Catfish's 1943 team were eleventh graders, their last year of school. With a twelfth grade recently added, the rules allowed them to return for one more year provided their eighteenth birthday did not occur before the start of classes in the upcoming September. Catfish saw an opportunity and met with the boys.

"What are your plans for summer?" he asked.

"With the war, we can't make plans," the boys replied. "When we reach eighteen, if we haven't already volunteered, we'll be drafted into the Army."

"You boys think your parents would sign for you to volunteer early?"

The boys shook their heads.

"Then, how would you like to play football another year, then serve your country however you choose."

They liked the idea, so Catfish told them to show up for spring drills.

For the first practice, thirty-six boys suited up, thirteen more than in the fall, delighting the coach. As Catfish immersed himself in the training and developing of his players, he realized that he not only had the nucleus from the prior fall's team, but he had some promising newcomers.

To his already outstanding corps of linemen, Dan Cargile, Charles Shurtleff, Harry Jack Pugh, and James Caudle, Catfish could add eight more youngsters. Frank "Two Ton" Parchman, was a "can't miss" at the tackle position, and Gene "Half-pint" Fleming was already a fine player but was clearly destined to be outstanding at a full pint. Young Charles Lowry had size beyond his years, along with intelligence and grit, while Gayle Tinsley was undersized, but his toughness and smarts made him a warrior to be reckoned with. Jack "Tractor" Horne, as his nickname implied, could plow over opponents, and James "Bigfoot" Pittman had size and strength in places other than his feet.

Then to his stable of proven running backs, Clarence "Swede" Crowston, Jerry "Jitterbug" Yokum, and Tom Irby, the coach added five talented runners. Speedy Charles Hogan showed that his tenacity not only served well on the basketball court, but on the gridiron, too. Kenneth Meek, wiry and only slightly over one hundred pounds, ran with an awkward-looking style that proved surprisingly effective. Catfish called him the "Rambler" and once jovially said of Meek, "If you need four yards, Kenneth will always get it for you. If you need six yards, he'll still get four yards for you." Buck Parchman's trademark was toughness, while C. J. "Tarzan" Bogue was the small version of his namesake. With an abundance of talented linemen on the squad, Robby Campbell asked to be moved to halfback, hoping to follow in the footsteps of his older brother and outstanding runner, Wayne "Bo" Campbell. Catfish liked the spunky kid and agreed. But most important, Glenn "Gumbo" Pierce was back at quarterback in the coach's T-formation. Catfish was indeed excited about the possibilities of a district championship in 1944.

To complete a successful spring practice, Catfish scheduled two intra-squad games, one April 14 and the other April 20. To form teams, he tried to equally divide the talent between a purple team led by Robby "Burr" Campbell, and a white squad led by Glenn Pierce.

"These practice sessions will be treated like real games," Catfish told the *Optic-Herald* editor. "Everybody is invited, and we'll forego our usual ten and fifteen cents for entry. We've got some outstanding talent, and I want my boys to get some game-like experience. The more fans there are in the stands, the more like a game it'll be for the players."

The fans responded as if the Tigers were playing for a championship, and they were not disappointed. The white team won both contests, but the competition was furious. Everyone left convinced that Coach Smith had two teams, either of which could win the district title, but when combined would produce a squad that would rival Mount Vernon's highly revered and undefeated 1938 Regional Championship team. With the second best basketball team in the state and the prospect of a championship football team, sports fans in Mount Vernon were abuzz. Everywhere Catfish went, he was congratulated and questioned about his talented boys.

Yet, amid all the hoopla and adulation, Catfish already had his sights set on something even greater than a championship, something he, at thirty-one years of age, had never before attempted, something that would have a dramatic impact on the remainder of his life.

12

April 21, 1944

"Mr. Milburn Albert Smith is to wed Miss Dorothy Neil Penn, Friday evening, April 21, at the home of Dr. J. M. Fleming," the newspaper article read. Continuing, the story named the bride's parents, Mr. and Mrs. E. F. Penn, and noted that Dorothy Nell was employed at the local Ration Office. Further, it cited the groom as the Athletic Director and Head Coach at Mount Vernon High School and mentioned that he was completing a most successful year of work.

The wedding, performed by Reverend S. M. Williams, occurred as planned and the couple traveled to Dallas for a weekend honeymoon trip, returning to their jobs on Monday.

The ramifications of the marriage reached well beyond the newlyweds and their families. First, the main topic of conversation and speculation in town had just been eliminated. Second, many of the sports-minded citizens rejoiced, believing the wedding vows Catfish repeated not only bound him to his bride, but also to Mount Vernon. Married to a girl with deep local roots, their coach would not be leaving any time soon.

Back at school, Catfish called his athletes together.

"The semester will be over soon, and I want you boys to stay in shape. The training rules still apply, so no smoking or drinking, and limited sweets. And get your rest at night. I don't want you to form a bunch of bad habits that I'll have you break in the fall. Also, I'm suggesting you start a softball team and compete throughout the summer. It's important that you boys stay together as a team and come back September first ready to start a championship season."

Early Friday morning Catfish dropped by the *Optic-Herald* office and picked up the spare newspapers that Devall had set aside for the history classes. Arriving at his classroom well before the students, the coach unfolded the top paper.

A bold-lettered headline immediately caught his eye.

LOCAL BOY AWARDED SILVER STAR

Sgt. Billy R. Radican is awarded the Silver Star for bravery by the Fifth Army in Italy. Sgt. Radican rescued a wounded comrade from within five feet of a burning ammunition carrier, saving his friend's life.

While blocking a crossroads at night, Radican and his section fired on an approaching enemy ammunition carrier. The vehicle caught fire and careened out of control, striking one of Radican's comrades before spilling into a ditch. Amid enemy gunfire, Radican, using light from the burning ammunition carrier, crawled to within five feet of the flaming vehicle and dragged his friend to safety just before the carrier exploded. While he performed this heroic work, the rest of his company kept the enemy distracted with constant gunfire so they could not pick off Sgt. Radican while illuminated by the flames.

With images of the event flashing through Catfish's mind, he sat unmoving with chill bumps popping up on his arms. Young Radican embodied the kind of courage he hoped to instill in his boys, many of whom very well might find themselves in a similar situation in a year or two. He wondered about his Army Air Force buddies. Where had they dropped their bombs? And the faces of the boys from Carey popped into his head: Middleton, Redwine, Hunt, Gresham, and Foust. What battlefield might they be on? Had the war claimed any of them? Had he adequately prepared them for what this turbulent world had thrown their way?

Slowly he folded the paper as students began filing in, some taking a copy off the small stack on the corner of his desk.

"Can anyone tell me how a soldier earns a Silver Star?" he asked when they were seated.

"Gallantry in action," a girl responded, one who had quickly scanned the newspaper.

"That's right," Catfish said. "Uncommon bravery and courage."

He then asked the girl to read the article about Sergeant Radican to the class.

"What made his action deserving of a Silver Star?" Catfish asked when she had finished.

"He risked his life to save his friend," the girl said immediately.

"Why would he do that?"

No one responded.

"Would he have done the same thing if it had been a different member of his company, someone other than a friend?"

"I think he would have," the girl replied, looking around at her classmates who nodded their agreement.

"So do I," Catfish said. "If we're right, then he was protecting something more than his friend. What would that be?"

"In war soldiers have to look out for all their buddies," a boy said. "I bet his friend would have done the same thing for him."

"Again, I agree," Catfish said. "So Sergeant Radican was not only saving his friend, but was protecting his company as well, something he was willing to risk his life for. And one could argue that ultimately his motivation was to protect his country."

"I guess they teach that in the Army," a boy said.

"Yes, they train them to look out for each other," Catfish said, "but I think Radican's motivation ran deeper than that. I think he learned well before he enlisted that there are things more important than his own safety.

"As a coach," he continued, "that is the most important thing I have to teach my boys. They have to put team success ahead of their own. I'm a coach because I believe it's essential to teach young men character, loyalty, and toughness, both mental and physical, especially in today's world."

"Sir," a girl said, raising her hand. "There's another interesting article in today's paper."

Catfish nodded for her to tell the class about it.

"It says Milburn Albert Smith has married Miss Dorothy Nell Penn."

Seeing the smile on Catfish's reddening face, the class had a good laugh.

"And it says," a boy continued reading from the article, "the couple went on a short wedding trip. Maybe you could tell us . . ."

"And I believe," Catfish replied, cutting the boy off, "that concludes the article. Now, who has other news of interest?"

War news dominated the remaining discussion with speculation that the Allied Forces would soon cross the English Channel and invade Northern France. Generally the students felt it would result in a rapid push to Berlin and thus the end of the conflict in Western Europe. The coach had doubts about a swift end to the war, but he kept those thoughts to himself.

As the students filed out and headed for their next class, Catfish pulled a package of matches from his front pocket. He smiled as he ran his index finger across the embossed lettering, "Baker Hotel, Dallas, Texas." He slipped the matches back into his pocket as mental images of the past weekend flashed through his mind.

*   *   *

By May 15 Catfish had finalized his football schedule for the fall of 1944. After school he took it to the *Optic-Herald* office and waited while Charles Devall looked it over.

"Wow!" the newsman said. "Nine games after playing only six last season."

"The first two are iffy," Catfish said, referring to two scrimmage games he had penciled in. "I hope to schedule a couple of AA schools in September. Even if we only play their reserves, they should provide stiff competition for us."

"Which AA teams do you have in mind?" Devall asked.

"I'd like to get Sulphur Springs for sure, and maybe Paris."

"If you start with Sulphur Springs and Paris, followed by Winnsboro, Mineola, and Mount Pleasant, I'd say you've got your boat loaded to the point of tipping over. Then there's Gilmer who beat you last fall, and a good Pittsburg team. If you can get through all that, you can surely whip Talco and Clarksville to end a perfect season. Coach, you'll be facing some of the strongest competition in East Texas."

"My boys say their season won't end there. They're going to win Regional, no matter who's on their schedule," Catfish replied.

"What does their coach say?" the newsman asked.

"The harder the fight, the greater the victory," Catfish replied, and then continued. "My boys are going to band together this summer, stay in shape, and return in the fall as a team, not individuals. Teams win championships, not a couple of star players."

"May I quote you on that?"

Catfish nodded, then turned and left.

*   *   *

The last Friday of school, the front page of the *Optic-Herald* featured a large diagram of the eastern coast of Great Britain, the English Channel, the North Sea, and the western coast of France, Belgium, and the Netherlands. The associated story indicated that thousands of troops and equipment were poised in England, waiting to invade Western Europe as part of Operation Overlord. "The map has every little village and hamlet along the western coast of Europe, so you can follow the moves of the invading parties," the caption read.

A photo showed rows of antiaircraft guns as part of the invasion equipment in England, being readied for Goering's dwindling air force, the *Luftwaffe*. "Here is one place your War Bond dollars have gone," the caption said. "And these guns will be bad news for the Axis airmen when they attempt to prevent the Allies from invading Fortress Europe."

Studying the map while waiting for his students, Catfish noticed the absence of symbols for German defenses along the westernmost coast of Europe. Yet he knew the Germans would be ready with their chain of fortifications, which they called the Atlantic Wall. Assigned by Hitler to protect against the invasion was the famous German military leader, Rommel. Without a doubt the general would have heavy artillery, sharpshooters, bombers, bunkered machinegun nests, and miles of barbed wire and treacherous mine fields to welcome the Allies. Obviously, keeping the time and place of the invasion secret was critical to the Allies. If somehow the Germans could manage to steal that bit of information with time to focus their defenses, the invasion would undoubtedly result in a massive human sacrifice by the Allies.

The students chattered excitedly about the pending invasion. They guessed it could happen most any day and predicted the Allies would sweep across Western Europe, giving the Germans a taste of *blitzkrieg*, American style. In the discussion with his students, Catfish did not mention his misgivings.

The final week of school passed quickly with the school administration preoccupied with preparations for the upcoming graduation ceremony. Arriving at this occasion Catfish was surprised to learn that one of his players, Jimmy Pierce, would not cross the stage and receive his diploma. He and two other boys, Robbie Bartley and Charles Pope, had already enlisted for military duty. Catfish took solace in the fact that the boys had volunteered too late to be thrown into the invasion force, yet he knew the day would come when they would confront the enemy amid the sobering reality of the battlefield.

*　　*　　*

The single room at Hasty Courts, which had served Catfish well, was too small for him and his bride. With school dismissed for the summer, finding a house to rent became his priority.

"Coach," said County Clerk L. E. Seay, "Hal Scott, the fellow with the lumberyard, has built a nice little house just east of town on the south side of highway sixty-seven, just past the cemetery. He just might rent it to you."

The lumberman was delighted to find a renter.

"It's a new house, freshly painted white, and it sits on three quarters of an acre with some nice shade trees," Scott explained. "You'll be less than half a mile from the plaza. I'll get everything arranged, and you can be moved in within the week."

Scott and Catfish quickly agreed on twenty-five dollars a month and an option to convert the deal to a purchase plan within a year. If the upcoming football team should live up to his expectations, he might be willing to become a homeowner.

Four days later the newlyweds were setting up housekeeping, ecstatic with their fresh new home. Dorothy Nell bought some colorful material, sewed and hung curtains, and stocked her kitchen while Catfish rounded up furniture that various people had offered, along with a new radio they purchased from Lowry's Furniture Store.

On Sunday, June 4, the radio brought news of Allied Forces rolling into Rome, liberating the city so long occupied by the Germans. Despite Mussolini's fall from power in July of the prior year and Italy's surrender two months later, the Germans had fought determinedly to maintain control of the peninsula, but the Allied Forces had proved even more determined to drive them out. The retreating enemy had cut dams and dikes, flooding the land and roads in their wake while burying mines along passable highways and leaving snipers at strategic points. Still, the American forces had pushed on, reclaiming the country for its residents.

On Tuesday morning, June 6, the couple arose early with Dorothy Nell dressing for work and Catfish preparing to mow the lawn. She had just turned on the radio and poured two cups of coffee when the scheduled program broke for a war bulletin.

The Allied forces led by General Dwight D. Eisenhower, under the shield of darkness and fog, have stormed the beaches at Normandy, France. This is the largest invasion of its kind in the history of the world. On its success hangs the freedom of millions of war-weary people in Western Europe. Early reports are sketchy but indicate that the fighting is the bloodiest of the war. Estimates are that over seventy-five percent of the first wave of Allied soldiers died, either in the water or on the beaches, under a horrendous barrage of German rifle and machinegun fire, along with land mines and heavy artillery shells. Many never made it to shore, drowning in surprisingly deep water, dragged down by their heavy packs and gear. Others were blown up by mines attached to underwater booby traps or became entangled in coils of barbed wire hidden below the choppy waves. Stay tuned for more news bulletins as they become available.

Hearing the first sentence, Dorothy Nell ran to Catfish who had just come through the doorway. At the mention of widespread deaths, she buried her face against his chest and sobbed while he wrapped his long arms around her and fought his own tears. Anger welled up inside him, accompanied with an almost uncontrollable urge to scream obscenities at Hitler, Mussolini, and Tojo. Never had he wanted to be aboard a bomber so much, dropping its massive payload onto the war machinery of Berlin and Tokyo. The frustration of that day when he had been told he would be discharged from the AAF came back, doubled.

"Three out of four dead," he mumbled. "What a high price to pay. I wish I was there." He closed his eyes and lowered his chin to his young wife's hair, his emotions about to burst through like water over a crumbling dam.

Midmorning, Catfish went to check on Dorothy Nell at the Rations Office. The mood there was somber with everyone seeming to move in slow motion while the radio was tuned for the news. At the least hint of a war bulletin, the volume was turned up and all movement stopped. Desperately, they hoped for good news.

Here is the latest from Normandy Beach.

Under cover of darkness, thousands of paratroopers were flown behind enemy lines; however, it is now reported that due to stormy weather, cloud cover, and darkness, many were dropped right over enemy strongholds. Slowly floating downward, they became target practice for the Germans. Also, we are told that the night before the landing, our soldiers, who would within hours be storming the beaches, were advised to write to their loved ones, to pen their last will and testament. Yet, for the cause of freedom these brave men splashed ashore and pushed forward, ignoring the horrific reality about them. Somehow they overcame the survivalist's urge to hang back and hide behind blown-out tanks and jeeps, rather than run headlong into the firestorm of bullets, scale the one-hundred-foot cliffs, and take out German machinegun nests, silence the big eighty-eight millimeter guns, and root out the hedgerow snipers. These brave soldiers will, no doubt, gain a foothold, and then pursue the enemy to his ultimate defeat.

All over town, the scenes were the same. The rah-rah spirit preceding the invasion was replaced with the grim reality of its necessary but gruesome price. Some went to their church and spent hours in prayer. Mothers and fathers, arm in arm, dropped to their knees, lowered their heads, and asked God's protection of their sons.

Through the following tense days, Catfish spent his time supporting the Fifth War Loan. Franklin County's quota was $207,000 of which $100,000 was assigned to Mount Vernon. Like everyone else, Catfish grasped for every shred of news he could garner regarding the progress of the war, both in Europe and the Pacific. Chairman of the War Loan, L. D. Lowry, Jr., expressed his commitment amid the growing reports of wounded, missing, and dead soldiers, airmen, and sailors.

"With untold thousands of our own boys facing the grim reality of war every day, wounded on the battlefront, spilling their life's blood for you and me, Mount Vernon and Franklin County must and will buy war bonds until it hurts, and then dig down and buy some more."

Picking up the newspaper of June 16, Catfish's eyes were drawn to an article about a former Mount Vernon student, Lieutenant Weldon Reeves, an Army Air Forces copilot serving in the South Pacific. Lieutenant Reeves of the 13th AAF was awarded a Bronze Oak Leaf Cluster for another outstanding achievement "while participating in sustained combat-operation missions of a hazardous duty during which enemy opposition was met." During his eleven-month stint in the AAF, Catfish had met many of the pilots and bombardiers in the 13th, and the award stirred his memory of images and faces of his former buddies.

Another story hit especially close to Catfish's emotional center. Lieutenant Colonel James Earl Rudder, Commanding Officer of the 2nd and 5th Ranger battalions, and a 1932 Texas A&M graduate and football coach, had entered the war in 1941. When told by his commanding officer that he was too valuable to lead his men onto Normandy beach on D-Day, up the sheer cliffs, and against the German concrete-fortified positions, he replied, "I am sorry to have to disobey you, sir." Rudder led his men, though he was almost blown to bits by a bursting British shell that fell short and sent him flying. The determined young man recovered and led an attack on German snipers protecting a machine gun nest, taking a bullet through his leg. Though hobbled, Rudder led on, inspiring his men with his courageous spirit. One ranger remarked that seeing Rudder leading the operation saved the day. Another said of his commander, "He was the strength of the whole operation."

If Catfish could not be there with his old pals and fellow coaches to fight the enemy, he would do his utmost to prepare young men under his charge for the harshness of war, while drilling them in the essentials of a cohesive working unit, an absolute requirement for success in battle. The bombers, the paratroopers, the Marines, the infantry, and the Navy destroyers had to coordinate their strengths, and the home front had to manufacture the airplanes, the battleships, beach-landing vehicles, the tanks, the guns, the ammunition, and every citizen had to buy as many war bonds as possible. Catfish translated this to his coaching. The next season he would stress teamwork above all else.

With two days left in the Fifth War Loan drive, July 7 and 8, the county was still short of its quota of $207,000. M. L. Edwards asked Catfish to help encourage people coming into town to make one last purchase.

"It's the closest we can come to fighting alongside our boys," Edwards said.

Saturday morning, while encouraging people around the square to help push the county to its goal, Catfish met Mr. and Mrs. Roy Bankston, along with their daughter-in-law, the former Martha Newberry.

"Our son Harold was a three-year letterman on the local football team when he graduated in nineteen forty," Mr. Bankston explained. "Now he's a turret gunner on the Flying Fortress, *Return Ticket*. He's just completed twenty-five bomber combat missions, and will be coming home soon with the Distinguished Flying Cross and an Air Medal with three Oak Leaf Clusters."

"Congratulations," Catfish said, and then glanced over at Martha. "I'm sure you can't wait to see him."

Embarrassed, she nodded. "I'm proud of the job he has done, but mostly I'm excited that he's coming home safe."

On Monday, L. D. Lowry, Jr., announced that Franklin County had exceeded its goal by $78,000, with every community in the county exceeding its allotted amount. But then he added a stirring note.

"Our local servicemen, having already given all that could be expected, purchased thirteen thousand one hundred dollars worth of bonds."

This news brought tears to Catfish's eyes and a deepened commitment to his heart.

13

Summer of 1944

While many of his boys labored in summer hayfields, Catfish finalized his fall football schedule by lining up two September home games: the Paris Reserves on the 14th and Sulphur Springs, a AA school, on the 22nd. True to his philosophy, "you've got to beat the best to be the best," Catfish felt his team would develop faster by playing these larger schools. Following these potentially bruising season openers, he accepted an open date to allow his boys some recovery time prior to jumping into league play.

September 14	Paris Reserves	Home
September 22	Sulphur Springs Reserves	Home
September 29	Open	
October 6	Mineola	Home
October 13	Winnsboro	Home
October 20	Mount Pleasant	Home
October 27	Pittsburg	Away
November 3	Gilmer	Away
November 10	Talco	Home
November 17	Clarksville	Away

On August 6, Catfish and Dorothy Nell packed up and headed to Wichita Falls for the annual school for Texas high school mentors. Driving west on highway eighty-two, he told his wife about the instructors.

"Sammy Baugh, the Texas Christian University quarterback who was a great passer and punter, heads the billing, but not far behind are Blair Cherry of the University of Texas and Bobby Dodd of Georgia Tech. Less known around here are Del Morgan of Texas Tech, Jeff

Craveth of the University of Southern California, and Jewel Wallace of San Angelo High.

"Honey, these are men who have proven they know how to compete and coach at the highest level, and that's what I'm aiming to do. Learning from them will get us there faster."

The names meant little to Dorothy Nell, but she smiled warmly at the enthusiasm they so easily stirred in her husband. While he talked on, she looked out the side window and watched the wooded hills of East Texas slowly fade away while the more open landscapes of Saint Jo, Nocona, and Henrietta prepared her for the windblown, heat-seared flatland of Wichita Falls.

As Catfish turned the car onto the campus of Midwestern University, Dorothy Nell spotted the town of Carey on the map and estimated it was only a hundred twenty miles farther west.

"Do you plan to drive on to Carey while we're out here?" she asked, knowing his fondness for the little town where he had started his coaching career.

"No," he replied. "I won't ever forget the fine people there or the good times, but in coaching, you quickly learn that what you accomplished last year, or the year before, won't win one game on your current schedule."

That week in Wichita Falls, with nights free to see the town, eat at fine restaurants, and visit with fellow coaches and friends, was their first vacation trip since the weekend honeymoon they had managed back in April. Then, on their way home Friday, they relived the highlights of the past five days through conversation, laughter, and lingering touches, but when they drove into Paris, Catfish became quiet.

"What a fine city," Dorothy Nell said.

"Yeah, and about five or six times the size of Mount Vernon," Catfish replied. "I expect their boys, even their reserves, will give us a stiff fight."

"Think you made a mistake scheduling them?"

"No," he said without hesitation. "My boys have plenty of fight in them, and more talent than last year. We're going to surprise some folks."

* * *

Fall practice began on Friday, September 1, with classes to start on the 11th, so Catfish had the boys to himself for ten days. After the first few days of morning and afternoon practices, the team thinned down to twenty-six players. Notable early surprises were Charles Hogan, Frank Parchman, and Jack Horne. The coach was delighted with what he saw, though a bystander would never have guessed it.

Dorothy Nell always showed up about the time practice ended, and waited in the car for her husband. She avoided an early arrival because the September heat was suffocating, even in the shade, but on Wednesday afternoon of the first week of two-a-days, Catfish worked the boys later than usual. For the first time, Dorothy Nell sat and watched the final half hour of the grueling drills, and heard her husband bellowing at the players and demanding that his sweat-soaked, exhausted boys repeat a technique or a play when it appeared their wobbly legs could hardly support them.

When it was over and the boys had gone, Catfish slid into the seat beside his wife and leaned across for the usual welcome kiss.

"What's wrong?" he asked when Dorothy Nell turned away.

With her face flushed and solemn, she stared ahead as her knuckles drained white under her unrelenting grip on the black steering wheel. Tired and hungry, Catfish waited, trying to guess why his wife was upset. Then he saw tears streaming down her cheeks.

"Honey," he said reaching for her arm, "what's the matter?"

She jerked her arm away, and then cut her eyes toward him.

"This is my home town," she said. "I love these people. They're my friends. Many were my classmates."

"I know that," he replied, "and they're my friends, too."

"They won't be when they see what you're doing to their boys," she said sharply. "They'll hate you, and they'll blame me."

"What do you mean?"

"The way you talk to them, yelling and screaming, and the way you work them in this horrible heat, the boys and their parents will run us both out of town."

"Dot," he said calmly, "kill the engine and listen to me for a minute."

She switched the key off, but refused to look at him.

"Honey, I'm teaching those boys how to win, how to be champions."

"Why is it so important to you to *always* win?" she asked, biting off the words. "Nobody can always win. We have to learn to accept defeat, too."

"You're right, Dot. They're not always going to win, but they have to always expect to win, and they should *never* be satisfied with losing.

Another thing. No one can expect to win unless they have prepared themselves better than their opponent, unless they have paid the price it takes to win.

"Honey, the most important thing I can do for my boys is to help them develop character. That's why I'm a coach. And winning does that, not losing. There's no better place in the world to develop character than right out there," he said, motioning toward the football field.

"Those boys will soon be stepping out into a world turned upside down by war. On the football field, we can correct a mistake with repetition and hard work; on the battlefield a mistake can be fatal. In a game we can call timeout and make adjustments; in war, there are no timeouts. We spend a week preparing for the next challenger; over there, the fighting goes on every day, every hour. Dot, now is the time and the place for my boys to learn to do the right thing, the right way, at the right time, and that they cheat themselves when they take a shortcut, when they settle for less than their best.

"Honey, the battlefield quickly becomes a cemetery for boys who take short cuts, who don't have the courage, the strength, and the endurance to persevere, to keep going when it seems impossible to go on, to never, ever give up. I don't want a single one of my boys to die because I didn't do everything in my power to prepare him for the challenges of life."

For a moment, they sat there in silence, both staring into the dusk of early evening, overwhelmed by their thoughts and emotions. Then, Catfish reached over and clasped Dorothy Nell's small hand between his. Slowly, he bowed his head and kissed the soft, delicate skin.

"You're right, though," he said, his voice barely audible. "Some of them may hate me right now. They may not understand why I push them, why I make them run a play over and over until all eleven boys do their job right, why I run them when they don't think they can take another step. But, that's okay. Some day, maybe a year from now, maybe five, ten, or even twenty, they'll understand, and they'll look back, and the hate will have turned to respect. For me, that's enough."

After staring out the windshield a few moments longer, Dorothy Nell started the engine and drove home. They ate in silence, but when she had gathered the dishes and put them in the sink, she eased over to the table where Catfish sat slumped, staring at the bare tabletop.

"Now I understand what you're doing," she said softly. "Still, it seems so harsh, but I'll just stay out of coaching from now on."

"Thanks," Catfish said, rising and hugging her. "It'll work out. You'll see."

The next day, a grim and distraught Jack Parchman showed up during practice. He immediately asked Catfish to excuse Frank and Buck Parchman from practice so he could talk to them. Catfish overheard the man explain that C. J. Parchman had been captured by the Germans and was being held in an unidentified prison camp.

"You boys go on home," Catfish said when Mr. Parchman turned to leave.

With tears in his eyes, the bulky lineman shook his head, and then pulled on his helmet. Young Buck followed suit, and practice continued, though the mood of the players grew increasingly somber as word was whispered from player to player.

Such reports were a weekly occurrence. Sergeant Robert Clark, a D-Day hero, had been recently reported as missing in action, leaving his wife Nell to agonize over the fate of her husband and father of her three-month-old daughter. Private First Class Lonnie Teague was listed as killed in France, as were L. J. Eubanks and Travis Banks, a 1932 graduate. Though bitterly painful to endure, these families struggled on, often submerging their grief in the hard work of daily life. During the quiet evenings or wee hours of the night, even the strongest parents would glimpse a school picture on the mantle or awaken from a dream filled with images of their once-alive and carefree child, and their buried anguish would surface and rob them of much-needed peace and rest.

Not all news was bad, however. By mid-August, General Patton's Third Army approached the outskirts of Paris, France. General Dietrich von Choltitz and twenty-five thousand German soldiers then held the city with orders to defend it at all costs. "Paris must not fall into the hands of the enemy except as a field of ruins," ordered Hitler. Then on August 25, the Americans, the French Second Armored Division, and Free French forces liberated the great city, driving the Germans out before they could carry out Hitler's orders to torch the city. Meanwhile, the British had swept into Belgium and captured Antwerp on September 4, and the Soviets were steadily pushing the Germans westward into the clamping jaws of the Allied forces. In the Pacific the Americans dealt a terrible blow to Japan's navy and air fleet in the Battle of the Philippine Sea, and the assault on the Marianas Islands had finally put Admiral Nimitz's forces within striking distance of mainland Japan, prompting Tojo, that nation's prime minister, to resign. Even as the

142

report came of C. J. Parchman's capture, Private Durwin Cox of nearby Talco was leading a daring escape from a Nazi prison camp.

Though Catfish was never satisfied with his boys' performance in practices, as the game with the Paris Reserves on Thursday, September 14, neared, he knew his team was much improved over the previous year's squad. Joining Pierce and Crowston in the backfield were Charles Hogan and Robby Campbell. In the line Frank Parchman, Jack Horne, and George Dickerson joined Shurtleff, Cargile, and Caudle, averaging one hundred seventy pounds on the forward wall. Among the backups were Jerry Yocum, a starting halfback a year earlier, Billy Grau, James Pittman, James Cherry, Leacho Tittle, and budding stars, Gene Fleming, Charles Lowry, Buck Parchman, and Gayle Tinsley.

With excitement as thick as a London fog in the air, the crowd gathered for the game while the players paced the concrete floor of the field house and mumbled words of encouragement to each other. Finally they took the field, and the fans stood for the kickoff and remained standing as the Tiger defense slammed the door on the Wildcat offense after only one first down.

The punt went to Hogan who caught the wobbly pigskin on the Mount Vernon thirty-six-yard line and returned it to the Wildcat forty. Before the crowd could settle, Robby Campbell had raced ten yards to the opponent's thirty. Then lightning struck. Pierce pitched the ball to Swede around left end, and he alternately dazzled and trampled defenders along the way to the end zone. The crowd moaned when they realized that a penalty had nullified the score, but Pierce quickly threw a pass to Pugh who lumbered to the one-yard line. Crowston then made short work of the remaining three feet. Campbell converted, and the score was 7-0.

Again the Tiger defense shut down the Paris offense, and the Wildcats punted once more. This time Swede received the kick and returned it to the opponent's twenty-yard line. From there Pierce chunked to Pugh to the eleven. Campbell then cut, like a hurled lance, off right tackle into the end zone. After a successful kick, the Tigers led by fourteen.

Unable to run the ball, Paris took to the air, but Pugh snagged the ball on the Tiger forty-eight. "Jitterbug" Yocum picked up four yards, and then Crowston rumbled to the Wildcat thirty-three. After a rare loss of yardage, Swede galloped forty-two yards to pay-dirt for the Tigers' third score.

Starting the second half, the Tigers kicked to the Wildcats, and then held them for no gain on three downs. Paris punted and the ball bounced out of bounds at the Tiger forty-six. Three plays moved the ball to the Paris eighteen. Crowston then notched his third touchdown run. Pierce converted, and the Tigers led 27-0.

The Tiger defense continued to stymie the Paris offense and soon had the ball again. Pierce fed the pigskin to Hogan who chewed up yards while the Wildcat defenders focused on Swede. When Hogan found himself bottled up at the Paris twenty-six, he lateraled to Campbell who sailed down the sideline to score, running the count to 33-0.

After Crowston scored his fourth touchdown, the second unit took the field. They held the Wildcats' offense to no gain, and took over the ball. Unable to advance, the Tigers punted for the first time in the game. Back on defense, Catfish's reserves forced Paris to try a pass, which reserve Charles Lowry snagged, preserving a 40-0 shutout.

Afterwards, Catfish cited his defense for controlling the line of scrimmage. Then he smiled and admitted that number twenty, Crowston, looked to be in top form. Before allowing the next question, he added that his quarterback had run the T-formation like he was born to it.

The anxiety of the game had flared Catfish's ulcers, which kept him up drinking milk most of the night. Early Friday morning, while leaving the office of the *Optic-Herald* with a stack of spare newspapers for his history class, he met Dr. Chandler whose office was next door.

"Doc," Catfish called out. "Do you have a minute?"

The doctor ushered the coach into his office.

"My ulcers are acting up again," Catfish said. "Do you have anything you can give me?"

The doctor pulled a box of phenobarbital tablets from a nearby shelf and handed them over.

"Those will help, but they won't cure you," Dr. Chandler said. "Take one before meals and at bedtime. Bland foods and a glass of milk with each meal are recommended for best results. Avoid seeds, raw fruit, uncooked vegetables, and coarse fibers."

"Thanks, Doc," Catfish said. "How much do I owe you?"

"Those are free samples," the doctor said while writing a prescription. "Drop back by Rutherford's later and get a week's supply. If you really want to get well, you'll have to do more than take a few pills. I'm sure you know that your profession isn't compatible with ulcers."

"And not with soldiering either, they tell me," Catfish replied. "I noticed in the paper that your daughter, Faye, is marrying a soldier."

"Yes, two weeks from today, she'll marry Joe Vaughn, stationed at Ward Island, Corpus Christi. Two years ago she resigned her teaching position here and moved down there. Before the war, Joe was a teacher, also."

"Congratulations," Catfish said. "We have an open date that week, so you can go down for the wedding and not miss a game."

"I never go to football games," Dr. Chandler replied solemnly.

"This year's team just might change your mind," Catfish said, smiling. "It's worth the price of a ticket just to watch Swede Crowston warm up."

"I had a son who could give your Crowston a run for his money," the doctor said. "But now he's buried out there in the cemetery near your house. Football injuries."

"I'm terribly sorry, Doc. I didn't know."

"Of course you didn't," Dr. Chandler said. "Now, you'd better get along, or you'll be tardy to class."

Injuries were a part of the game of football, but the story of Doctor Chandler's son disturbed Catfish. He believed deeply that the sport helped prepare young men to meet the challenges of life and to survive when one less physically fit might not. He had given little thought to the possibility of one of his boys sustaining a life-ending injury.

That afternoon Catfish worked his team almost exclusively on conditioning drills, believing that physical fitness was the best guard against injuries. Also, he feared his boys were overconfident, and he intended to work it out of them. The players responded without complaint, and never lost that confident edge to their voice or spring in their step. They were ready for anybody, they believed.

If his boys were cocky, it did not matter. The Sulphur Springs reserves fared no better than the Paris subs.

Crowston romped for four touchdowns, including an interception that he returned twenty-seven yards for a score. Charles Hogan had two scores, while Leacho Tittle and Robby Campbell had one each. The defense was relentless, forcing the opponent to punt after three downs, time after time. The game was decided by halftime with the Tigers leading, 31-0.

The highlight of the game came with Sulphur Springs making their only scoring threat from the Mount Vernon two-yard line. The Tigers dug in, determined that the Wildcats would not cross their unblemished goal line. Trying to run behind his right guard, the enemy ball carrier was swarmed a yard behind the line of scrimmage by Tiger defenders. Amid the grabbing and hitting, the ball popped free, and suddenly Robby Campbell burst out of the scrum, having somehow stolen the ball, and scampered ninety-seven yards for a touchdown. Catfish's earlier move of Campbell from the line to halfback made him look like a coaching genius, and the development of basketball-playing Hogan as a running back added to the coach's reputation. The Tigers won, 51-0.

Monday afternoon Catfish met with his players before they headed for the practice field.

"Boys, we've got two weeks of hard work ahead of us," he said. "Yeah, you've looked good against two teams of subs, but come October sixth, you'll be facing the Mineola Yellow Jackets, and they're no patchwork team."

Catfish slowly transformed his face into a scowl and balled his fists.

"Mount Vernon has never defeated Mineola. Not ever," he bellowed. "I don't know how you feel about that, but it makes me want to fight. If you're gonna be winners, you've got to start by showing the Yellow Jackets that they'd better find a new whipping boy, because the purple-and-white Tigers ain't gonna be nobody's whipping boy."

The furious coach slowly stalked down the open aisle between the two lines of players, then turned and glared.

"Now get out there on that practice field, and let's get ready to battle the Yellow Jackets until we're the only ones left standing."

For two weeks, Catfish was relentless in pushing his players, in reminding them that Mineola had trampled on past Tiger teams, treating them like a dirty doormat. "You'll never be considered winners until you change that," he warned them over and over.

Meanwhile, Catfish worked the newspaper editor, Charles Devall, to bill the game as a battle for respectability. "The Mount Vernon fans are a part of this fight," he was quoted as saying. "Be there, fill the stands, and show our boys that you're behind them one hundred percent." He even managed to time the arrival of new uniforms for the game.

Whatever the explanation for what happened, the result was a stunning 38-6 victory against the once-mighty Yellow Jackets. Again the Tiger linemen dominated their opponent, and credit for victory started there: Shurtleff, Cargile, Pugh, Parchman, Horne, Dickerson, and even the younger players, Fleming and Lowry.

The Tigers scored on the fourth play of the game when Hogan took the ball on the thirteen-yard line of the Yellow Jackets, skirted around right end, and when trapped at the five, pitched the ball to Cargile who plowed into the end zone.

After forcing the Mineola offense to punt, the Tigers took over on their own forty-yard line. The Swede got ten yards, and then Pierce tossed a pass to Hogan who could not be corralled until he had reached the Yellow Jackets' ten. Robby Campbell scored on the next play and added the point-after.

Again the Tiger defense stifled the Mineola offense on three plays. The Yellow Jackets then punted the ball, but this time Campbell bolted through the enemy's line, blocked the kick, and fell on the ball at the opponent's thirty-one-yard line. After Crowston rambled to the fourteen, Hogan slipped into the end zone, untouched.

The next Mineola offensive effort failed when Pierce intercepted a pass on the Tigers' forty-eight. Penalties stopped the Tigers, so they punted to the Yellow Jacket twenty-three. When the opponent tried an end sweep, Shurtleff trapped the ball carrier back on the eleven, forcing the Yellow Jackets to punt again.

Starting from Mineola's forty-six, Yocum and Hogan ripped off big chunks of yards down to the twenty-yard line. From there, Campbell scored, and the Tigers led by twenty-six points, but they were not satisfied. Again their defense stymied the Yellow Jacket offense and took over on their own forty-nine. On first down, Crowston punished would-be tacklers down to the Mineola twenty-seven, from where Yocum twisted and squirmed into the end zone.

With the game well in hand, Crowston followed a wipeout block by Pugh to sprint thirty-one yards for the last Tiger score, running the Mount Vernon total to thirty-eight points. Finally, against Tiger reserves and aided by penalties, the Yellow Jackets scored on a pass by their quarterback, Hughes, for their only points of the game. Final score: 38-6.

The Yellow Jackets' domination of the Tigers was over, but amid their elation, Catfish and his boys glanced ahead along the path to the district championship, and there stood the Winnsboro Red Raiders.

14

October 13, 1944

On Friday morning in Catfish's first period history class, a quick scan of the newspaper revealed that Sergeant Robert Clark, earlier reported missing in action, had been confirmed among the casualties of the D-Day invasion. He was twenty-four years old, husband of Bobbie Nell, and father of a five-month old daughter. Equally dark news reached the family of William Huckeba, Warrant Officer, who had lost his life in action in the South Pacific after serving twenty-eight months. Another war report stated that Billie Padgett, son of Mr. and Mrs. C. L. Padgett, was missing in action following the crash of his plane in the Pacific. As did so many Mount Vernon families, the Padgett parents had two more sons in the war: Eunice and Rex.

These dismal losses were followed with a report on Lieutenant Charlie Brown, former County Extension Agent in Mount Vernon and popular announcer of Tiger football games. He served as commander of the Navy Armed Guard gunners on a Merchant Marine ship that had made seven separate deliveries of supplies to the Normandy invasion force. In doing so, Brown and his crew had endured heavy bombing, shelling, and even a brush with robot bombs. His wife, Abbie, waiting and worrying in Mount Vernon, was glad to receive the news, but fretted that her husband, having entered the war in August 1943, might yet have a fatal encounter with the enemy before his tour was over.

"So many of our young men have traded their boyhood dreams for a military uniform and an M1 rifle," Catfish said.

A girl raised her hand, and Catfish nodded at her.

"And many girls have given up their hopes, too. They work the fields, build airplanes and tanks, or sew uniforms when all they had ever wanted was to marry and take care of their families."

"You're right," the coach said, reminded that someone should be preparing these girls for the different kind of world they would soon enter.

In the pep rally that morning, after Bobbie Jean Davis was introduced as the football queen, Catfish made the emotional announcement that the Winnsboro game was being dedicated to all former Mount Vernon players now serving in the war, as well as those who had died in the service of their country.

"Some people believe war time is no time for athletic contests," he said. "They'd have us cancel all sporting events out of respect for our men and women in uniform. I don't agree.

"First, if I were over there fighting, I'd want the folks back home to go on with their lives, especially the young ones. After all, what are we fighting for? Among the reasons is that of preserving our freedoms, our way of life.

"Second, these boys sitting up here on this stage behind me, as well as many out there among you, may soon find themselves proudly pulling on a military uniform. Athletics is one of the best possible ways to prepare young men, body and spirit, for the challenges that lie ahead.

"Third, our ballgames offer us the opportunity, for a short time each week, to push the horrors of war out of our minds. They become a diversion from the worries that so many parents, teachers, and families bear constantly.

"Last, as we are doing today, our sporting events bring us together to remember our servicemen and women. Today, we lift high onto a pedestal of honor our former students, who have taken up the sword and the rifle, and we promise to give our all tonight to make them proud to say, 'Mount Vernon High is my school, and the Tigers are my team.'"

What would have normally been a joyous time for students returning to their classes instead became a somber one. In those solemn moments, many silently committed to do their part to uphold the proud tradition of their school, not only on the gridiron, but in the classroom and throughout the community.

Just prior to the kickoff, Catfish had the dedication announced to the fans, followed by a prayer for all servicemen. The crowd became subdued and attentive, fans from each side showing a quiet determination for their cause. The Tiger players resolved that they must not fail while competing on behalf of such an honorable cause.

The Tigers struck early in the first quarter when Swede Crowston sped fifty-five yards to the Red Raiders' seventeen-yard line. After a four-yard run by Hogan, the Swede rumbled the final thirteen yards into the end zone. Robby Campbell added the extra point, and the uncaged Tigers were on the prowl.

Following the kickoff, the Tiger defense pushed the Red Raiders back eight yards on their first two plays. Sensing the opponent's desperation, Campbell drifted into the left flat, dashed in front of a Winnsboro receiver at the eighteen to steal the pass, and sailed into the end zone for his team's second touchdown.

After the Red Raiders made two futile drives into Tiger territory, one stopped by a fumble and the other on downs, Pierce hooked up with Jack Horne on three consecutive passes for eighty-four yards, and the Tigers' third touchdown.

With Mount Vernon's stubborn defense stiffening, the Red Raiders' quarterback chunked an errant pass that an alert Robby Campbell grabbed on the enemy's thirty-two-yard line. Pierce needed only one play to fling an arching spiral to a streaking Charles Hogan for the Tigers' fourth score, and the first half ended with Mount Vernon leading, 28-0.

The second half began with Campbell shagging the Red Raider kickoff and racing sixty yards to the Winnsboro twenty-yard line before enemy tacklers converged on him. However, before going down, the shifty runner flipped the ball to Captain Charles Shurtleff who rambled down to the five where he pitched it to Dan Cargile before chopping down the last defender, clearing the way for his fellow-lineman to trot into the end zone. What looked like razzle-dazzle was becoming routine for the Tigers.

When the Red Raiders received the kickoff and could not muster a first down, they punted to the Tiger twenty-six from where Mount Vernon's stable of runners began their next march. Two plays brought the ball to the Tiger forty-eight, setting up Campbell's fifty-two-yard touchdown sprint.

Crowston and Campbell completed the scoring. The Swede needed only three runs to cover forty-six yards for a counter, and Campbell, late in the final period, accounted for his third touchdown of the game.

In honor of their servicemen, the Tigers hung up fifty-two points while allowing none for their opponent.

Always looking for a motivational edge, Catfish considered his team's next opponent, Mount Pleasant. The Titus County Tigers' lair lay only twelve miles to the east, and the city's limits housed three to four times the population of Mount Vernon. Business, family, and social connections between the two towns abounded, all of which stimulated their competitive juices when confronting each other in the sports arena, but the inspiration the coach capitalized on was the black and gold Tigers' victory over his charges the previous season, one of only two losses to be avenged.

In Friday morning's pep rally, Catfish beat the war drums, recounting the above call to battle with his unique style and fervor, but he was soon to be upstaged when Captain Shurtleff asked to speak.

"Coach Smith has just given us plenty reasons to play our best tonight, but this team has another incentive. As you know, Mount Pleasant is his high school alma mater. We let him down in last year's game, but this year will be different. We'll be victorious for our coach who has taught us how to win, how to be winners," Captain Shurtleff said, and then turned to Catfish. "Coach, your team dedicates this game to you."

The players leaped to their feet, clapping and whooping with the student body following their example. Catfish quickly stepped back to the podium, brushing his sleeve across his eyes as he asked for quiet.

"I couldn't be prouder of a group of players. Win or lose, you are my team, my boys," the coach said, turning toward his players and smiling while the assembly stood and applauded.

"Tonight, my alma mater is our enemy," the coach said as the students quieted. "They've been picked by some folks to win the district crown, but I know the fighting spirit of this team. While we celebrate victory tonight, those prognosticators will be scrounging for another choice, and we'll give them one."

Applause continued as the coach stepped back and Principal Bolger's amplified voice sent the students and teachers to their overdue classes.

That night the scoring started eight minutes into the first quarter when quarterback Pierce stood at midfield and heaved an aerial to Hogan on the ten-yard line. The feisty back fought his way into the end zone, and Campbell kicked the point-after.

As in prior games, Catfish's ironclad defense forced the black-and-gold Tigers to punt, but here the script changed. Following a thunderous tackle, Mount Pleasant recovered the loose ball and began a long march toward pay-dirt. Three passes from Miller to Kenny keyed their pushing the ball to the purple-and-white Tigers' thirteen-yard line. After three more plays gained only two yards, Miller flipped a pass to Trice for the Titus County Tigers' score. The Mount Pleasant eleven then lined up to boot the point-after to tie the score, but instead the kicker faked a kick while Kenny sped around right end with the ball and the score-knotting point.

The battle was on, and it continued as a seesaw affair fought in the middle of the field. At halftime the weary combatants trudged to their dressing rooms, neither with an advantage.

The second half brought change. Whether a result of Catfish utilizing his well-known oratory skills, making tactical adjustments, or simply renewed determination, the Franklin County Tigers stonewalled their opponent's offense. After Mount Pleasant returned the kickoff to their forty-four-yard line, Catfish's defense tore through the opposing forward wall, throwing runners for successive losses and forcing a punt from Mount Pleasant's thirty-four.

From Mount Vernon's thirty-seven, the purple-and-white team began its determined march. Robby Campbell ripped off a gain to the opponent's twenty-seven. From there Swede took over and rammed his way into the end zone. The critical extra point failed.

The favored Mount Pleasant team showed its mettle by driving the ball down the field, the key play being a long run to the Mount Vernon thirteen-yard line by Kenny on a faked punt. Three line plunges pushed the ball down to the nine-yard line. On the desperate fourth down, the black-and-gold Tigers tried an end sweep, but big Harry Jack Pugh plowed through their blockers and put one of those picture-perfect tackles on the runner. The ball squirted loose, and Glenn Pierce pounced on it at the seventeen-yard line, ending the threat.

Following a couple of punt exchanges, Swede showed he could play both sides of the ball with a bone-jarring tackle of a black-clad runner, separating him from his senses and the ball. Jack Horne made the recovery.

An inspired Crowston and his running partner, Campbell, needed only three plays to turn their opponent's tragedy into their triumph. The Swede delivered the decisive blow with a thundering thirty-five-yard run into the end zone.

Turning to face his excited teammates, Swede spotted three prone, would-be tacklers strewn in his wake. These weary black-clad warriors symbolized their defeat that was suddenly apparent to the frenzied fans filling the stadium.

Catfish's boys handed to him a 20-7 victory over his alma mater, and in the locker room he declared that the district now had a new contender for its coveted crown, and the "prognosticators" now had little choice but to adopt his team.

The coach was always quick to forget past victories and irritate his ulcerated stomach with worry over the upcoming opponent, in this case, the Pittsburg Pirates. However, few joined him in his woeful exhortations regarding the danger looming on the horizon. The Mount Vernon team, now the exalted league favorite, was just too talented, too skilled, and too well-coached to fall to an opponent they had shut out, 13-0, the prior season. Still, Catfish fretted.

"Fall in love with last week's victory, and you'll hate this week's loss," he reminded his players before every practice. "One critical defeat will sour all your wins."

Even his dedication of the game to Bob Suggs, the team's most loyal fan, seemed flat and uninspiring. The Friday morning pep rally was more a celebration of the prior week's victory than preparation for battle with the Pirates.

"It's been easy with all these home games," Catfish told the assembly, "but tonight we travel to our enemy's turf. There's never been a team that didn't fight harder on its own field."

The argument was not convincing. Pittsburg, about fifteen miles away, was no foreign land, and the Pirates lacked the weapons to win, regardless of their pride in defending home turf.

"Now that we're at the top of the district race, Pittsburg will see this game as their opportunity to leapfrog to respectability by knocking us down," Catfish said, still trying to instill the fear of losing.

The students and fans did not buy that theory, either. The Pirates might leapfrog over a bump in their path, like Talco, but climbing Tiger Mountain, which loomed like a purple Mount Everest capped in white, required skills and talents unheard of recently within the black Pirates' realm.

To Catfish's surprise, the enemy supplied the inspiration that he had been unable to muster in his team and fans.

Early in the game, the Tigers' Swede Crowston snowplowed thirty-five yards to the Pittsburg twenty-five, where a swarm of frustrated Pirates became excessive in pounding him into submission. A fifteen-yard penalty resulted and moved the ball forward to the five-yard line.

With Crowston recovering on the sideline, the angry but stunned Tigers could not push the ball into the end zone, and gave it up on downs. The purple-and-white defense held, however, and forced the Pirates to punt. Hogan returned the kick fifteen yards to the Pirate forty-yard line. That is when the Swede reentered the game to wild cheers from Tiger fans, and Glenn Pierce immediately concocted a shrewd plan.

The Tiger quarterback faked a handoff to Crowston, drawing the Pirate defensemen to the powerful running back like ants to sugar, then dropped back and lofted a perfect spiral to Robby Campbell down on the ten-yard line. The crafty back trotted into the end zone, triggering a scoring avalanche, like thundering tons of snow burying everything in its path.

After the Tigers stopped Pittsburg again, the Pirates punted to Hogan who raced twenty yards to midfield. From there, Pierce again sent the football spiraling through the night air to Hogan who broke a tackle and sprinted fifteen yards for another touchdown, making the score 13-0 at halftime.

Little Robby Campbell, one of Catfish's former undersized bulldogs, took over in the second half. He broke several tackles in route to a forty-yard score, and then followed that with an interception, which he returned thirty-five yards to pay-dirt. What Catfish had feared would be a game-long struggle had suddenly become a lopsided 27-0 Tiger advantage.

The Swede, possibly fired by revenge, kicked the ball deep into Pittsburg territory, where the Tiger defense, smelling blood, slammed the door shut on everything the Pirates tried. Appropriately, the Tiger tackler leading the way, making the most vicious hits of the season, was Swede Crowston.

That defensive stand was followed by Pierce's fourth touchdown pass of the game to a streaking Jack Horne. The point-after settled the score, 40-0.

Bob Suggs, first on the team bus, beamed as he shook hands with each player as they boarded. When Catfish climbed on the bus, the two embraced.

"Mr. Suggs," the coach said as the two took their seats, "don't you ever miss a game. You're our good luck charm."

"Coach," Suggs replied, "it's a lot more than luck that makes these boys win."

Evidently Catfish agreed. In his review of the game with the *Optic-Herald*'s editor, he pointed with pride to his players' scholastic achievements.

"With grades from the first six-weeks posted, we've got nine players whose grade-averages are ninety or above: Charles Lowry, Gene Fleming,

154

Glenn Pierce, Gayle Tinsley, George Dickerson, Wayne Hightower, Kenneth Meek, Charles Shurtleff, and Jerry Yocum. The average for the entire team is eighty-eight point one. League rules require a player to pass at least three subjects to be eligible for participation in sports. That's an insult to this bunch of boys."

"Does that make it easier on the coach?" Devall asked, joking.

"Sure it does. It saves time on the practice field, but there's more to it than that. During the game, these boys use more than brawn and speed. Take our quarterback. He runs the T-formation like he designed it. He calls the right play, knows everybody's assignments, and avoids mistakes. He knew the Pirates were keying on Crowston, so he faked the ball to him, then threw those touchdown passes."

"What about Gilmer this week? They beat you last year."

"The Buckeyes are tough again this season," Catfish replied. "Two years ago, they beat us thirty-three to nothing. After the one-point loss last year, I told my boys that we were knocking on the door. This year we're gonna kick that door down."

"You're predicting a victory?" the shocked editor asked, knowing the coach always praised his opponents as world-beaters.

"Gilmer has sat on the throne long enough. It's our time," Catfish said, as he smiled and walked away.

That afternoon Catfish called Glenn Pierce. "Let's go do a little fishing."

Pierce understood. Before big games his coach frequently took him to the pond on the Smith's old home place.

Catfish hummed and whistled most of the drive to Winfield. After fishing for half an hour, the coach got down to business.

"This is the biggest game of the season," he said, referring to the upcoming Gilmer contest. "Think we're up to it?"

"Yes, sir."

"You've been doing a good job passing the ball. I think we can throw on them, don't you?"

"Yes, sir."

"What if it rains?"

"We'll run the ball. Nobody can stop Swede, Charles, and Robby, not with our line."

"Do the boys realize this game is likely for the district championship?"

"I think so."

"Don't forget the tackle-eligible pass to Cargile. We might need a big play early to get the lead. The Buckeyes aren't used to playing from behind, and I'd like to see if they can handle the pressure. If the weather's fit, the hook and lateral might work, too."

"Yes, sir."

"They have a strong defense. We may need a way to unsettle them. Got any ideas?"

"My brother and I have talked about calling multiple plays in the huddle. If we can surprise their defense, we might hit them before they're ready."

"Think our boys can handle it?"

"Yes, sir."

"Try it if you see the right opportunity."

After visiting with Catfish's mother, they drove back to Mount Vernon.

With Franklin Roosevelt and his running mate, Harry Truman, sweeping the presidential election with four hundred thirty-two electoral votes and a margin of three million popular votes, the country was optimistic about victory in Europe. The war in the Pacific, however, was brutal and the outcome less sure. In Catfish's Friday history class, after allowing election discussions, he made General Douglas MacArthur's return to the Philippines the subject.

"When the General left the islands in March of nineteen forty-two, some ridiculed him as 'Dugout Doug,' because he had holed up in the tunnels on Corregidor, but he promised he would return. The American soldiers had never known defeat, but weakened by months of subsistence on reduced rations, their ammunition near depletion, hemmed up at the tip of the Bataan Peninsula, and all avenues of re-supply shut off, they had little choice but to surrender on April ninth. Even so, they could not have guessed what was in store for them.

"The Japanese were not prepared to accept seventy-five thousand prisoners, so they set the Americans on a sixty-five-mile march along the blistering east coast of the peninsula and into the steaming jungles to Camp O'Donnell, a prison facility. The defeated soldiers, suffering from various forms of malnutrition, malaria, typhoid, typhus, beriberi, dysentery, and jungle rot, were in no condition for such a grueling march. Seven hundred fifty to eight hundred prisoners died along the road, some from disease but others bayoneted or decapitated when they could no longer keep pace. If laid out evenly along the road, one would find a dead soldier every one hundred and fifty yards. Conditions

156

in the prison camps are thought to be so dismal that few of those who survived the march are believed to still be alive.

"But not all the soldiers chose to make the Bataan Death March. Some in the more remote areas were given the option to select from available weapons, ammunition, food, and clothing and head into the jungle to fight alongside the underground Filipino warriors and survive the best they could. One such individual is Sergeant Alvis O. Loveless, an Army Air Forces mechanic from Mount Vernon assigned to the Twenty-seventh Bomber Group.

"The planes for his group never arrived in the Philippines, and he, along with most of our airmen, was handed a rifle and retrained as infantry. We can only imagine what Sergeant Loveless has endured, if he has survived; but when General MacArthur keeps his promise and liberates the islands, I pray that Mr. Loveless can leave the dark shadows of the jungle and step boldly into the sunlight."

When the coach had concluded, his students sat quietly, sobered once again by an instance of war being brought home to them. They were somewhat familiar with the price of victory. Many of the boys had already openly declared their intent, upon graduation, to join the glorious battle, but the horrors of defeat, POWs, and starvation struck them to the core of their souls.

The dismal subject was amplified by the dreary weather. A cold, relentless rain drenched everything, causing Catfish to allow an extra half hour for the team to travel to Gilmer later that afternoon. Any hope that the weather would be better forty miles away was lost upon their arrival at the opponent's sloppy field. The coach knew he must change his game plan.

Glenn Pierce had thrown a crucial touchdown pass against Mount Pleasant two weeks earlier and a week later had heaved four more against Pittsburg. Also, their four days of practice had focused on the use of the aerial game to defeat the stout Buckeyes. A cold, wet, muddy gridiron, he explained to his team, meant old-fashioned running, blocking, and tackling to secure a victory.

"The weather is the same for them," Catfish explained, "and it's never been an excuse for losing. Champions find a way to win regardless of the conditions, the officials, the opponent."

He had no idea how prophetic his words were.

Mount Vernon received the initial kickoff and drove down the field as if it were a bright sunny day; however, the drive stalled on the Buckeye two-yard line. Gilmer took over on downs, but could not move the ball against the stiff Tiger defense. The Buckeyes punted, and the Tigers again marched down the field until a fumble stopped them inside the ten. Throughout the first two quarters, the Tigers' offense pounded away at the Gilmer eleven, but each drive fizzled short of the goal line.

The third stanza went much like the first two with the Tigers moving the ball to the Buckeye twelve. On second down with six needed for a first down, Crowston drove ahead to the nine-yard line. On third down, he slipped and barely gained the line of scrimmage. Hogan, on fourth down, came within an inch of a first down, but again they had failed to score.

Gilmer ran three plays and gained no yards, so they dropped back in punt formation. No one considered that the punter was the Buckeyes' speedy fullback, Henry. The kicker crossed up the Tigers with a fake kick, and scampered out to the forty-one. Angry with themselves, the Tiger defense held the Buckeyes there, forcing yet another punt situation. This time the Tigers were not only alert, but crashed in and blocked the kick.

Again the Tigers took over but stalled after one first down. Gilmer had the ball and the game clock was running down in a scoreless battle.

The Buckeye quarterback tried to catch the Tigers off guard with a rare pass, but instead Glenn Pierce turned the tables on him by cutting in front of the intended receiver and snaring the ball on the Tiger twenty-eight-yard line. Pierce wasted no time in pulling another surprise on the Buckeyes, to the everlasting delight of his coach.

"Boys," Pierce said, hurrying his mud-splattered teammates into the huddle. "Pay attention. I'm going to call three plays. We won't huddle again until we've run them. After each one, just line up again."

Campbell gained three on the first play. Before the sluggish Gilmer defense could reset, the Tigers had lined up, and Pierce was shouting signals. He took the snap and pitched to Swede who went tearing around left end. Crowston would not be stopped until he reached the Buckeye thirty-one, a thirty-eight-yard gain. Again hurrying his teammates to the line of scrimmage, Pierce handed the ball to Campbell who burst through the shocked Gilmer line for eleven yards, down to the twenty. There the Tigers' quarterback quickly huddled his team.

"We're running out of time, so don't waste a second between plays. When we get inside the five, Swede will get the ball on thirty-five counter," he said, and then called three plays.

Every rain-soaked fan stood, some holding their breath, some

158

shouting, some with eyes closed and fingers crossed when Crowston plowed nine yards to the eleven. Hogan ripped his way off right tackle to the three-yard line. Like a mother hen, Pierce shooed his teammates to the line of scrimmage, reminding them that time was about expired. He took one lingering look at Swede, as if to say, "This is our last chance. You've got to score."

With mud covering his face, the big fullback nodded with a grin as he dropped into his stance. Pierce clucked the cadence. The wet, muddy ball popped into his hands. Slowly he turned to his right as Horne, Parchman, Shurtleff, Dickerson, Caudle, Cargile, and Pugh lunged forward into the Buckeyes' stubborn front wall. When Pierce planted his left foot to spin clockwise, it slipped in the mud, but while falling into the slush, he stretched his right arm out and slipped the ball between Crowston's cradled arms.

Before Pierce saw what happened, he heard the collision. The entire Buckeye team, too many for Shurtleff and his fellow linemen to block, had swarmed to stop Swede.

For Catfish, standing on the sideline with his gut twisted by tension and his ulcers pulsating with acid, it was like a replay of the first run he had seen his fullback make the previous season. Crowston lowered his shoulder and sent the first Gilmer tackler sprawling backwards. The next, he met with a wicked stiff-arm that tore the Buckeye's helmet off. The third, Swede sidestepped, and then he lunged through a sliver of an opening into the end zone.

Half the fans went delirious with joy, while the other half stood frozen by shock. With bedlam all around him, Pierce lined his team up for the extra point attempt. Campbell converted, time was out, and the outcome was settled: 7-0, Tigers.

"It took you four quarters to do it," Catfish said when he had quieted his team in the dressing room, "but like true champions, you finally kicked that door down."

His mud-clad boys roared.

"Two more doors stand between you and the district title," Catfish said. "We can't let up now."

As the coach had told the news reporter a week earlier, sometimes quick, clear thinking is required, and his quarterback had proven him right. Pierce's grasp of the situation and his unprecedented play calling had saved precious time and had befuddled the opponent. That, and the savvy of his teammates to execute the plan under the worst of conditions and at the most critical time, had won the game.

For Catfish, that hard-fought win, requiring all the physical and mental toughness he had preached for two seasons, was treasured above all the 40-0 victories his teams had accumulated in the past.

*   *   *

On Friday, November 17, in his history class one of the female students asked to read an article from the front page of the *Optic-Herald*.

Mrs. Sidney Legendre, according to German radio, has been captured by the Nazis. She was last seen being taken by a staff officer to the German town of Wallendorf, near Trier. She is said to be the first American woman captured by the Nazis. Mrs. Legendre was in France on assignment as liaison officer between the Allied European Forces Club and the United States Army.

"I just want to point out that women are not just helping back here, but on the warfront, too," the student said. "They are risking their lives just like our men."

"You are right, of course," Catfish said. "Not only do women such as Lela Parrish, a neighbor of mine, stay home and take care of their families while their men fight, but they serve in other vital ways. When General MacArthur was ordered out of the Philippines, he not only left behind an army, he also left seventy-seven nurses, women suffering with the same ills as the soldiers and completely unequipped to defend themselves. When General King surrendered, these women were taken to Corregidor, an island in the mouth of Manila Bay. They lived in Dugout Doug's tunnels, a multi-fingered cavern chiseled into the rock of Malinta Hill for protection and storage of supplies. But on May sixth when this stronghold was surrendered to the Japanese, the nurses were then imprisoned at Santo Tomas, a walled-in former university, where they continued to care for those in worse shape than they.

"Filipino sympathizers say that today, with prisoners dying for lack of crucial medicines, they remove the heart of melons, intended to feed the prisoners, fill them with much-needed medical supplies, and then get Catholic priests to smuggle them inside. The nurses use these to save lives, even to perform operations when no doctor is available, doing so with ether as the only anesthetic. We don't know how many

160

have survived, but we can hope and pray that General MacArthur will liberate them quickly when he keeps his promise to return."

In practice that week, Catfish had made little effort to convince his team that they were the underdog against their next opponent, the Talco Trojans. The Tigers had handily defeated their neighbors the past two seasons, 20-7 and 45-0.

Five minutes into the game, Swede bolted through the line and scored on a fifty-five-yard run. The Tiger defense held the Trojans, forcing a punt. Shurtleff then blocked the kick, knocking the ball into the end zone where Campbell fell on it for a touchdown. Then Crowston started the second quarter with a twenty-yard touchdown run. Frustrated, Talco went to the air, but Hogan stole the first aerial and ran thirty-five yards for the Tigers' fourth touchdown.

After the following kickoff, Mount Vernon's defense held the Trojans' offense for no gain, and the Tigers' Campbell received the punt and raced forty yards for another score. The same runner closed out the third period with a twenty-yard touchdown. Mount Vernon led by a score of 41-0, and the reserves finished out the game, protecting the lead.

To the surprise of some, Catfish gave his highest praise to his quarterback.

"Everybody played well, but 'Curly' Pierce had a great night. He always does his part, offensively and defensively."

The Tigers finished the regular season by defeating Clarksville 47-0. They were undefeated district champions with possibly the most impressive statistics for any Mount Vernon team ever. For the season, they had scored three hundred thirty-six points, averaging thirty-seven per game, while allowing only thirteen, a fraction over one point per game.

As impressive as the Tigers' statistics were, they were overshadowed by those of their bi-district opponent, McLeod, who had scored three hundred thirty-eight points and allowed none. On Thanksgiving afternoon, November 30, the Tigers would travel twelve miles east to Mount Pleasant to face the most formidable Class-A defense in the state, and some said the McLeod offense was the only one that could score against its awesome defenders.

15

November 20, 1944

With ten days to prepare his team for the bi-district showdown, Catfish fretted over his lack of insight into the much-ballyhooed McLeod team. Mount Vernon and McLeod had played no common rival, and the coach knew no one familiar with the upcoming opponent. At the same time Catfish relished the opportunity. In recent games his team had been the prohibitive favorite, a situation that had driven him crazy. His ulcers would fare better with his team the underdog.

"The harder the fight, the greater the victory," was taped onto the Tigers' dressing room wall when the players arrived for practice the next week, and day after day the coach tried to convince his players that they were in for the fight of their lives.

Yet, Catfish believed his balanced offense could score on anybody, even McLeod. His biggest worry was how to throttle McLeod's scoring machine. What insight he had gleaned indicated that his opponent disdained the pass, so he focused his defensive preparations on stopping their running attack, though he knew success would ultimately depend on game-time adjustments and the smarts of his players.

The first quarter was a battle royal between the two defenses, neither offense able to challenge the other's goal line until the final two minutes of the period when the purple-and-white boys began a steady march that took them to the opponent's one-yard line. An early score against the previously unblemished McLeod defense would give the Tigers a great psychological edge, not to mention the touchdown advantage. But it was not to be. The proud McLeod defenders justified their reputation, holding the potent Tigers out of their end zone.

The second quarter started ominously when McLeod punted the ball past the Tiger return men, and it settled on Mount Vernon's three-yard line. It was the kind of break that usually determined games contested between equally powerful teams. The slightest bobble of the ball by Pierce and his offense could now give away the game.

Huddling his teammates, the quarterback had a plan. He gave the ball to Swede whose powerful arms and hands clamped onto the ball like the iron jaws of a vise, but the fullback gained only two yards. Again Crowston tried the line, and this time he fought his way to the ten-yard marker, three steps short of the most crucial first down of the game. Without a new set of downs, the Tigers would have to punt from their own end zone, and with even a mediocre return, McLeod would have the ball deep in Mount Vernon territory.

With a capacity crowd focused on the big blond fullback, Pierce faked a handoff to him, then pitched to Hogan who quick-kicked the ball to midfield, completely catching the opponent's defense off-guard and eliminating any return.

The McLeod offense lined up on the fifty-yard line and ran the ball at Shurtleff. But the Tiger guard slipped his block, slammed a shoulder into the ball carrier's chest, and drove him backwards, a picture-perfect tackle. A fast-closing Crowston saw the ball pop out and pounced on it. Was this the game-turning break? Catfish wondered.

Mount Vernon then drove the ball down inside the ten-yard line, but the game clock ticked to all zeroes as the Tigers scrambled to the line of scrimmage for one last play. The first half ended in a scoreless deadlock between two teams, each of which had averaged nearly forty points a game.

During the second quarter, however, Catfish thought he had seen the tide turning. His boys were wearing the opponent down. During intermission, he made no changes, assuring his team that the points would come.

"I believe we're in better physical shape than they are," he told his players. "Come the fourth quarter, all those wind-sprints you've run will pay off."

With the start of the second half, Catfish's prediction appeared to take life.

McLeod had a great kicker, and he booted the ball to the Mount Vernon twelve-yard line where the Swede gathered in the end-over-end kick and headed upfield. The long kick gave Crowston extra time to scan his opponents as they converged on him like a pack of wolves. He spotted a crevice and headed for it, breaking through and having only the kicker and one other defender to beat. The McLeod kicker finally attempted a tackle fifty-nine yards later at his twenty-nine-yard line, but only caused Swede to break stride momentarily. At that instant, however, the second tackler made a desperate dive for the runner's feet and got a hand on Swede's ankle. Already off balance, Crowston stumbled to the twenty-three before he went down.

From there Campbell carried to the twenty-one but fumbled amid a gang of tacklers. That miscue was turned into good fortune, however, when Horne recovered the loose ball on the seventeen. Hogan then burst through to the ten-yard line and a first down.

At that point Pierce decided to see just how good the McLeod defense was. He gave the ball to Crowston in the middle of the line on two consecutive plays, pushing the McLeod boys back to the three. On third down, Pierce again went to Crowston. The enemy, having pulled their entire team into the middle of the line, swarmed him for no gain. Now the Tigers faced fourth down and three tough yards needed.

Pierce gathered his offense in the huddle and called the play, thirty-two dive, another handoff to Crowston up the middle. As the Tigers broke from the huddle, the quarterback signaled Harry Jack Pugh and Crowston to hold up.

"Swede, take a step or two forward toward the two-gap, then break to the outside," Pierce said, pointing toward the right sideline. "Harry Jack, that big outside linebacker is killing us. Let the end in front of you go unblocked, and go get that linebacker."

When the ball was snapped, the Tigers' forward wall attacked their opponents, trying desperately to create a small opening just to the right of the center for their fullback to plunge through. As on the previous play, Pierce turned to hand the ball to Swede who took two steps forward, then suddenly veered toward the right sideline. The quarterback waited a split second to lure the unblocked defensive end toward him, and then flipped the ball to his fullback as McLeod's defense swirled to the middle like water drawn to the spout of a funnel. After catching the ball, Crowston stiff-armed the confused end and then cut upfield where Pugh, an outstanding blocker, surprised the big outside linebacker with a shoulder block that flipped him upside down. Swede pranced into the end zone, untouched. The cerebral quarterback had once again worked his magic.

The extra point failed, but the Tigers led, 6-0. Though not evident on the scoreboard, something bigger had happened. The formidable McLeod defense had been scored upon, something that had not happened to them all year. Catfish wondered if it would trigger the opponent to fight with even greater ferocity, or if they might have an emotional letdown, like a crack in a dam that gradually widens into a major breakthrough.

After kicking the ball to the McLeod eleven, the Tigers' defense held once again and forced a punt that traveled to the Tiger twenty-nine. On the first play, Hogan burst out to the thirty-seven. Then Swede blasted his way to midfield. Sensing a stunned opponent, Pierce quickly faked a running play and threw to big Harry Pugh down to the thirty-five. The quarterback then surprised everyone with a keeper for five yards, following Swede over left guard. Seeing a confused McLeod defense, Pierce rushed his team into the huddle and back to the line of scrimmage. Rattling off the cadence, he then pitched the ball to Hogan who dodged and darted into the end zone. The extra point pushed the score to 13-0, and three thousand fans knew serious damage had been done.

McLeod's defiant defense, after refusing nine consecutive opponents the thrill of penetrating their goal line, had grudgingly given up two touchdowns, and it seemed to be in a state of shock. The crack in the dam had widened.

After Catfish's defense stopped the McLeod offense again, the Tigers began another long march that reached the three-yard line of their weary and battered opponent. On first down, only three steps from the goal line, the Tigers fumbled away a likely third touchdown.

The missed opportunity did not seem to fluster the Tigers. Instead, they exuded confidence, convinced that the vaunted McLeod defense could not stop them, something the opponent must have feared, also. The Tiger defense again shut down the powerful McLeod offense, forcing yet another punt.

Sensing victory now, the Tigers pounded away at the McLeod defense, repeatedly sending Crowston, Hogan, and Campbell into the line. The Mount Vernon forward wall overpowered their opponents, making steady progress. The game ended with the Tigers methodically pushing toward their opponent's goal line. Mount Vernon's offense had proven it could not be stopped, and the Tigers' defense had shown that it was more than a match for their highly rated counterpart from McLeod.

The victory catapulted the Mount Vernon Tigers into the Regional Championship game against either Commerce or Van, the equivalent of a state championship contest for Division A football.

After showering and dressing at the Mount Pleasant facility, the Tiger team celebrated on the bus the entire twelve miles back home.

Being Thanksgiving, all the boys living at the Miller Hotel rode home with their parents, except Swede Crowston. Catfish gladly played chauffer for his blond fullback, driving him to his farm home near Hagansport to spend the extended weekend with his family.

Though Friday was a holiday from school, Catfish rose early and made his way to the newspaper office. Editor Devall was at his desk, writing his weekly article, covering the game.

"Good morning, Coach," the reporter said. "Do you think Commerce will beat Van?"

"I don't know a thing about either team," Catfish replied. "We'll be glad to play either one."

"Everybody says you've just beaten the best team around," the editor said, referring to the McLeod squad.

"Don't put that in your article," Catfish warned. "The toughest opponent is always your next one."

"What do you have to say about yesterday's game?"

"A great team effort," the coach replied. "I can't praise our defense enough. They shut down an offensive juggernaut, giving our offense time to get going. Starting this season, I knew Pierce and Crowston were solid in the backfield, and Shurtleff, Pugh, and Cargile in the line, but I could not have hoped for the effort we have had from Campbell, Hogan, and Yocum in the backfield. Then Parchman, Dickerson, Caudle, and Horne stepped up and made our forward wall the best I've ever had. They are all top-notch kids, a direct reflection of their parents."

As Catfish got up to leave, the reporter grabbed a newspaper off a stack and pitched it to him.

"There's a war article in there about one of our local boys. Thought you might want to share it with you students."

Sitting in his car, Catfish unfolded the paper and scanned the pages. His eyes settled on an article about a fellow Army Air Forces pilot.

Second Lieutenant Creel Leon Chandler, son of Dr. and Mrs. H. E. Chandler and husband of Rebecca Ann Chandler, 208 Green Street, Quannah, Texas, has been assigned to the recently activated AAF Convalescent Hospital at Miami Beach. Lt. Chandler is a graduate of Mount Vernon schools, attended Texas A&M College before transferring to East Texas State where he earned both his Bachelor of Science and Master of Science degrees. Prior to his induction into the AAF he was superintendent of Saltillo schools. He and his wife have three children, Leon Jr., Doris Jean, and Charles. Dr. H. E. Chandler, longtime Mount Vernon physician, says his son is recovering well from his wounds and should be released soon for a visit with his family.

Catfish knew Dr. Chandler well and had attended college with his son Truett, brother of Lieutenant Leon Chandler. A couple of months earlier the doctor had mentioned having a son who had died from football injuries, so Catfish had done some checking. From Pauline Rogers, girlfriend of the boy at the time of the incident, the coach learned that the player's name was J. T., and his death had occurred in October 1931 in a dramatic and heroic fashion. Before the second game of the season, Truett had learned of a plot by the opposing team to injure his brother, an outstanding runner. Truett, with similar build and a member of the same backfield, secretly swapped numbers with J. T., hoping to protect his brother. J. T. had noticed the switch and insisted on wearing his regular jersey. His subsequent injury and death had so upset the team and community that the remainder of the football season was cancelled.

Article in hand, Catfish stepped out of his car and walked to the doctor's office, which stood next door to the *Optic-Herald's* entrance. Dr. Chandler was with a patient, so Catfish wrote a note wishing the doctor's son a speedy recovery and left.

At home, the coach handed the paper to his wife, indicating she might be interested in the article. Instead, Dorothy Nell focused on an article entitled, "Eleven Yanks Rescue Eighty-one Kids Trapped in No-Man's Land."

The United States 35th Infantry Division in France faced the well-fortified Germans across a narrow strip of land, mostly open, when they received word from the local French that a small chateau in no-man's land housed eighty-one children, aged two to six. Concerned parents from Nancy had sent their little ones there, thinking they would be safer in the countryside. Now they lay directly between two massive armies poised to clash.

The American colonel promised to do his best to avoid shelling the chateau but explained that he had to capture nearby Hans to protect a division of American soldiers. Captain George Schneider then went to Company A of the 134th Regiment and asked for volunteers to sneak into no-man's land by night and rescue the children.

Without hesitation, ten men stepped forward and formed the "baby patrol." At nine that night, they trudged into the freezing, wet darkness and reached the chateau without being spotted by the Germans. The men, each carrying two toddlers and shepherding others, headed back toward the American lines. In the black night with many of the children barefoot, the pace was slow and strenuous.

When they came within a thousand yards of friendly lines, the Germans spotted them and cut loose with their mortars and artillery. The baby patrol had no choice but to hunker down and move forward by crawling.

Amid the bombardment they reached an icy stream where the soldiers carried the children across, one and two at a time. Miraculously, not one child or volunteer was injured.

Later, the ten brave men were awarded the bronze star; however, only five were on hand. The others had since become casualties of war.

Dorothy Nell dropped the paper onto the table, tears filling her eyes.

"What's the matter, honey?" Catfish asked, kneeling beside her.

"I hope this inhumane war is over soon," she answered, choked with emotion as she pointed toward the article.

Catfish scanned the story, and then stood up.

"If one of my boys had been there," he said, referring to his players, "I hope he would have had the courage to save those children. Winning games is great, but it's character that really counts."

At that moment, the phone rang.

"Cat," Superintendent Fleming said, "your boys will be playing Commerce for the Regional Championship."

"So Commerce whipped the Van Vandals," Catfish replied

"Not exactly," Fleming said. "A thirteen-to-thirteen tie, but Commerce had a six-to-two edge in penetrations."

"Where and when will we play?" Catfish asked.

"We'll negotiate the site and time for the game tomorrow morning in Sulphur Springs. You're welcome to come along."

"I prefer a neutral site rather than risk playing on the opponent's home field," Catfish replied. "And with this colder weather, I'd like to play in the afternoon, but I'll leave the negotiations to you."

Superintendent Fleming traveled to Sulphur Springs and settled the specifics for the game, which would be played at two-thirty on Friday afternoon, December 15, on the Wildcats' field in Sulphur Springs. This gave Catfish and his team almost two weeks to prepare, and then bus his squad twenty miles west to the neighboring town.

Catfish made a few phone calls to coaching friends who confirmed that the Commerce Tigers lacked the stellar reputation of the McLeod team that his Tigers had defeated for bi-district. The Commerce team had won district 17-A by defeating Cooper 28-0, Leonard 21-0, and by receiving a forfeit from Honey Grove. Only a couple of weeks prior to winning their district, they had played Ladonia, champions of district 17-B, to a 13-13 deadlock. The Commerce club then tied Van in their bi-district tilt, but had advanced on penetrations. The game had ended with Commerce throwing a desperation pass, which was almost intercepted by a Van player who had clear sailing to score if he had held on.

"Commerce will throw the ball a little," Catfish was advised by East Texas State coach, Bob Berry. "William Brookshire, number eighty-five, is their quarterback, and he passes mostly to Jack Wright, the right end, but also to Jackson out of the backfield. They especially like to pass the ball down near your goal line. Tosses by Brookshire accounted for both scores against Van, and he'll throw for the point-after, too. Also, they have a trick play where a halfback, Stanley, ends up with the ball off left tackle. He's scored on it several times this season.

"Their left guard, Whitlock, is their best lineman and team captain. They like to run behind him with Brookshire, Jackson, Weems, and Stanley. They've been prone to fumble with a good lick on the ball carrier. They bobbled the ball five times in the bi-district game, but the field was wet and slippery.

"They're coached by Ed Myrick, and they're fundamentally sound. I think your boys have some size on them, especially in the forward wall."

"I'm told three of the game officials are from Commerce," Catfish said. "Will that be a problem for me?"

"No," Berry replied. "They're good, honest, hard-working refs, and you'll get a fair shake from them."

The Commerce team did not sport the impressive record of

McLeod, and talk around Mount Vernon concerned a celebration planned for when the Tigers would be crowned champions, not if they would be. Predictably this drove Catfish crazy, and he counteracted it as best he could by preaching to his players that any team that makes it to the regional level is an outstanding opponent. "The most dangerous enemy is the one you underestimate," he told his players over and over.

Catfish considered one last barometer. Commerce had defeated Sulphur Springs' reserves 13-0 while his Tigers had rolled over the young Wildcats, 51-0. Everything indicated his team's superiority, a popular opinion that undoubtedly had made it to his players' ears. For two weeks Catfish's ulcers fed well off his worrying.

Following the kickoff, the suspense of the championship game did not last long. Mount Vernon scored three times in the first quarter, building a 20-0 lead.

Hogan started the scoring binge after Mount Vernon recovered a Commerce fumble. The little halfback dashed up the middle for forty-three yards and a touchdown, completing a seventy-two yard drive.

After kicking the ball to Commerce, one of their halfbacks, Hevron, fumbled and the purple-clad boys recovered the ball on the opponents' seventeen-yard line. After two running plays, Pierce tossed a touchdown pass to Jack Horne for the Tigers' second score.

Again, Mount Vernon kicked to Commerce and then held their opponent to five yards in three plays. Commerce attempted a punt, but a Tiger defender blocked it and recovered the ball on the opponent's nineteen. From there, Hogan skirted right end for Mount Vernon's third counter.

Mount Vernon started the second quarter by scoring in six plays, Swede Crowston getting the tally on a five-yard plunge through the line. However, later in the quarter, the Commerce eleven made a determined drive of eighty-eight yards to pay-dirt, culminating in a touchdown pass from Brookshire to Jack Wright, making the halftime score, 26-7.

The third stanza found Mount Vernon gobbling up another Commerce fumble which they turned into a touchdown by way of a twenty-eight-yard pass from Pierce to Pugh. Commerce then tried the airways, but Brookshire's pass was intercepted by Pierce and returned to the opponents' forty-two. From there Crowston burst through the line for twenty-two yards, down to the twenty-yard line. Three plays later, Campbell scored.

In the final period, Brookshire again tried a pass, this time to the right flat. Leacho Tittle, a reserve running back, intercepted this one and ran thirty yards for another Mount Vernon score. Fortunately, the touchdown barrage ended when Crowston completed a sixty-three-yard drive with a twenty-five-yard sprint to the end zone.

In the waning moments of the game, Brookshire completed a touchdown pass to Jack Wright, the leading scorer in Commerce's district, for their second and last tally. When the final gun sounded, Catfish's boys had clinched the regional title, 53-14.

The game statistics indicated Mount Vernon's dominance: two hundred fifty-seven yards rushing to eighty-nine for Commerce, sixteen first downs to eleven, and five interceptions of Commerce aerials while giving up none. Mount Vernon's district, 19-A, had prepared them well for the playoffs. Of the ten A-level regional winners in Texas, Catfish's team was arguably the best.

Catfish had his first championship and undefeated football team. No longer could his detractors refer to him as a basketball coach just passing time with football until round-ball season began. He had now reached the highest level in both sports.

With the lengthened football season completed, Catfish had to quickly focus on the upcoming basketball schedule. Most of the other schools had already completed two weeks of practice, some having managed scrimmage games. Starting late did not suit him, and he spent the weekend in a grumpy mood.

Additional pressure came from the fact that Catfish's basketball Tigers had played for the state title the prior spring, losing by a point in overtime. Newspaper articles and Mount Vernon fans had already voiced high expectations for a return trip to Austin and a state championship trophy as their reward. Catfish's 1945 squad would find little opportunity to play the preferred role of underdog.

Catfish could hardly wait to get his boys back on the hardwood and start making up for lost time.

1944 Basketball Team
State Finalists

Front Row: Billy Stinson, Harry Jack Pugh, Lollis Loyd, Glenn Pierce, J. C. Cannaday, Clarence "Swede" Crowston, Charles Hogan

Back Row: Coach Catfish Smith, Mgr. Robby Campbell, Mgr. George Dickerson, J. C. Morgan, Charles Shurtleff, Robbie Knotts, James Caudle, J. M. Connley, Billy Ingram, Supt. Millard Fleming, Mr. Bob Suggs

1944 Football Team
Undefeated Regional Champions

Front Row: Gerald McCook, Robby Campbell, George Wims, Buck Parchman, Jack Henry, Charles Shurtleff, Charles Hogan, Leacho Tittle, C. J. Bogue, Kenneth Meek, Gayle Tinsley, Jinkins Moore, Bob Suggs

Middle Row: Mgr. Olan Ray Brewer, Russell Adams, Glenn Minshew, Glenn Pierce, Clarence "Swede" Crowston, James Pittman, Jerry Yocum, Wayne Hightower, Billy Grau, Gene Fleming, Howard Rogers, George Dickerson, Mgr. Billy Rex Cody

Back Row: Coach Catfish Smith, S/Sgt. Wayne "Bo" Campbell, Harry Jack Pugh, Charles Lowry, Loyd Chaffin, Frank Parchman, Coy Sims, Merle Simons, Dan Cargile, Jack Horne, James Caudle, James Cherry, Assistant Coach Acie Cannaday

16

December 16, 1944

Up early on Saturday morning, Catfish grabbed the newspaper from the coffee table, not realizing it was from the prior week. He quickly skimmed over most of the stale news, but one article caught his attention.

Moore and Sons Operate Successful Dairy

A move from cotton farming to dairy operations is occurring in Franklin County. The county now has thirteen Grade-A dairies that represent a monthly income of $6,000. The largest of these is owned by Hoffman Moore who milks forty-two cows that produced an income of $2,355 in September and October. After $720 of expenses, the dairy operation cleared $1,635. The Moore dairy is located on four hundred twenty acres north of town, one hundred twenty acres of which is dedicated to feed-grain.

The dairy herd consists of fifty-five grown jersey cows, fifteen two-year-old heifers, and twenty one-year-olds. Along with one hired hand, the dairy operation is carried on by the Moore family, including three sons, fifteen-year-old Dewey, thirteen-year-old Dale, and eleven-year-old Johnny.

Catfish had no plans of entering the dairy business, so he had little interest in agrarian trends, but he lingered over the last sentence in the article. The image of three hearty farm boys in purple and white uniforms temporarily lifted him out of the doldrums.

A later check of the school's records revealed that the Moore brothers already attended Mount Vernon schools. Dewey was a freshman, while Dale was in the sixth grade, and Johnny attended the fifth. Catfish made a mental note to be sure that Dewey came out for spring football.

*　　*　　*

Due to the basketball team's success the prior year, twenty-four young men turned out on Monday afternoon, December 18, for the 1945 squad. Catfish's 1944 team had played its first game on December 17, so he was anxious to get started and make up for lost time. To do that, he needed to cut the team down to a manageable number, and after only a few practices those who sought glory without paying the price were pursuing other interests. By the end of December, the varsity team was set.

Glenn Pierce	# 10 Senior	Captain, 1944
Charles Hogan	# 11 Senior	Captain, 1945
Harry Jack Pugh	# 18 Senior	All-Region, 1944
J. C. Cannaday	# 12 Senior	All-State, 1944
Clarence "Swede" Crowston	# 16 Junior	Starter, 1944
Glynn Minshew	# 85 Junior	
Jinkins Moore	# 19 Senior	
James Caudle	# 15 Junior	
Charles Shurtleff	# 17 Senior	
J. C. Morgan	# 14 Senior	

Mount Vernon's opponents must have looked at the Tiger lineup in despair. From the 1944 state championship finalist quintet, Catfish had lost only one player, Lollis Loyd. Into that slot stepped Charles Hogan, Catfish's personal choice for All-State defensive guard. With Glenn Pierce, Harry Jack Pugh, J. C. Cannaday, and Swede Crowston a year older and a season smarter, the Tigers looked unbeatable.

While Catfish reveled in the prospects of his varsity unit, Acie Cannaday, assistant coach and former captain of the 1944 Southern Methodist University basketball team, handled the junior varsity team, a group that he believed to be better than some varsity teams for other area schools. Players like Pat Loyd, Gerald Skidmore, Robert Banks, Gene Fleming, Kenneth Meek, Billy Ingram, and Robbie Knotts gave promise of a bright future for Mount Vernon basketball.

Before the first ball was bounced on the hardwood, Catfish

174

scanned the schedule and knew the games that would make or break his season. Fourth on the schedule was Deport, a team that had pushed his 1944 squad to the limit in a 12-11 affair in the district tournament. Deport was followed by Sulphur Springs, a class AA school. The prior spring, three times his Tigers had squeaked by Mount Pleasant by a single point. And then there was Blossom, the only team to defeat his Tigers prior to the state championship contest, and the Lamar County team had decisively whipped his boys twice.

The season opened against Avinger, a small community that played basketball all year long, and the rusty Tigers barely skimped by, 18-17. After defeating Saltillo by fifty points, 58-8, they played Avinger again, improving their victory margin to 24-12.

With the short preseason over, the Tigers then jumped into district play, first defeating Talco, 39-17. Then they faced the dangerous Deport team, a nemesis of a year earlier, and Catfish's boys passed the first major test with flying colors, whipping them 46-22. Catfish then took his boys to Sulphur Springs, and walked away with a surprising 41-29 victory. This brought the Tigers to back-to-back encounters with Mount Pleasant. Mount Vernon captured the initial contest, 43-24, and followed that two nights later with a 35-19 win.

After breezing through Talco (52-23), Avinger (38-18), and Winnsboro (31-21), Catfish and his boys came face to face with their largest challenge of the young season, a Blossom team that was runner-up to the state champions in Class B the prior spring. When that game was over, the Tigers had a 34-21 victory, and Catfish knew he had a special team.

After repeat wins over Winnsboro (21-15), Sulphur Springs (40-34), and Talco (34-25), games in which his boys played uninspired basketball, Catfish's squad whipped Naples (42-29) and then Winnsboro (35-25) for a third time.

With the regular season completed, the undefeated Mount Vernon Tigers traveled to the semi-district tournament to face a desperate Deport squad. Catfish's spirited boys prevailed 41-28, and appeared to be at peak performance when they thrashed Mount Pleasant (33-19), and Winnsboro (41-25) to win the tournament.

Next was the district championship in an unusual format that pitted the Tigers in a two-of-three challenge against the Hooks Hornets, a team they had not previously played. The third game became unnecessary as Catfish's boys grabbed the first two contests, 43-20 and 41-25.

Through the district schedule, Mount Vernon had averaged thirty-eight points per game while allowing twenty-five, and then in the playoffs, the Tigers had averaged forty points while giving up only twenty-three, an impressive seventeen-point margin.

Tiger fans, and many of their opponents, were openly talking about Catfish's squad reaching the ultimate: an undefeated season and a state championship. The coach was worried, and his ulcers were having a heyday.

The red-hot Tigers, having faced no serious challenge through twenty-two games, took their perfect record on the road to Greenville for the regional tournament. Waiting for the previous game to end, Catfish grabbed a copy of the local paper, the *Greenville Evening Banner*, and scanned it, always looking for a story of interest to his history students. There it was on the front page.

The story cited Audie Murphy, a young man from Kingston, Texas, just north of Greenville, who initially had been rejected by his country's armed services because of his smallish size. Recently, the already highly decorated soldier had been recommended for the country's highest military award, the Medal of Honor.

Reminded of his dismissal from the AAF, Catfish read on and learned that the diminutive soldier had been accepted by the Army, and though underage, he had quickly distinguished himself as a fearless fighter and was promoted to second lieutenant. Then only a couple of weeks earlier, on January 26 in Colmar, France, Murphy had sent his charges toward safety while he climbed atop a burning tank destroyer and faced a field of advancing Germans. With his retreating buddies screaming for him to get off the vehicle before it exploded, Murphy grabbed the mounted machinegun and blazed away. When it was over, fifty Germans lay dead while their comrades retreated in disarray, and Murphy leaped through the flames and hobbled toward his waiting buddies, who then realized that at some point during the fighting, a German bullet had pierced Murphy's body.

Folding the paper and stuffing it in his coat pocket, Catfish thought back over his own life. How different might it have been if he had been able to complete his service in the AAF. Instead, he had students to teach and a basketball team to coach.

Mount Vernon's first opponent in the Regional Championship Tournament was the Grand Prairie Gophers. The Tigers played poorly, but won, 31-24. This matched them once again against Coach Goolsby's

Quitman Bulldogs, a team they had defeated by three points the prior year.

The way the Tigers had won that contest had grated on the Bulldogs' Ingram boys for a miserably long year, raising their thirst for revenge to full pitch. Down by only one point, Quitman had had the ball out of bounds with the time clock showing ten seconds, when Crowston had tricked them into passing the ball to him. His final shot had given the Tigers an undeserved victory, so believed the Bulldogs.

Meanwhile, Catfish's boys gave little thought to those year-old dramatics. They coasted into the regional finals, confident they would prevail and move on to avenge their one-point loss to Nocona in the prior state championship game.

Whatever the reason, the Quitman five played with a fervor seldom seen by the Tigers, leaving Catfish's boys befuddled and overwhelmed. The Bulldogs defeated the purple-clad boys by a whopping nineteen points, 44-25. The loss proved as painful for the Mount Vernon boys as it was glorious revenge for the Quitman team.

While Quitman went on to play for the state championship, defeating East Mountain and finishing as runner-up to Sidney Lanier, 30-24, Catfish moped for a week, telling himself and everyone who would listen that he had failed his boys.

"This team deserved better," he told Dorothy Nell while pacing the floor. "They should be in Austin playing in the state tournament this weekend. That loss, the only one of the season for my boys, kept us out.

"First, I should have put together a tougher schedule, should have included Quitman a couple of times. The Bulldogs could have vented all their anger on us when it didn't count so much. We might have lost a game, but we'd have known what to expect later.

"Second, we beat everybody so easily, the boys didn't know how to respond when we fell behind, and I didn't know how to coach them. Early on, I should have played some of our backup players more, allowing the score to stay close, letting us feel the pressure at the end. If you haven't been there and fought your way back, when you see the time slipping away, you panic.

"Well, it won't happen again. I'll make sure we have a tough schedule every year. I'll never let my boys down like that again."

Before Catfish could dwell further on his problems, a phone call came from Charles Devall, editor and owner of the local paper.

"Cat," the newsman said, "I've just received some news that I don't think should wait until Friday's paper. Dr. H. E. Chandler's wife Mamie has just passed away."

Stunned, Catfish thanked Devall, and glanced at a calendar. Sunday, March 18. Not only had the coach frequented the doctor's office for medical help, he also considered him a friend. Mamie was the sister of William H. Parrish who lived with his wife Bessie near Winfield, Catfish's hometown. The Parrishes attended the same church as Catfish's mother. Before church that evening, the coach dropped by the Chandler home on south Kaufman and expressed his condolences to the doctor and other family members.

The death and sadness brought upon the doctor and his family helped the coach to put events in perspective and to let go of the guilt he felt about the disappointing end to the basketball season. With his brooding over, he focused on the upcoming spring football drills. He sought out his returning players, as well as those he hoped would give the game a try, and began piecing together the team that would try to match the perfect season of the 1944 Tiger squad.

Frank Parchman would be back at left tackle, Caudle at right guard, and George Dickerson at center. The rest of that formidable line was gone. He would lose his valued quarterback and both halfbacks, but would have Swede returning at fullback. Also, he had some promising younger players, but they were unproven for championship level play. The dairyman's oldest son, Dewey Moore, had agreed to give football a try, and Catfish had a feeling he would be a tough one, though lightweight. And a strong-bodied Hopewell boy, Herb Zimmerman, had said he wanted to join the squad. Likewise, Charles Lowry and Gene Fleming were big strong boys whose abilities should improve rapidly with experience, something they were sure to get.

Just as Catfish penciled-in his 1945 lineup, fitting the pieces together in his mind, he received some devastating news.

"Coach," Clarence Crowston said, "I'll turn eighteen in the fall, and I aim to enlist in the Army and do my part to win this war."

No Swede at fullback? Catfish had never been caught so off-guard in all his life. He wanted to talk his prize player into staying. He would convince him that playing football another year would better prepare him for a college career, would give him more time to mature before he faced a cruel world, but in good conscience the coach could not.

In his heart, Catfish knew it was his own doing. Steadfastly, he had preached good citizenship to his players, and he had taken every opportunity to applaud and honor his country's servicemen. He had repeated to his players every Silver Star and every Purple Heart story he had come across. The clincher was, given the opportunity, he undoubtedly would do the same as his young fullback.

"Son," he finally managed to say, "you've been a great athlete for me and your school. Now, go be an outstanding soldier for your country."

Spring drills not only served to evaluate new players, introducing blocking and tackling techniques and the T-formation, but they also gave insight into hopes for the fall squad. Losses to graduation told Catfish that he had to rebuild his team. Further, he knew that the eleven players he would field in September would not match the regional champs of 1944. Rebuilding had to start at quarterback, but it must permeate the line and the backfield, too. Billy Rex Cody showed some promise as the man under center, Leacho Tittle played tough, and James Cherry would fit into the lineup, but nobody could match the Swede, or replace Campbell, or Hogan. With his fullback gone, Catfish moved Caudle to the backfield where he immediately displayed surprising skills.

With the Caudle move, along with switching Dickerson from center to right end, only one starter from the 1944 forward wall would be returning to his position: Frank Parchman, left tackle. But Catfish did not make these changes without a plan. He believed young Charles Lowry, with size and intelligence, could anchor the middle of the offensive line, and James Pittman could fill the left end position. Parchman's counterpart at right tackle would be the mild-mannered but aggressive Gene Fleming. Guards Herb Zimmerman and Howard Rogers would round out the forward wall, a young but promising group.

While Catfish and his boys had busied themselves with winning basketball games and preparing for another year of football, the world around them heaved in the throes of war and its endless fatalities. In an unprecedented string of deaths of world leaders, on Thursday afternoon, April 12, only eighty-three days into his fourth term, President Franklin D. Roosevelt died in Warm Springs, Georgia. On April 28 Benito Mussolini, dictator of Italy, was shot to death by his countrymen. Two days later on April 30, Hitler was dead. Even the stalwart Churchill would be out of power by July.

More than a president, Roosevelt was the steadfast emotional leader of his country. First elected Commander in Chief in the fall of 1932, for many he was more like a king or monarch than a leader elected for a term. Thirteen-year-olds had never known the United States without him at the helm. Initially, America's new leader, Harry S.

Truman, having served in the long shadow of Roosevelt, stirred none of the determination and inimitable willpower of his predecessor.

"Fortunately," some said, "the war in Europe is about won, and with the full might of the United States against Japan, she won't last much longer."

In late April of 1945, while the world adjusted to its leadership changes, the Mount Vernon Tiger Band ushered out its officers and elected new ones for the coming school year. Also, that is when a junior cornet player named Martha Hill approached the band director, Mrs. Vera Mitchell.

"I'd like to try out for majorette," Martha said.

"You'll have to show you can twirl."

"Yes, ma'am."

"I'll give you a tryout after school this afternoon."

Martha showed up at the band hall after her last class and eased into the director's little office.

"Where is your baton?" Mrs. Mitchell asked, glancing up from the paperwork on her desk.

"I'll need to borrow one," Martha said, her eyes dropping to the floor.

"You don't own a baton?"

"No ma'am."

The skeptical director found an old one in the corner of her office, and they stepped outside.

Martha picked a basic routine to get past the jitters.

"That's okay, but our techniques are more complex than that."

The girl smiled and began twirling again, flawlessly copying one of the more intricate routines that she had memorized with her broomstick.

"That's enough," the director said. "Young lady, it looks like I'll have to find another cornet player."

Martha Hill joined majorettes Dorothy Gilbert, Peggy Self, Faye Eula Gilbert, and Patsy Pugh, along with the new drum major, Patsy Irby, captain, Jerry Cannaday, and first lieutenant, Charles Moffett. Clearly, the Tiger band was more prepared for the upcoming fall than the football team.

In Catfish's final history class of the spring semester, he led his students in one last discussion, focusing on the progress of the war.

First, he explained how throughout the spring the Allied forces had squeezed Hitler's army tighter and tighter in their relentless pincers, but Catfish claimed the collapse had begun over a year earlier.

"Some would argue that Hitler was doomed from November nineteen forty-three when President Roosevelt, Winston Churchill, and Joseph Stalin met in Tehran, Iran and hammered out the Overlord agreement. Stalin wanted an all-out push by the Americans and British on the western front to ease pressure on his army. Roosevelt wanted Stalin's pledge to make no separate peace agreement with Hitler, and he required Russia's promise to declare war on Japan after Germany was defeated. Churchill did not like the plan for a massive invasion of Western Europe, but he was voted down, signaling Great Britain's decline as a world power and the rise of the United States and Russia.

"By that time on the Russian front, Stalin's forces had won a five-month battle at Stalingrad and had defeated Hitler's forces near Kursk in one of the largest tank battles of all time. In Stalingrad, the Nazis' surrendered, but not until thousands of German soldiers, surrounded and cutoff from life-sustaining supplies, had frozen or starved to death. Additionally, the Nazis' siege of Leningrad had failed, though over a million Soviet citizens had died, mostly from hunger and cold. In Kursk and Leningrad, the war turned in no small part due to American Lend-Lease war machines, food, and clothing.

"In January nineteen forty-four, the heart of Russia's winter, the German supply lines had been stretched beyond the point of maintenance, and Stalin's Soviets had begun an offensive to drive the frostbitten and depleted German army out of their country.

"Recently," Catfish said, "the Russians have pushed the Nazis back to Berlin."

He then described the second pincer, British and Canadian forces who had poured down through the Netherlands into northern Germany.

"The Americans made up the third and most powerful pincer," Catfish said. "Pushing up through Italy and France, the Americans and French stormed toward the Elbe River in central Germany, and drove right on toward Berlin.

"In March, with celebrations of victory in Europe at the Allies' fingertips," Catfish continued, "confirmation of Nazi atrocities squelched the world's celebratory spirit. Concentration camps filled with starving Jews were found, revealing a horror of misery and death beyond imagination. Then death pits filled with the bulldozed bodies of those executed en masse were found, and the gas chambers, and the human-experiment labs."

To personalize the point, Catfish then told how, on April 12, General Eisenhower had reacted upon his first sight of a concentration camp, the one at Ohrdruf Nord. "I never dreamed that such cruelty . . . and savagery could really exist in this world," Eisenhower had said. "Consider," Catfish added, "that this is the reaction of a man hardened to the horrors of war, the architect of D-Day."

He then went on to describe how Ollie Kirby, a young United States intelligence officer and code-breaker, had described his first sighting of a death camp: corpses stacked like cordwood and starving and dying survivors who peered at him hopelessly through sunken eyes. These sickening images would fill the officer's most lasting and haunting memories of a war replete with ghastly sights.

"Hearing these reports," Catfish said, pacing back and forth before his class, "an anxious world waited for Berlin to fall and the German leader to capitulate."

Catfish deplored Hitler's form of leadership, and his fury showed in his eyes as he focused on those most responsible for the world's current chaos.

"On April twenty-fifth, the Allies had Berlin surrounded, yet Hitler, burrowed deep in his underground bunker, ordered his soldiers to fight on. On April thirtieth, while his weary army continued to battle the Allies, *der Fuhrer* committed suicide. Reports claim that he died believing his cause was just, but that the German people had failed him. Some believe he and Eva Braun escaped and now plot a future world catastrophe.

"Grand Admiral Karl Doenitz succeeded Hitler just long enough to arrange Germany's surrender on May seventh, signed by Colonel General Alfred Jodl, chief of staff of the German Armed Forces. The unconditional surrender occurred at General Eisenhower's headquarters in Reims, France. May eighth, nineteen forty-five, has been declared Victory in Europe Day, an unforgettable triumph for our soldiers and the families of those who have perished in this colossal struggle for freedom.

"If not for the Ultra Secret project," Catfish said, "the European war would still be going on. British and American code-breakers, using a German encryption machine, the Enigma, supplied by Polish spies, deciphered thousands of Hitler's secret war plans. Careful use of this invaluable information concealed the fact that the Allies were reading the Nazis' mail, but undoubtedly knowing the German's plans shortened the war."

"Were we ever in danger of Hitler reaching us over here?" a girl asked.

"The Germans desperately wanted to bomb Washington, D. C., and New York," Catfish replied. "Their planes lacked the range, but still they considered dropping bombs over here and then ditching their bombers into the ocean, the pilots to be picked up by their U-2 boats. Also, they were developing an all-winged plane, the Ho-229, that could have done the job. A prototype of this plane, designed by Reimar and Walter Horton, was captured in the Gotha factory by United States forces just last month. Powered by two turbojet engines and covered with a radar-absorbing material, it could have flown undetected over our cities, dropped its one-thousand-kilogram bombs, and flown home."

Catfish then switched his focus to the Pacific theater.

"Our men and women there, and their families, will have to wait until Japan has surrendered before they celebrate. Fortunately, the tide of war in the East has turned."

Catfish described how McArthur had returned to the Philippines, invaded the island of Luzon, and in March had taken back Manila. The nurses imprisoned there had survived and were freed.

"The whereabouts of Mount Vernon's Alvis O. Loveless remains unknown," he said. "If he's alive, he's likely hiding somewhere deep in the jungle with Filipino guerilla fighters, striking at the straggling bands of Japanese soldiers who continue fighting, or he could be languishing in a prison camp in Japan."

The coach went on to tell how the island-hopping Americans had advanced to Okinawa, only three hundred fifty miles from the main island of Japan. At Okinawa, Japanese *kamikazes* or "divine winds" had crashed their crafts into American ships, sinking thirty and damaging another three hundred fifty. Like the original "divine wind," a typhoon that had destroyed a Mongol fleet sent to attack Japan in 1281, the damage inflicted was immense. Over fifty thousand Americans had died while more than twice that number of Japanese lives ended there.

"Among those wounded at Okinawa was Mount Vernon's Private First Class Milton Steed," Catfish explained. "After serving thirty-two months, he received a serious thigh wound and is currently being treated at the base hospital in Hawaii. Steed recently mailed his Purple Heart and Combat Infantry Badge to his anxious wife back here."

Catfish then addressed expected warfront developments for the summer months when more Mount Vernon boys would be enlisting in the various branches of the military.

"Possibly the worst and bloodiest phase of the war is just ahead. The military's timetable calls for a massive invasion of the Japanese mainland in November. In such an assault, planners estimate a million more American soldiers will die, and Japanese deaths might double or triple that number.

"World history is being written in big bold letters," he told them, "and you have a front-row view of it, if you'll just open your eyes and minds. Maybe your generation will learn how to avoid such horrible wars."

However, in a thousand years, neither he nor his students could have imagined the potential for world catastrophe being developed by the Manhattan Project. Not even the soldier crouching in his foxhole, the airman flying his B-29 bomber, or the seaman riding the waves could have guessed what lay ahead.

17

May 25, 1945

High School graduation celebrations were tempered by the news that thirteen young men from Franklin County had been inducted into the armed services, including Carson Jacobs and Cecil Newsome. Many would be replacement soldiers for the dead and wounded, those like Sergeant Loyd South of Mount Vernon, survivor of three battle wounds. Sergeant South was currently being treated in Brooke General and Convalescent Hospital at Fort Sam Houston. The award of four battle stars, an Oak Leaf Cluster, and a Purple Heart awaited his recovery.

One Saturday afternoon in early June, Catfish was in the M. L. Edwards store looking at shoes, when he felt a tug at his elbow.

"Hi, Coach Smith," Herb Zimmerman said.

After visiting a minute, the youngster motioned Catfish to ease over behind a tall shoe display.

"Coach, I don't think I'm gonna be able to play football this fall."

In spring drills, Zimmerman had earned a starting guard position, and was one of the most promising players on the forward wall. The coach thought enough of him, along with Billy Jack Guthrie and Pat Loyd, that he had driven them to Hopewell every afternoon after spring practices.

"What's the problem?" the coach asked.

"My brother is still in the war, and my dad needs my help on the farm."

Not only did Herb's father need him to help tend their crops, but also his mother did not want him playing such a violent sport. She had one son in the war, and she wanted the other safe at home.

"Maybe I should talk to your father," Catfish said, craning his neck to see over the shoe display. "Is that him over there?"

The boy nodded and followed Catfish across the store.

"Sir," Catfish said. "I'm Coach Smith."

"Bob Zimmerman," the man responded.

"I think your son has got a chance for a college football scholarship, Mr. Zimmerman, if he's given the opportunity to play and applies himself."

"I'm a farmer, Coach Smith, and fall is harvest time," Mr. Zimmerman replied. "With Hank off to war, I need help in the field."

"I understand," the coach said, nodding. "I just hate to see your boy lose a chance to get a college education."

"You really think Herb could win a scholarship?" Mr. Zimmerman asked, after a few moments.

"I sure do," Catfish said. "And a college diploma will open lots of doors in his lifetime, doors that'll be shut in his face otherwise."

"Let me think about it," Mr. Zimmerman said, motioning his son to come along as he headed for the door.

A week later, having heard nothing from the Zimmermans, Catfish drove out to their farm at Hopewell.

"Heard anything from H. B. lately?" Catfish asked, settling into a chair.

"Last thing we heard, his outfit was headed for Luzon," Mr. Zimmerman said. "He's already fought at Bougainville and Cebu, but I expect he'll end up making the invasion of Japan, if he survives until then."

Catfish recalled that H. B. Zimmerman had earned a Bronze Star on Bougainville Island, helping capture Hill 260.

"Got a letter from him after they'd wrapped things up in Cebu," the father said, making his way to a little lamp table across the room.

Returning, Mr. Zimmerman handed over a folded, three-page letter.

Catfish scanned the pages, shaking his head as he read.

We swung over the side of our infantry transport ship and climbed down the heavy nets to the landing craft. Being a communications specialist, I was loaded down with a roll of telephone wire, in addition to the usual things. We crouched low in the craft because enemy mortar and machinegun fire zinged all around us, splashing geysers thirty feet into the air. Our battleships had pounded the island fortifications for hours earlier, but evidently, they didn't knock out many of the enemy's guns.

About a hundred yards from shore, somebody opened the ramp door in the bow of the boat, and like cattle through a chute, we poured

186

into the water, which was chest deep. Holding our weapons over our heads, and me lugging that roll of wire, we pushed toward shore. I was afraid I'd step in a hole over my head, and with all the gear I had on, I'd have sunk like an anchor. But drowning was not as big a worry as stopping some of the lead the Japanese were firing at us.

I don't know how to describe what it was like seeing my buddies take a bullet and disappear beneath the water. You want to stop and help them, but there were so many, and the lieutenant was screaming for us to get ashore as quickly as possible.

We finally established a beachhead, and mopped up the enemy on the island. We've been here eighty-two days now, and there are rumors that we're shipping out for Leyte or maybe Luzon. If we get through all that, I expect we'll load up and hit the main island of Japan this fall.

When the letter turned to family matters, Catfish folded the pages and handed them back to Mr. Zimmerman.

"I've thought about what you said last week," the farmer said. "I'd like for my boy to have that shot at a college education. I just don't know how to get him to town and back for practices and games."

"Sir," Catfish said, "I think I can find him a nice place in town, if that's okay with you. And I'll get him home on weekends."

Within minutes, a deal was struck, and Catfish headed home, unable to get the images from the letter off his mind.

While Catfish was busy preparing for the coming football season and rounding up a few more country boys for his team, Mount Vernon's city fathers decided the regional champion Tigers deserved a new and improved football stadium. Plans called for enhancement of the west grandstands with an enclosed press box perched on top and the addition of bleachers on the east side. Also, to improve visibility at night games, floodlights would be added, along with repositioning of existing ones. Accordingly, ticket prices were bumped up to fifty cents for adults and twenty-five cents for students.

On June 22, Catfish announced the ten-game fall football schedule.

September 14	Tyler Yannigans	home
September 21	Sulphur Springs B	home
September 28	Mineola	away
October 5	Deport	home

October 12	Winnsboro	away
October 19	Mount Pleasant	away
October 26	Pittsburg	home
November 2	Gilmer	home
November 9	Talco	away
November 16	Clarksville	home

Having never played the Tyler team, the season opener presented a certain intrigue that goes with the unknown, and Catfish hoped for stiff competition from a town much larger than Mount Vernon. The last time the Tigers had played Deport, an addition to the district, had been in 1934 and resulted in a six-point Tiger loss, yet no one expected the newcomers to challenge for the 1945 district title. The Tigers had not defeated Mineola until the prior season, and the coach anticipated the Yellow Jackets would be out for revenge. Without a doubt, the heart of the district schedule was Winnsboro, Mount Pleasant, and Gilmer.

Along with the lineup of games, Catfish proudly announced that Charles Shurtleff, his senior left guard, had been selected to play for the south in the Texas Coaches High School All-Star Game, August 10, in Abilene. Shurtleff, one of only forty-four footballers in the state of Texas to be chosen, was the first since Glyn Jones in 1939 to be so honored from Mount Vernon. Shurtleff, headed for Southern Methodist University in the fall to continue his football career, expressed delight at the opportunity. Coach "Dutch" Meyer from Texas Christian University, Tom Dennis of Rice, and Bill James from Texas A&M had agreed to coach the high school boys, and Catfish promised he would be there to encourage his protégé. Additionally, Shurtleff had received an invitation to play in the Oil Bowl at Wichita Falls, a rivalry between the best high school football players from Texas against the elite from Oklahoma.

Just weeks later, Dave Bolger saw the fruits of his labor with the poliomyelitis project take a decidedly negative turn. Allen Seay, two-year-old son of Mr. and Mrs. Edward Seay of Rock Hill, a community in south Franklin County, succumbed to the dreaded disease. Taken ill on Monday, July 23, the boy's health quickly deteriorated until he died on Thursday, July 26, four days shy of his third birthday. The family, including brothers, James, Donald, and Jimmie, was stunned by the sudden loss.

One day after the boy's death, Dave Bolger endured another

setback when thieves broke through a rear window at his car dealership and stole tires valued at six hundred dollars. Then ten days later, on Monday, August 6, while Catfish and Charles Shurtleff were traveling to Abilene to the annual coaches meeting and All-Star Game, the startling news of a distant mushroom cloud, the most frightening happening of the century, came over the car radio.

That morning an American B-29 bomber, the *Enola Gay*, flown by Colonel Paul Tibbets, Jr., and named after his mother, had penetrated the sky over Japan, as hundreds of others had done on bombing missions, but this plane carried the Manhattan Project's super-bomb. The recently developed atomic weapon, unknown and unimagined by the world's general citizenry, exploded over Hiroshima, a city of three hundred forty thousand people, obliterating everything within a five-square-mile area and killing an estimated seventy thousand people. Soon, about thirty thousand others, with severe burns or buried beneath collapsed structures, were added to the death toll.

Though ninety thousand had been killed with conventional bombs in a single raid on Tokyo on March 9, the devastation from the atomic explosion, one bomb from one plane, was stark and inconceivable. A purple mushroom cloud boiled into the sky as if it were a rapidly enlarging monster, quickly reaching an altitude of forty-five thousand feet, over eight miles. The force from the bomb, "Little Boy," sent shock waves racing after its delivery vehicle and shook her violently, "like a giant had struck our plane with a telephone pole," co-pilot Bob Lewis said.

The phone lines sizzled with the news. Hopes were high that this one gigantic blow meant the end of the war with Japan, but American elation was tempered by fears associated with this seemingly all-powerful weapon. "What long-term effects might it have?" people asked. "Would Japan's leaders see the futility of continuing the war? Was the atomic bomb the ultimate weapon to end all wars? Would its future use mean self-destruction?"

For H. B. Zimmerman and his buddies in the Philippines, the question was somewhat different. "Does this mean the dreaded invasion of mainland Japan, planned for November, will not be necessary?" He and tens of thousands of soldiers in the Pacific hoped so, because they knew the likely consequences of an invasion. "If not for the atomic bomb, I doubt I would have made it home," H. B. confided years later.

Still, Japanese leaders refused to capitulate, though warned by the United States that failure to surrender immediately would lead to similar destruction of additional cities. On Wednesday, August 8, Russia seized the opportunity, declared war on Japan as promised in Tehran, and invaded Manchuria. Still Japanese leaders held on. On August 9, another American bomber dropped its super-bomb, an even larger one, over Nagasaki, killing approximately seventy-five thousand people.

The horror experienced by the Japanese was worse than the rest of the world could possibly imagine. People literally evaporated in the intense heat of the explosion, but the worst was borne by those who were burned and mangled and yet clung to life while in indescribable misery and pain, with little hope of relief or help.

With an anxious world wondering how humanity had come to this, many prayed it would lead to a quick end to the conflict.

Meanwhile, the coaches meeting continued but without the usual enthusiasm. In the highlight of the week, the All-Star Game on Friday, August 10, Shurtleff and his south team prevailed, 13-12, but what had once been a sports highlight, now dimmed in comparison to world events.

With the outlook for Japan at its most dismal point, its emperor, Hirohito, pleaded with warlords for a quick surrender. Meanwhile, some of that country's military leaders chose suicide rather than face the inevitable. Finally, at six o'clock in the evening on Tuesday, August 14, President Truman delivered a nation-wide radio address.

I have received this afternoon a message from the Japanese government in reply to the message forwarded to that government by the secretary of state on August eleventh. I deem this reply a full acceptance of the Potsdam declaration, which specifies the unconditional surrender of Japan. In this reply there is no qualification. Arrangements are now being made for the formal signing of surrender terms at the earliest possible moment. General MacArthur has been appointed the supreme Allied Commander to receive the Japanese surrender. Great Britian, Russia, and China will be represented by their high-ranking officers. Meantime, the Allied armed forces have been ordered to suspend specific action. The proclamation of Victory over Japan Day must wait upon the formal signing of the surrender terms by Japan.

As the news swept across the United States, Americans celebrated throughout the night and the following day. In Mount Vernon, tears of joy were shed openly, businesses closed on Wednesday, and many churches held special services for prayers of thanksgiving. The most far-reaching and destructive war of all time was finally over.

General MacArthur did not wait for the official surrender papers to be signed to move troops into Japan. He sent the 4th Marine Combat Team ashore at Tokyo Bay, and the 11th Airborne Division landed at Atsugi Airfield on Wednesday, August 29, while the General arrived aboard his silver airship, *Bataan*. Though prepared for combat, the Americans met no resistance.

Official signing of the terms of surrender by Japan's leaders and its warlords occurred aboard the United States Battleship *Missouri*, which lay at anchor in Tokyo Bay on Sunday, September 2, thus determining V-J Day. Obviously, the honored ship was not randomly chosen, as President Truman was a native of the "show me" state.

Catfish had begun the fall football practices at nine o'clock the prior morning by issuing uniforms to twenty-four boys and scheduling the first drills that afternoon at three-thirty. As the coach had done with Clarence Crowston and some of his other country boys, he had made arrangements for Herb Zimmerman and a few other rural players to stay in town so they would not miss practices. To pay their way, the boys swept out the school every evening, dumped the trash, cleaned the chalkboards, dusted erasers, and made the classrooms ready for the next day.

Saturday afternoon when the *Optic-Herald* editor questioned the coach about his starting lineup, Catfish replied, "We have a lot of rebuilding to do and only thirteen days to get the job done. The boy who works hard and gets himself ready to play is the one who will start against the Tyler Yannigans."

A week prior to the first day of classes, Catfish stopped by the *Optic-Herald* office and thanked Charles Devall, editor and owner, for supporting his current-events project in his history classes.

"I think it has been enormously beneficial to the students, and though the war is over now, I'd like to continue it, if you can spare the papers."

Devall agreed and then handed Catfish a copy of the September 7 edition.

"I want you to read 'Pop's Corner,'" the editor said, referring to Olin Hardy's regular column on the front page. "You'll see just how important the hometown paper can be."

Tribute must be paid where it is due, and none is due more than to L. D. Lowry, Jr. of our community. Knowing the burning desire of every boy on the battlefield to hear news from home, Mr. Lowry has, at his own expense, seen that every Franklin County soldier, some five-hundred of them, has received the Optic-Herald, his hometown paper. "It has been the greatest pleasure of my life," Mr. Lowry said.

Catfish glanced up at Devall. "What a thoughtful and patriotic gesture. I'm beginning to see what a special town Mount Vernon is."

As he climbed into his car, Catfish plopped the paper down on the seat. As he turned away, he glimpsed a familiar name in another article.

San Diego Naval Training Center
Dear Reverend J. C. Mann,

Today is Sunday, and somehow everything seems to be different from the other six days of the week. Maybe it's just me, but I feel a subdued undertone in all the noise around me. We are quieter, it seems; we march to chow in a meditative mood. Everything in the universe seems more in harmony; turmoil and strife so recently prevalent seem far removed. I believe there is in the hearts of Americans a prayer of thanksgiving.

It's funny, but when a boy goes away from home on his own, and situations arise that he has never been faced with before, certain things that he has experienced as a kid come back to help him. I think I have an advantage because of the lessons from my parents and those teachings I received at church. The saying, "As bent the twig, so grows the tree," has proved true in my case. No matter how much I may try to ignore my upbringing, it always comes back, like a wall. For this I must thank first my parents, then all those who labor with young people day after day to give them some meter with which to measure right and wrong.

Every boy has a different notion of right and wrong. For each of us, the standard is molded by our environment, our parents, and our teachers. I think mine is more refined, more crystallized, than for most boys. For that, I again want to thank all those who have played a part in my upbringing. I particularly appreciate the religious training I have received, and the part you have played in that.

Billy Stinson, S2-c

Billy Stinson had played on Catfish's 1944 basketball team, the one that challenged Nocona for the state title. Not an outstanding player, he always supported his teammates and celebrated their accomplishments without envy. The letter was especially touching for the coach, supporting his belief that helping prepare young men for life, whether minister, teacher, or coach, was an honorable life work.

For the Mount Vernon fans, the season opener seemed to pick up right where the prior year's team left off, winning decisively. The Tigers defeated the team from Tyler 25-6.

Of the starting eleven, only three had played regularly on the 1944 regional championship team, and two of those now played different positions. Unlike the enthused fans, Catfish knew his team was nowhere near ready to challenge for a district title, and certainly not a regional crown.

The first quarter ended as it had begun, a scoreless deadlock marred by fumbles and mistakes; however, in the second stanza the Tigers scored twice. An outstanding Tiger punt that tumbled out of bounds on the opponents' five-yard line set up the first Mount Vernon touchdown. Catfish's defense kept the opponent pinned down, and the Tyler punter only got the ball out to the twenty. From there, Leacho Tittle broke loose and scored. The point-after failed.

After the following kickoff, the visitors tried a pass on their second play from scrimmage. The Tigers' Billy Rex Cody intercepted it on the opponents' forty-eight-yard line. Tittle and Caudle, on four tries, moved the ball to the enemy's twenty. From there Caudle scored on a strong run that justified Catfish's move of him from guard to fullback. Again the point-after failed, and the Tigers went to the locker room with a 12-0 lead.

The third quarter began with the Tyler team making a steady sixty-yard march to the end zone. Suddenly, a comfortable Tiger lead had been cut in half, 12-6, and Catfish was pacing the sideline like a caged animal.

With the close of the third stanza, Tittle left the game with an injury, seriously limiting the Tigers' offensive options. However, the defense rose up, and Frank Parchman blocked a Tyler punt, recovering the ball on the visitors' five-yard line. From there Caudle made another hard run that took him into the end zone. Still unable to convert the point-after, the score read, 18-6.

In the final period, trailing by two touchdowns, Tyler resorted to passing the ball in an attempt to quickly close the scoring gap. The plan backfired when Dickerson, playing end, intercepted an aerial on the Tyler twenty-nine. After a seven-yard gain, Caudle dashed to the end zone from the twenty-two, but a penalty negated the score and moved the ball back ten yards. Four plays gained nothing, and Tyler took over.

Behind with time slipping away, the visiting team fired a quick pass on first down, and just as suddenly, Caudle stole the aerial and fought his way to the two-yard line. Two plays later, the pugnacious runner crossed the double stripe. The try for extra point looked like another failure when Caudle fumbled, but the Tigers' big tackle, Parchman, got a paw on the ball and lugged it into the end zone as time ran out. The successful point-after set the final score at 25-6.

The most exciting play of the game, an eighty-five yard touchdown run by Billy Rex Cody, the Tigers' quarterback, was erased by a clipping penalty. His ball handling was a bit ragged, resulting in fumbles, but he played especially well on the defensive side of the ball.

Frank Parchman turned in a stellar performance, and newcomers, Fleming and Pittman, proved they belonged in the forward wall. The fans left satisfied; the coach did not.

"I didn't know a win could be so ugly," Catfish told his players after the game. "I don't care what you hear from folks around town, we're not a good football team yet. We can't even make an extra point, the simplest play in the game."

Then he called out his quarterback and halfbacks, and handed each an old football to take home.

"Keep that ball in your hands every minute from now until practice Monday," he bellowed. "If you drop it, do ten pushups. If you wake up at night and don't have it in your hands, hit the floor. You show up here Monday without that ball tucked under your arm, you're off the team."

Practice the next week was like starting all over. Catfish ran his boys until they stood bent over wheezing, and he then lined them up for blocking and tackling drills. When they thought they were about dead, he ran them some more.

"If it's this painful to win, what will it be like if we lose a game?" one of the younger players asked Parchman when they had finished the last wind-sprint.

"I don't know," Parchman replied, bent double with his hands gripping his knees. "Last year we never lost."

194

The Tigers played better against the subs of Sulphur Springs, especially the defense. Caudle scored in both the first and second quarters, and added several strong runs in the second half. To the coach, the fullback's aggressive, hardnosed style brought back flashes of Swede, though Catfish was not yet ready to put him in that class.

The second score of the final quarter brought the crowd to their feet. After Cody had sneaked across from the two-yard stripe for the first touchdown of the period, the Tigers got the ball back on their thirty-four. The first play was a twenty-yard run by Caudle, which ended with a lateral to James Cherry who rambled on another eleven yards to the Wildcats' thirty-five. Cody then fired a pass to Pittman who immediately became entangled with a defender; however, when the right end, Dickerson, came loping by, Pittman pitched the ball to him, and he dashed to the two-yard line before the enemy could corral him. The Tigers then scored their third touchdown.

The last counter came on a nineteen-yard pass from Cody to Kenneth "Rambler" Meek, a wiry lad of barely one hundred pounds. Final score: 24-6.

Reviewing the game, the coach saw improvement, but raved about four touchdowns without a single successful point-after. "How do you hope to win a close ballgame?" he bellowed.

The following week, Catfish lined his offense up on the three-yard line, the point-after stripe, and then folded the right side of the line around to defense. Right behind his first-line defenders, he placed the remaining dozen or so reserves.

"Now, offense," he called out, "let's see you make an extra point. For every time you fail, you'll run an extra lap after practice."

The result was more like a free-for-all than football. When the third attempt failed, Parchman got in a fight with Fleming, the defender who had slipped his block and stopped the ball carrier. After that, every play was followed with a scrape of some magnitude. To everyone's surprise, Catfish did not complain about the fighting. He just bellowed at the offense, telling them that they could make the three yards every time if they wanted it bad enough.

After an hour of that, the coach pulled the right side of the line around to offense and put the left on defense, again supported by the full cast of reserves, and the battle continued. Though the offense never converted more than one out of four attempts, the coach was pleased. After all, in the first two games, they had made only one of eight.

Friday night the Tigers traveled to Mineola, their first real test, and Catfish was worried. He had worked his team so hard that week, he knew they were worn out and banged up. Besides, Mineola was probably as good as any team on their schedule, maybe the best.

Starting the first quarter, Mount Vernon kicked to the Yellow Jackets, and the defense held. The Tigers received the punt on their own twenty-four-yard line. The first play moved the ball forward two yards. The next ended with a jarring tackle that shook the ball loose. Mineola recovered on the Tigers' thirty-six.

On first down the Yellow Jackets ran the ball to the twenty. Six more running plays produced a touchdown, and Mineola led by six points.

The Tigers found only two options for moving the ball. Caudle, running out of the fullback position, pounded into the line for tough yard after tough yard. Taking advantage of the new passing rule whereby the quarterback was not required to drop back five yards before tossing the ball, Cody found he could pop quick aerials to his ends, especially Dickerson, for easy yardage. However, every drive fizzled, whether by fumble, penalty, or incomplete pass.

With time running out in the final quarter, the Tigers recovered a Yellow Jacket fumble only twenty yards from pay-dirt. Catfish's boys knew this was their last chance to tie or win the game. Looking much like they had while running the extra point drill all week, time after time Caudle smashed into the mass of Yellow Jacket defenders. To the left behind Parchman and young Zimmerman, then to the right behind Rogers and Fleming, the Tigers moved the ball forward three and four yards at a time until it rested on the one-yard line. While breaking from the final huddle, eleven confident Tigers hurried to the line of scrimmage knowing they were going to score, but at that moment the game-ending gun sounded, finalizing the score at 6-0, Yellow Jackets.

Unlike Pierce from the regional champs, young Cody had huddled his team after each play, losing valuable seconds.

Walking to the dressing room, editor Devall caught up with Catfish and asked his assessment of the game.

"I can say this for my boys," the coach said, lengthening his stride, "we didn't miss a single extra point tonight."

In the dressing room, Catfish paced back and forth among his silent players, sitting with their heads down.

"Tonight," the coach said, "you boys showed the fighting spirit of a champion. I'm prouder of you right this minute than after either of your two wins. Now, this one's over. Next game we play our first district opponent, so lift those chins and tell me who we're gonna beat."

"Deport, Deport, Deport!" his players yelled, jumping to their feet.

The wake had become a celebration. These Tigers had earned the respect of their coach tonight, and he was no ordinary coach. He knew what it took to win a championship.

18

October 5, 1945

After two weeks of upbeat practice, the Tigers took the field against the Deport team, a new member of District 19-A. From the prior two basketball seasons, the Tigers knew several of the opposing players: McDowra, the Westbrook brothers, Skaggs, Bailey, Bell, McLemore, and Hulett. The tough competition in round-ball had created a sense of rivalry beyond just another league opponent.

Deport kicked off to the Tigers to start the fray, and Mount Vernon returned the ball to their own thirty-seven. From there they took off on an eight-play drive that ended with a four-yard touchdown plunge by halfback James Cherry, who had his best showing of the season. Cherry then added the point-after.

Receiving the kickoff, the visitors moved the ball to their forty-nine-yard line before having to punt. Cody returned the wobbly kick to the Tigers' thirty-five from where he led his team on another scoring jaunt, this one culminating in a touchdown by halfback Russell Adams. The quarterback then tossed an aerial to Cherry for the point-after.

Again the Tiger defense stifled the visitors' offense, mostly on spectacular tackling by young Gene Fleming. Deport punted again, setting up the Tiger offense on their forty-yard line. The fans went wild when, on the first play from scrimmage, James Cherry took a handoff, split through the defenders' line, and sprinted sixty yards to pay-dirt. This time Cody lobbed the ball to Dickerson for the extra point.

The impotent Deport offense failed again, and kicked the ball back to the Tigers. For the first time in the game, Catfish's boys could not generate ten yards on three downs and faced a fourth down situation. They lined up to punt the ball away, but Deport managed to block the kick, setting up their offense only eighteen yards from the Tigers' goal line. To compound their problems, Mount Vernon's defenders committed three infractions that helped the visitors to advance to the Tigers' three-yard line. There, Catfish's defense stiffened, and the Deport team ran out of downs with the ball stuck on the three-yard stripe. The half ended with the Tigers leading, 21-0.

After holding the visitors on their first offensive attempt in the second half, the Tigers scored again on a fifty-eight-yard rumble by Caudle. Cody then tossed to Dickerson for the point-after.

Following the kickoff, Deport took the ball to midfield on one of their better offensive efforts, but there they stalled. Their punter got off a high spiral that bounced out of bounds on the Tiger eighteen, but bad field position did not daunt Catfish's boys. On first down, Caudle romped eighty-two yards for his second long touchdown run.

With the Tiger reserves taking the field, the Deport team fared no better, and faced another punt. Herb Zimmerman, the Tigers' young left guard, broke through and blocked the kick, then pounced on it after it had tumbled back to the visitors' eleven-yard line. From there, reserve Wallace Hunnicutt slashed through the enemy line for a score.

The visitors made one last valiant effort to put points on the scoreboard, but the march fizzled at the Tigers' forty-eight. From there they punted the ball to Mount Vernon's twenty-six-yard line. The Tigers then tried a flashy new play in which the quarterback went in motion to the right. The ball was hiked to Cherry who, after drifting a few steps to his right, pulled up and winged a spiral to Russell Adams for yet another touchdown. The extra point made the score 47-0.

Young Kenneth Meek accounted for the final Tiger tally midway in the fourth quarter on a four-yard run, capping a fifty-eight-yard drive. Another pass to Dickerson for the point-after bumped the final score to 54-0.

In the dressing room following the game, Catfish immediately reminded his young team that Deport's effort was not typical of a District 19-A opponent.

"Forget this game right now," he stressed, and then repeated his saying about the perils of falling in love with a win. "We've got Winnsboro next week, and I've been told that they defeated Mineola tonight, twelve to nothing."

The Tigers had not forgotten that Mineola had beaten them earlier, the one mar on their record. Thus the coach's message was clear: the Winnsboro Red Raiders would be their toughest opponent yet.

Regardless of what Catfish told his players, he was not quite ready to file away and forget the Deport game. He wanted his young Tigers to face up to the challenge ahead, but also he made sure they knew that he believed in them.

"We're headed into a four-game stretch that will make or break our season," Catfish told the *Optic-Herald* reporter. "Some folks will look back at our game against Mineola and conclude that we don't have a chance against Winnsboro, but that would be overlooking the fact that we're an improved team."

Catfish then noted that several young players had stepped up big in the win over Deport, both linemen and backs. Fleming, Zimmerman, Lowry, Rogers, Gilbert, and Pittman, along with the seasoned Parchman and Dickerson, had provided a solid front wall. The bigger area of concern, the backfield, looked hopeful, also. James Cherry, Russell Adams, Wallace Hunnicutt, Joe Zane Condrey, and Kenneth Meek had given James Caudle, the workhorse, some relief in lugging the ball, while quarterback Cody had shown progress, especially in completing passes.

Shaking a clenched fist, Catfish privately dangled the underdog carrot in front of his players. "How satisfying it is to win when nobody thinks you can do it."

The Red Raiders were the first hurdle, but then Mount Pleasant, Pittsburg, and Gilmer followed them. If Catfish could somehow coach his boys to victory in these key contests, he was confident of finishing the schedule with wins over Talco and Clarksville. Winning a district championship with his young upstart team would require a masterful coaching job, and he could already taste the sweet satisfaction.

First, he had to take his Tigers to Winnsboro and defeat a team that statistically outranked his by three touchdowns.

"Boys," he explained to his players at Monday's practice. "We lost to Mineola by six points, a team Winnsboro beat by twelve. We've got to play eighteen points better than we did in Mineola just to break even with the Red Raiders."

When the *Optic-Herald* editor reminded Catfish that his Tigers had defeated Winnsboro 52-0 the prior season, the coach jumped to his feet.

"That was a different team," he bellowed. "Only three players from our regional championship bunch will be on the field Friday night. Besides, the Red Raiders are a better team than their last year's bunch. They're not only undefeated, they haven't allowed a single touchdown this year."

Catfish would not allow the newsman to spoil his underdog role.

200

If his pessimistic assessment was wrong, the coach wanted his players to prove it on the gridiron.

The game began with the two defenses dominating until the second quarter when James Cherry's punt pushed the Red Raiders back to their one-yard line. Unable to fight their way out of that hole, Winnsboro booted the ball only to their thirty. Five plays later Caudle and Cherry had rammed the ball down to the Red Raiders' three-yard line. From there, Caudle exploded into the middle of the line, but fumbled. Fortunately, the pigskin squirted into the end zone where Leacho Tittle fell on it for the score. A Cody to Cherry pass added the point-after.

Taking the kickoff, the Winnsboro eleven moved the ball to their forty-four before bogging down. Cody returned the opponent's fourth-down kick to the Tigers' thirty-three. On first down, Cody again went in motion, and the ball was snapped to Cherry who tossed a pass to Tittle to the forty-five. After that bit of trickery, the Tigers bulldozed their way across the goal line with Cherry carrying for the final two yards. With only seconds remaining in the first half, Cody passed to Pittman for the extra point, making the score 14-0.

Again in the third period, the defenses dominated play, leaving the score unchanged. Early in the final period, Mount Vernon pushed the ball to the Red Raider thirty-yard line, and then fumbled the pigskin away. From there Winnsboro began their only successful march of the game, featuring quarterback Vance Vogle. The final two yards came on a pass from Vogle to King, and the point-after failed.

The Red Raider celebration would be short-lived.

Cody received the Winnsboro kickoff on his own twenty-one and followed his blockers upfield. When it looked like he would be tackled about the forty-yard line, Caudle laid a jarring block on a Red Raider who tumbled into the legs of two of his oncoming teammates, taking them down, too. Cody scored, untouched, puncturing Winnsboro's ballooning hopes.

Desperate to make a quick comeback, the Red Raiders took to the air, but Russell Adams soon threw a wet blanket over that plan with an interception on the Tigers' forty-three. Penalties then pushed Mount Vernon back to their own twenty-three, leaving them with second down and thirty yards needed for a first down. James Cherry solved that problem with a spirited jaunt out to the forty-seven, followed by a Caudle run to the Red Raiders' twenty. Again a penalty pushed the Tigers back ten yards, but after a nine-yard run by Cherry and a Cody pass to Pittman, the ball rested only two yards from the goal line. After a one-yard gain, Cody sneaked in and finished the scoring for the night. The Tigers had captured a twenty-point win, 26-6, one of the most impressive coaching efforts of Catfish's young career.

The victory came at a price, however, as Leacho Tittle had been forced out of the game with a knee injury that would sideline him for an indefinite time. Compounding the Tigers' problems, in practice the following week the starting center, Charles Lowry, broke his shoulder while making a tackle, putting him out of the lineup for the remainder of the season. Fortunately, several running backs had shown promise and could take up the slack in the backfield, while an older, but much lighter, Billy Grau would step in at center.

At about two-thirty on Monday morning, the fire alarm woke most of the town. Flames had engulfed the McGill & Grau grocery, market, and café, housed in the Cecil Davis building. Faulty wiring was blamed for the fire that destroyed all stock and fixtures of the business, which were only partially covered by insurance, leaving reopening in doubt.

Young Billy Grau, eager to prove himself worthy of his new starting role, showed up at practice on Tuesday, apparently unaffected, and Catfish pushed his Tigers to focus on the next opponent, the Mount Pleasant Tigers. Regardless of won-lost records or season expectations, these two teams seemed to always battle each other more ferociously than they did any other opponent. This game would be no different.

Playing in Mount Pleasant, the first half turned into a war between two powerful forward walls. The closest Mount Vernon came to a score was a drive to the sixteen-yard line of the host Tigers, while the Mount Pleasant boys fought their way to the visitors' twenty-one.

During halftime, Catfish decided that pounding his runners into the line was not going to produce a win. He told his quarterback to look for opportunities to pass the ball to his ends, Pittman and Dickerson.

After Fleming kicked the ball to Mount Pleasant, the black-and-gold Tigers gained only two yards on three runs, so they punted the ball to Cody standing back on Mount Vernon's twenty-two. On the first play, Cody threw to Dickerson out to the thirty-eight and a first down. The quarterback followed that with a strike to Pittman to the host's forty-nine. With the defense leery of another pass, Cody then repeatedly gave the ball to Caudle and Cherry who churned down to the Mount Pleasant seven-yard stripe. After three runs and only three yards to show for it, the purple-and-white Tigers huddled and planned their final attempt to break the scoreless deadlock. Remembering his coach's halftime advice, Cody zipped a pass to Pittman for the score, but then another for the point-after failed.

Through the remainder of the third and halfway through the fourth quarter, the two teams battled but neither could advance to the other's end zone. The game might have ended that way except for a bone-rattling hit by George Dickerson on the Mount Pleasant quarterback. Two-hundred-pound Frank Parchman claimed the fumbled ball on the enemy's thirty-three-yard line, giving Mount Vernon their best shot at adding to their point total.

After Caudle failed to move the ball on a run, Cody again looked to Pittman, his left end, who snared the pass at the Mount Pleasant twenty. That loosened the defense, and Caudle then rambled down to the three-yard stripe. When the sturdy fullback plunged into the line again, he was tripped up at the line of scrimmage. Once more Cody abandoned the run and tossed to Pittman for the touchdown. Caudle then hammered into the end zone for the point-after, and the Tigers had a hard-earned 13-0 lead, a score that would stand until the final whistle.

On Saturday morning, Devall ambled down to the Miller Hotel and took a seat beside Catfish who was enjoying a cup of coffee.

"You've got your third district win," he said. "What was the key to this latest one?"

"Our linemen," the coach responded immediately. "They shut down Mount Pleasant's offense and blocked good enough for us to score a couple of times."

"Any standouts?"

"Parchman was outstanding," Catfish said smiling. "And Dickerson made a picture-perfect tackle on their quarterback that sealed the deal. But I want to mention Fleming, Rogers, and Grau, too. With the family business destroyed and his first start, this was a big game for Billy. He plugged the hole in the dike for us."

"Pittsburg is next," the editor said. "You whipped them forty to nothing last year."

"Don't you mention that in the paper," Catfish said wryly. "I've got a young team, and I don't want their heads growing faster than their abilities."

Friday's paper carried the usual article about the previous week's win and a buildup for the game to be played that night. As requested, the editor did not mention the forty-point win of the prior season, but praised the Tiger players as not only good athletes, but outstanding young men. The writer went on to say that Mount Vernon had two superb coaches, Milburn "Catfish" Smith and Acie Cannaday. "They are second to none," the article claimed.

Pittsburg had more than the purple-and-white Tigers to worry about. On Sunday morning a tornado hit their town, ripping through the northwest section, injuring thirty-three and claiming the life of Sam Bynum while leaving eight other residents in critical condition. Twenty-five homes were destroyed, several businesses damaged, electricity and telephone lines downed, and the hospital was operating by candlelight.

The outlook for the damaged city did not improve on Friday night when its Pirates invaded Mount Vernon. The Tigers scored early and frequently on their way to a 47-0 win, their fourth district victory in a row.

On Mount Vernon's second play from scrimmage, James Cherry scampered forty yards for a touchdown. That was quickly followed by a stout Tiger defense that forced a Pittsburg fourth and long. The punter fumbled the deep snap, and a Tiger gobbled up the loose pigskin on the Pirates' thirty-five. Caudle plowed ahead for ten yards on the first play and scored on the second. A Cody to Dickerson toss made it 13-0.

After again holding the inept Pirate offense, Cody slipped the ball to Caudle who blasted his way through the enemy line for a fifty-four-yard score. Cody to Dickerson made it 20-0 at halftime.

The second half began much like the first. Caudle hauled in the Pirate kickoff on his twenty-one-yard line and headed the other way. Seventy-nine yards later, he crossed the goal line. That score was followed by a Pirate bungled punt attempt on their forty-yard stripe. The Tigers, mostly made up of reserves now, marched to another score with Cherry and Meek accounting for most of the yards. Cherry finished the drive from six yards out.

When Pittsburg received the kickoff and tried to pass, Meek intercepted on the thirty-five and hustled back to the Pirate twenty. Caudle then ripped up the middle for his fourth touchdown of the game.

With the third quarter waning, the Pirates' offense stalled on their own thirty-six. They punted to the Tiger twenty-six. After reserve Joe Zane Condrey rushed to the thirty-seven, Wallace Hunnicutt circled left end and sprinted fifty-eight yards to the enemy's five-yard stripe. Condrey then covered the last five steps, and Hunnicutt made the extra point, accounting for the Tigers' forty-seventh point.

The final stanza passed quietly, and the Tigers had their fourth district win. Catfish's reserves played much of the second half, and a new star appeared on the horizon.

"Young Gayle Tinsley," Catfish said, "had a great game. He's smart, and pound for pound, he's as tough as I've ever seen."

Upon watching the Tigers' fullback, James Caudle, decimate their defense with runs of twenty-five, fifty-four, seventy-nine, and twenty yards, the Pittsburg people complained, "he's Swede Crowston's shadow." Wearing the Swede's jersey, number twenty, Caudle not only looked like his predecessor, but had begun to punish defenses like the blond Norseman.

By Saturday morning, Catfish had heard enough accolades. Gilmer was next on the schedule, and based on the Buckeyes' record, the victors in Friday's contest would, in all likelihood, ultimately wear the district crown. The coach might not be able to sell his Tigers as underdogs, but he emphasized that the upcoming game would separate the "winners from the wishers."

Anyone who had ever played for Catfish Smith could have told those boys what their week of preparation would be like. The man lived for championship contests. He thrived on competing against the best. He was in his element, and his players would join the heat of battle, even if he had to prod and poke them there, using every motivational scheme he knew.

Just in case all the inspirational mumbo jumbo did not work, Catfish put in a few new plays, actually adding options to plays already in their repertoire. One alteration was to the quarterback-in-motion play where halfback Cherry received the snap and drifted to his right as if to pass. When the defense dropped back to defend the aerial, Cherry was to pull the ball down and run. Another addition was to put Cherry in motion and have Cody throw him a sideline pass. The last was a fake punt by Cherry on fourth down, a play he was told to try if faced with a critical short-yardage situation.

In Friday morning's *Optic-Herald*, Charles Devall deemed that the "pre-game dope has Gilmer a slight favorite in a score-scarce contest." Catfish certainly did not question the newsman's source, though it was most likely homegrown. If nothing else, it proved the editor knew his coach.

Well before the kickoff, the stands creaked under a mass of fans, the fence around the field swayed with spectators hanging on its top rail, and the gates bulged with more coming in. Bands played, drums beat, and car horns honked. The dew-kissed turf glistened under the added floodlights, streamers atop the goal posts rippled in the soft north breeze, and cheerleaders jumped, yelled, and turned cartwheels. Then the players, like a stampede of buffalo, romped onto the field amid a thunderous cheer.

Gilmer kicked to the Tigers to open the game, and Cody gathered in the pigskin on the goal line and brought it out to the twenty. Three running plays pushed the line of scrimmage to the Tigers' forty-five and a first down. Three more plays put the ball on the Buckeyes' forty-six, setting up fourth down and one. Too early for the fake punt, Cherry decided. Besides, the Tigers' running game was working, so the rehabilitated Tittle was given the task of gaining that tough yard. He came through, along with twenty-eight more around left end, making it first-and-ten on the Buckeye seventeen. Then, with the opposing defense set for the run, Cody called the special pass play to Cherry. The halfback went in motion to the right, cut upfield when the ball was snapped, and blew by the defensive back as Cody faked a handoff to Caudle. The quarterback then stepped back and lifted a spiral toward the goal line. Cherry pulled it in as he crossed the double-stripe. The critical point-after failed, but the Tigers had the lead.

Clark of Gilmer received the ensuing kickoff on his left sideline, reversed field, and set sail, stopping in the far end zone. With a successful point-after, the Buckeyes could take the lead, but it was not to be. The Tigers stuffed a quarterback sneak, leaving the score deadlocked.

Following a couple of defensive stands, the Buckeyes found themselves facing fourth down at midfield. Their punter lifted a high one that rode the wind into the end zone, giving the Tigers the ball on their twenty. On the first play, Caudle lugged the ball out to midfield. A couple more runs moved it down to the thirty-five of Gilmer as the quarter ended. After a five-yard penalty, Cody again called the motion pass to Cherry. Again it worked, and the Tigers led, 12-6. Caudle made one of his most determined runs to convert the extra point, breaking three tackles before he crossed the goal line.

On the kickoff return, like lightning, it looked like Gilmer would strike again in the same place, but the runner was finally hauled down on the Tigers' forty-five. Mount Vernon's defense stiffened against the Buckeye running attack, pushing them back to the forty-six after two plays. A third down pass was broken up, but a back-breaking interference call against Mount Vernon gave the Buckeyes a first down

206

on the Tigers' seventeen. Gilmer immediately threw another pass that was hauled in by their left end, Hogg, who raced into the end zone. This was the first time this Tiger eleven had given up more than one touchdown in a game. The point-after knotted the score, 13-13, and that is how the half ended.

Well into the third quarter, the Tigers began a march from their own twenty-two. The key play of the drive was a twenty-four-yard gain on the Cherry fake pass, especially designed for the Gilmer game. With the ball on their own forty-six, Caudle fought for twelve yards down to the Buckeye forty-two. After sending Adams into the line with a run, Cody once again called the motion pass to Cherry. For the third time it worked, moving the ball to the Gilmer four-yard line. Caudle rammed into the line three times before he found a slight crevice of light and wedged through for the touchdown. Determined that Caudle was the Swede reincarnated, Cody once again gave it to him for the crucial point-after, and the tough fullback rewarded his quarterback's trust.

The Tigers had reclaimed the lead, 20-13, with a power running attack, but after the scoring play, Zimmerman, their tough left guard hobbled off the field with a torn hamstring. Not only was Herb a powerful blocker, he also was a fierce tackler, and more than ever, the Tigers needed their defense to shut down the Buckeye offense.

On the kickoff, the Tigers held the Buckeye return man short of midfield, dragging him to the turf at his own thirty-five. However, in two plays, Gilmer moved the ball to their own forty-eight, and then hit a big one down to the Tigers' twenty-eight-yard line. There, Mount Vernon held for two plays, bringing up a crucial third down. With the Tiger reserves exhorting their teammates on the field, Fleming trapped the Buckeye ball carrier for a two-yard loss, bringing up fourth and twelve. Even with Catfish's defense expecting a pass, Gilmer completed one to the Tigers' fifteen and a first down. A stubborn Mount Vernon defense gave ground grudgingly to their nine-yard line, bringing up another key fourth down. Clark then took a pitchout around left end and fought his way into the end zone. Determined to protect their one point lead, the Tigers gathered along the line of scrimmage, but Clark again foiled them, sneaking in for the score-knotting point.

The Tigers took the kickoff and began one more long drive. Play after play, they moved the ball forward, but the clock was ticking away. Finally, the Tigers reached the Buckeye's eleven-yard line. They tried two passes to the end zone, but both failed and time expired with the scoreboard showing a 20-20 tie.

The players filed into the dressing room, their heads hung in disappointment and frustration, and waited for their coach, knowing a tie did not settle anything. In their coach's mind, were they winners or wishers?

Catfish ducked through the doorway, smiling. "Boys, if you beat Talco and Clarksville in your next two games, tonight's game is as good as a win."

The tiebreaker was penetrations, the number of times a team crosses its opponent's twenty-yard line, and Mount Vernon held a 4-2 advantage.

What his boys heard registered in their minds, but it did little for their emotional state. They had allowed Gilmer to chalk up three touchdowns and had failed to score at the end of the game with the end zone within easy reach.

Catfish knew his team should defeat Talco without a serious challenge. That left Clarksville, a team they had defeated 47-0 the prior year. Just two more wins, and his Tigers, a rebuilding project, would repeat as district champions.

When the Tigers showed up for practice Monday afternoon, Catfish knew he had a problem. Regardless of what he said, his players could not shake the disappointment of allowing the Buckeyes to tie them in a crucial game. They were disappointed in themselves, and nothing but a district championship would drive out that sick feeling.

Friday blew in on a cold northeast wind, while Catfish penciled in replacements for the injured Pittman, Rogers, and Tittle and his ill quarterback. Somehow he had to patch together an offense that could whip a Talco Trojan defense that had given up only one touchdown all season. That single score had come at the hands of unbeaten Gilmer, so if the Tigers should falter tonight, they could wave goodbye to the district championship.

After kicking the ball to the Trojans, the Tiger defense held. Talco punted to Mount Vernon's thirty-five, from where Caudle and Cherry made steady gains until the ball rested on the opposing three-yard line. Cherry then ran through a hole in the left side of the line so large he could have walked in backwards. Caudle pounded the line for the extra point, and Catfish smiled for the first time in a week.

Until near the end of the first half, the two vaunted defenses dominated play, but then the Trojans' quarterback, Dickerson, unloaded a long pass to Nugent all the way to the Tigers' twenty-yard line. The end snagged the pass behind Mount Vernon's defense and scampered in for the score. Suddenly, at the midpoint of the game, Talco was in a position to tie the score.

With a stadium full of fans on their feet, holding their breath, the Trojans lined up to kick the extra point. The center passed the ball back to the holder who had trouble with the hard, cold pigskin, but he got it set in time for the kicker to get his toe into it. Meanwhile, George Dickerson and Pat Loyd came crashing in from their end positions, heading for a point four feet in front of the kicker. With their fully extended arms coming together to form a mesh-like screen, the ball rose to head-height and then caromed off to the side. The Tigers went into halftime leading by one point, 7-6.

The third quarter brought more problems. The Trojans moved the ball with apparent ease against a defense that had consistently shut down more potent offenses, and reached the Tigers' ten-yard line before stalling and having to hand over the ball.

By then a cold rain had begun to fall, negating the Tigers' passing game, but Caudle and Cherry hammered away on runs until they had worked the ball away from their goal line. Still, the Tigers could not maintain a drive and had to punt the ball away. Again Talco marched down the field, reaching the Tigers' ten this time. On a desperate fourth-down play, the Trojans tried a pitchout around right end, where the ball carrier broke two slippery tackles and was headed for the end zone when Russell Adams flew out of nowhere and cut his legs from beneath him. It was the third time Adams had been the only line of defense between a Trojan ball carrier and a touchdown.

Taking over on downs, an ailing Cody fed the ball to Caudle and Cherry, and once again they worked the ball away from the Tigers' end zone, but as before they could not sustain the drive and had to punt.

Between the Tigers' defense and the miserable weather, Talco could not mount another assault on Mount Vernon's goal, and the game ended with the Tigers capturing their fifth district win without a loss.

Just one more victory, and the Tigers would wear the District 19-A crown again, an accomplishment no one, other than Tiger fans blinded by loyalty, would have predicted back in September.

19

November 11, 1945

On Saturday morning, Catfish rose early and drove to the Miller Hotel for breakfast. Before going inside, he stepped over to the *Optic-Herald* office and grabbed a copy of the paper, which he scanned while eating. After delivering his country boys to their parents, he returned home and slid the paper across the table toward Dorothy Nell who put down her coffee cup and began flipping through the pages.

"Rutherford Drug Store is giving free New Testaments to children," she said, pointing at a notice. "I think I'll go get one."

"I don't believe you'll have much luck passing yourself off as a child, honey," Catfish said, laughing.

"We'll see," she replied smugly.

Later that morning, the two of them drove downtown to do some Christmas shopping. Dorothy motioned for her husband to park in front of Rutherford Drug Store. She then headed for the door, Catfish hurrying to open it for her.

"I would like one of the New Testaments," she said to the druggist.

"But what child is it for, Dorothy Nell?" G. W. Rutherford asked.

"This one," she said, patting her flat stomach and glancing up at Catfish.

While her dumbstruck husband stood open-mouthed, the druggist reached into a box under the counter and handed over a red-letter New Testament.

"Congratulations to both of you," Rutherford said.

"Are you saying . . ." Catfish stammered, staring wide-eyed at his smiling wife.

She nodded while looping her arm through his and headed for the door, but near the entrance, Catfish pulled Dorothy Nell aside, shielded from view by a tall shelf loaded with medical supplies. He wrapped his arms around her, and for a couple of minutes, they remained in a tender embrace. The coach had been so occupied with the football season, school, and his boys, that he was totally surprised by the news.

"If it's a boy . . ." he said as they got to the car.

"Wait!" she interrupted. "First, it just might be a girl, but even if we have a boy, you'll first be his daddy, not his coach."

Their shopping plans quickly changed to looking at baby things and maternity clothes. That afternoon they drove to Mount Pleasant for more shopping, stopping by Winfield on the way back. After checking on Catfish's mother, they drove to the old farm south of town. Catfish told Dorothy Nell how as a child he had climbed and played on the Indian mounds, and he showed her the old tree where his father had attached a barrel hoop for him to practice basketball.

"What got you so interested in basketball?" Dorothy Nell asked.

"The Doris Candy Kids," he replied.

"Who?"

"When I was just a kid, old Dr. Taylor built a gym north of Jim Beck's store," Catfish explained. "The Doris Candy Company sponsored a basketball team coached by D. R. Lilenstern. How those boys could play ball. They took on anybody who came to town and almost always won."

"Did you play for them?"

"No. I was too young, but Roger Bounds, Tobe Thomas, Joe Mehane, G. A. Taylor, C. S. Taylor, R. A. Tetter, Bunyon Reed, and Little Howard Cody did. I loved to watch those fellows play basketball."

"I suppose I can see how a boy might get excited watching his friends win all the time."

"And the cheerleaders," Catfish said, shaking his head.

"They had cheerleaders?" Dorothy Nell asked, sensing a tall tale.

"Mary Miller was the cutest one," he replied.

"What ever happened to her?"

"Oh, she went to summer school and skipped ahead of my grade. Then she went off to college. Made a school teacher I heard, and taught over at Possum Trot."

"Possum Trot?" Dorothy Nell said, snickering. "I don't believe a word of it."

"She married a fellow named Russell Smith," Catfish said, staring ahead. "Brakes failed when he was crossing a bridge over near Cooper, wrecked his car, and killed him. Mary had to get away from the memory, so she moved out to West Texas, Midway I think, and taught oilfield kids."

Dorothy Nell slid over close and leaned her head against his shoulder, neither one talking for a while.

"Now," Dorothy Nell finally said, as they headed back home, "I'll tell you about when I was a little girl, so you'll know what to expect from your own."

Catfish smiled as he stretched his arm across the back of the car seat and looped it around her shoulders.

*   *   *

About eight o'clock the following Monday morning, Mal Moore, cashier at the First National Bank, and another worker pulled into the parking lot behind the building as usual. As they approached the rear entrance, they spotted the bank's janitor, Dan Snell, crumpled against the base of the door, clutching his blood-soaked midsection. They grabbed up the unconscious man, laid him in the backseat of Moore's car, and sped away to Crutcher Hospital. While the doctor tended to the janitor's multiple stab wounds, a nurse called the police, and Moore hurried back to the bank. After determining that the bank had not been robbed, the banker traced the trail of blood, which led to the Cotton Belt train depot two blocks to the southwest. The police then joined the search and quickly identified the crime scene at the northeast corner of the depot, but found no witnesses. With the victim in no condition to provide any leads, the police searched for evidence while the townspeople became increasingly concerned.

Typically, Snell would have let himself into the bank about four that morning and performed his cleaning chores, finishing before eight o'clock. Since the trashcans inside the bank had not been emptied, the investigators concluded that Snell had been attacked as he arrived, some four to five hours earlier. Also, Snell's key to the bank was missing. Had his assailant intended to rob the bank? Where was the bank key? Would the assailant return later, or was a personal vendetta involved?

Later that day, Snell regained consciousness and vaguely described his assailant as a poorly dressed man whom he did not recognize. Attacked from behind in the darkness, he had seen almost no details that would be useful to the police in identifying the assailant. Furthermore, no one else had seen a man fitting the given description around the depot or knew any such person. Snell had been following his regular route to work, walking alone beside the depot, when the man had jumped him. Adding to the confusion, Snell could not recall what happened to the bank key.

With the townspeople nervous that a vagabond killer might be loose in town and others concerned that a bank robbery could yet be attempted, the police posted a watchman at the hospital to guard against a second attack on Snell and at the bank during its closed hours.

The next day, everyone sighed in relief when the investigator found the bank key in some weeds under the edge of the depot, and within days, the excitement had faded as Snell's condition dramatically improved and a man assumed to be the assailant was apprehended for vagrancy while snooping around the train depot in nearby Mount Pleasant.

While most of the local fans were distracted by the stabbing incident, Catfish went about preparing his team to face Clarksville for the final district game. The one-point scare at Talco had renewed the Tigers' focus, bringing a crisp and spirited effort to their practice sessions. The close call also shook fan confidence, though the coach assured them his young team would bounce back. To help the cause, Catfish added another trick play, one that would become a mainstay of his future teams and a point of considerable controversy among opposing coaches. He called it the "stingaree" play. Upon taking the snap from center, the quarterback would turn counterclockwise as if to hand the ball to the right halfback on a slant play to the left; however, as he turned, he would slip the ball into the hands of his big left guard, Gene Fleming, who appeared to be pulling to block. With all backfield motion toward the left, Fleming would sneak down the line and around right end, hopefully undetected by the defense.

On Friday night, Catfish's boys quickly rewarded the fans that arrived early, braving a strong southerly wind. Tiger fullback, James Caudle, went on a rampage, scoring twenty unanswered points in the first quarter.

The first time Caudle touched the ball, he raced forty-four yards to pay-dirt. His other scoring runs covered twenty-four and fourteen yards, and he accounted for the two extra points on punishing runs through a stunned Clarksville defense.

Catfish's boys added another touchdown in the second period, coming at the end of a sixty-yard drive led by Cherry, Cody, Condrey, and even Fleming who rumbled for twelve yards on the tricky stingaree play. From the one-yard line, Cody sneaked across the goal line, and Caudle added the point-after, running the score to 27-0 at halftime.

Later, George Dickerson returned a short Trojan kickoff to the Mount Vernon forty-yard line. After only a couple of runs, Caudle broke loose for thirty-eight yards down to the enemy's ten. After Adams came up one yard short of the end zone, Cody followed his center across the goal line. Caudle added the point-after.

Late in the third period, the Tigers pounded out eighty yards through the Clarksville defense for their final counter. Condrey and Caudle did most of the work, but another stingaree by Fleming brought the crowd to their feet when the big guard churned out twenty-seven yards. Cherry capped the drive with a four-yard scamper to pay-dirt, settling the score at 40-0.

The closest Clarksville came to a score was a drive that took them to the Tigers' thirty-eight, where the march stalled and the visitors tried to punt. A Tiger lineman broke through and blocked the attempt, putting the final stitch in the victory pennant.

Amid the excitement of clenching the district championship, young Gene Fleming's performance gave notice of his emergence as a Tiger star. Beyond his offensive efforts, the big lineman turned in strong defensive play, and his booming kickoffs repeatedly pinned the Clarksville offense within the shadow of their goalposts.

The win gave the surprising Tigers their eighth victory of the season against the non-conference loss to Mineola and the bitter tie with Gilmer. More important than that, Mount Vernon was the undisputed champion of District 19-A, pitting them against the Atlanta Rabbits, winner of District 20-A, for the bi-district title.

"Boys," Catfish said in the locker room, "you deserve all the credit. With so little experience, no one believed you could do it, but you have proven that the will to win, which is the heart and soul of a champion, is the most important ingredient in competition."

He let his players whoop and holler over their victory, then he quieted them, determined to focus his young, upstart team on the next goal.

"Now, you can't be satisfied with a district championship. The Tigers of last year raised the standard; they set the expectation for all following teams. So, put this game behind you and start thinking about that bi-district title right now. Boys, there are thirty-nine other district winners in Texas Class A football. There will only be twenty bi-district titleholders. You can put yourselves among that elite group with one

214

more win and, at the same time, grab the chance to be a Regional Champion."

"On to bi-district!" Catfish bellowed, while thrusting his clenched fist high over his head. His players mimicked him, and thus he took their attention away from their district accomplishment and focused them on the goal ahead.

*   *   *

Officials from Mount Vernon and Atlanta settled on Mount Pleasant as the site for the bi-district contest, to be played on Friday night at seven-thirty.

Then a damper was put on the upcoming contest when the Tigers learned on Wednesday morning of the misfortune that had befallen their rival's town. A fire in downtown Atlanta had destroyed ten businesses, leaving damages estimated at $300,000. Thought to have started in the Atlanta Electric Company facility, the neighboring town was in shock.

Meanwhile, Catfish set his priorities for the coming four days of preparation. First, he wanted to develop a fervor in his boys for the bi-district title. To do that, he continued the elite-twenty theme he had used after the prior game. Second, he focused on repetition of plays and the use of backup players. He wanted them to know their assignments without thinking, and he wanted substitutes ready in case of an injury to a prime player. Third, he emphasized the importance of the point-after. Playoff games tend to be close, and he did not intend to lose by one point because his team could not convert from three yards out.

Catfish must have pushed the right buttons.

After Cody ran the initial kickoff back to the Tigers' twenty-eight, Caudle bulled his way for twenty yards. Cherry then dazzled the Rabbits' defense for thirty-six more, down to the Atlanta sixteen. Caudle and Cherry then pushed the ball to the nine where Cherry ran an off-tackle slant into the end zone. Caudle bulldozed in for the point-after and the Tigers had struck first blood.

After kicking the ball to the Rabbits, Parchman rattled the opposing quarterback with a jarring tackle, sending the ball spinning backwards to the fourteen, where he pounced on it. On two runs, the Tigers hammered the ball down to the four-yard line, and an apparent first down, but the Tigers committed a holding violation on the play and were penalized back to the fifteen. An incomplete pass then brought up fourth down, and a golden opportunity to score now depended on one desperate play.

Cody sent Cherry in motion, faked a handoff to the hard-charging Caudle over right guard, and then tossed a spiral toward the goal line where Cherry ran under it and waltzed into the end zone. Again Caudle found a seam in the defensive wall and made the point-after, inflicting the second wound.

Then on the final play of the first quarter, the Rabbits fumbled again, and George Dickerson gobbled up the ball only nineteen yards from pay-dirt. Cherry ran for six yards and Cody for four, placing the ball on the nine-yard line. From there, Cherry duplicated his earlier run, and the Tigers had left a third scar on the Cottontails.

After receiving the kickoff, Atlanta moved the ball with passes, reaching midfield before bogging down. On third and seven, the Rabbits surprised the Tigers with a quick kick that rolled dead on the six-yard line.

Caudle pushed it out to the ten with two runs. Trying to repay the favor given them, the Tigers tried a surprise kick, but the Rabbits' Coulter Kennamer, a burly lad, anticipated the trick, retreated quickly, grabbed the bounding ball, and returned it to the Tigers' thirty. There, Mount Vernon's defense stiffened and pushed the Atlanta offense back to the thirty-nine, from where the Rabbits countered with a pass to a towering Duncan Thompson who thundered into the end zone, nicking the Tigers' heretofore unblemished hide. Kennamer added the point-after.

Mount Vernon grabbed the ensuing kickoff and took it out to the thirty. Caudle, Cherry, and Adams battered away at the Rabbits' line for sixty-five yards, setting up a first down on the enemy's five-yard stripe. Cherry, seemingly unstoppable, made it look easy from there, and Caudle again pleased his coach by hurtling into the end zone with the point-after, making the score 27-7 at halftime.

Atlanta gained some revenge starting the second half. The Rabbits methodically pounded away with Coulter "Mule" Kennamer, sustaining a sixty-six yard march to pay-dirt. The burly Cottontail then added the point-after, bringing his team within two touchdowns and a conversion of tying the score.

Following the kickoff, Atlanta's inspired defense held the Tigers and forced a punt. With a quarter and a half remaining to play, the Rabbits had recovered from a bruising first half, and were set to drive for another score. Now, the championship-minded Tigers must meet the challenge or allow the momentum to swing to their opponents.

The determined Rabbits pounded their way to midfield, where Fleming and Kennamer collided in the hardest hit of the night. When the bodies were untangled, the Tigers had recovered a loose ball near midfield. From there Caudle, Cherry, and Adams attacked the opposing defense with renewed ferocity. Behind solid blocking, the Tiger runners racked up two first downs and had a fresh set of downs at the four-yard line. Rather than hand the ball to Caudle, Cody followed his center, Grau, into the end zone. Caudle failed to get in for the extra point, but the Tigers had recaptured control of the game, 33-14.

For the remainder of the contest, Mount Vernon's forward wall, led by Dickerson, Gilbert, Rogers, Parchman, and Fleming, did not allow the Rabbits past their forty. When the gun sounded, the Tigers were bi-district champs and headed for the ultimate game, the Regional Championship.

True to his nature, Catfish challenged his boys to move up one more notch, from the elite twenty to the select few. After the convincing defeat of Atlanta, the Tigers felt they were no longer a bunch of upstart underclassmen. They were a legitimate contender.

Edgewood played Commerce to decide who would face Mount Vernon for the ultimate championship, and the Bulldogs easily defeated the team the Tigers had overpowered in the 1944 regional game. Edgewood and Mount Vernon school officials then met to determine the site, date, and time of the contest. Edgewood insisted on a coin flip to see whether the game would be at Mount Vernon or on their home field. The Tigers won the toss, and set the contest for two-thirty Friday afternoon at Tiger Stadium.

As he had done the previous season, Catfish reached his Commerce contacts for information about the Edgewood team.

"They're a talented bunch," he was told. "Their forward wall averages only one hundred and forty-seven pounds, but they're scrappy. They have a bruiser of a fullback in James Ray Edwards, who weighs one-ninety. But Reggie Gilbert at quarterback and Judd Ramsey at halfback are the wheels on which that team rolls."

Beyond that Catfish learned that the Bulldogs win or lose running the ball.

Devall's game-morning article proclaimed Edgewood, based on past games, a slight favorite over the Tigers. However, the article went on to mention a bigger problem. Several of Mount Vernon's players had missed three days of school and practice with influenza. "Several substitutes will be forced to play," he quoted the coach as saying.

Though his backups had performed well, Catfish already had a weakened team with Lowry out of the lineup with a broken shoulder, Tittle and Pittman hampered with knee injuries, and Zimmerman nursing a torn hamstring. Billy Grau had performed admirably at center, Russell Adams had filled in at halfback, and Mack Gilbert, a two-hundred pounder, had come in at right tackle, allowing Fleming to move over to Zimmerman's left guard slot.

With a hopeful crowd filling Tiger Stadium on the afternoon of December 14, the Bulldogs kicked the football to Mount Vernon to start the game. Running their first play from their twenty-eight-yard line, disaster struck when Cherry was gang tackled after advancing the ball five yards. The football popped out, and Edgewood grabbed it only thirty-two yards from pay-dirt.

As scouted, the Bulldogs hammered away with Ramsey, Edwards, and Kenneth Gates running the ball nine straight times, the latter reaching the end zone. Gilbert added the extra point, and the visitors quickly had a seven-point lead.

With Caudle sidelined with fever, Cherry and Adams picked up the ball-carrying load for the Tigers. Catfish's boys moved the ball steadily, but sorely missed the bruising punch customarily provided by their fullback. The first quarter ended without a change in score, but well into the second period, the Tigers put together a drive and pounded the ball down to the enemy six-yard line. From there, the swivel-hipped Cherry scooted into the end zone. Without Caudle to ram home the point-after, Cody tried a pass that fell incomplete, leaving the Tigers with a one-point disadvantage.

The remainder of the first half and through the third period, the Tigers' defense held the Bulldogs at bay while the Mount Vernon offense made several valiant efforts to catch up, each falling short.

In the final stanza, with the clock ticking away, the Tigers again failed on third down near midfield. Facing fourth down, Cherry booted the ball forty-seven yards to the opponent's five, but the Bulldogs' scrappy Judd Ramsey brought it back to the twenty-two. With the Tigers' defense set to stop the Edgewood running game and grasp one last opportunity to score, Reggie Gilbert, the Bulldogs' quarterback, crossed them up with a pass to Robert Hooks, his left end. Russell Adams finally chased down the one-hundred-sixty-five-pound receiver at the Tigers' twenty-four, a huge fifty-one-yard gain. Returning to the ground game, the Bulldogs fought their way to a first down on the eleven. A pitch out around right end to Ramsey pushed the ball down to the one-foot line from where he needed only one more try to ram his way into the end zone. The extra point put the Bulldogs up by eight, pushing the game out of reach.

With less than two minutes remaining in the contest, the Tigers tried desperately to score, but the Bulldogs met their challenge. The game ended with the Tigers losing 14-6, unable to match the accomplishment of the great 1944 Tiger team.

Catfish lauded praise upon his young Tigers, telling them he was every bit as proud of them as if they had won the championship. Indeed, he was pleased with their season, and as he told his assistant coach, Acie Cannaday, "We couldn't have expected more from this young team, but if our boys had all been healthy, I believe they would be regional champions right now."

*   *   *

Sunday evening, December 16, brought devastating news to the citizens of Mount Vernon. Dr. Zack Fuguay, after practicing medicine locally for thirty-five years, serving on the school board for more than twenty years, and on the board of stewards at the Methodist Church for thirty years, succumbed to heart failure at six forty-five. Typical of this faithful medical servant, he spent his last minutes on this earth preparing to make a call on one of his patients.

Born September 12, 1887 at Hopewell, a small community south of Mount Vernon, he had graduated from Tulane University prior to completing his medical degree at Baylor Medical College in 1910. He and his wife, the former Myrtle Kidwell, were two of the town's most revered and devoted citizens. At his funeral service Tuesday morning, Reverend Mann remembered the doctor as one of the most respected and unselfish men ever to grace any community. "No man ever held himself to a higher standard of ethics, better performed his duties as a citizen, or was more humble than Dr. Fuquay," said Devall in the *Optic-Herald.*

In small towns such as Mount Vernon, a few citizens like Drs. Fuquay, Fleming, and Chandler, along with businessmen like L. D. Lowry, Jr., M. L. Edwards, Sr. and Jr., G. W. Rutherford, Lester and Roy Smith, Jeffy Meredith, four generations of Teagues, and the Bolger brothers, Dave and Rufus, dramatically affect the quality of life. Such

219

unselfish leaders, with their time, money and influence, see that their town flourishes, that it provides a stimulating social environment, that its citizens rise to overcome community disasters, and that its schools offer a superior education. When one of their civic giants is taken from them, the townspeople close their businesses, come to pay tribute, and mourn their loss. The death of Dr. Zack Fuquay was such an occasion.

Fortunately Mount Vernon had ample leaders, and upon the loss of one, it seemed that another soon stepped up. Emerging business leaders such as Landon Ramsay, Hoffman Moore, Finley Moore, Charles Teague, and Bill Meek stood at the threshold.

Currently the town had two major issues facing it. They desperately needed a new post office building to accommodate the one hundred fifty-four percent growth in mail traffic over the past ten years, and at the urging of city leaders, Congressman Wright Patman had headed the fight to secure $95,000 for a Federal Building and Post Office to be located in Mount Vernon. The second was a new hospital. The Crutcher facility, originally a private home, was forty-years old and woefully inadequate. The citizens signed petitions asking the Commissioners Court to call an election for approval of the construction of a $50,000 hospital.

Meanwhile, the weekend brought a challenge of another kind to Catfish and Dorothy Nell. The stress of the playoffs had irritated his stomach ulcers, causing bleeding which he had not mentioned to anyone. Saturday night the pain became unbearable, and Dorothy Nell rushed him to Crutcher Hospital where Dr. Rouse explained that most likely one of his ulcers had perforated.

"You've lost a great deal of blood," the doctor explained. "I recommend you get to Dallas in a hurry. Without proper treatment, you could be in serious trouble."

20

December 15, 1945

Dorothy Nell's brother was out of town, so she called Reverend Whitt and asked for help. The pastor agreed to drive them to the Medical Arts Center in Dallas, where Dr. Rouse had arranged for a physician to see Catfish.

Riding in the back seat with Catfish's head in her lap, Dorothy Nell hardly said a word during the trip to Dallas. Upon arrival, Reverend Whitt opened the car door for her and noticed her hand trembling.

"Are you all right?" he asked.

"Just feel faint," Dorothy Nell explained.

The pastor quickly waved over an attendant and requested a wheel chair, which he helped Catfish into and wheeled him into an examination room. After a few questions and a check of the patient's vitals, the physician gave Catfish medication to curtail the bleeding and to ease his pain. With Catfish sedated and asleep in room 1638, the doctor recommended that Dorothy Nell return home and check back later.

"He's going to be all right, but he'll likely be here three or four days," the physician explained.

"I'm concerned about his wife," Reverend Whitt whispered to the physician. "Coming over here, she got sick at her stomach and about fainted on me."

"Either fright or motion sickness," the doctor guessed, unaware of her pregnancy. "I can give her something for the queasiness."

When Dorothy Nell felt better, she and her pastor headed home. Driving along in a cold, dark rain, the pastor observed Dorothy Nell's gloominess.

"Now, don't you get sick on me again," he teased. "I've got to get back and prepare a sermon for tomorrow morning. I don't want to have to leave you out beside the road and hope some Good Samaritan comes along."

"I thought *you* were my Good Samaritan," she replied weakly.

"That's right, but if you'll remember, he took his patient to an inn and left him. I guess I could leave you at one of these farm houses along the road."

"He also offered to pay the bill," she said, forcing a smile.

"I guess I could take up a collection at church. Your friends might pitch in enough to pay for your room and board."

"I'm feeling better already," she said.

"That's good. Now, what do you recommend I choose as the subject of my sermon for tomorrow?"

"Healing," she said.

"Healing ulcers?" the pastor asked. "Why, from what I hear around town, your husband can walk on water. Getting over a little ulcer or two shouldn't be a problem."

"Even the Apostle Paul had his thorn in the flesh," she replied.

"And he prayed to have it removed," the pastor said. "I guess that's what we'd better do for your husband."

"It didn't work for Paul. He had to live with it."

"And maybe your husband will have to learn to live with his problem."

"Sometimes I think it's God's way of telling him to slow down."

"That could be," the pastor said as he pulled into the Smith's driveway. "If so, that means He plans for your husband to hang around down here a while longer."

"I sure hope so," Dorothy Nell said, stepping out of the car. "Thank you so much for your help."

With Catfish in the hospital a hundred miles away, Dorothy Nell slept fitfully, and rose early the following morning. In addition to household chores and checking on her husband, she had agreed to gather up and wash the boys' basketball uniforms. Her first step was to ask Olan Ray Brewer, the team manager, for help.

On Sunday afternoon, Dorothy drove out to "Little Brewer's" to get a key to the storage room where the uniforms were packed. Olan did not have the key, but guessed that George Dickerson did. As she turned the car to leave, the rear wheels sank in an area softened by recent heavy rains. After a half-hour delay, she got back on the road and finally located Dickerson, who quickly recruited Gayle Tinsley, Leacho Tittle, and Kenneth Meek to assist. The boys sacked up the uniforms and loaded them into the trunk of Dorothy Nell's car for her to take home and launder.

After visiting Catfish Monday morning, she spent the afternoon washing and drying basketball uniforms. That night she sat down and wrote a letter to her husband. She missed him, but was glad he was receiving the care he needed. She explained how worried she had been when he had been doubled over in pain. "But soon you'll be home and feeling fine," she wrote. She ended by telling him that Brother Whitt had talked to Dr. Rouse who guessed that Catfish would not be released until Thursday. She promised to write again Tuesday night, then signed off with an expression of her love.

By Thursday, the Medical Arts physician had eased Catfish's pain, but before releasing him, he warned the patient to eat right and avoid stressful situations.

While Catfish recovered from his ulcer problems, his assistant coach, Acie Cannaday, handled the basketball team. With Glenn Pierce, Harry Jack Pugh, J. C. Cannaday, Swede Crowston, and Charles Hogan, his great 1945 team, all having graduated, Catfish had to find five new starters. As with his football team, it promised to be a challenging season.

To build a team, Catfish brought in some country boys. Billy Rex Cody came from Winfield, Pat Loyd and Robert Banks from Hopewell, while Mack Gilbert, Glynn Minshew, and Russell Adams lived in south Franklin County. The coach arranged for rooms in town for those that needed one, with Minshew and Adams staying with Pat and Loraine Scott who lived right across the street from the high school.

Mack Gilbert, the six-foot-two, two-hundred-pound tackle from the football team, proved to not only have the size but also the skills to play center on the basketball team. Young Pat Loyd, whose older brother had been an All-State player on the 1944 squad, quickly fit in at forward. Billy Rex Cody became the other forward, while Glynn Minshew was solid at guard. Either the fleet Russell Adams or powerful Gene Fleming could fill the second guard position. James Cherry, a lanky boy with deceptive speed, pushed constantly for a starting position at guard or forward.

With time lost to the extended football season and the coach sidelined with health problems, the untried Tigers' basketball team appeared to be in trouble. No one understood this better than Catfish who fretted and fumed to the point Dorothy Nell threatened to take him back to the hospital.

Lacking the willpower to completely stay away from the game, Catfish dropped by the gym one Tuesday night and watched the elementary basketball team play. Since Jack Henry's return from military service, the principal had taken an intense interest in athletics and had a fine squad. Catfish watched as Billy Jack Meredith, number eighty-eight, Johnny Moore, number eighty, Leon Maples, number seventy-five, Larry Edwards, number seventy-four, and Stanley Jaggers, number seventy-eight, trounced their Saltillo opponent. Meredith was the tallest player as well as the best ball-handler on the court. Catfish smiled, sure that he was watching future Tigers who would one day win a varsity championship of their own.

*   *   *

With the war over, rationing lifted, and young men returning from the military, business boomed in the little town. The number of ads in the newspaper was at an all-time high. Crescent Drug Store advertised Shaffer lifetime fountain pens for ten dollars. B & L Groceries had five pounds of sugar for thirty-seven cents, five pounds of flour for forty cents, and fifty pounds of Robin Hood flour in a print bag for two dollars and sixty cents. Charles K. Devall offered six months of the *Optic-Herald* for eighty-five cents, while the Lady's Shop advertised Sue Ann blouses for two dollars and ninety-eight cents. Parchman & Meredith sold print dresses for less than two dollars and Big Smith work pants for less than three dollars. M. L. Edwards listed men's blue Chambray work shirts for a dollar and sixteen cents. McGill and Grau, their business having burned in mid-October, reopened their grocery and café operation on the west side of the square. The Joy Theatre listed *Sunset in Eldorado* with Roy Rogers, *Anchors Aweigh* with Frank Sinatra, and *Kiss and Tell* with Shirley Temple.

Soon after the arrival of the new year, County Judge A. C. Moffett announced the approval by the Commissioners Court of the issuance of $50,000 in hospital bonds to support a new medical facility to be located north of town along the east side of highway thirty-seven. The court set the vote for March 2, and with Catfish's recent bout with ulcers and Dorothy Nell's pregnancy, they became big supporters of the project.

Meanwhile, Hoffman Moore had sold his dairy when his cattle became infected with bangs, opened a Ford dealership on the north side of West Main, and moved his family to Mount Vernon. He replaced the deceased Dr. Fuquay on the school board, joining L. L. Thomas, furniture dealer and president, Roy Smith, druggist, Jeffy B. Meredith, dry goods, W. H. Bruce, former newspaperman and farmer, and C. E. Harvey, undertaker.

Of special interest to Catfish were Moore's three sons, Dewey, Dale, and Johnny, along with Meredith's two boys, Billy Jack and Donnie. Dewey, a freshman, was on the basketball team and had already indicated his interest in football, while Dale's sports exploits as a seventh grader had come to Catfish's attention, as had those of Billy Jack and Johnny, though only sixth graders. In Mount Vernon organized teams of football and basketball started as early as the third grade, usually coached by the grade school principal. As reward for a winning season, Principal Henry took a group of his boys to a college basketball game in Commerce. By the time these "future Tigers" would reach high school age, they would have completed five or six years of competitive sports, the better ones having distinguished themselves in town through articles in the *Optic-Herald*. Athletics in Mount Vernon was more than a pastime, its star athletes more than students.

With three to five inches of snow on the ground, more than one hundred citizens attended the football banquet held on Monday night, January 14. After the meal and crowning of Patsy Irby as Football Queen, Charlie Brown, again county agent after having returned from his military duties, spoke to the players and guests. Brown praised the coaches and players for their extraordinary accomplishments, and then compared the training and development of athletes to that of drilling and preparing soldiers for combat. Having commanded Navy gunners onboard a Merchant Marine supply ship during the Normandy invasion, his comments carried considerable weight with the locals. Catfish then continued the theme when he emphasized the need for early development of both the spiritual and physical sides of young men, preparing them for life's sobering challenges, and the ideal role athletics can play in the process.

By then the basketball Tigers, without a single starter from the prior season, had already won their first three district contests and were looking ahead to a highly favored Gilmer quintet on Thursday night.

Catfish's inexperienced squad defeated the more celebrated visitors by a score of 23-20. Though Mount Vernon trailed most of the game, a late scoring flurry led by Pat Loyd, who scored back-to-back goals, pushed the Tigers ahead. With a one-point lead and time running down, Glynn Minshew dribbled the ball down against a harassing Gilmer full-court press. As Minshew made a quick move to evade a defender, the Buckeye stuck out his foot and tripped him. Angry, Glynn jumped to his feet, anticipating a foul call against the defender, but no whistle blew. After chasing the offending Buckeye down court, Minshew stole a pass and again headed for Mount Vernon's goal. Determined to get even, he darted and dashed back and forth until the clock showed only three seconds. Suddenly, he slipped past the defender and let go a thirty-foot shot. Watching the ball arch upward and begin its inevitable descent, the fans stood and held their breath until the ball swished through the net. The gun sounded, and the upstart Tigers had defeated the favored Buckeyes. Big Mack Gilbert led the team in scoring with seven points, followed by Loyd with six and Billy Rex Cody with five.

After losing a non-district contest to Blossom, 24-23, the Tigers prepared to meet Deport on Tuesday, January 22. This would be the second Tiger game against an undefeated conference opponent within a week.

Again the Tigers passed the test, winning by a lopsided score of 43-20. "Cheezy" Gilbert tossed in eighteen points, only two less than the entire Deport team, while Loyd added nine, Cody eight, and Minshew six. The victory left the Tigers with only two more district opponents, Clarksville and Pittsburg, in the round-robin style of play. Neither of these upcoming rivals had won a district contest.

With his history students, Catfish continued to monitor postwar events such as the trial of Lieutenant General Masaharu Homma, the commander of Japanese forces in the Philippines in 1941 and 1942. After some discussion, the majority of the students concluded that Homma was as responsible for the unnecessary deaths of American and Filipino soldiers on the forced march to Camp O'Donnell as those who actually wielded the bayonets and swords against their weak and diseased prisoners.

Back in late January 1945, Catfish had told his students about a special Rangers force, a highly trained group of volunteers, making a miraculous rescue of over five hundred survivors of the Bataan Death March who were imprisoned at Cabanatuan. Images of the malnourished skeletal forms still burned in the minds of many Americans, anger lingering even a year later.

General Tomoyuki Yamashita had recently been found guilty of hideous war crimes and sentenced to death by hanging in Manila, Philippines. The general appealed to the United States Supreme Court, claiming an unfair judgment against him. Chief Justice Stone refused to interfere with the trial and sentencing by the military tribunal. When the Japanese general asked President Truman to intervene, he ignored the plea, sealing the wartime leader's doom.

Meanwhile, Rudolf Hess, Hermann Goering, Julius Streicher, and Franz von Papen were held in Nuremberg, Germany and charged with war crimes. In Landes Haus, German doctors, nurses, and administrators who had run the mental institution at Hadamar, Germany, were on trial for the mass murder of five hundred Polish and Russian slave laborers. On every front, the price of waging war was still being paid.

The students showed little sympathy for those on trial. Catfish pointed out that if the United States had lost the war, our own military leaders, such as Generals Eisenhower, Patton, and MacArthur, would likely be facing similar judgments. The students saw differences: the Germans and Japanese had initiated war and had committed inhumane acts against their victims. Yet, the class acknowledged that the bombing of German cities and the atomic destruction of Hiroshima and Nagasaki must undoubtedly be considered war crimes by our enemies.

Catfish pressed the point, citing the sanctions against Germany and splitting up of that proud country, until he felt his students could fully appreciate the ramifications of war, even those that linger well beyond the fighting.

On a happier note, Catfish took delight in announcing to his students that Sergeant A. O. Loveless, who had avoided the Death March and joined Filipino guerilla fighters, had recently returned home. His three-year ordeal, though not yet fully revealed, was surely the stuff from which books and movies are made.

With February's arrival, Catfish's boys kept winning and soon were headed into the district tournament in Clarksville, undefeated in conference play. Even with James Cherry substituting for Pat Loyd, who had an injured foot, the Tigers qualified for the finals by defeating Bogata 34-17, receiving a forfeit from Gilmer, and whipping Mount Pleasant 27-22.

Facing Talco in the finals Saturday night, the Tigers trailed 16-10 at halftime, but in the third quarter, young Cherry broke loose for seven points, putting Mount Vernon ahead. The Tigers followed that with twelve points in the final period to capture the district title, 29-22. Mack Gilbert led all tournament scorers with thirty-nine in the three games.

With a 22-3 record for the season, and another basketball district crown, Catfish gave credit to his assistant. "Early in the season, I dumped the whole thing in Acie's lap," he said, recalling how Cannaday had taken over while he lay in a hospital bed. "He's done a great job. Acie's an ex-Tiger and that explains everything."

Competition for the bi-district title pitted Mount Vernon against the Hooks Hornets in a two-of-three series, with the first game scheduled for Tuesday night at seven-thirty on Mount Vernon's court.

The Hornets, coached by Roland Loyd, former Mount Vernon player and older brother of Pat, proved too much for the young Tigers. Mount Vernon then traveled to Hooks for the second game, losing a heartbreaker by one point. Typical of Catfish, he made up his mind right then to get Hooks on his basketball schedule for the following season. He would not be satisfied until his Tigers had defeated the Hornets.

*   *   *

In the early morning hours of a Saturday in late February, the ringing of his phone stirred Catfish from his sleep. Dorothy Nell was up and reaching for the receiver when her husband finally became coherent enough to comprehend the situation. She kept saying, "Calm down, mother, I can't understand you."

"What's the matter?" Catfish asked, bailing out of bed.

"Mother says it looks like the whole south side of town is on fire," she said.

Catfish jumped in some pants and headed for the door. Looking toward town, he spotted a huge red and orange glow reflecting off heavy clouds, making the fire look larger than it was. Checking closely, Catfish could see that the fire was very close to where Dorothy Nell's family lived on Holbrook Street.

"Let's get on over there," Catfish said, rushing back inside.

"Mother, we'll be right there," Dorothy Nell said, and hung up.

As they turned onto Holbrook, Catfish immediately saw Dave Bolger's car dealership engulfed in flames and smoke. The size and proximity of the blaze to the Penn's home, combined with its reflection off clouds, undoubtedly created the illusion that Lizzie Penn had described on the phone.

With the street blocked by police and firefighters, Catfish and Dorothy Nell parked and headed for her parents' home on foot. By the time they arrived, Frank had checked out the fire and had calmed Lizzie, so Catfish eased over to where Dave Bolger stood.

"I'm sure sorry about this," the coach said, hardly knowing what to say to a man watching his livelihood go up in smoke. "Any idea what started it?"

"Not sure," Bolger said, "but I don't think it was electrical or anything like that. It might be related to the robbery I had a while back. Somebody broke in through the back window, and it looks like the fire started back there."

"What'll you do?"

"Get another location and open back up as quick as I can."

Within days Catfish heard that Dave Bolger had purchased land on the northeast corner of the square, facing south, and would be opening his Chevrolet dealership there.

No sooner had Bolger got his business open than on Sunday night, March 3, McGill & Grau's new Grocery and Café business burned on the northwest corner of the square, their second fire in less than five months. This time they estimated their loss at forty-five hundred dollars, while M. L. Edwards, the building owner, guessed his at seven hundred fifty. On the heels of that disaster, Thursday, March 7, Dave Bolger died in a car accident near Bogata, leaving his family and friends in shock. Only forty years old, Bolger left his wife, Henrielen, better known as "Snow," alone with young David, Jr., to raise without a father's help.

A year that had started so promising had suddenly turned dismal for the citizens of Mount Vernon. Though no one could have known at that time, this tragic event would lead to the establishment of an automobile dealership in Mount Vernon that would become an icon of the town's durability and steadfastness and would still be flourishing over half a century later.

21

March 8, 1946

Early Friday morning, Catfish dropped by the *Optic-Herald* office, picked up his allotted stack of newspapers, and headed for school. Seated at his desk before students arrived, he opened the paper and scanned a few articles.

H. B. Zimmerman, Bronze Star veteran of the war in the Pacific and older brother of Herb Zimmerman, had returned home in December 1945. A civilian again, he and Carolyn Majors had recently been issued a marriage license. Also, Dr. W. H. Daubs, general practitioner and surgeon, had opened an office in Crescent Drug Store, and Hiram Teague and his son Charles had begun the process of acquiring the Chevrolet dealership from Snow Bolger, a business soon to become Teague & Son Chevrolet.

Also, the newspaper announced the start of spring football drills, along with a review of Catfish's three-year coaching accomplishments at Mount Vernon. In three seasons, the Tiger coach had won twenty-four football games while losing only four, each loss by one touchdown or less, and had captured two district titles, two bi-district crowns, and one regional championship. In basketball, his teams had won seventy-four games while losing only nine, with two district championships, two bi-district crowns, a regional title, and runner up to the state champion in 1944.

Then Catfish turned the page and noticed the Joy Theatre advertisement. *Sheriff of Cimarron* starring Sunset Carson was listed, along with *Come Along Jones* with Gary Cooper and Loretta Young, and finally *Back to Bataan* starring John Wayne and Anthony Quinn. The last one grabbed his attention. It was the story of the amazing rescue of the prisoners of war who had survived the infamous Death March in the Philippines. The daring feat had been accomplished by a volunteer group of American Rangers and Filipino scouts.

I've got to go see that one, he thought, and I'll recommend it to my students. He felt their seeing the movie would be more educational than anything he could tell them.

While watching the heroics on film, Catfish got a chilling glimpse into what the war in the Pacific must have been like. Knowing he could have been one of those five hundred thirteen POWs rescued from a slow death of starvation and disease made it even more real, and the fact that he could also have been among the one hundred fifty American prisoners drenched with fuel and torched in the trenches at Puerto Princesa Prison Camp in December, a month prior to the Cabanatuan rescue, sent goose bumps rippling up and down his arms. That massacre had convinced the Americans that they must risk the lives of one hundred twenty-one Rangers, along with sympathetic Filipino warriors, to grab the remaining POWs before they suffered a similar fate.

That night, and several nights thereafter, Catfish lay awake reliving the story, remembering his Army Air Force buddies and wondering how many of them had endured, or succumbed to, the horrors flashing through his mind. It took spring football to shake him free of the gripping images.

Though graduation would take his starting tackles, Frank Parchman and Mack Gilbert, and his entire backfield of James Caudle, Leacho Tittle, James Cherry, Russell Adams, and quarterback, Billy Rex Cody, the coach was excited about some of his younger players. Gene Fleming, All-District the prior season, and Coy Sims would fill the tackle slots. Pat Loyd, who had played well for the injured Pittman the prior season, would join George Dickerson, All-District receiver, as the ends. At guard would be Charles Lowry and Herb Zimmerman who, prior to their season-ending injuries, had proven their worth in the forward wall. The backfield, however, posed a problem.

First, Catfish had no proven quarterback. Next, he had no runner comparable to Swede Crowston or James Caudle. Though he had a stable of fast and gritty backs in Kenneth Meek, Joe Zane Condrey, Wallace Hunnicutt, Roy Cunningham, and Buck Parchman, he lacked a proven running back.

With so much rebuilding to do, the coach treasured every practice session, feeling they were so few that he could not possibly evaluate and train his new athletes in the allotted time. He demanded that his players not miss a single one, so when Kenneth Meek played hooky one afternoon, the coach immediately sought an explanation when the sophomore showed up for practice the following afternoon.

"I went to the circus over in Mount Pleasant," Meek said, his eyes downcast.

"I hope it was worth the price," Catfish said caustically.

"Yes, sir, it was," Meek replied with an irrepressible smile.

"We'll see what you think about that after a while," Catfish said.

With the offense lined up against a stout defense, Catfish called for the attention of both units. "I want everybody to know we're gonna give the ball to Mr. Meek on every play." Then turning to Meek, Catfish continued, "Rambler, don't you stop until you've gained ten yards. If someone tackles you, get back on your feet and run some more."

By the time that practice was over, Kenneth had knots, scrapes, whelps, and bruises all over his one-hundred-ten-pound body. As he headed for the locker room, Catfish called out to him.

"Mr. Meek, I just want you to know it's going to be this way every day. I don't care if you come back or not, but if you miss one more practice, you're off the team."

Young Meek never skipped another practice.

As the spring sessions ticked away, Catfish saw a solid offensive line forming, along with some capable backups in Frank Carr, big C. L. Stroman, Robbie Cannaday, and Billy Jack Guthrie. Also, the coach got a pleasant surprise at the critical center position, where freshman Dewey Moore proved to be reliable, tough, and deceptively strong. The real shocker, however, came at the most critical position: quarterback. Catfish expected Robert Chambers, an effective runner and passer, to fill that slot, but an eighth grader, Dale Moore, showed surprising promise. The Moore-brother combination, recently from the dairy farm, would have to wait until the fall for their debut, however, as Dewey, along with C. J. Bogue and Buck Parchman, became ill and missed the game against the 1945 team that concluded spring drills.

With his ailing brother on the sidelines, young Dale wasted no time proving himself in the April 11 contest, drilling a bullet pass to George Dickerson for an early touchdown. Graduates Caudle, Cody, and Cherry soon knotted the score, but the younger boys held on, stopping the veterans until, in the final stanza, Robert Chambers came into the game and tossed a twenty-five-yard touchdown to Dickerson, sealing a victory, two-touchdowns to one.

"Though these boys were teammates a few months ago," Catfish said afterwards, "tonight they fought each other like bitter rivals. We'll field a young team next fall, but watch out. They're gonna surprise some folks."

With spring drills complete, Catfish dropped by one afternoon to see Jack Henry's elementary team, the "Little Tigers." He was shocked to count thirty-five boys ranging from third to eighth graders. Again, the standout player was Billy Jack Meredith, however, several others caught Catfish's eye: Don Yates, Dale Brakebill, Billy Clinton, Buster Simms, Johnny Moore, Eddie Turner, Billy Hunt, Glen Slaughter, and Joe Long. Catfish walked over to Henry, complimented him on his team, and then pointed to one of the younger players who showed an uncanny ability to get to the ball carrier and to bring him down, smiling and laughing all the while.

"Who's that spunky youngster?" Catfish asked.

"Don Meredith," Henry replied, "Billy Jack's younger brother."

In the Meredith brothers, Catfish saw unusual athletic talent and the nucleus for future teams. In this case, the future was much closer than the coach realized.

*   *   *

In late April, fire struck Mount Vernon again. Crescent Drug Store, owned and operated by Lester and Roy Smith, suffered heavy damage before the local fire department, aided by their counterparts from Mount Pleasant and Bogata, could extinguish the blaze. The flames, smoke, and water destroyed the entire stock of the business, along with the offices of Drs. Fleming and Daubs. The fire spread to the drug store's neighbors, the dry goods business of Parchman & Meredith and Ed Holton's auto supply. Local firefighters said that without help from neighboring fire departments, the flames could have destroyed the entire south side of the square. The cause of the fire was not immediately determined, leaving local businessmen with a growing concern.

After the citizens of Franklin County had approved the hospital bond issue in March, Dr. Daubs leased Crutcher Hospital effective May 6th and opened his office there, leaving Catfish and Dorothy Nell somewhat concerned. With the delivery of their first child only a month away, the couple took special interest in the continued operation of the old medical facility. They were somewhat relieved when they read in the *Optic-Herald* that the medical unit would remain functional until completion of the new hospital; however, their doctor recommended the Kennedy Clinic for the delivery of the baby.

Taking the doctor's advice, Catfish rushed his wife there on June 8th where Ronnie Gayle Smith, eight pounds and thirteen ounces, made his entry into their world. Naming his son after Gayle Tinsley, the father puffed up his chest and crowed as if he had performed the miracle himself; however, after a moment of reflection he saw a practical side to it also.

"I'm going to the school board and ask for a raise," he quipped. "It's one thing to coach the football and basketball teams, but it's quite another when you start raising the players."

With this new bundle of life less than a month old, Dorothy Nell received some bad news. Her uncle, Alfred "Bud" Penn, had died unexpectedly. Sixty-four years of age, he left his wife Clara, four sons, two daughters, his mother, and six siblings to mourn his passing. During the service, Dorothy Nell promised herself that she would spend more time visiting her aged parents. With their new grandson around, she need not have worried.

That summer brought more change. L. D. Lowry, Jr., purchased a huge building site on the south side of West Main. Though he did not reveal his plans, most guessed he would move his expanding business from Smoky Row down to the new location. Then the Ford dealer, Hoffman Moore, contributed a new pickup to help support the construction of a local American Legion Hall. Catfish volunteered to work the downtown area, raffling off one-dollar tickets to shoppers for a chance at winning the vehicle. The organization sold all the tickets within ten days.

With football season less than a month away, Catfish traveled to Sulphur Springs to fill the catcher position for the neighboring town's baseball team. On Catfish's first plate appearance, the Paris hurler sailed a high inside pitch that ricocheted off the coach's head, striking just above his left eye and knocking him out cold. He regained consciousness an hour later in the Sulphur Springs hospital with a large, discolored lump above his eye, blurred vision, and a headache. After observation he was released, whereupon he announced that he would be back behind the plate Friday night catching pitches from Wayne Pierce, recently returned from the Navy. The game pitted the local All-Stars against an East Texas State team. It was the sort of toughness he expected from his players.

From Wayne, Catfish learned that Glenn Pierce, his outstanding quarterback and captain of his teams for two years, would marry Gwendolyne Orren of Saltillo at the First Baptist Church in Mount

234

Vernon on August 23. On furlough from the Army base at Aberdeen Proving Grounds in Maryland, the younger Pierce, after a brief honeymoon in Shreveport, Louisiana, would then head for Seattle, Washington to be shipped to Korea for the duration of his service time. Until his return, his bride planned to reside in Sulphur Springs where she was employed. With considerable satisfaction, Catfish contacted the young couple and wished them a long and happy marriage.

By this time the coach had his football schedule set, including a couple of new opponents to raise the level of competition. First, he replaced the Sulphur Springs reserves, which had provided little challenge, with Edgewood, the team that had defeated his Tigers in the Regional game the previous season. Second, he signed up Grand Saline, another up-and-coming team.

September 12	Paris (reserves)	home
September 20	Edgewood	home
September 27	Grand Saline	away
October 4	Mineola	home
October 11	Winnsboro	home
October 18	Mount Pleasant	home
October 25	Pittsburg	away
November 1	Gilmer	away
November 8	Talco	home
November 15	Bogata	home

"My biggest concern," Catfish told Devall of the *Optic-Herald* when discussing the upcoming preseason practices, "is I have only eight days to work my boys into shape and get them ready for competition." He especially fretted over pushing his freshman quarterback and sophomore center, key ball-handlers, into battle with so little preparation time, but he had a plan. Rather than have his raw-talent quarterback call plays, he would give that responsibility to the dependable and heady Gene Fleming.

A worry that Catfish did not mention to the newsman was the loss of his trusted assistant coach, Acie Cannaday, who had become Winnsboro's head mentor. Weldon Brewer, a 1938 Mount Vernon graduate and a former Navy Lieutenant, replaced Cannaday, but could not be expected to immediately fill the considerable shoes left by his predecessor, whose experience and familiarity with Catfish's system was substantial and proven. The most recent example had been

Cannaday's leading of the basketball team back in December and early January while Catfish recuperated from his ulcer attack. Brewer, with no coaching experience, was not ready for that kind of responsibility, but with a college degree in economics and journalism, he was a public relations whiz.

Beginning Monday, September 2, the coach held two practices a day in the heat of late summer. Conditions were grueling, but most of Catfish's players were country boys who had spent much of the summer in hay fields from dawn to dusk. An open practice field, even in a one-hundred-degree heat wave, offered relief from a one-hundred-forty-degree barn loft, its stagnant air thick with dust and the pungent scent of fresh hay. Also, like bait dangled before a fish, the excitement of a new football season and the anticipation of a championship run, with its first victory only a week away, enticed the boys to endure the wind-sprints, to batter each other in blocking and tackling drills, and to practice their plays over and over until they knew them by heart.

Friday morning, September 5, Catfish scanned the newspaper before heading for football practice, and a notice caught his eye. Billy Stinson was to marry Patsy Irby that night. Billy had been a member of Catfish's 1944 state-finalist basketball team. Patsy, Tiger band member and football queen in 1945, was equally well known around town. With the war over and men returning weekly, each issue of the *Optic-Herald* announced engagements and weddings, prompting Catfish to comment to Dorothy Nell that he much preferred reading about his boys getting married rather than their war efforts.

Three days before the first game, school opened with six hundred twenty-five students, and that afternoon the team elected their captains: Gene Fleming, George Dickerson, and Charles Lowry. Fleming and Dickerson had been chosen to the All-District team the prior year, while Lowry had been the starting center until midseason when a broken shoulder sidelined him for the remaining games.

Thursday, September 12, the Paris Reserves came to town to meet the Tigers' starting lineup, consisting of George Dickerson and Pat Loyd at the end positions, Coy Sims and Charles Lowry at the tackle slots, Gene Fleming and Herb Zimmerman at the guard posts, Dewey Moore at center, halfbacks Kenneth Meek and Joe Zane Condrey on either side of fullback James Pittman, and young Dale Moore as the quarterback. The offensive line was young, but averaged a robust one hundred seventy-three pounds. Catfish had moved Pittman, one hundred eighty pounds, to the backfield to add experience and heft to an otherwise lightweight rookie crew.

"We've got a tough bunch of linemen from Hopewell," Catfish said, referring to Herb Zimmerman, Pat Loyd, Billy Jack Guthrie, and alternate tackle, C. L. Stroman. "Also, I predict that no average high school player will last a full game against Lowry, while on the other side of the line is Fleming who's almost as big and has more experience."

As in their previous meeting, the Tigers handily defeated their Lamar County opponent, 31-0. True to Catfish's prediction, his forward wall proved to be the strength of the Tiger team, clamping its jaws down on Wildcat runners before they could cross the line of scrimmage, and swatting away enemy defenders while its own fleet backs ran wild. While Catfish's ferocious defense limited the Wildcats to only four first downs, each Tiger back ran for at least one touchdown while Condrey accounted for three, including a seventy-yard interception return.

Not only did powerful Gene Fleming call plays and block and tackle like a premier district guard, he also slapped down a Paris punt, setting up a thirteen-yard touchdown run by rambling Kenneth Meek.

Though Catfish's big linemen hogged the limelight, the coach also took considerable satisfaction in the showing of his stable of speed-merchant runners. He was so impressed that the only lineup change he made for the upcoming Edgewood contest was to move James Pittman back to his end position, where he had been one of the conference's best performers the prior season. Wallace Hunnicutt then moved into the vacant fullback slot.

Friday morning when Catfish dropped by the newspaper office to pick up his quota of papers, Devall opened the top copy and pointed proudly to a full-page ad. In the spirit of the upcoming battle, the editor had worked with forty-six businesses in town to spring the surprise page, which declared war against the returning villains. "BEAT EDGEWOOD is the Battle Cry," it said in huge bold print. "Mount Vernon has not forgotten the loss of the regional title last year and now we expect to avenge that defeat." Clearly, fan fervor matched or exceeded that of the team.

Saturday morning when Catfish dropped by the hotel to pick up his country boys, Devall told him that his next opponent, Edgewood, had defeated Winnsboro by a score of 31-6. With most of the Bulldogs' starters back from their 1945 regional championship team, Edgewood looked even more impressive than a year earlier when they had defeated Catfish's boys by a touchdown. The *Dallas News* had already picked

Edgewood to repeat as the region's best, and favored them over Mount Vernon by two touchdowns in the upcoming contest. Catfish loved it.

As underdogs against the current regional titleholders, his Tigers would quickly forget their big win in the season opener, and the coach had plenty ammunition to "fire up" his players to the point of explosion.

"Our line will not be pushed around," Catfish was quoted as saying. "We have only three starters from last year, but we can still win this game."

Friday morning of the big game, another full-page ad hit the newspaper. The same sponsors urged all Tiger fans to be at the stadium and to cheer their players. They repeated their earlier battle cry, pitting the Champion Bulldog team that had "trampled" Winnsboro by twenty-six points against their Tigers who had won over Paris by thirty-one.

The game was billed to define the 1946 Mount Vernon Tigers.

22

September 20, 1946

If the Edgewood game was to be the measure of the Tigers' 1946 season, without a doubt it was to be a woeful one. Mount Vernon lost 19-6, the worst defeat ever of a Catfish-coached Tiger team. The three Bulldog touchdowns were the most that one of his teams had allowed in three years, and represented only the second time in thirty-two contests where a Tiger defense had allowed an opponent more than one touchdown in a game. However, the coach said, "I honestly didn't know I had such a good ball club. The boys never stopped fighting, and that's what makes a great team."

Reggie Gilbert, quarterback of the Bulldogs, proved to be the nemesis, running for a touchdown and throwing for two. After firing a scoring aerial to end Robert Hooks in the first half, the Bulldog passer sailed another to his other end in the second half.

Meanwhile, Kenneth Meek scored from sixteen yards out for Mount Vernon, while Condrey, Fleming, and the young center, Dewey Moore, performed admirably. The Tigers' freshman quarterback held his own until he received a solid lick to his head.

"You okay?" Fleming asked when Dale wobbled back to the huddle.

"Sure. What down is it?" the quarterback asked, his eyes glazed.

"Third and four to go," Fleming replied. "Forty-five slant on one."

As the Tigers lined up, Dale ambled up behind his offensive linemen, already in their three-point stance, but hesitated, obviously confused. Fleming looked back and told his quarterback to hurry up, and Dale headed toward him.

"Get over here," Dewey growled at his brother, having settled over the ball. "What's wrong with you?"

Dale heeded his brother and began the cadence. Dewey snapped the ball, and the linemen lunged forward. The quarterback ignored the halfback as he slid by, expecting the handoff. Instead, Dale dropped back and let go a beautiful forty-five-yard spiral. But no Tiger receiver was within thirty yards of where the ball crashed to the turf.

Startled, the Tigers huddled.

"Call the same play," Dale said, a silly smile on his face. "I'll get this one to you, Dickerson."

"Why, you're plumb goofy," Fleming said. "It's fourth down. We've got to punt the ball."

Dewey then ushered his addled brother to the sideline.

Without their quarterback and lacking a power runner, the Tiger attack was badly weakened. After the game, Catfish indicated he would evaluate Gene Fleming at fullback, and fill his guard slot with C. L. Stroman.

"At one hundred and ninety pounds," Catfish said, "Fleming is reminiscent of Bo Campbell, the two-hundred-and-six-pound fullback who led the 1938 team to the championship.

"And let's not overlook the fact that Edgewood has a fine football team. When you consider that they handily defeated Acie's Winnsboro boys, who tonight battled Mineola even-up for three quarters, you have to conclude that Edgewood is the premier team in our region. The way I look at this game, it serves as a measuring stick for us. We now know what we have to do to compete against the best.

"Another thing. We open district play in two weeks, and we'll be facing stiff competition every Friday night. Talco has whipped Daingerfield by forty points; Pittsburg has downed Hughes Springs by twelve; and Mount Pleasant got by Clarksville by a touchdown. All this indicates that we've got a solid conference this year. Also, Gilmer and Winnsboro have already won their early district contests."

The coach seemed to be the only one in Mount Vernon able to take something positive from the game and move on to the next opponent, Grand Saline, though Devall of the *Optic-Herald* wrote that the Tigers, ". . . looked good, fighting the Bulldogs to a standstill most of the game." Even the Mount Vernon players were dispirited, knowing they had disappointed their fans and had lost a shot at matching those great, undefeated Tiger teams of the past.

After a week of grueling practices, Catfish took his boys to the "Salt City" where they redeemed themselves, 34-13. The win seemed to salve the wounds of the Mount Vernon fans, and they now focused on the upcoming district games with renewed hope.

Mineola, always tough on the Tigers, was next, and Catfish saw the game as more important than the Edgewood tilt. If his Tigers could finish district play on top, they would likely get another shot at the Edgewood Bulldogs, whereas a loss to Mineola could end their hopes of an extended season. However, the Yellow Jackets, led by deluxe runner Rex Hughes, would be as rugged as ever.

While the Tigers shut down Hughes, sending him to the bench prematurely, big Gene Fleming, guard-turned-fullback, crunched Yellow Jacket defenders like a bulldozer rolling over saplings and racked up two first-half touchdowns, one a sixteen-yard jaunt. He plowed his way into the end zone on the first extra point, but failed when he attempted to kick the second.

In the second quarter, the Yellow Jackets counterattacked when Minick scored and added the extra point, but immediately the Tiger offense proved their earlier successes were not flukes. With Condrey darting one way and then another for hefty chunks of yards and Fleming pounding the line for four and five at a time, the Tigers marched almost unimpeded across enemy yard-stripe after yard-stripe. With the first-half clock winding down, Dale Moore crossed up the defense when he dropped back and sent a spiral to Condrey to the Yellow Jackets twenty-three. But, before the Tigers could run another play, the halftime whistle blew with Catfish's boys leading, 13-7.

Frustrated at failing to score on the final drive of the first half, Catfish led his Tigers onto the field for the third quarter with a scowl and a challenge to "land the first blow quickly and then keep them on their heels." Mirroring the mood of their coach, the Tiger defense smothered the opposing offense, setting the stage for the knockout punch.

Following the formula of that final first-half drive, the Tigers battered their way down to the Yellow Jacket one-yard line where freshman quarterback Dale Moore sneaked in for the score. The Tigers' bull-like fullback, Fleming, then crashed into the end zone for the point-after, and Catfish's boys led, 20-7.

From that point, the Tiger forward wall shut down the Yellow Jacket attack, and the outcome was settled. Catfish and his boys had their all-important win, and that district championship feeling was alive and well in Tigerland.

Meanwhile, Jack Henry's "Little Tigers" were playing their own schedule, with Catfish receiving weekly reports. Billy Jack Meredith, a one-hundred-forty-pound fullback was making a name for himself, and Catfish could not resist projecting ahead to the next season. With the exception of George Dickerson, the coach's entire forward wall would return, along with his speedy stable of runners. He was sure Meredith would fit somewhere in the backfield, which would allow him to move Fleming back to the interior line, where he belonged. With another year of experience, his ball club just might compare favorably to his 1944 regional champions. But for now, he had to concentrate on the Winnsboro Red Raiders, the Tigers' next district opponent.

Under their new coach, Acie Cannaday, the Red Raiders were improved, as evidenced by their earlier Mineola game and their recent 27-7 victory over Talco, a team that had defeated Daingerfield 40-0. With Winnsboro's offense built around their ace runner, Cowser, a one-hundred-sixty-pound halfback, and with Cannaday leading them, Catfish knew this contest would be like no prior one against this rival. Catfish's former assistant knew the Tigers' personnel, their playbook, including their trick plays, and Catfish's tendencies. The Winnsboro boys would sense their advantage and be sky-high.

Mount Vernon would counter emotionally with the spirit of homecoming, where Mildred Scheirman would be crowned Football Queen at halftime. Every team fought harder to win on this occasion, playing at home before an overflow crowd that included dozens of former players. Additionally, as Devall reported in the *Optic-Herald*, the district championship would likely be determined by this contest. The upstart Tigers were heading into another make-or-break game.

Catfish's lineup remained unchanged from the prior week, keeping Fleming at fullback, though Hunnicutt would substitute for him when speed was at a premium. As usual, Dale Moore, Condrey, and Meek would surround Fleming in the backfield. Loyd and Dickerson would bookend the line, while Sims and Lowry would line up as the tackles, Zimmerman and Stroman as the guards, all anchored by Dewey Moore at center. Pittman would swap out with Loyd at end, and Dudley Miller was set to kick extra points.

The game opened ominously. The Red Raiders took the kickoff and marched down the field, Cowser warranting the rave reviews preceding him. However, upon getting inside the Tigers' ten-yard line, Mount Vernon's forward wall stiffened and held, taking over on downs at the seven.

Catfish's offense attacked with Fleming and Condrey, the Tigers' version of thunder and lightning. They marched eighty-five yards to the eight-yard line of the Red Raiders and appeared unstoppable, but then Fleming plunged into the line and coughed up the ball. Subsequently, the game slowly deteriorated into a battle fought to a standstill in the middle of the field. Coach Cannaday clearly had his boys ready for the Tigers, while Mount Vernon's defenders recognized their own offensive plays in those run by their opponent. Nothing worked for either offense, the defenses essentially having read their rival's playbook.

The second half found the stalemate firmer than ever, with the Winnsboro offense garnering only two first downs, while the Tigers managed only one. When it was over, the score deadlocked at zero, each team had one penetration, and the Red Raiders had seven first downs to the Tigers' six. Should the two teams tie for the district title, Winnsboro would be crowned champions and advance into the playoffs by the slim margin of one first down.

Before the Tigers could worry about that eventuality, they had to beat the undefeated Mount Pleasant Tigers who had whipped Talco, Clarksville, and Gaston by a touchdown each, and Bogata by a whopping score of 107-0.

The first two quarters of the Mount Pleasant game looked like a continuation of the defense-dominated battle with Winnsboro. To make matters worse for the purple-and-white, Zimmerman smashed his hand near the end of the first quarter and watched the remainder of the half from the sidelines. Neither team could mount and sustain an offensive drive, but then with thirty seconds remaining in the half, Mount Pleasant fooled the purple-clad Tigers. Trice, quarterback and triple threat for the black-and-gold Tigers, was considered their best offensive weapon, but Legg, their fullback, pulled off the play of the game with a surprise pass to halfback Dooley for a touchdown. The point-after failed, and the teams went into intermission with Mount Pleasant leading, 6-0.

After a scoreless third quarter, the teams entered the last frame with Mount Pleasant holding on to that fragile advantage. Then, halfback Dooley broke loose on a twenty-one-yard run and pushed the Titus County boys' lead to twelve points, where it stayed after a failed point-after.

Catfish called to Zimmerman, standing off to the side holding his throbbing hand.

"Zim, if we put a splint on your hand and tape it up, do you think you can play?"

"Yes, sir."

The manager quickly wrapped the bruised and swollen hand with tape.

"Get in there and tell those boys we need a touchdown right now,"

Catfish said, giving Zimmerman a sendoff onto the field with a hefty nudge in the back.

The Mount Vernon boys, as if suddenly inspired by the return of their wounded teammate, marched sixty yards for a score. Hunnicutt accounted for forty-seven of those steps from the fullback position, subbing for Fleming who had proven too slow-footed to reach the temporary breaches his linemen carved out of the opponent's forward wall. Catfish desperately needed another solid blocker up front, and Fleming was a dandy. Later, the coach wished he had made the change much earlier, thinking Fleming's blocking might have changed the 12-6 loss into a victory.

The Tigers now had their first conference loss against a tie and no wins, while Mount Pleasant remained undefeated with their third district victory. The prospects for a Mount Vernon conference championship were dismal, but the Tiger faithful were about to receive even worse news.

County Agent Charlie Brown announced that an anthrax epidemic had hit thirteen counties clustered in northeast Texas, including Franklin. Cattle were quarantined with sale and movement of cows across county lines forbidden. Ranchers were required to have their herds vaccinated with the anthrax serum, which would render their cattle immune twelve days after treatment. Fortunately the medication was available at all area drug stores, and Brown helped Franklin County cattlemen with the laborious roundup and vaccination of their animals.

The countywide quarantine would remain until two weeks after all herds were treated, a lengthy process. The schedule was extended for everyone by the usual grumblers who saw no indication of the disease in their cows and preferred to isolate their herd and avoid the expense and effort. The strong-willed and active county agent proved persuasive and invaluable in resolving this problem. Meanwhile, the financial impact on the area, dominated with beef and dairy cattle, mounted daily.

One group benefited from the cost burden on some ranchers. Returning servicemen could go to C. E. Cowan, local real estate dealer, who had a list of farms available for purchase, and he would assist in getting their GI Bill loans approved. In fact, the low-interest mortgage, a small reward for their productive time lost at war and intended to speed up their re-entry into the community, applied not only to land but also to homes and farm equipment. Several local war veterans took advantage of this benefit that put more money into circulation, somewhat offsetting the impact of the anthrax epidemic.

Meanwhile, Catfish went about the task of preparing his boys to face the Pittsburg Pirates, intent on salvaging a respectable season. With Zimmerman still hampered with his mangled hand, the coach made permanent the switch of Fleming back to the line and Hunnicutt to the fullback slot. Otherwise, the lineup remained unchanged.

Friday morning Catfish's history students produced a couple of interesting topics. First, a girl pointed out that Ronnie, Catfish and Dorothy Nell's four-month-old son, had received the Scovell Award as the Outstanding Boy of 1946. Field Scovell, for whom the award was named and by whom it was given, lived in Austin, Catfish explained, and was a friend who used the award as a way to recognize Ronnie. The coach then declined to bring his now-famous son to class for introductions, as requested by his students.

The next news story dealt with the seventy-second anniversary of the *Optic-Herald* newspaper in Mount Vernon. With its beginning in 1874 as the *Franklin Herald*, the paper had been a mainstay of the community. W. H. Bruce and Charles R. Devall, age eighteen, had purchased the old *Herald* paper in 1893. The elder Devall then combined it with the *Mount Vernon Optic* in 1906 to form the *Optic-Herald*, currently owned and edited by Charles K. Devall who took over following his father's death in 1931.

"The newspaper is a business," Catfish pointed out to his students, "but it's more than that, especially here in our little town. The public service it renders to our community, the announcements, notices, and local and world news, is the best bargain in town. Without it, our field of vision would stop at our own limited horizons."

The final news item reported that the ten leading Nazi war leaders had all been hanged following the Nuremberg Trials. Only Hermann Goering avoided the noose. He took his own life minutes prior to his scheduled execution. For many it took this, in addition to the death of Adolf Hitler, to feel safe from another German-led world war.

With the Pittsburg game dedicated to Bob Suggs, the Tigers traveled to that neighboring town to take on the Pirates. After a sluggish start, the Mount Vernon boys scored four times in the second quarter on runs by Hunnicutt, Meek, and Condrey, in addition to a twenty-five-yard interception return by Fleming. Meek turned a simple dive play into a thrilling thirty-five-yard scamper, while the others were of the shorter variety. The Tigers finished the scoring in the second half when Dickerson took an end-around and sprinted thirty-one yards to pay-dirt. The scoreboard flashed 33-0 when the final gun sounded, and the Tigers had chalked up their first district win.

Next for the Tigers were the Buckeyes of Gilmer, a team the Mount Vernon boys had repeatedly struggled to defeat. The previous year the contest had ended knotted at twenty points each. Even the regional champs of 1944 had found the Buckeyes tough, winning by a touchdown on a last-ditch drive inspired by the shrewd play-calling of Glenn Pierce.

The current Buckeyes, with two wins and one loss, ranked right behind Mount Pleasant in the conference race. Led by quarterback Hoffman and halfback Nations, the Gilmer eleven must beat Mount Vernon to maintain their hopes of a district championship. Likewise, Catfish's Tigers faced a must-win situation. Always looking for an inspirational edge, the coach dedicated the game to Superintendent Fleming, a twelve-year leader of Mount Vernon schools and an ardent sports fan.

Consistent with the Tigers' recent trend, defensive play dominated the first half, which ended in a scoreless tie. Returning to the field, the Mount Vernon offense received the kickoff and drove eighty-two yards, the march ending when Fleming bulled his way into the end zone from the one-yard line. Dickerson failed on the extra point, and the Tigers held a precarious six-point advantage.

When the Buckeyes could not sustain their next drive, the Tigers took over again on their twenty-six. As they had done earlier, they moved the ball steadily to Gilmer's twenty-four-yard line, where Dale Moore dropped back and tossed a scoring pass to Dickerson. The point-after failed, but the Mount Vernon boys had a two-touchdown lead with time needed for a Buckeye comeback slipping away.

Gilmer then took off on a desperate march, led by quarterback Hoffman's passing. After completing four consecutive aerials, the Buckeyes pushed to the doorstep of the Tigers' end zone, but Mount Vernon's defense stiffened and took over on downs. Catfish's boys then easily ran out the clock and captured their second district victory, 12-0, eliminating Gilmer from the title race.

Reviewing the game, Catfish noted that his team had rushed for two hundred fifteen yards, and his young quarterback had thrown three passes, one for a touchdown, without an interception. From this solid performance against a contending team, the coach saw a rising sun on the Tigers' horizon.

The victory celebration in town was tempered by an automobile accident that had occurred during the contest. Hiram Teague and his wife, driving down highway sixty-nine in a rainstorm between Alto and Rusk, rammed their car into the rear of a logging truck. Blinded by the headlights of an approaching car, Mr. Teague lost sight of the slow-moving vehicle ahead. Realizing he was blinded, he hit the brakes and skidded into the truck, breaking his wife's arm, lacerating his own, and both sustaining severe bruises. Mrs. Teague's condition kept her hospitalized until Tuesday when she returned home in an M. L. Edwards ambulance.

This accident and need for follow-up care pointed out a medical-service vacuum in Mount Vernon. Crutcher Hospital, leased to Dr. Daubs in May, had been sold in early July to Mr. and Mrs. I. J. Welch of Santa Barbara, California, and converted into the Colonial Inn. With the opening of the new hospital facility nearly a year away, citizens of Mount Vernon would have to travel elsewhere for hospital care, throwing an ominous shadow over the growing and otherwise progressive town.

Meanwhile, Mount Pleasant remained undefeated with four district wins, and Winnsboro claimed second place, the only mar on their schedule being the tie with the Tigers. With Talco next on Catfish's schedule, the coach sat down with editor Devall.

"Does your team have anything else to play for?" the newsman asked, noting that even if Mount Pleasant should falter and Winnsboro somehow pass them, the Red Raiders held that first-down tiebreaker with Mount Vernon.

"Absolutely!" Catfish roared. "Pride, if nothing else."

"Talco has only one win," the newsman continued. "Do you expect a good game?"

"The Trojans are better than their record indicates," Catfish replied. "They've outplayed every one of their opponents, including Mount Pleasant. Another thing. They beat Gilmer nineteen-to-six while we struggled to get two touchdowns against the Buckeyes."

"Since Fleming scored the first touchdown against Gilmer," Devall said, "will you move him back to fullback?"

"No. I'll use him back there when the situation calls for it, but otherwise I'll keep our regular lineup for Talco."

Receiving the opening kickoff, the Tigers used their running game to march seventy-five yards. Hunnicutt finished off the drive with a nifty six-yard touchdown run. Fleming kicked the point-after.

After stopping the Trojans' offense, the Tigers took over at the

Talco forty-eight. With the opposition expecting a run, Dale Moore faked a handoff to Condrey, dropped back, and threw a thirty-six-yard pass to Dickerson to the twelve, from where Meek rambled into the end zone. Fleming missed the point-after.

Again the Tigers' defense held, but the Trojans surprised them with a wind-aided quick-kick that tumbled down to the Tigers' twelve. With the first-half clock winding down, Catfish's offense hurried to the line of scrimmage and snapped the ball, but in their haste, the Tigers fumbled. When the tangle of players was separated, Talco had the pigskin on Mount Vernon's fourteen. From there, Harry Dixon, a first-class speed merchant, needed only three tries to reach pay-dirt. A successful point-after made the halftime score 13-7.

The second half started with Mount Vernon's defense again shutting down the Trojans' offense. After a punt, the Tigers started another drive that reached the Talco seven-yard line, where Fleming was moved to fullback and given the ball. He rammed it across the goal line, and after missing the extra point, the Tigers led, 19-7.

The next time the Tigers got the ball, Dale Moore chunked a twenty-six-yard aerial to James Pittman, the Tigers' outstanding end of 1945. The one-hundred-eighty-pounder made a determined run to the two-yard line. Again Fleming slipped back to the fullback post and bulldozed into the end zone. Condrey ran for the point-after, but a penalty canceled it.

In the final quarter, Condrey intercepted a Trojan pass, and the Tigers marched seventy yards for the next score. Then, with the game well in-hand, Dale Moore scored on a remarkable eighty-yard run that set the final tally at 37-7.

While winning another district contest, Catfish's Tigers rang up twenty first downs while allowing the Trojans only three. Moore, Condrey, Meek, and Hunnicutt ripped off two hundred forty yards on the ground while the Tiger defense allowed only twenty-one.

The Tigers had made their best offensive effort of the season against the Trojans, while the defense had played equally well, something immensely pleasing to Catfish. With no district championship in the balance, his young club could have let down, but instead they played with a fierce sense of pride. In the coach's eyes, his team proved it had "the heart of a champion."

What had seemed a meaningless game in the district standings turned out to be significant. Winnsboro lost to Mount Pleasant, 7-6, tying them with Mount Vernon in the district standings. With a tough

Gilmer team left on their schedule, the Red Raiders stood in jeopardy of dropping to third place, if the Tigers could win their last contest. With Mount Pleasant assured of the district crown, Catfish took great pride in coming in second and avoiding the worst finish of any of his teams.

While preparing for the Tigers' final game against Bogata, Catfish read in the *Optic-Herald* that Billy Jack Meredith had led his "Little Tigers" to a tie against the Sulphur Springs Wildcats. The eighth-grader had two outstanding runs, one that took him to the opponents' four-yard line as the first half ended, and the second was a forty-five-yard scamper after picking off a Sulphur Springs aerial at midfield. Already thinking about the 1947 season, Catfish looked eagerly toward spring drills.

The coach had little to do to prepare his team for the winless Bogata eleven. Mount Pleasant had scored over one hundred points against this hapless opponent, so Catfish focused on providing opportunities for his faithful reserves.

Mount Vernon's second string started the game and played three quarters, building a 32-13 lead. Letting some of his seniors play in the fourth quarter of their final game as a Mount Vernon Tiger, Catfish's boys added twenty-six more points. Eleven different Tigers scored, including one-hundred-pound Paul Dean Gilbert. Gayle Tinsley scored twice, as did Roy Cunningham, Robert Banks, and Buck Parchman. Gene Fleming, Herb Zimmerman, Kenneth Meek, and Joe Zane Condrey each added a touchdown, but the highlight of the game came when Catfish put a uniform on his loyal business manager, Olan Ray Brewer, and sent him into the fray in the waning moments of the first half.

This slight youngster, recognized as one of the Tigers' most heady and dedicated managers ever, loved the game and long had dreamed of playing quarterback for the mighty purple-and-white Tigers. With only two seconds remaining before intermission and to the surprise and delight of Mount Vernon players and fans, Brewer dropped back and sailed a pass downfield where lanky Robert Banks grabbed it and pranced into the end zone. Olan Ray's teammates swarmed him, lifted him to their shoulders, and carried him off the field as a triumphant warrior.

Catfish's lopsided win over Bogata, 58-13, turned out to be significant. As fate would have it, Winnsboro lost to Gilmer, 27-0, leaving the Tigers alone in second place in the final district standing with four wins, one loss, and a tie. The next week Mount Pleasant, the district winner, lost its final game to the same Gilmer Buckeyes, 18-12. Ironically, only the tie with Winnsboro separated Catfish's team from first place.

While Mount Vernon's fans celebrated their football season, the local ranchers had their own hurrah. The anthrax quarantine of cattle in Franklin County was lifted after area ranchers had spent a hectic month vaccinating their herds. Renewed movement and sale of their cattle brought welcomed relief to the stockmen and economic help to the community.

In post-season voting by District 19-A football coaches, twelve Tigers were honored. Gene Fleming and George Dickerson, both repeat honorees, along with Joe Zane Condrey, claimed All-District, first-team slots. Second team selections were James Pittman, Pat Loyd, Charles Lowry, and Herb Zimmerman. Honorable mention positions went to Dewey Moore, the sophomore center, Coy Sims, Kenneth Meek, Roy Cunningham, and freshman quarterback, Dale Moore. The entire Mount Vernon starting team made the district list.

While Mount Pleasant prepared to compete for the bi-district crown against an undefeated Edgewood team that had averaged forty points per game, Catfish reviewed the two teams' records. He shook his head, recalling how Mount Pleasant had defeated his boys with a surprise fullback pass with only thirty seconds remaining in the first half. Then he noticed that his Tigers had held the mighty Bulldogs to their least offensive output of the season, nineteen points, while accounting for one of only six touchdowns the Edgewood squad had allowed.

"Just wait until next year," Catfish muttered.

23

December 7, 1946

While reviewing his basketball schedule, Catfish checked on the outcome of the bi-district football contest between Mount Pleasant and Edgewood, both likely opponents for his 1947 Tigers. Devall of the *Optic-Herald* explained that Edgewood had defeated Mount Pleasant, 26-7, leaving Terrell as the only remaining challenger to the Bulldogs' undefeated, regional-championship season. Few outside of Terrell doubted the outcome, since Edgewood had earlier whipped the Terrell eleven by a whopping 50-6 score.

With a few practices under their belts, Catfish's basketball players had him smiling. He knew he could count on Gene Fleming and Pat Loyd, both standing at six-foot-one, and he liked what he saw in the tenacious Herb Zimmerman, skillful Gerald Skidmore, and sure-shot Robert Banks, a lanky six-foot-two post player. Beyond that group, Catfish had the swift Joe Zane Condrey, fiery Kenneth Meek, and ball-handling Billy Burton, yet he faced the most agonizing dilemma of his coaching career.

Number seventeen, newcomer Maurice Campbell, showed more scoring ability than anyone else on the team. A gifted shooter, this ambidextrous kid showed basketball dexterity and savvy beyond his years. However, he was a junior transfer from Winnsboro and thus ineligible for the current season. Catfish would have to settle for watching him lead the junior varsity unit, coached by Assistant Weldon Brewer.

Campbell, living at New Hope in south Franklin County, had tired of playing his heart out with so little hope of a championship. His father was a county commissioner, which afforded Maurice the opportunity to get to know several Mount Vernon students, who were always talking about the Tigers and their district and regional titles. Maurice decided to give up a year of eligibility to play for Catfish and get one last shot at being part of a championship team, and maybe a trip to the state tournament.

With Campbell living a dozen miles from Mount Vernon, Catfish got the youngster a room at the Miller Hotel, a job sweeping up at the school, and Maurice "Bud" Campbell became a Mount Vernon Tiger.

Catfish's boys started their season by splitting games with Pickton, winning 23-17 at home and losing 21-15 on Pickton's home court. In the win, Catfish got balanced scoring from Fleming (7), Skidmore (6), and Loyd (5) while holding Pickton's leader, Parret, to four points. In the loss, his team managed only four points in the first half, finding themselves down by nine. With six points, Banks showed improved play in the second half, but no one else managed more than four points. Worse, in the win Catfish's boys committed fifteen fouls and drew a dozen, reflective of their aggressive play, but in the loss, they were charged with eleven fouls but drew only six. Appearing lethargic, the Tigers made only one of seven free throws, not what Catfish had in mind.

"How do you expect to win district when you lose a game like this?" he quizzed his players while pacing before them. "And if you should skimp through district, teams like Quitman and Hooks will run you right off the court.

"Why, Coach Brewer's junior varsity could have beaten us. If you don't play with more pride and more fighting spirit than I saw tonight, you'll embarrass your parents, your school, and yourselves.

"Boys, our fans expect more of you. I believe you expect more of yourselves, and I know I expect more of you.

"Yantis is next. If I were in your shoes, I'd make an example of them. At their expense, I'd send a message to every basketball team in northeast Texas. 'That wasn't the real Tiger team that lost to Pickton.'"

The following day in practice, Catfish was an unholy terror.

"When you miss a shot at your goal," he bellowed at mid-court with his players gathered around, "then I'd better see you hustle back and stop your opponent from making a bucket. And I'm not just talking about the shooter. You're a team on both ends of the court. Now, I want you to show me how you're gonna play the next game."

"Cut 'im off, cut 'im off," the coach yelled at Pat Loyd who was guarding a driving Gerald Skidmore along the baseline.

On the rerun of the play, Loyd shuffled his feet laterally and blocked Skidmore's path to the goal, forcing his teammate to pull up short.

252

"No, no!" Catfish yelled. "Skidmore, drive the ball on him. Don't let him take your lane to the goal."

Again they ran the play, whipping the ball around to Gerald in the right corner.

"Drive, Skidmore, drive!" the coach hollered.

When young Skidmore pulled up rather than run over Loyd, Catfish rushed over to Gerald and grasped his shoulder.

"Do you know what 'drive' means?" he asked, his nose almost touching Skidmore's.

"Yes, sir, I think so."

Suddenly, Catfish lowered his right shoulder and rammed it into Skidmore's chest, sending the young forward flying backward and slamming into the wall.

"That's what drive means! Now, let's see you drive the ball to the goal."

Skidmore never knew if in a game it would have been called a foul on him or Loyd, but when he plowed over his teammate, Catfish shook his balled fist and bellowed his approval.

"That's the determination I want to see!"

In their next game, the Tigers reflected their coach's attitude. They did not shoot well, but they played aggressively on offense and like a pack of demons on defense, beating a good Yantis team, 24-15. Fleming pitched in eight points, Loyd seven, and Zimmerman five. Their aggressive play cost them fourteen fouls and drew fifteen from the Owls, and they converted six free shots. The Tigers followed that with a victory over Winfield, 33-18, in which Loyd scored eleven points, getting help from five other players, each with at least four points. The Bearcats' high scorer, Narramore, was held to eight.

Over the holidays, Catfish gave his boys three days off, but otherwise had them practicing. The highlight for the team was a New Year's Eve volleyball tournament in the gymnasium with teams named "spring," "summer," "fall," and "winter" and players assigned to a season based on date of birth. After "spring" defeated "winter" for the championship, they then had a free-throw contest. Dale Moore, Pat Loyd, Gene Fleming, and Herb Zimmerman came through their groups undefeated. Then Zimmerman made fifteen in a row to cap the evening.

Coming out of the Christmas break, the Tigers headed into the Mount Pleasant invitational tournament. They drew DeKalb first and won, 32-24, with balanced scoring from Fleming with ten, Skidmore eight, Loyd six, and Zimmerman five. Next came Arp. The Tigers slipped by narrowly, 24-22. Fleming led with ten points, followed by Skidmore and Loyd with six and five respectively. This took the Tigers into the championship game and their first big test against the Hooks Hornets.

Hooks, coached by Roland Loyd, older brother of Pat and former Mount Vernon player, had knocked the Tigers out of the playoffs the prior year, and Catfish had hoped to schedule them for a rematch. This was the opportunity he had waited for.

Though his boys played inspired basketball, they came up short, 36-31. Pat Loyd had twelve for the Tigers and Condrey eight. Gilbert and Griffin led the Hornets with ten and nine respectively, but four other players balanced their attack, each with four or more.

The Tiger loss was disappointing, but not discouraging. Catfish's team had been down by only one point at halftime, and he saw progress by his boys against a playoff-caliber team. Each Tiger player received a silver basketball, and the team accepted the second-place trophy, but there was no celebrating because everybody knew how Catfish felt about second-place trophies.

This took Mount Vernon to their first district contest, which matched them against Winnsboro and Acie Cannaday, the assistant who had coached the Mount Vernon boys the prior year while Catfish had recovered from a perforated ulcer. Also, Winnsboro had knocked the Tigers out of the football district title race with a tie, so the competition was likely to spark fireworks.

Catfish's starting quintet had settled down to Fleming at center, Loyd and Skidmore as forwards, Zimmerman and Condrey filling the guard slots, and Robert Banks substituting at center and forward, playing about as much as the starters. Four of these were football players, and they wanted revenge.

In a hard-fought, emotional contest, the Tigers slipped by the Red Raiders, 19-18, capturing their first district victory of the season. Throughout the game, neither team led by more then two points, with Fleming tossing in the final goal at the buzzer for the win. Twenty-nine fouls were assessed, indicating the intensity with which this game was contested. The Tigers converted seven foul shots while Winnsboro made six, the difference in the final score.

As in football, the Tigers found Bogata an easy opponent, 41-10. Banks dropped in seventeen points while Loyd added ten. The Tigers then trounced Talco for their next district victory, 38-16, with Fleming accounting for eleven, Banks eight, and Skidmore seven. Pittman (7) and Jones (5) were the only Trojans with more than two points.

This led to Mount Vernon's eight-team tournament on the weekend of January 17-18. Catfish wanted a strong field, and limited the contestants to Clarksville, Yantis, Hooks, Mount Pleasant, Winfield, Linden, and Pickton. The Tigers humbled Clarksville, 24-16, in the first round. Banks (9), Skidmore (6), Fleming (5), and Loyd (4) provided Mount Vernon's points, while Taylor sank nine for the opponents. A confident Hooks team used their substitutes to defeat Yantis, 33-21, while Winfield overcame Linden, 25-21, and Mount Pleasant eliminated Pickton.

In the second round, Mount Vernon squeezed by Mount Pleasant, 23-21. Skidmore and Zimmerman racked up eight points each to lead the Franklin County Tigers, while Chastain (7) and McRea (6) headed up scoring for the Titus County boys. Then, Hooks used their varsity lineup to overcome Winfield, 25-22, bracketing the Tigers and Hornets in the finals.

With five consecutive wins under their belts, Catfish's boys anxiously awaited the rematch with Hooks, a team Catfish saw as a midseason measuring stick for his squad. However, the test became tainted when the Tigers' leading scorer, Pat Loyd, came down sick and missed the game against his brother's team.

As in the Mount Pleasant tourney finals, the Hornets prevailed, 28-21, defeating Catfish's team for the fourth consecutive time. The game was a battle with a total of thirty-five fouls. The Tigers cashed in on twelve attempts at the foul stripe, while Hooks managed only four of nineteen. Banks dropped in ten points before he fouled out of the contest with twice as many points as any other Tiger. On the other side, the Hornets had balanced scoring between Tiller (9), Griffin (8), and Templeton (6).

This time, Catfish came away upset. His Tigers did not play well, possibly being intimidated by their opponent. The coach saw no progress against this stalwart foe, and he found that unacceptable.

"I spoke to Roland Loyd after the game and scheduled another contest with his team," Catfish announced after the game. "We missed Pat tonight, no doubt about that, but we'll have him back when we see them again. Banks showed improved play, as did Meek. I expect we'll give them a better fight next time."

Well into district play now, Mount Vernon stood tall with four wins and no losses. Deport leered up at the Tigers from second place with two wins and no losses. Catfish pointed out to his boys that their upcoming opponent had recently lost by only one-point to mighty Hooks.

The district race was shaping up to be a fight between Mount Vernon and Deport, and the outcome of their next contest was sure to weigh heavily on the eventual league championship.

Whether a result of their recent loss to the Hornets or claims that Deport was the district favorite, the Tigers took the court and made a statement. "Just because Hooks beat us, don't think you can."

The Tigers almost doubled Deport, 43-22. Banks (12), Fleming (12), and Skidmore (10) dominated the scoring. Zimmerman added six, more than every Deport player other than Salters (11). Remarkably, the Tigers did it without Pat Loyd, their leading scorer.

"We have a good ball club," Catfish told the *Optic-Herald* editor, "one that can go places in the playoffs, if they keep playing like champions. Their hearts are in the game. The worry I have is overconfidence. It's ruined many good teams that might otherwise have won a championship.

"Now, we go to Gilmer Friday night, then come back here for Quitman on Saturday, and tackle Pittsburg on Tuesday. What our boys did in Deport won't make it any easier against these opponents. One at a time; that's our spirit."

"Is this the best team you've had at Mount Vernon?"

"That remains to be seen," Catfish replied. "I'll say this. If they'll play all their remaining games like they did at Deport, they won't lose another one."

"How do you prevent overconfidence?" the reporter asked.

"You lose," Catfish quipped. "So, I'd rather see a little chest-beating. They know they're good, but they aren't so sure they're the best. That's my job. I can't let them be satisfied with being good. They've got to want to be the best, to be champions."

"What conference opponent do you fear the most?" Devall asked.

"If there's one team in District 16-A that I'd hate to have to play for the championship, it's our junior varsity," he said, smiling. "They're undefeated, so far."

The Tigers traveled to Gilmer, and sneaked out of town with a two-point win, 34-32. Fleming played big with fourteen points, and a healed Pat Loyd added six, but the Tigers found Hoffman of the Buckeyes to be a handful. He pitched in seventeen points with help from Lee (7) and Richardson (5). With a combined thirty-one fouls, it was another hard-fought contest, but the bottom line was the Tigers' chalked up their sixth district victory without a loss.

A tired Mount Vernon quintet returned home to face Quitman

the next day, Saturday. The Bulldogs had defeated Hooks the prior year in the championship game of the regional tournament, and their current season's performance pointed toward a return to the state playoffs. No doubt, Quitman would be a barometer to see where the upstart Tigers stood against the elite of Class A.

The Tigers got off to a fast start with Banks and Skidmore combining for nine first-quarter points, yet the offense was not the story. The Tigers' defense held the Bulldogs to two points, a pair of free throws, and Catfish's squad grabbed an 11-2 advantage, which they grew to 17-5 by intermission. After a half of play, the Quitman quintet had not scored a single bucket, all their points coming from the charity stripe.

Quitman's heralded team made a charge in the third quarter, outscoring the Tigers 6-4, but in the final stanza, the Tigers put the game out of sight and won 33-17.

Catfish praised his squad's defensive work, while also pointing toward their balanced scoring attack. Banks pitched in ten, Fleming nine, Skidmore eight, and Loyd four. Meanwhile, the Tigers held the Bulldogs' high scorer to five points. This impressive win sent shockwaves through District 16-A and the surrounding area.

Tuesday, Clarksville came to town, and the adrenaline-filled Tigers went wild. They led 13-3 after the first quarter, and Catfish's reserves took over in the fourth period, growing a 33-13 lead to a final score of 46-15. Roberts Banks led all scorers with sixteen but got help from Skidmore (11) and Loyd (8). Fleming's six points matched Clarksville's scoring leader, Albritton. They then followed that victory with a thrashing of Pittsburg, 48-10. Fleming led with a dozen, Banks with eleven, and Condrey with eight.

And just like that, the Tigers were district champions again, sporting an 8-0 record, 15-3 overall.

While waiting for the start of the district tournament, the Tigers prepared for the rematch with the Hooks Hornets that Catfish had arranged after the earlier seven-point loss to Roland Loyd's team. In fact, the Hornets had knocked the Tigers out of the playoffs the prior season and had whipped them in their last four consecutive meetings.

Catfish's team was playing its best ball of the season, and he knew this bunch had the potential to advance in the playoffs. However, those losses to Hooks galled him, and if his boys could defeat the Hornets, a playoff-caliber squad comparable to Quitman, their confidence level would be bumped up a notch at just the right time.

Interestingly, he never seemed to consider the potential impact of a loss, and his boys rewarded their coach's faith in them with a 31-19 victory.

On that strong note, Mount Vernon headed into the playoffs again, but Catfish had more to be proud of. His junior varsity had just competed an undefeated season. Led by the sensational Bud Campbell, they had demolished opponents by scores of 30-4, 35-9, and 37-6. Over a fourteen game season, they had averaged thirty-two points a game while allowing only thirteen. Many Mount Vernon fans and a few league coaches would have agreed that the Tigers had the two best District 16-A teams in 1947.

The district tournament was played using an unusual format. If the winner of the regular season, Mount Vernon, should win the tourney, they would be undisputed champions. However, if the Tigers should lose, they would then play the tournament winner in a best-of-three series.

Winnsboro became their first challenger, a team the Tigers had defeated earlier by one point. Since that time, the improved Red Raiders had whipped Gilmer, 54-26, and Clarksville, 44-14. By comparison, the Tigers had sneaked by Gilmer by only two points.

Acie Cannaday and his Red Raiders got their revenge, giving the Tigers their first district loss, 34-32, eliminating Catfish's team from the tournament championship. An amazing total of thirty-seven fouls indicated the degree to which the players fought for the win. Banks and Condrey fouled out of the game, while foul shooting won the contest for Winnsboro. The Red Raiders cashed in fourteen while the Tigers managed only six of seventeen from the charity stripe, an eight-point difference in a two-point game. Fleming contributed ten for the Tigers, Skidmore nine, and three others added four each. Martin (10), Morris (8), and Coppedge (7) carried the scoring load for the Red Raiders.

"All year, we've come up short on our foul-shot opportunities," Catfish lamented. "If we'd have made half of them tonight, we would have won."

To be exact, the Tigers shot thirty-five percent against the Red Raiders, where they had shot forty-six percent for the year. Gene Fleming, an above-average, fifty-four-percent foul shooter, missed four of four against Winnsboro, while the other players made six of thirteen, their normal forty-six percent.

Rather than sit back and idle while the other teams decided the tournament champion, the team to challenge Mount Vernon for the right to proceed into the playoffs, Catfish scheduled another game with the Hooks Hornets for the coming Thursday.

Whether the result of losing out in the district tournament or the stress of a twenty-game season, Catfish's ulcerated stomach brought him to his knees, and he spent most of the week in the hospital, missing the Hooks contest.

Once more Roland Loyd's quintet defeated the Tigers, 32-29 this time, with Superintendent Fleming coaching the team in Catfish's absence.

Meanwhile, Deport won the 16-A tournament and hosted the playoff to determine which team would represent the district in the regional tournament. Though the Tigers had defeated the Deport quintet easily in regular season play, the tournament champions proved they were an improved squad with a win in the first playoff game, 26-20. Leading 17-16 going into the final quarter, Mount Vernon managed only six shots for three points while Deport threw up ten shots for ten points, five by Thomas. The Tigers had their worst offensive showing of the season in a battle that saw forty-six fouls assessed, a new high for the season. Pat Loyd was the leading scorer for the Tigers with six points, prior to being eliminated with five fouls. Thomas and Salters of Deport had ten points each.

The Tigers redeemed themselves in the second game, 26-18, tying the series at a game each. Banks, held to four points in the first game, broke out with ten while every Tiger contributed at least three points. Martin had eight for Deport, while Thomas contributed six, but Salters, their leader, was limited to four points, none in the last quarter. Salters, the key scorer for Deport, was shut down by the ferocious defensive play of Gerald Skidmore.

The final and deciding game was moved to Talco, a neutral site, and set for Friday, February 21. Emotions ran high on both teams, and the contest promised to be a war.

The Tigers got off to a good start with Pat Loyd firing in two goals and a pair of free throws in the first quarter, while Banks added a pair of buckets giving Mount Vernon a 14-11 lead. The Tigers widened the gap in the second quarter with Fleming adding four of his team's eleven points. Meanwhile, Salters carried the load for his team with eight in each stanza, scoring all but three of his team's total. The squads headed for their locker rooms at halftime with the Tigers leading, 25-19. The third quarter saw Deport shave four points off Mount Vernon's lead, pulling to within two at 29-27 and setting up the final quarter as a fight to the finish.

With four minutes to go in the game, Banks, Loyd, and Fleming each had four fouls, one short of disqualification. That trio had to back off their aggressive play, but the Hopewell duo of Herb Zimmerman and Pat Loyd saved the day for the Tigers with Zim sinking four points and Loyd three. Ed Salters had a twenty-point night; however, he was shut out in the final and game-deciding quarter. For the Tigers, Pat Loyd countered with fifteen, and each of Catfish's boys contributed at least four. Mount Vernon pulled out the district-championship, 38-34, but the battle was not over.

Fans from Deport stormed the court, and a brawl ensued. Not only did the Deport contingent go after the Tiger players, they became so abusive with the referees that, upon later review, league officials would suspend the Deport team from district competition for the following year.

Cool-headed, hard-working Gerald Skidmore received All-Tournament recognition, though he scored only thirteen points over the three games. "That number twelve is a much better player than some fans realize," an official said of Skidmore. "I'd take him on my team any day." Pat Loyd scored twenty-five tournament points, sinking every shot taken during the final quarter of the deciding game. Robert "Slats" Banks had twenty-two points, six of which turned the tide in the third quarter of the second game when Deport had closed to within a point of the Tigers. Catfish said of Banks, "My only complaint is that he needs to shoot more." Herb Zimmerman sank fourteen points, seven in the final contest, while his hustle was unsurpassed in the league. "I don't care who scores the points, just so we win," Zim said. Big Gene Fleming had eleven counters, low by his standards, but his leadership never faltered. Joe Zane Condrey and Kenneth Meek remained dependable substitutes, though they played little in these crucial games.

Meanwhile, the fierce Quitman Bulldogs lost to Van in a shocker, 34-30, so the Tigers were scheduled to face the Vandals in the first round of regional competition. The game would be played Saturday, March 1, in Greenville at three o'clock; however, two days before the playoff game, Catfish learned that he might have to enter the regional tournament without one of his most outstanding players.

On Thursday, February 27, a three-page, mimeographed school newspaper, *The Tiger's Tale*, showed up in the hands of many of the students. Superintendent Fleming sought out a copy, scanned its columns, and frowned his discontent. In a humorous and somewhat unprofessional manner, the paper revealed the latest gossip about dating couples and who was saying what about whom, some of which was questionable. With little effort Superintendent Fleming determined the primary culprit behind the scheme.

"Catfish," he said to the coach between classes, "one of your boys has taken it upon himself to publish school news. I'm going to have to talk to him and maybe discipline him."

"Which one?" Catfish asked, wrinkling his brow.

"Gerald Skidmore."

"Gerald? He's such a good kid," Catfish said. "Will you suspend him?"

"That depends upon how he reacts when I confront him."

The coach wagged his bowed head slowly and turned back toward his classroom, wondering if he might be without one of his most valuable players going into the state playoffs.

"Son," Superintendent Fleming said when he had young Skidmore seated on the opposite side of his desk, "who gave you permission to start a school paper?"

"No one, sir."

"What is your purpose?"

"Well, I discussed it with a friend of mine, and we thought our school was a little behind the times. Lots of schools have a newspaper, and the students really enjoy reading about their classmates, what they think about things, and school plans."

"School plans?" Fleming questioned. "Don't you think you should have consulted with me or Principal Bolger before you took on that subject?"

"Yes, sir," Skidmore replied, casting his eyes down to his clammy hands.

"What I see here," Fleming said, glancing at the newspaper, "is mostly student gossip. While it might be entertaining and funny to most of the students, it could be very hurtful to another. Do you think that's fair to the student being offended?"

"No, sir. I didn't think about it like that."

"I want you to get with your fellow-conspirator and give this situation some thought. Then, the two of you meet me back here first thing tomorrow morning," the superintendent said, getting to his feet. "Meanwhile, I'll consider what action I'll have to take."

Fleming did not have to consult school records to know that

Skidmore's academic rating was one of the highest among his classmates. Though the young man had no formal journalism training, the articles were surprisingly well written, and the overall concept was impressive. Nor did the superintendent have to be told that Gerald was a superb athlete and vital to the school's hopes of advancing in the upcoming playoffs.

Puzzled as to Skidmore's silent partner, Fleming checked with Miss Binnion, who could be counted on to know more about individual students than any other member of his staff. What he learned surprised him.

Mildred Scheirman, a senior, had moved to Mount Vernon for her tenth year of school. Having lost both parents when she was ten, she had arrived in town with her aunt and uncle, who served as the pastor of the Christian Church on Yates Street. A popular girl, Mildred was the reigning football queen, selected "Best All-Around Girl" by her peers, senior class treasurer by her classmates, served on the school yearbook staff, and was a talented musician. Evidently, she also aspired to be a news reporter.

Gerald and Mildred stepped into the superintendent's office at eight o'clock the next morning, hesitating at the doorway.

"Come in," Fleming said and waited for the students to take a seat. "Now, you've had some time to consider your actions, as have I. Tell me what you think should be done."

"Sir," Gerald said, glancing at Mildred, "first, we will try to collect all the papers we've distributed. Second, we'll apologize to those we may have offended by what we wrote. Third, I'll write an essay to you explaining why I think the school needs a newspaper, what it should contain, and we'll request your permission to do it the right way."

The superintendent fought back a smile, not wanting to betray the seriousness of the meeting. What more, or less, could he have expected of these prize students? Their acceptance of responsibility for their error, their willingness to right any wrong, and their determination, the drive, to go forward with what they believed in, immediately diffused any lingering concerns Fleming might have had.

Millard Fleming was a thirty-year educator, twelve of those in Mount Vernon, and no one loved students more than he. A man who saw hope in almost every situation, he focused on the bright side, even when many could not see the slightest glimmer of light.

"Gerald and Mildred," he said, "I accept your solution; however, I want to add a couple of points.

262

"I applaud your ambition, your creativity, and your enterprise, but with those comes responsibility. The higher your position in life and the greater your influence, the more you must be diligent and fair to all concerned in the exercise of those powers and the control entrusted to you.

"Now, I see talent in your first attempt, and you have opened my eyes to the need for a forum for disseminating school news. If you choose to go forward with your idea, then I want to help you."

Fleming hesitated, reading their faces.

"You do want to publish the paper, don't you?" the superintendent questioned.

The two students broke into a smile and nodded.

"Good, because I have already talked to Miss Binnion about this, and she's willing to sponsor you and guide you. Also, I'll give whatever help I can, providing materials and access to typewriters."

"Thank you, sir," Skidmore said. "I can't tell you how much I appreciate this."

"One more thing," Fleming said. "How would you like to have the guidance of a real journalism teacher?"

"Oh, yes, sir."

"I believe Mr. Weldon Brewer can help," the superintendent said rising. "I'll speak to him."

The two students beamed as they left the meeting, while a smiling Millard Fleming stepped to the hallway and watched them head for class. When they disappeared around the corner, the superintendent ambled down to Catfish's classroom and motioned him into the hallway.

"Thought you'd like to know Gerald will be available for the game tomorrow," he said.

Catfish smiled as he drew his hand across his brow.

During study hall that afternoon, Miss Binnion and Weldon Brewer met with the two newspaper enthusiasts, and while showing her excitement for the project, Irene also gave a word of warning.

"Of utmost value to anyone is their dignity," she said. "What may seem frivolous, funny, and entertaining to everyone else, might hurt someone deeply. Always remember that your moment of fun can be the source of another's lifetime of pain."

The two solemn-faced students nodded agreement.

"I want to invite you to my house tonight," Weldon Brewer added. "We'll look at the design of the paper, how to write catchy headlines, how to organize some reporters to gather the news, and how to get your paper published."

Gerald and Mildred collected the original issue of the paper, made their apologies, and he wrote his essay, though it's original purpose had long since become irrelevant. If nothing else, the exercise provided the opportunity for the pair to clearly state their objective and to share the inspiration that had driven them to spend their afternoon hours typing, their nights proofreading, and their evenings cranking the handle of the mimeograph machine.

Soon a journalism class was started, taught by Weldon Brewer, and attended by twenty-four students who unanimously elected Gerald Skidmore as their editor. Brewer and his wife, Anita, proved to be a goldmine for the aspiring news reporters. Weldon had the necessary formal training and loved journalism. In his class he challenged his students to clip a sentence from any publication available, underline one word, and give the clipping to him. If he could not give the correct definition of the highlighted word, the student won a point. At the end of the school term, the student with the most points won a prize, a new dictionary. Anita's brother, Stanley Walker, had been a *New York Herald Tribune* editor for several years, and her love of journalism matched that of her husband.

On the way home, Gerald marveled at how so much good had come from stepping up and doing something, though the initial reaction had been anything but encouraging. Also, he thought how fortunate he was that Millard Fleming was his superintendent, that Irene Binnion was a compassionate, student-loving teacher, and that Weldon and Anita Brewer were willing to lend their talents and time to a couple of high school students trying to find their way in life.

The next day, Van got off to a good start behind the shooting of T. Ingram with five first-quarter points, while his teammate, Miller, added three. Loyd with four points was the only Tiger to make a bucket, and the Vandals led 11-6 starting the second period. Pierce of the Vandals took over in the second quarter and pitched in eight of his team's eleven. Halftime showed the Tigers woefully behind, 22-11. With balanced scoring, including four from Skidmore, Mount Vernon gained two points in the third, but still trailed, 30-21. In the final quarter, "Slats" Banks pitched in seven points to rally the Tigers to within four of the lead, but T. Ingram responded with six counters and led his team to victory, 39-29.

Though not the difference in the game, deficient foul shooting came back to haunt the Tigers in the biggest game of the season. They made only five of fourteen while Van converted eleven of fourteen. Banks chipped in eleven points, but missed four of five foul shots. Loyd contributed eight points, but was shut out in the final stanza. A good Tiger team lost to a better Van quintet that eventually got eliminated from the state tournament by East Mountain who ran away with the 1947 state title, eliminating Bowie, 35-22.

Catfish never experienced a loss that he did not hate, but realistically, his 1947 unseasoned team had accomplished more than anyone could have expected. With all juniors in the Tigers' starting lineup, more would be expected of them next season, especially with the sensational Bud Campbell becoming eligible.

For the junior varsity team, Campbell had scored one hundred sixty-three points, eight more than the combined total of all opposition teams! He had averaged thirteen per game. "Ambidextrous, ubiquitous, and gregarious, he would have made the varsity team this year, if he had been eligible," Devall wrote in the *Optic-Herald*.

There was more. Kenneth Meek, "the toughest man wearing tennis shoes," pitched in ninety-three points for the junior squad. The Moore brothers, Dewey and Dale, scored forty-two and fifty-one respectively. Added to this impressive list was Billy Jack Meredith from Jack Henry's squad, likely the best grade-school athlete in Mount Vernon history.

Considering all this, it is not surprising that after the game when Catfish shook hands with the Vandals' coach, his parting words were, "See you back here next year."

24

March 24, 1947

By the spring of 1947, Catfish had earned a reputation second to none among Texas high school coaches. Easily one of the most recognizable men in East Texas, he received a steady flow of invitations to speak at social gatherings and to promote every conceivable cause throughout the area. His folksy, witty personality added to his stature as a cagey coach and exceptional motivator.

Some of the locals watched with concern, fully aware that their coach could move on to a larger town, bigger school, and higher pay. Their nervousness elevated when college coaches arrived in town. For instance, the postman, while poking letters into the individual letter boxes, would have had to be blind to not notice the source of much of Catfish's mail.

"What's Matty Bell doing in town?" the postman asked Catfish when he dropped by to check his post office box.

"Says he's interested in Swede Crowston," Catfish replied.

Many of Mount Vernon's favorite sons had returned from the war more mature and seeking new lives and young wives, prompting the influx of college recruiters. Bell, the head coach at Southern Methodist University, was indeed looking for the ex-Tiger great, but his interest did not stop there.

"You've had quite a successful four years here," Bell said to the coach. "You get interested in moving on, I believe I can help."

"I'll keep that in mind," Catfish replied.

"Mount Vernon seems to produce more good athletes than most other towns its size. At SMU we've been fortunate enough to get a few of them."

Bo Campbell and Lendon "Skinny" Davis of the undefeated 1938 Tiger team had played on Bell's football squads, while Acie Cannaday and J. C. Cannaday had played for the Mustangs' basketball club.

"I hear this Crowston kid led your 1944 team to an undefeated season," Bell said. "I'd like to have him do the same for the Mustangs."

"Best running back I've ever coached," Catfish replied, and then gave directions to the Crowston farm.

"Coach," Bell said as he turned to leave, "I'm interested in some of your current players, too, including Gene Fleming, Charles Lowry, and that Zimmerman kid, though I hear they have another year of high school eligibility."

"That's right," Catfish replied firmly, clearly indicating those boys were currently off limits. "They'll be ready to talk to you next year."

Matty Bell was not the only college recruiter in town. Coach Wagstaff of Tyler had his eye on Mack Gilbert, the six-foot-three, two-hundred-twenty-pound 1946 graduate, and Harry Jack Pugh, a two-sport star from the 1944 teams.

The town radiated with pride in its athletes and welcomed the recruiters, but the reaction was quite different when another rumor hit the local barbershops.

"He wouldn't leave Mount Vernon," one fan replied when told Catfish was being wooed to coach at a big AA school. "Why Dorothy Nell grew up here. She'd never allow it."

"This town has a population just over two thousand," the barber countered. "We can't match what some Dallas school or big oil community, five or six times our size, can pay him."

"But he's done so well here, winning over thirty football games in four years, losing only six, and Lord knows how many basketball games he's won. He might not find another town with athletes like we have in Mount Vernon."

"But that's the point," the barber replied. "His teams win. He won the state championship at Carey and never lost a game at Winfield before he came here."

"I just don't believe he'll leave, not with what he's got coming back next year. He'll win it all next season."

"Football or basketball?"

"Both. Then he'll likely have some big college job waiting for him."

Catfish had received offers, but the first man was right. Dorothy Nell was happy with their situation. She loved Mount Vernon, and Catfish believed his best team was right around the corner. Besides, the businessmen in town enjoyed and profited from the notoriety that winning teams brought to their community, and some had sons wearing the purple and white. Though their boys were fine athletes, they might not win with another coach, but with Catfish on the sidelines, not one doubted that Mount Vernon would continue to accumulate championships. They would never allow him to walk away without a handsome counteroffer.

Meanwhile businesses were growing and new ones popping up. The local Home Ice Company announced the installation of a fifteen-ton ice plant. L. D. Lowry, Jr., had purchased surplus military storage tanks and established a growing propane delivery operation to add to his furniture business. Lucky Ramsay had opened a Dodge and Plymouth dealership combined with a Texaco station on West Main. The First Baptist Church on South Kaufman and the Church of Christ on West Main were breaking ground for new facilities. A new Federal post office was on its way, and a modern eight-bed hospital with an up-to-date operating room was under construction.

With all this prosperity, some men decided the town needed a semi-pro baseball team. Charlie Brown was elected president of the club, Ed Holton vice president, and Joe Moore, secretary-treasurer. The board of directors included Hoffman Moore, Austin Brakebill, Alton Shurtleff, Billie Ford, Tom Newsom, and W. A. Nash. Harlan "Skeeter" Lawrence was named manager with Catfish as assistant manager and coach. But before the coach could get too involved in this baseball enterprise, he had spring football drills to complete.

*   *   *

Catfish took a good look at the boys waiting for uniforms. They were familiar, almost to the last one. Gene Fleming, Herb Zimmerman, Charles Lowry, Pat Loyd, Gayle Tinsley, Dewey Moore, Robert "Slats" Banks, Dale Moore, Wallace Hunnicutt, Joe Condrey, Kenneth Meek, Buck Parchman, and Roy Cunningham. Only George Dickerson and Coy Sims were missing from his 1946 starting lineup.

Less familiar faces were Dudley Miller, a good lineman, Billy Jack Guthrie, Pat King, two-hundred-pound Billy Jack Carter, Charles Stretcher, George Wims, little Johnny Moore, and the promising Billy Jack Meredith.

Catfish knew what his regulars could do, so he focused on the newcomers. To his amazement, Billy Jack Meredith could throw a football like a quarterback, run like a fullback, catch like an end, and punt with exceptional consistency and accuracy. Dudley Miller proved to be a reliable center, deep snapper, and place kicker. Carter, with his size and mobility, had the potential to be an All-District lineman, and the versatile Guthrie could play guard or fill in at running back.

The coach's projected forward wall was awesome. Size, speed, versatility, intelligence, and especially experience were applicable attributes. The backfield was less proven with Dale Moore as a sophomore quarterback, Billy Jack Meredith as a triple-threat freshman, and some gritty runners in Kenneth Meek, Buck Parchman, and Roy Cunningham. Wallace Hunnicutt was the closest the coach had to a power back, but Catfish was not satisfied. He wanted a proven, dynamite runner, a game-breaker, and he had an idea how he might get one.

Joe Zane Condrey's family had moved to Galveston, leaving him to room and board with various families in Mount Vernon throughout the current school year. Upon completing the eleventh grade in May, the boy would join his parents in South Texas for the summer and likely would not return, though the rules allowed him one more year.

"Son," Catfish said to Condrey, "I believe you are just one season away from becoming a college-level back. How would you like to return for one final season?"

"Coach, if you'll help me get a football scholarship next year, I'll come back."

Catfish agreed to do what he could, and a deal was struck. Now, the coach had that experienced runner with exceptional open-field ability and with breakaway speed, and he had a backfield to complement that awesome forward wall.

"The game with the exes should be interesting," Catfish told Superintendent Fleming, referring to the traditional scrimmage contest that signaled the end of spring practice.

Swede Crowston coached and played for the exes, which included Harry Jack Pugh, Dan Cargile, Mack Gilbert, Coy Sims, Ray Clark, Howard Rogers, Frank Parchman, George Dickerson, Charles Hogan, Billy Rex Cody, Glynn Minshew, and Leacho Tittle. The list looked like "Who's Who" among past Mount Vernon Tigers.

The afternoon of the contest, Herb Zimmerman, living at the Miller Hotel, went home with Gayle Tinsley after school to share a pre-game meal. Reaching the Tinsley home on Yates Street, Zimmerman met Gayle's mother, Bea, his father, Pep Tinsley, and older brother, Tommy.

After dinner, Herb and Gayle started back toward the football field.

"Gayle," Zimmerman asked, "what happened to your dad's leg?" Herb had noticed that Pep Tinsley wore a peg leg.

"Lost it in a hunting accident thirty years ago," Gayle explained. "Almost died."

"How'd it happen?"

"Dad was plowing when he saw a couple of squirrels playing in a tree at the edge of the field. He grabbed his gun from the wagon and headed that way, but had to cross a gully. Hurrying down the embankment, he tripped and the gun went off. He'd have bled to death except for a woman who was taking a jar of water to her husband plowing in the next field. The woman heard the shot and came running. She made a tourniquet out of her apron and then ran to get her husband. They lifted Dad into the wagon, hitched the team, and took him home. The man then unhitched one of the horses, and rode him bareback to get the local doctor."

"I guess your dad feels like he owes his life to that couple."

"That's right. Mr. and Mrs. Johnson, a black couple, were the best neighbors a person could ever have."

In the scrimmage game, the young Tigers proved to be in better physical shape than their opponent, and they held their own, with Catfish's big offensive line controlling the line of scrimmage. Late in the second period, the younger team drove the ball sixty yards, with Gayle Tinsley taking the pigskin into the end zone for the first score.

The battle continued in the second half with the exes moving the ball well, but their lack of team practice time resulted in too many mistakes to sustain a long drive against a strong and stubborn defense. When the exes ran out of downs in the final quarter, Catfish's tireless juniors hammered away against the veterans until the goal line was only twenty yards away. Then freshman Dale Moore surprised everybody by dropping back to pass, but surprise turned to cheers when he sent a perfect spiral to the sideline, where Joe Zane Condrey snatched the ball and galloped into the end zone. The youngsters led 12-0.

Bigger and stronger now than in his playing days, Crowston was practically unstoppable, but he had not played football in three years, so he could not carry the ball down after down as he had once done. Watching Swede run, Catfish thought of the back-to-back, undefeated regional championships his Tigers might have had if number twenty had stayed for the 1945 season. But this night, the Swede and his glorious teammates just could not overcome the stamina, skill, and courage of Catfish's young team.

"That was mighty good for my boys tonight," Catfish said after the game, beaming. "Swede and his boys were not in top form, but I expect they gave us about as much competition as we'll face in the fall. You folks have something special to look forward to, come September."

*   *   *

At the high school graduation in May, Catfish stood and applauded Olan Ray Brewer, his sports manager, who was declared valedictorian, one of only two boys in the top ten. Sara Anderson was salutatorian with Betty Birdsong and Archie Johnson in close pursuit. Others in the elite group included Evelyn Birdsong, Dorothy Hightower, Maxine Gilbert, Martha Hill, Robbie Nell Norris, Dorothy Lynn Gilbert, Mildred Schierman, and Deryl Jean Sparks.

On the honored list at the elementary school was Billy Jack Meredith with a 95.125 average. Catfish would be adding another brainy player to his squad in the fall.

The semi-pro baseball season got underway in late May with Catfish as manager and catcher. In the opening inning of their first game, against Winnsboro, he got a hit and drove in a run from his cleanup position. The opposing pitcher intentionally walked him upon his next appearance at the plate, and with the score knotted at 3-3 in the critical eleventh inning, Catfish stepped into the batter's box with a runner on second. Again, the opposition gave him a free pass to first. Bo Campbell, a late arrival at the park, strode to the plate as a pinch hitter, bringing the crowd to its feet. The Tiger great promptly belted a double off the leftfield fence, driving across the winning run.

In the return game against Winnsboro, Catfish got two hits in four attempts and scored two runs in a 7-1 win, but Bo Campbell proved to be the team's slugger, pounding out the longest homers anyone around had seen. Robby Campbell also showed he knew how to handle a bat, along with Glenn Penn. Pop Griffin and Mike Mikeska were the mainstays of the pitching staff, but they got relief from Skeeter Lawrence when they found themselves in a jam.

At a critical point in the following Pittsburg game, Catfish chased after a towering popup in foul ground to the third-base side. Just as the ball settled into his mitt, he collided with a guy wire attached to a light pole, loosening a couple of teeth. He held on for the out and preserved the win. However, for Catfish and his teammates, it was not to be a championship season.

League officials, after much heated debate, ruled Pop Griffin ineligible because he had once played major league baseball, and they also questioned the proximity of his home to Mount Vernon. Following the decision, Catfish's Lions withdrew from the league, but agreed to play their remaining home games out of respect for their fans.

Catfish banged out three hits against Sulphur Springs, but his most memorable act was rattling the opposing pitcher with his constant chatter. With two outs and the bases filled with Mount Vernon runners, Catfish elevated his level of harassment from the third-base coach's box.

"He's stealing home," he yelled just as the hurler started his pitch to the plate. The pitcher glanced toward third, saw the base runner heading toward the plate, and stopped.

"Balk, balk," Catfish yelled, pointing at the pitcher.

The umpire agreed, waved the runner home, and the other runners to second and third. The frustrated pitcher glared at Catfish, and then proceeded to give up three consecutive hits, leading to a 10-2 victory for the Mount Vernon squad.

After swatting three hits in four at-bats against Gilmer in a 9-7 losing cause, Catfish then banged two hits and scored a pair of runs against Mount Pleasant in a 14-8 win.

With the baseball season over, Catfish sought and got a commitment from Bo Campbell to be his assistant coach, handling the backfield and the kicking game, and the two headed for El Paso for the annual clinic for high school coaches.

About midweek at the Del Norte Hotel, Catfish received a letter from Dorothy Nell. In beautiful script, she explained that little Ronnie had a cold and was unable to sleep. He had been repeatedly calling for his daddy. Her mother had spent Sunday night with her, but when Dorothy Nell came out to leave after taking her mother home, she noticed a flat tire on her car. Her brother had driven her home where she called Hoffman Moore who arranged for someone to repair the tire. She missed her husband, she said, but he was not to worry about all the problems. She would contact him if Ronnie's condition worsened, and she promised to write again the following night. She signed off with an expression of her love, followed by, "Dot."

Concerned, Catfish returned home two days earlier than planned and found Ronnie fully recovered, so the coach turned his attention to the upcoming football schedule.

September 12	Clarksville	home
September 20	Paris Reserves	home
September 26	Grand Saline	home
October 3	Mineola	there
October 10	Winnsboro	there
October 17	Mount Pleasant	there
October 24	Pittsburg	home
October 31	Open	
November 7	Talco	there
November 14	Gilmer	home

Catfish was not happy with the upcoming competition. First, he was unable to schedule a game with Edgewood, the team he expected his Tigers to meet if they made the playoffs. Second, he had that open date on Halloween. Originally, Talco had filled that slot, but with district realignments, the Trojans had been assigned to another league.

When thirty-five players showed up for the first practice at eight-thirty on Monday morning, September 1, the coach was both surprised and pleased to see "Bud" Campbell, the basketball whiz, among them. Catfish, having been a basketball player and a football end, immediately saw the potential: sure hands, a sense of how to fake a defender and get open, jumping ability, and dexterity. In Campbell's case, the coach would find ambidextrous hands developed as a kid when Bud had broken his right hand, his naturally dominant one, but had refused to quit playing basketball at New Hope. Forced to dribble, pass, shoot, and catch left handed, he had become as adept with his left as his right.

Other notables showed up, also: Gerald Skidmore, another basketballer, Donald Yates, Dale Brakebill, Kenneth Kimbrell, Glen Slaughter, and Louis Agee. With the exception of Skidmore, these were younger players, generally slight of build, but tough and aggressive. They would become the coach's newest pack of feisty bulldogs.

Campbell and Zimmerman needed a place in town, so Catfish arranged for their room and board at the Miller Hotel, along with Condrey and a couple other boys.

This team would be different from any other. With proven players at every position, competent backups for most, and outstanding newcomers, it had all-star quality. With so much talent among his boys, the coach worried about individual egos getting in the way of team spirit.

"Boys," the tall, lean Catfish said while pacing slowly before his squad gathered for early practice beneath an umbrella-shaped red oak, "I consider it a privilege to be your coach. I want to thank you for making the commitment to be a part of this team, to wear that uniform with pride and honor, to work to become the best football player you can be. And I want you to pass along my appreciation to your parents for trusting me to teach their sons, not only about football, but about living life with dignity, pride, and above all, with character.

"I want to make sure each of you understands one thing right now. Your commitment is not to me, not to your school," he said, stopping and slowly scanning the face of each boy, his piercing eyes momentarily locking with theirs. "Your commitment is to the boy to your right, to your left, to the one in front of you, and the one behind you. It's to every young man gathered here: your teammates. From this moment forward, everything we do is for this team. As a team we will win, and if we lose, we'll bear that burden together, too. We'll accept victory with humility. We'll face defeat without excuses but with determination to overcome our weaknesses and faults.

"We may meet teams with outstanding players, with larger boys, and with better raw athletic talent. We can't do anything about that. Oh, we'll work hard, get stronger, and develop our skills to the best of our ability, but we can't change the limits Mother Nature has put on us."

For a moment the coach stood grim-faced and silent. Then his face broke into a slow, wide-spreading smile. "But we'll win."

"How?" he asked rhetorically. "Boys, winning is all about character, and character is all about heart. And I promise you, nobody will display more character or play with more determination than the purple and white Tigers. You see, this is not just about winning football games. It's about life, and it's character that sustains you throughout life, not athletic talent.

"Now, if any one of you has second thoughts about making this commitment to your teammates, about always representing your parents, your school, and your town with honor, you need to take off that uniform right this minute, because I will not settle for less."

As the stern-faced coach waited for his words to soak in, for any defections, he again scanned their faces. No one said a word.

"Now, strap on those helmets, and follow Dale in ten laps around the field," the coach said, referring to his quarterback from the prior

274

season. "Whoever comes in last, will run ten more. And Dale, if you let anyone finish ahead of you, you'll run ten more."

The lanky, confident sophomore took the lead, sprinting alongside the perimeter of the field. Others filed in behind him, a stocky youngster in the rear. As the players circled the field, Curly Newsom walked over to where the coach stood watching his team.

"Hello, Curly," the coach said, continuing to watch his circling players.

"Howdy, Catfish," the man replied. "You know, I never liked this drill, especially the part making the straggler run ten more. It never seemed fair."

"There's good reason," Catfish replied. "Being satisfied with last place is not acceptable. Running more laps isn't punishment; it's improvement. It says 'I'm gonna get better.' Whether better shape, better running technique, or better endurance, it means working harder and longer than those who finished ahead of you."

"But always, somebody has to come in last," Curly replied.

"That's right, and I won't have a single player on my team who's satisfied with it being him!"

"How come you picked young Dale Moore to lead?"

"Every team has to have a leader, somebody the players turn to when things are their worst. It's gotta be somebody who always sees a way to come back, to persevere, to win. Dale believes in himself, isn't afraid to take responsibility, and is eternally optimistic. He's our quarterback, and he can be that leader for us."

"But there's a couple of boys out there who can outrun him, so aren't you setting him up to have to run the extra laps?"

"The fastest man doesn't always win the race. The best athlete doesn't always come out on top. If Dale is to lead this team, he's gotta show the others that he can win even when he's not the most capable."

"How can he?" Curly replied, pointing to the runners. "Condrey is right on his heels, and on the final lap, he'll zip right past Dale."

"If I know my quarterback, he won't let it come down to that. Even now he's picking up the pace, pushing those right behind to run harder than they want to. Let's watch and see how he does it."

It was lap six when Dale spurted ahead, putting seven or eight yards between himself and his closest rival. Within half a lap, Condrey and a couple others closed the gap, but then Moore put on another burst of speed, rebuilding his lead. Again his pursuers closed the gap, but it took them a full lap to do it this time.

With grimaces etched on the faces of his pursuers, young Moore again built a lead, a full ten yards this time. Then it was lap nine, and the others had little time to catch up, but they gave it a try. Condrey and Cunningham were on Dale's heels with a quarter of a lap to go.

"Dollar say's Condrey passes Dale," Curly said.

"Make it breakfast at Miller's I tomorrow morning," Coach Smith replied, smiling. "I'm broke and a free meal sounds mighty good."

As Condrey tried to ease up beside Dale, the cagey quarterback drifted over to block him. Joe Zane tried the other side, but was blocked again. Obviously, Condrey had enough speed to outrun Moore those last fifteen yards, so he took a wide angle and attempted to pass with five yards left. Dale then took a different tactic. He put his head down and leaned forward, taking the shortest distance to the finish line, and then plunged ahead. With his body airborne, he crossed the goal a half step ahead of his pursuer.

As Dale struggled to his feet and Condrey clutched his knees, gasping, Catfish headed toward his spent players, but then glanced back, smiling.

"I usually eat breakfast about seven," he said to Newsom. "My appetite is always best about that time."

Bunched in twos and threes, players struggled across the finish line. The short, stocky youngster plodded along at the very back with Gene Fleming just ahead of him. Heaving players and their coach watched as the two approached the goal.

Fleming slowed down, though he clearly was not exhausted. The straggler closed the gap as the big tackle glanced over his shoulder. Fleming said something to the kid. Then it was over, and the chubby boy had lost by half a step.

"What'd you say to that kid?" Curly asked Fleming.

"I told him to gut it out, and not to give up," the big tackle said. "I just wanted him to know we're pulling for him."

Curly thought, now there's a man I would follow.

25

September 1, 1947

With a veteran starting lineup, Catfish quickly turned the grueling practices into offense-versus-defense sessions. One of his favorite scenarios was to simulate the adrenalin-pumping dramatics of the ending of a close ballgame, convinced that it elevated his players' emotions above the drudgery of practice, and it also prepared them for that specific situation in a future contest.

"For any critical game situation, if you've practiced it, you're always more confident," the coach preached to his players. "Every down in scrimmage, imagine you're facing a fourth and four against Winnsboro, three yards for a touchdown against Mount Pleasant, or third and long yardage to maintain control of the ball."

His seasoned players had heard the speech before, had faced those game-deciding challenges, and most of them relished the opportunity to prove themselves. Likewise, most of them knew the formations, the plays, and the defensive sets, so Catfish dispensed with the typical repetitious drilling on fundamentals.

The first week of preseason drills, the coach emphasized conditioning and evaluating his new players. After assigning positions to the newcomers, Catfish had the veterans run plays with the rookies learning by watching their counterparts. Soon, he had his second unit executing the plays and practicing their assignments on defense.

The second week, Catfish was ready to throw the first team against the second unit, though he knew it would be a mismatch. Monday afternoon, he stepped over to the offensive huddle and dropped to one knee, scanning the sweaty faces of his boys.

"It's the last minute of the game. We're behind. It's third down on Winnsboro's thirty-five-yard line, and we need five yards to keep the drive alive," he said, then hesitated. "Who wants the ball?"

"I do," Meek said immediately, followed by Hunnicutt and Condrey.

"Okay, Rambler gets the ball. Now, who wants to clear the way for him?"

"Just follow me," Fleming said sternly.

"That's it, then. Forty-four dive on two," Catfish said, as the players broke the huddle and hurried to the line of scrimmage.

Dale Moore bent under center, his eyes straight ahead, and started the cadence.

"Set, hut one, hut two," he barked, and clamped down on the ball when Dewey slapped it into his hands. As his brother shot forward, Dale turned and stuffed the ball into Meek's midsection, then watched the runner plow ahead behind the big tackle.

Fleming, with the help of Tinsley and Bud Campbell, blew the second string defense off the line of scrimmage, bowling them over. Meek broke past his big linemen with nothing but green grass ahead, that game-time feeling coursing through his sleek body.

The coach's shrill whistle signaled the end of the play, and the boys, with pride written all over their faces, jogged back and surrounded their coach.

"That looked good," Catfish said solemnly, then smiled, "but that's not Winnsboro's defense over there. Now, Zim, Lowry, Loyd, and Dewey, you boys switch to defense and let's see if Mr. Fleming and his pals can get that five yards against some real competition."

The left side of the offensive line rushed over and took their defensive positions, slapping each other on the back. Dewey lurked behind them as a lone linebacker.

"They won't make one yard," Zimmerman said, lining head up with Dudley Miller, the backup center. "We know who's getting the ball, and we know where he's going."

As the right side of the offense lined up, Lowry stomped his cleats into the hard ground, and stared across at Fleming. Loyd cheated a little, lining up on the left shoulder of Bud Campbell, and Dewey eased within a yard of the gap between Lowry and Loyd. Zimmerman had his eyes locked on Meek.

Dale barked the cadence, and Miller snapped the ball. Hot sweaty bodies collided amid groans and the popping of pads and helmets. As the ball settled into Meek's gut, his eyes darted for an opening, even a small crack of daylight. From the corner of his eye, he saw a slit of a window open and veered to his left, to the inside of Fleming who was matched in a fierce standoff with Lowry. Dewey had cheated to his left, toward the four hole, and could not get back in time to stop the speedy Meek.

Just as Meek put it in high gear, he saw a flash from his left, then his whole body vibrated as Zimmerman stuck a shoulder into his ribs, lifted him off his feet and drove him to the ground. The ball carrier lay flat on his back on the original line of scrimmage.

As the players untangled, the offense realized they had failed, and the defense congratulated each other with back-claps and helmet slaps.

"You boys want to try that again?" Catfish asked, disgust twisting his face.

His players knew it was no question. They lined up once more.

Again bodies collided and leather popped as Meek disappeared into the mass of straining, struggling men in front of him. The whistle blew and when the players untangled, the ball showed one yard gained.

"Boys, we just lost to Winnsboro," their coach said, scowling at his offense. "And I don't like losing, especially to Cannaday."

"The left side can do it," Zimmerman muttered.

Fleming, Tinsley, and Campbell turned, and if glares could fire arrows of anger, Zim would have looked like a porcupine. Meanwhile, Lowry and Loyd smiled uncomfortably.

For a moment, Catfish studied his players, and then nodded his head. The right side of the line slowly moved to their defensive positions while Zimmerman, Lowry, and Loyd crossed over to offense.

As the left half of the line took their positions across from the right half, their opposing helmets only inches apart, smoldering anger reddened their grim faces as they clenched their fists and bulged their muscles. Then Dale began calling signals, his voice sharp and crisp like a drill sergeant.

Suddenly Miller slapped the ball up into the quarterback's hands and guttural sounds filled the air as the players hit, pushed, grabbed, pulled and strained. As had Meek earlier, halfback Condrey shot forward, looking for a crease. He lowered his head and rammed his way between Loyd and Lowry, but tripped over the powerful legs of the stymied linemen. He had gained only two yards.

"Anybody on this team think they can carry that football five yards without stumbling over their own feet?" Catfish bellowed.

Quickly Buck Parchman and Wallace Hunnicutt stepped forward, snapping their chinstraps in place.

"Okay, Buck, let's see if you can do it, but I want you to run right behind Zinnerman," the coach said, intentionally mispronouncing the guard's name. "He shot off his mouth a while ago, so let's see if he's all talk."

"Let's huddle up," Zimmerman said, motioning to his fellow linemen.

When they had gathered around him, he stared at each of them. "Dudley, you can block the man in front of you, can't you?"

"He won't get the tackle, I promise you that," Miller responded, glad to be a key part of the offensive line in what had built to a game-like situation.

"Okay," Zimmerman said, "Pat, forget Campbell. You move out a little farther than usual and make sure Bud's on your outside shoulder, and then go after Dewey, the linebacker. Buck is coming on a dive right behind me, so the end can't get there in time. I'll help Charles with Fleming, and Buck, when you're past the line of scrimmage, watch for Pat, and cut outside off his block. You'll get the five yards."

They broke from the huddle and trotted to the line of scrimmage, while Catfish turned to his assistant, Bo Campbell.

"Zim's gonna make a fine coach, one of these days," he whispered.

Dale called out the cadence, Miller snapped the ball, and again powerful bodies clashed. Lowry countered the initial charge of the powerful Fleming. Miller maneuvered the noseguard onto his right shoulder and shielded him from the ball carrier. Loyd brushed Campbell, and then streaked toward the unsuspecting linebacker. Seeing Parchman approaching the line, Fleming made a move to his left but suddenly was smacked in the ribcage by Zimmerman and driven outside, bumping into Campbell and blocking his path to the ball carrier. Parchman slipped through the opening and spotted Dewey Moore coming straight at him, ready to slam a shoulder through his chest. Suddenly, from Moore's right came Loyd who blindsided the linebacker. Parchman cut left behind the wipeout block, and broke free in a dead run, stopping when the shrill whistle blew.

Back at the line of scrimmage, Fleming shoved Lowry. Zimmerman grabbed Fleming by the shoulder pads and yanked him away. Campbell yelled at Zimmerman. Dewey Moore jumped to his feet and yelled, "Illegal block."

"We whipped your tails, fair and square," Zimmerman said.

"You want to try it again?" Fleming challenged.

"Coach," Bo Campbell whispered to Catfish, "you got your first down, but I'm afraid the team is split. We'll be lucky if they don't kill each other."

"Yeah, they're not a team yet, but I'm gonna fix that tomorrow," Catfish replied. Turning to the players, he yelled, "Line up on the goal line. Time for wind-sprints."

The angry players shuttled to form a long line, their minds suddenly shifted to the pain of running ten one-hundred-yard, gut-wrenching sprints, maybe more. With the whistle they took off.

After a dozen trips up and down the field, during which Catfish yelled at each player at least once, telling one that he was running like an old wash maid, another that his grandmother could run faster, still another that he had never seen a more pathetic sight, he then sent his team to the locker room.

As the players showered and dressed, Catfish wandered through, noticing the absence of their usual horseplay and bantering. Tension showed on the boys' faces, and hung in the air. Fleming was visibly angry, and Dewey Moore's eyes were narrowed and his face flame-red. Zimmerman and Lowry stared at the floor rather than meet the gaze of their teammates. Loyd dressed quickly and left while Bud Campbell sat motionless, staring at the gray, blank wall.

Slowly the locker room emptied and only Catfish remained, pondering his fractured team. It had to be remedied, but the situation was not all bad. Though he would not yet tell his players, he knew he had an exceptional team. There was not a better line in the district, offensive or defensive, or in the region. Considering like-sized schools, there might not be a better forward wall in the state. Today, they had been tested against a formidable adversary, probably as good as they would meet on their schedule. And they had found a way to succeed, and had done so without his help. That was what pleased him most. In a critical situation in the heat of battle, that kind of on-field ingenuity, determination, and will-to-win could make all the difference.

Practice the following day started like any other. The tension from the prior day had turned the team into silent, eyes-straight-ahead warriors. After calisthenics and wind-sprints, Catfish called his boys around him.

"We've got to be in shape, boys," he started. "I don't ever want to lose a game because of poor conditioning, because you couldn't go all-out to the very last play of the game. And you've got to be mentally tough, too. So, we're going to do a little drill. It's called the bullring.

"Now, I want you to make a big circle around me," he said,

watching the boys push back until they formed a spacious ring with him in the center. "Zinnerman, come here."

The coach sometimes mispronounced players' names, especially when he had something special in store for them. Though suspicious, Zimmerman obediently joined his coach in the center of the circle where Catfish laid his right arm across the guard's broad shoulders.

"Coach Campbell is gonna call out jersey numbers, and when your number is called, you come after Zinnerman and knock him down, any way you can do it," Catfish said to the circle of players, and then turned to Zimmerman. "Your job is to fight them off, staying on your feet, no matter what."

Catfish patted Herb on the shoulder, walked outside the circle, turned and nodded to Coach Campbell. Then Catfish folded his arms across his chest and, towering over his players, watched.

"Ninety-five," the assistant called out, and Gene Fleming broke from the circle, heading for Zimmerman.

Herb turned and readied himself for the two-hundred-pound tackle bearing down on him. When their helmets hit, it sounded like a gunshot. Zimmerman staggered back three steps but did not go down. His eyes aflame, Fleming coiled to unload on Zimmerman again but turned back to the circle when he heard Coach Campbell call out the next number.

"Four," the assistant said, and Gayle Tinsley flew along a radius to hit the opposite guard with everything he could muster. Zimmerman, stunned from the head-on collision with Fleming, caught the hard-charging Tinsley with his left shoulder, but still had to drop a hand to the ground to maintain balance.

"Eighty-one," Coach Campbell yelled, and Bud Campbell charged forward, coming from directly behind Zimmerman.

Zim frantically searched for his attacker but spotted him too late. Campbell hit the big left guard across his shoulder blades and sent him sprawling to the ground.

"Fifty-five," the assistant called out, and Dewey Moore barreled toward Zim, who was frantically pushing up from the hot turf.

Caught before he could get his feet set, and with no leverage, Zimmerman was flattened again by the fiercely competitive Dewey Moore. Struggling to get up, Zim suddenly realized that he had just been hit by every member of the right side of the line, along with the center.

"Ninety-eight," Coach Campbell said, sending Charles Lowry after his battered teammate.

Though Lowry did not deliver his best shot, Zimmerman staggered backwards.

"Twenty-two," the assistant called out, then quickly yelled, "eleven."

Pat Loyd headed for Zimmerman, with Kenneth Meek coming from the guard's right. The one-two punch sent Zim tumbling.

"Seventy-five, forty-one, seven," Campbell called out steadily.

One, two, three, they plastered Zimmerman, each before Herb could recover from the previous hit and get to his feet.

Amid the pounding, Coach Smith glanced at Zimmerman's teammates. He especially noticed Gene Fleming who wore a pained, angry look. Catfish eased over behind the big tackle.

"I'd never let anybody treat my teammate . . ." the coach growled through clenched teeth.

Before Catfish could finish the thought, Fleming took off as though shot out of a cannon, headed for Zimmerman. As he neared the target, he veered to his right and plastered one of the approaching attackers, sending him tumbling into the shins of the circled players nearby. Fleming then backed toward the fallen Zimmerman and crouched like a wild tiger, searching the circle for the next attacker.

"Sixty-one," Bo Campbell called out, sending Billy Jack Carter into the fray.

Fleming went to meet the backup lineman, and knocked him on his backside.

"Ninety-six, eighty-nine, ninety," the assistant called, sending more attackers after Zimmerman than he and his lone defender could handle.

Before the second one reached Zimmerman, Lowry had joined Fleming in guarding their weary teammate. Then Gayle Tinsley joined them, along with Dewey Moore. They fended off the stream of attackers until Bud Campbell and Pat Loyd joined the inner circle around Zimmerman. With angry sneers on their faces and tears in their eyes, the offensive linemen formed an impenetrable wall around their comrade.

"Fifty-four, ninety-nine, forty-six, thirty-three . . ." the assistant called out hurriedly, but not one boy in the sparse circle attempted to make an attack.

A shrill whistle blew.

"That's all, boys," Catfish said. "Now, let's scrimmage a while."

While the offense huddled and the reserves gathered on defense, Catfish eased over to Bo Campbell.

"Coach, now they're a team," he said with that unique Catfish smile spanning his face.

*   *   *

The prior season, Dale Moore had been involved in three head-on collisions that had resulted in concussions. He would get knocked "goofy" and could not remember the plays or down-and-yardage. As in the prior season, Gene Fleming would control the huddle and call plays, both because of Dale's affliction and Fleming's leadership skills. To protect the young quarterback, some businessmen, L. D. Lowry, Jr., Hoffman Moore, Jeffy Meredith, and others, decided Dale needed a special helmet. With Catfish's help, they chose a Riddell that offered considerably more protection. Rather than have one player with an odd headgear, these men ordered new ones for the entire team, helmets that matched their new, shiny, white pants and jerseys. A group of boys never looked prouder than the 1947 Tigers decked out in those immaculate uniforms in their team picture.

As the first game approached, the lineup was solid. Bud Campbell had taken over at right end, with Pat Loyd his counterpart. The tackles were Fleming and Lowry, the guards Tinsley and Zimmerman, and Dewey Moore anchored the center position. The halfbacks were Kenneth "Rambler" Meek and Joe Condrey. Hunnicutt was penciled in at fullback, but a tonsil operation sidelined him, making room for freshman Billy Jack Meredith and the basketballer, Gerald Skidmore.

Clarksville had won its district the prior season, primarily because of the powerful running of one-hundred-eighty-pound Jess Stiles. A senior now, he was bigger and stronger and heralded as unstoppable. Regardless, fan expectations in Mount Vernon soared, with locals convinced their Tigers were about to claim their first of a long string of victories.

Two thousand fans filled the stands and lined the fence, cheering the local team. Regardless of their expectations, they could not have been prepared for what they were about to witness.

In the first quarter, the Tiger defense threw the Clarksville runners for more yards in losses than gained, a net negative two yards. In the second stanza, it got worse, a net negative twelve. The third and fourth periods got no better, a net negative eight and nine yards respectively, for a net thirty-one yards lost running the ball. Mount Vernon's forward wall was as impressive as the noted "seven stones of granite." Stiles, his running game stymied, threw twenty-one passes; however, three Tigers, Dewey Moore, Kenneth Meek, and Dale Moore, each intercepted one, returning them for a total of more than one hundred yards.

Meanwhile, the Tiger offense racked up two hundred thirty-five yards with Condrey accounting for one hundred nine on a dozen carries, Meek with fifty-five, Skidmore thirty-nine, and Parchman fourteen. Dale Moore chunked eight passes, completing three for fifty-six yards.

On the final play of the game, Stiles launched a desperate pass intended for his teammate Emery; however, Dale Moore snatched the ball, then zigzagged back to the Clarksville twenty-yard line, almost breaking loose for another score.

One-hundred-thirty-eight-pound Meek, the lightest player on the field, scored all four Tiger touchdowns, giving Mount Vernon their first victory of 1947, a 24-0 shutout.

For the next game against the Paris reserves, the weather could not have been more disagreeable. A cold rain fell all day, soaking the field and making a well of every hole and a pond of every depression, but it seemed that nothing could faze Catfish's team.

Paris gained only eighteen yards from scrimmage in the game, while losing thirty-one, a net loss of thirteen yards. Zimmerman and Bud Campbell lived in the opponent's backfield, accounting for most of the negative yardage. The Wildcats' offense never crossed their line of scrimmage in the second half. Their only first down came on a fifteen-yard penalty against the Tigers. Meanwhile, Catfish's boys racked up eighteen first downs, two hundred fifty-seven yards rushing, twenty-six more passing, and scored five times.

In the first quarter, Buck Parchman polished off a long drive with Mount Vernon's first touchdown. Dale Moore then hauled in a punt and raced seventy yards for another score. Condrey, Meek, and Loyd all added six-pointers, and Fleming toed four of five extra points, an improvement credited to Bo Campbell's expert instruction. When the scoreboard clock showed zeroes, the Tigers had their second shutout, 34-0.

The next game was homecoming against the Grand Saline Indians, a contest the team especially wanted to win for all the former Tigers who would be in attendance.

Practices that week were a little more intense until Thursday when

Catfish decided to have the team shed their helmets while the offense ran plays without an opposing defense. Somehow Gayle Tinsley got his feet entangled with Gene Fleming's and tumbled to the ground. In trying to regain his balance, Fleming unintentionally stepped on Tinsley's head, and his cleats ripped a long gash laterally above Gayle's right ear.

"Hold up, boys," Catfish hollered, rushing over to Tinsley.

A closer examination revealed that the cut would require stitches, so the coach had his right guard rushed to the nearest medical clinic. After a doctor had cleaned, stitched, and bandaged Tinsley, not only was the wound covered with tape, but a wide band of gauze encircled his head, holding the bandage in place.

When Catfish saw Tinsley the next day just prior to the game, the coach could not believe his eyes. Gayle looked like a casualty of war.

"Son," Catfish said, calling Tinsley aside, "we need you to play tonight."

"Okay," Gayle replied, having never considered otherwise.

"I tell you what," Catfish said. "Put your helmet on before leaving the dressing room and keep it on. Don't take it off for anything. If the fans see your head all bandaged up, they'll be yelping at me for using a hurt player."

The class that had collected the most money for the athletic fund would have their choice, previously determined by vote, crowned as the football queen. The plan was to announce the honored young lady during halftime ceremonies, whether Joy Jones for the seniors, Patsy Bogue for the juniors, Cynthia Moulton for the sophomores, or Margaret Bean for the freshmen. The queen would then be allowed to sit with the players on the Tigers' bench. However, due to rain, which after a half of football would leave the field a mush of mud, the ceremonies were held prior to the game. The senior class had gathered in four hundred sixty-three dollars, and thus Joy Jones was hailed as football queen. Little Jim Mac Stinson was crown bearer, and Kenneth Meek escorted "her royalty" while Charlie Brown narrated. The white clad Tigers lined up along the sideline while the band played, "Let Me Call You Sweetheart" followed by "To Our School."

Near the center of the line of players stood Gayle Tinsley, the only player wearing his helmet. While the band played "The Star Spangled Banner," Tinsley was the only human in the stadium with his head covered, setting off a general grumble in the stands and leaving the undersized guard feeling like a Nazi engulfed in a sea of Marines.

When his teammates tugged on their headgears to start the game, Tinsley breathed a sigh of relief. Throughout the first half, he wore the helmet, though he was sure the bandage had come loose and the support band inside his headgear was rubbing the wound. Sure enough, during halftime, he removed his helmet in the privacy of the locker room and found blood smeared inside it, and all across the side of his head. Catfish immediately had the manager clean and re-bandage the cut. Though Mount Vernon was leading by thirty points, the coach seemed to give no thought to having Tinsley sit out the second half.

While Gayle was being tended to, Mrs. Vera Mitchell was directing the halftime performance of the smartly dressed Tiger band, which had recently received rave reviews. Led by Drum Major J. W. Combs, it included Charles Moffett as captain and lead trumpeter, bass and snare drummers, baritones, trumpeters, trombonists, clarinetists, saxophonists, lyrist and cymbalists, along with a color guard and baton-twirling majorettes. A highlight of their performance was the playing of the school song.

The boys from "Salt City" proved no match for Catfish's Tigers. Mount Vernon's offense exploded for eight touchdowns and fifty-three points; however, the heretofore-impenetrable Mount Vernon defense, with reserves playing, finally gave up a score on a desperation pass in the final quarter, along with the point-after. In spite of that breakdown, the defense again threw their opponent for more yards lost than gained, a net negative two. Meanwhile, the Tigers rushed for two hundred eighty-one yards and passed for another one hundred fifty-four, while racking up nineteen first downs.

A beautiful punt by Billy Jack Meredith set up the first score. From his own forty-eight, the freshman sent a spiral that trickled out of bounds on the Indians' one-yard line. The Tigers' defense held, giving their offense a short field to cover for the initial touchdown.

The second score was bizarre. Fleming boomed his kickoff over the heads of the Grand Saline deep receivers and into their end zone. The Indian return man pursued the ball but slipped down, and the speedy Joe Zane Condrey covered the ball for another Tiger six-pointer.

The next kickoff thrilled the fans again, when Fleming sent the ball sixty-three yards through the air, with it bounding out of the back of the end zone. Bo Campbell's work with the big kicker was paying high, and long, dividends. Later this kick was to be overshadowed with a seventy-plus yarder that cleared the goalpost crossbar and landed beyond the back of the end zone.

With their ground game stalled, the Indians' quarterback, Dewey Pierce, went to the air, completing nine consecutive passes; however, the longest aerial came off the hand of Dale Moore to Pat Loyd for a forty-eight-yard score, and the most impressive one was snatched by Bud Campbell on a leaping one-hand grab for a twenty-seven-yard touchdown.

Campbell also led the Tigers in sacking their opponent in their own backfield, tripping them up three times. With some help from his friends, Lowry, Zimmerman, Tinsley, Loyd, and Fleming, the basketballer and his buddies trapped the Indians for thirty-nine yards in losses.

After missing the first two games, recovering from a tonsillectomy, Wallace Hunnicutt added power running to the Tigers' formidable attack. When combined with Condrey's speedy ten-yards-per-carry average and Meek's tenacious and deceptive running style, the Tiger's stable of runners was impressive.

The fourth Mount Vernon opponent, the Mineola Yellow Jackets, was their last non-conference and first out-of-town contest of the season. Though typically a tough adversary, the Yellow Jackets had already suffered two close losses, by seven points to Gilmer and six to Winnsboro.

In the initial quarter, the Tigers took the ball on their forty-six-yard line and marched for five first downs on ten consecutive running plays with Condrey and Meek carrying the load and the Rambler accounting for the touchdown. Starting the second period, Billy Jack Meredith provided a bright spot, again hitting a coffin-corner kick to Mineola's one-yard line, pinning the Yellow Jackets in a hole from which they could not escape.

After intermission, Dale Moore set up the second score when he intercepted a pass and returned it to midfield. Hunnicutt powered his way for fifty yards on five plays, one an eighteen-yard scamper, and three first downs. Meek again finished off the march with a one-yard plunge to pay-dirt.

In the final stanza, Meredith pulled off a quick kick that again hemmed up Mineola dangerously deep in their territory. After the Tiger defense held, giving the ball to Mount Vernon on their opponent's forty, Dale Moore heaved a pass to Pat Loyd who, when he found himself trapped on the fifteen, pitched the ball to Hunnicutt who galloped on to the seven-yard line. After a couple of line plunges by Hunnicutt, Condrey skirted right end for the final tally.

The Tigers were not sharp, suffering ten penalties for seventy yards, yet they prevailed, 19-0.

Mineola's running game netted thirty-five yards on twenty-one attempts, to which they added thirty-seven passing yards, all producing only three first downs. In contrast, the Tigers ground out one hundred ninety-six yards rushing and thirteen through the air, collecting sixteen first downs.

With the Winnsboro Red Raiders next on the Tigers' schedule, Catfish billed the game as possibly the district-championship decider. Acie Cannaday, Catfish's prior assistant, had spoiled the Tigers' 1946 season with a deadlocked game that prevented Mount Vernon from sharing the district title. This year the Red Raiders were coming into the game with three impressive wins, having defeated Mineola, Talco, and the perennial regional champ, Edgewood. The stunner was that Cannaday's boys had shut out the highly regarded Edgewood Bulldogs.

Catfish knew he must prepare for a battle.

26

October 6, 1947

For the Tigers, the week of the Winnsboro game was particularly troublesome. First, the death of Bud Campbell's uncle, D. H. Campbell, caused him to miss two practices. Second, the senior class of 1946 had purchased a new score clock for the gymnasium. It arrived that week and was installed in a special ceremony that shifted attention to the upcoming basketball season. Then the town celebrated the opening of its much-awaited new hospital with an event Catfish felt obligated to attend, making him late to practice. On top of that, Rutherford Drug Store had an open house commemorating seventy-eight years of service, having opened in 1869. While Catfish fretted and strived to keep his players focused, it seemed that one distraction after another came along.

Evidently, none of these sidetracked his Tigers. They destroyed the Red Raiders, 27-0, while their defense allowed only one first down and a net four yards gained. Meanwhile the Tiger offense amassed nineteen first downs, two hundred fifteen yards rushing, ninety-seven passing, and intercepted two Red Raider passes. Loyd, Meek, Condrey, and Parchman each crossed the double-stripe for the Tigers.

The first score came on a methodical eighty-yard drive. Dale Moore, Hunnicutt, Condrey, and Loyd moved the ball down to the Red Raider's twenty-eight, where the Tigers unleashed a trick play that was to become a trademark of this team.

Quarterback Moore took the snap from Dewey, turned counterclockwise, then followed his backfield in a power sweep around left end. Going unnoticed, as Dale had turned from center he had slipped the ball to his left guard, Zimmerman. With all backfield motion to the left, the guard slid down the line to the right, cut upfield, and headed for the end zone. A Winnsboro safety finally tripped him up at the six-yard line. From there, Dale Moore tossed a pass to Pat Loyd for the first score of the game.

After an exchange of possessions, Billy Jack Meredith, for the third week in a row, angled a kick out of bounds deep in enemy territory, on their nine-yard line this time. Unable to move the ball, the Red Raiders punted, a weak one that only reached their twenty-four. Using the same guard-around play, Zimmerman clicked off twelve yards. After a quick pass to Loyd to the two-yard stripe, Meek rambled into the end zone.

After Catfish's defense again shut down the Winnsboro offense, Dale Moore returned a punt to the Red Raiders' thirty-one. The Tigers then blasted away with their stable of runners until Condrey tore loose for an eight-yard score. The half ended with the Tigers up, 20-0.

Starting the third period, Catfish's offense powered down to the enemy's ten-yard line before incurring a penalty that killed the drive. After shutting down the Red Raiders' offense, the Tigers again marched deep into Winnsboro territory, stalling at the three-yard line after another disastrous penalty. The highlight of that drive was a "hook and lateral," using Loyd and Hunnicutt, followed by the tricky guard-around play to Zim for a third time. Catfish delighted in revealing an expanded playbook to his former assistant.

The final score came on a forty-yard drive that featured a twelve-yard pass to Loyd, taking the ball down to the two-yard line. From there, Hunnicutt rammed home the touchdown. The game ended with Mount Vernon marching again, having pushed the ball to the Red Raiders' thirteen when the horn sounded.

The win ran the Tigers' victory string to five in a row, four of those being shutouts. Catfish's offense had averaged over thirty-one points per game, while his defense had yielded only the single touchdown to Grand Saline. With four games remaining on Mount Vernon's schedule, folks were already comparing this 1947 team to the undefeated regional championship squad of 1944 that averaged thirty-seven points per contest while allowing only two scores against them through the regular season.

With Coach Coody's Mount Pleasant team, the district's defending champions, next on his schedule, Catfish refused to make such comparisons, stressing that his boys must not look past their next opponent. However, the exuberant Mount Vernon fans pointed out that the Titus County Tigers had already suffered two setbacks, a 30-18 loss to the Talco Trojans and a two-touchdown defeat by Clarksville. The 1946 champs were already essentially dethroned.

Always the worrier, Catfish tortured himself with the fear that his players were reveling too much in their press clippings. As highly regarded as his team was, the coach knew he could never convince his boys that they were underdogs. His way of bringing his players down from the clouds was to work them extra hard in practice.

Adding to Catfish's concerns were injuries to his quarterback, a severe ankle sprain, and his power runner, Hunnicutt, who had a six-stitch cut over his right eye. As he had done with Zimmerman's broken hand the prior season, Catfish hoped to tape both up and send his wounded warriors into the fray.

Mount Pleasant won the coin toss, and Fleming kicked the ball down to the opponent's twelve-yard line, from where Cook managed only a five-yard return to the seventeen. On the first play from scrimmage, the Mount Pleasant runner met a brick wall in the form of Zimmerman. The ball popped loose, and Fleming pounced on it two yards behind the line of scrimmage.

On Mount Vernon's initial offensive play, Condrey burst through a hole carved out by Lowry and Zimmerman and glided untouched into the end zone. Fleming missed the point-after, but Catfish applauded his boys for immediately taking control of the game.

This time Lamb received Fleming's forty-eight-yard kick and wriggled out to the twenty-eight-yard line. After a failed running play, Milton Marshall, Mount Pleasant's quarterback, tried two passes, both incomplete. The Titus County boys punted the ball to Roy Cunningham who cut left across the field, crisscrossing with Condrey. At the last second, Roy pitched the ball to Joe Zane who rambled for fifteen yards to the Mount Vernon forty-six.

On a pitchout, Condrey then looped around left end for fourteen, and Meek ran behind Fleming and Tinsley for eight, putting the ball on the enemy's thirty-two. Meek then fumbled, and the ball bounded forward to the twenty-eight, inciting a mad scramble to make the all-important recovery. Dewey Moore emerged from the pileup with the ball. After the trick play to Zimmerman netted only two yards and a dive by Condrey was stopped for no gain, the Tigers faced third down and eight to keep the drive alive.

With Billy Jack Meredith at fullback, Dale Moore tossed the ball to the freshman triple-threat, but Soward of Mount Pleasant broke through and dropped Meredith back on the thirty-five. Facing fourth and eighteen, Billy Jack dropped back to punt, but squib-kicked the ball only ten yards. Leading by only six points, Catfish's boys had let a great opportunity to pad their lead slip away.

As Mount Vernon's defense had done so many times in prior games, it smothered its opponent's offense, pushing them backward on three consecutive plays, forcing Milton Marshall to punt to Mount Vernon's Condrey.

Joe Zane hauled in the wobbly spiral on his own thirty-four, and darted through a crack in the opponent's defensive wall. If not for a desperate shoestring tackle, he would have gone the distance, but he lost his footing and tumbled to the ground after an eighteen-yard return, positioning the Tiger offense just inside Mount Pleasant territory.

After Cunningham fought for two yards, Meredith dodged and weaved for six, setting the stage for Condrey who made a brilliant sixteen-yard run to the four-yard line. The Zimmerman trick play, so successful against Winnsboro, garnered only two. A silent-snap, quarterback sneak pushed the ball to the one. After Meredith was stopped at the line of scrimmage, Mount Vernon faced fourth down and one, but before they could run another play, the first quarter ended. While jogging the length of the field, Fleming used the extra time to consider his most crucial play call of the game.

The purple-and-white Tigers lined up in a straight T-formation, no flanker, nobody in motion. Fleming had decided it was time for hard-nosed football, power against power. Possibly he recalled that preseason practice when Catfish had created just this sort of scenario and demanded that his offense repeat a play until they got the necessary yardage, temporarily splitting the team.

With Cunningham in at fullback, the lightning-quick Condrey set up at left halfback, and the little-used Parchman at right half, Dale barked the cadence, and Dewey snapped the ball to his younger brother. To the surprise of most everyone, the quarterback slid the ball into the cradled arms of Buck Parchman, just as he had back in that practice session when Lowry, Zimmerman, and Loyd had cleared the way. Now, however, Fleming chose to put the burden on himself, Tinsley, and Campbell. Using the blocking scheme Zim had devised that day, they cleared a four-foot path for Parchman to burst into the end zone. The point-after sailed wide left, but the Tigers had a two-touchdown advantage.

After kicking the ball to Mount Pleasant, the Tiger defense again shut down the Titus County offense. Marshall punted the ball to Condrey who crisscrossed with Hunnicutt, faking a reverse, and then sailed sixty-yards to pay-dirt, giving Catfish's boys a three-touchdown lead.

When Mount Pleasant again failed to move the ball on the ground, Marshall went to the air, completing an eleven-yarder to Rains. On the next play, Pat Loyd stole a pass and raced forty yards to pay-dirt, sealing the deal, or so it appeared. However, a penalty cancelled the score, giving the ball back to the Titus County boys on their forty-seven.

With time running out in the first half and Mount Pleasant's ground game shut down, Marshall again resorted to a pass, but this time Billy Jack Meredith slipped in front of the receiver on his own forty-two, snatched the aerial, and raced twenty-three yards before being hauled to the turf. With time enough for a quick score, the Tigers rushed to the line of scrimmage, but their good fortune turned sour in a hurry.

Moving gingerly on his gimpy ankle, Dale Moore failed to make a clean handoff to Kenneth Meek, and the pigskin bounded erratically on the turf. Lacy Morris of the enemy camp slipped between them, snatched up the ball, and raced seventy-one yards untouched. A successful point-after by Soward brought the black-and-gold team within two touchdowns of Catfish's boys with two quarters remaining.

The second half start portended a disaster. After receiving the kickoff, Meredith pitched to Condrey who brought the ball out to the thirty-six. After a stymied running play to Condrey, quarterback Moore threw an aerial that Rains picked off and scrambled back to midfield. A Mount Pleasant touchdown and point-after would make it a four-point game, but the bedrock of Catfish's team came to the rescue.

The powerful Mount Vernon defense refused to give ground, and Marshall had to punt to Condrey back on the Franklin County boys' sixteen. The swift back slithered out to the thirty, again threatening to break away for a score. After a five-yard run by Meek, Catfish's boys thought they had weathered the storm and were on their way. Then Dale threw another interception that Mount Pleasant returned across midfield to the forty.

After a nifty first down, Marshall picked up twenty-two to the Mount Vernon eight, and suddenly Catfish's team was on its heels. The same play ran into a determined Zimmerman and Lowry for no gain. Following a three-yard run, Marshall tossed a pass to Morris in the left flat. Only one man could keep the receiver out of the end zone. Pat Loyd plastered the runner with a vicious hit, driving him backward from the two-yard line. The black-clad Tigers faced fourth and two, but still with a golden chance to get back into the game. Marshall hit up the middle, but Zimmerman and Tinsley met him at the one-yard line, straightening him up and driving him to the ground.

With the Tigers backed up to their goal line, on first down Meredith surprised the Titus County boys with a quick kick that finally died at midfield. Glad to be out of the shadow of their goal, Mount Vernon was preparing to play defense when the referee called for their captain. Mount Pleasant had lined up offside, a five-yard infraction. Fleming accepted the penalty, retaining the ball for his Tigers.

After three more attempts to run the ball for a first down, Meredith had to punt again. This time he sailed the ball out to the forty, where Rains latched onto it and headed back, slip-hipping his way to the Mount Vernon eighteen.

One more time Catfish's defense held, taking over on downs at their fifteen. After Condrey failed to gain, Meredith romped seventeen yards for a first down on the thirty-three. He then ripped off eleven yards to the forty-four, and Mount Vernon had battled their way out of a dangerous situation.

After Meek gained seven yards, freshman Meredith picked up another seven, putting the ball on Mount Pleasant's forty-two when the third quarter ended.

The final stanza started with Meredith gobbling up another eleven yards to the thirty-one, then the fullback followed that with a dazzling seventeen yarder to the enemy's fourteen. To cap the drive, the amazing freshman then circled right end for an apparent game-clinching touchdown, but again the officials threw a flag. Illegal motion cancelled the score and moved the Mount Vernon boys back to the nineteen.

The misfortune did not faze young Meredith. He ripped off ten yards and then four more to the five-yard line. The next two plays ended in penalties, one against each team, leaving the ball on the three-yard line. After Meredith fought to the one, quarterback Moore fooled the defense once more. With the whole stadium focused on Meredith, number eighty-eight, Parchman slipped into the end zone. Meredith, the eighth-grader Catfish had so anxiously anticipated for a year, was now an emerging star. Fleming booted the ball through the uprights, giving Mount Vernon a commanding lead, 25-7.

With the game under control, Dewey Moore appeared to seal the victory with an interception on Mount Pleasant's twenty-eight, following Fleming's fifty-five-yard kickoff. However, this game had a couple more twists.

With Catfish's team unable to make a first down, Meredith dropped back to punt the ball, hopefully another coffin-corner job. Instead, Mount Pleasant blocked the kick and the ball was smothered on the thirty-three by Sanders wearing black and gold.

An alert Gene Fleming realized that Gayle Tinsley had uncharacteristically missed his block, allowing the enemy to break through and swat down the punt.

"You all right?" Fleming asked, seeing the glazed look in Tinsley's eyes.

"Yeah," the feisty guard responded. "Just got my bell rung on that last kickoff."

Again Catfish's defense rose up to stop the Titus County boys, forcing a punt. Marshall sailed the ball out of bounds on the Mount Vernon forty, eliminating any opportunity for a dramatic kick return. Then came the final twist.

With the Tigers needing a sustained drive, Tinsley was flagged for lining up offsides on the first play, putting his team in a first-and-fifteen situation.

"Tinsley," Fleming barked, "just look at the ball and make sure you're behind it."

"Which one?" Gayle asked. "I saw two balls, and neither one would stay still."

With Tinsley addled and his team needing a big play, Fleming decided to roll the dice. If successful, the game would be iced. If not, the Tigers could run the clock down and punt deep into enemy territory.

As they headed to the line of scrimmage, Fleming asked Tinsley if he knew his assignment on the play.

"What's the play? I've forgot."

"Just block the man to your outside," Fleming said.

The play surprised not only a confused Tinsley, but caught the Mount Pleasant defense off-guard also.

Dale Moore dropped back and sailed a beauty to Pat Loyd for fifty-two yards, setting up Catfish's team with a first down on Mount Pleasant's thirteen. While the black-and-gold defense tried to recover, Meredith burst through for nine to the four, then Meek knifed in for the final score. The point-after made the final score 32-7. Catfish's boys had survived a determined opponent, as well as their own mistakes, to win their sixth game.

Afterwards, Gayle Tinsley could not remember a single play or event in the game subsequent to the kickoff when he had received a blow to the head. The tough guard had refused to leave the field, so Fleming had explained what he was to do on every play.

Pittsburg was next, followed by an open date. With wins over the Pirates, Talco, and ever-tough Gilmer, the Tigers would have an undefeated district championship.

Though the Pirates' record was not impressive, their losses had been by narrow margins. In fact, recently they had come within one touchdown of Gilmer and had soundly defeated the Naples Buffaloes, 12-0.

Catfish announced that his starting lineup for the Pittsburg contest would have Meredith at the fullback slot and Buck Parchman at the right halfback position. Condrey, who was nursing an ailing shoulder, could play if necessary, and Hunnicutt would see limited action for the second consecutive contest due to stitches over his eye.

Pittsburg could almost match the size and weight of the Tigers' forward wall. With a couple of one-hundred-seventy-five-pound tackles, a center at one-seventy, guards at one-forty to one-sixty, and ends at one-fifty-five, the Pirates would not be easily pushed around. Their one-hundred-fifty-pound backs overmatched the Tigers' lightweights who tipped the scales at one thirty-eight and one forty-five. The Pirates' one-hundred-eighty-pound fullback, Steele, would not play, according to their coach, Red Russell.

Size was the only area in which the Pirates matched the Tigers on Friday night. In a "T-party" deluxe, as described by editor Devall, Billy Jack Meredith claimed two touchdowns, as did Buck Parchman and the ailing Condrey, while Bud Campbell added a seventh score on a spectacular grab of a pass. The Tigers prevailed 44-0.

The show did not just highlight Catfish's T-formation, however. The "seven stones of granite" rolled the Pirates' rushing attack backward a net twenty-one yards and blocked a punt, while holding Pittsburg's offense to six first downs. On offense, the Tiger linemen ripped holes in the Pittsburg defense for almost three hundred yards on the ground and seven short of two hundred in the air, totaling four hundred eighty-five net yards.

The Tigers did all this while watching most of their substitutes get significant playing time, including players like Pat King, Billy Jack Carter, Billy Jack Guthrie, Dudley Miller, George Wims, Stanley Jaggers, Charles "Birddog" Stretcher, Frank Carr, and Dale Brakebill.

Having completed the toughest part of their schedule with a 7-0 record and with an open date to let some of their nagging wounds heal,

297

the Tigers looked like a prohibitive favorite to romp over the Talco Trojans and stumbling Gilmer Buckeyes for a clean sweep of District 19-A. Clearly, this team, dominant over some of East Texas' best, was destined to be one of Catfish's all-time great ones.

Not the coach, his boys, nor their fans could ever have guessed how different their world would look in just two weeks.

27

October 29, 1947

The Tigers' troubles started on Wednesday of the off week. Prior to practice, some of the players got into a game of kickball. When both Dewey Moore and Herb Zimmerman rushed toward the ball, Zim reached it first and gave it a whack. Trying to protect himself, Dewey extended his hands in front of his body. The ball shot up and struck the tip of the middle finger on his right hand, and something snapped. With a yelp, Dewey grabbed the hand at the base of the finger, which was bent backward and skewed to one side, obviously broken. Dewey cradled his injured hand against his chest, muttered inaudibly, and headed for the locker room. Thoughts flashed through his mind like successive lightning strikes, alternating between the throbbing pain and the injury that would sideline him, likely for the rest of the season.

With little game experience, sophomore Dudley Moore moved into the all-important snapper position. A dedicated, hard-working boy, he became the center of attention in practice that afternoon. Performing flawlessly, the black-haired, dark-eyed lad impressed both his coach and teammates, but understandably they would worry until he proved he could do the job under game-time pressure against the Trojans.

Eighteen new white Riddell helmets arrived the next day, giving a boost to player morale. Dale Moore could now abandon the special one he had been wearing, and the team's headgear would now match their snappy uniforms.

The next problem came on Sunday when Glenn Penn dropped by to see Catfish.

"Cat," he said, standing on the front porch and dropping his gaze to his shoe tops, "I was out late last night and saw a couple of your boys."

Catfish felt a rush of blood to his head as he pushed through the screen door and stared at his brother-in-law, fearing the worst.

"I know you're a stickler for the rules," Penn continued, "and you prohibit . . ."

"Which boys?" Catfish asked, wanting to cut through the details.

"Joe Zane Condrey and Wallace Hunnicutt," Penn muttered. "I hate telling on 'em, Cat, but I know you'd be awful mad if you found out I knew and didn't tell you."

Without a word, Catfish turned and stared into the trees across the road. He could see his perfect season blowing up in his face. Losing his two best running backs, Condrey the fastest and Hunnicutt the most powerful, could jeopardize everything.

"Thanks," he finally said as Penn headed for the steps.

Catfish spent a sleepless night and arrived at school early Monday morning. He explained the situation to Superintendent Fleming and made arrangements for Condrey and Hunnicutt to meet him in the gymnasium during their study hall period. The coach questioned the pair at length about their weekend activities, but made no decision regarding their playing status.

Before practice that afternoon, Catfish called his team together under a big oak in front of the field house.

"Boys," he said, "you've all known our rules since September first, and you know they don't mean a thing unless they're followed and enforced. When I became a coach, I made a commitment to discipline any player who breaks team rules, no matter his importance.

"Two players have violated our rules: Joe Zane Condrey and Wallace Hunnicutt. I won't embarrass them with the details. Normally, I would dismiss the players from the team, and that would be the end of it. But making tough choices is part of life, so I'm leaving this decision to you, their teammates. You're a team, and this team is more important than any player, any two players. Now, I'm going to walk away for a few minutes and let you boys discuss the problem and decide what's best for this team."

Catfish stepped inside the field house and tried to concentrate on some handwritten notes for the afternoon practice session. Within ten minutes, Gene Fleming appeared in the doorway.

"Coach Smith, could you come out here?"

As Catfish approached the group, he noticed that Condrey and Hunnicutt were gone.

"Before we voted," Fleming said, "they both apologized and wanted to stay on the team, but Joe Zane told us he knew what we had to do.

He said, 'I'll save you the trouble of kicking me off.' Wallace followed Condrey. They're gone, Coach."

Catfish scanned their faces and saw that his players were shaken by the sudden loss and the unanswered questions it left. He wished he could tell them that everything would be okay, but the same doubts and concerns etched on their faces gnawed at his insides.

"Go put on your uniforms, boys, and let's get ready for Talco," he said through clenched teeth.

While the players dressed, Catfish stood under the big oak, wondering how he could hold this team together and sustain their run for the championship. Through seven games, Condrey had scored ten touchdowns, had averaged ten yards per carry, and was the premier kick-return man in the district. Hunnicutt had added two scores and represented the only power back on the team. Without these two, where would the Tigers' offense come from?

"Coach," he heard someone call from his left.

Catfish turned and there stood Joe Zane, his gaze glued to the ground.

"I'm sorry, son," Catfish said. "I had hoped to see you get that scholarship and play college ball."

"It's not your fault, Coach," the boy said.

"Come spring and the recruiters show up, I'll still put in a good word for you. Meanwhile, you keep in shape, and keep up your school work."

"Think I'll go home, Coach," Joe Zane said, tears welling up in his eyes. "But before I go, I just want you to know I think you're the best coach a boy could ever play for."

"Thanks," Catfish replied, his voice quivering.

As Joe Zane walked away, it occurred to Catfish that the boy had probably saved the team. He knew that the remaining players had strong feelings regarding rules violations, some believing expulsion was necessary and others preferring some lesser punishment. A close vote could have split his team and doomed the season.

The next day Condrey checked out of his room at the hotel and hitchhiked to Galveston. Without a high school diploma, all hope for a college scholarship was gone.

Wallace Hunnicutt remained in school, disappointed but supportive of his teammates.

With three starters gone from his lineup, Catfish gathered his team and stressed that others had to step up and carry more of the load. He pulled out every slogan he could think of. "You don't know what you're made of until you're back is against the wall," he told them. "Life is full of adversity. It's how you respond to it that determines success or failure." "Real champions rise up when everybody thinks they're down for the count," and, "They say a chain is only as strong as its weakest link, but I say the strongest link, a good leader, can make all the others stronger by example."

"If you let down now," he continued, "everybody will say you're just a bunch of quitters, fair-weather players. People will say, 'If they can't overcome a little adversity, they weren't much of a team.' If I were you, I'd prove to every doubter out there that as long as the Mount Vernon Tigers have eleven players left, they'll beat anybody who's got the guts to line up against them."

"We're sure gonna miss Condrey," one of the boys said walking home after practice that afternoon. "With him on the field, we could score from anywhere, at any time."

"I think we'll miss Wallace just as much," another said. "He's almost as fast, and has more power."

"I don't know if we can beat Talco without them," another whined. "If the Trojans whip us, they can take the district championship. They're gonna play their best against us, and that Harry Dixon is almost impossible to stop."

"Wait a minute," Gayle Tinsley said, stepping ahead of the boys, turning to face them, and extending his arms like a policeman holding up traffic. "Sure we'll miss them, but who pulled out the Mount Pleasant game for us? Billy Jack, that's who. Wallace missed that game and the Pittsburg one, too. Meek and Parchman have carried their part of the load. And another thing. We trounced Winnsboro, who beat Talco earlier."

"But we've lost Dewey, too," another reminded.

"We've all seen Dudley fill in this week, and he hasn't messed up one time," Tinsley said. "Don't worry about those players who are gone. Think about those who are left."

"Maybe Gayle's right," one of the doubters said. "Even without Dewey, there's not a better line in the district, offense or defense."

"Zim and Gayle stopped Mount Pleasant on the goal line, and the hit Pat made on Morris in that game is the best open-field tackle I've ever seen."

"And now that Dale's ankle is better, he'll play his best football of the year."

302

"We're still the top football team going," Tinsley said, smiling. "And to anybody that says different, I say let 'em line up and prove it."

If Catfish had been there, he would have hugged Gayle Tinsley.

Instead, as the coach drove home, he spotted Dewey Moore stepping out of Crescent Drug Store. The recuperating center had decided to treat himself to an ice cream cone.

"Want a ride?" Catfish asked, pulling over by the curb.

Using his left hand, Dewey worked the door latch and slipped inside.

"How's the finger?" Catfish asked, glancing down at the bandaged right hand that now held the untouched ice cream cone. Before Dewey could answer, Catfish bellowed, "What's that in your hand?"

"Ice cream."

"Throw it out the window!"

"But coach, I can't play for several weeks. I didn't think I had to . . ."

Catfish reached across, grabbed the cone, and tossed it out. Stone-faced, the coach then remained silent until he delivered Dewey to his doorstep.

"You be at practice early tomorrow," Catfish growled.

"Yes, sir."

Arriving for practice ten minutes early the next day, Dewey eased into the locker room and took a seat. Catfish let him sit and worry for about five minutes before walking over.

"Put on your uniform," the coach said.

"Coach, the doctor said . . ."

"I'm coaching this team, and as long as you're a member of it, you'll do what I say."

As the other players strolled in, they noticed Dewey pulling on his shoulder pads and sensed trouble.

"What's the deal?" his brother asked.

"Catfish got mad when he saw me with that ice cream yesterday. I guess he's gonna make me practice."

"You can't," Dale said. "With that splint, you can't grip the ball."

"Little brother," Dewey said, "you try explaining that to him."

As the boys filed onto the field, Catfish lined the players up for wind-sprints, Dewey among them. With every jolting stride, the finger pulsed with pain, but the center knew that if he stopped, the next step would be turning in his uniform.

Then the coach lined the boys up for scrimmage. Dewey ambled over to the huddle, confusing Dudley Miller.

"Stickfinger," Catfish said to Dewey, "get out of here. Start running laps around the field."

While the team prepared for Talco, Dewey lapped the field, again and again. Finally, out of breath and with his finger throbbing, he stopped and bent double at the waist.

"Stickfinger," Catfish bellowed, "it's your finger that's broken, not your legs. Now, get back to running."

Over the next three days, Dewey ran more than he had ever run in his life. His finger ached all the time, and he was sick of it. He could picture Catfish having him lap the field throughout the Talco game.

Thursday afternoon, Superintendent Fleming knocked on the door of Catfish's classroom. He motioned the coach into the hall.

"We might have a big problem," he said.

"Another player hurt?" Catfish asked, as fingers of panic gripped his throat.

"No. The Chicago Cardinals have offered your assistant coach a job kicking for them. They'll pay him four hundred dollars a game and an extra thousand if the team makes the playoffs. That's a lot of money to turn down."

"What does Bo say he's going to do?" Catfish asked, his midsection tightening now.

"He's considering it. You might want to talk to him."

"Can you cover for me in there?" Catfish asked, nodding toward his students.

Fleming took over, and Catfish headed down the hallway to see Bo Campbell.

"We really need you, Bo. We're in the middle of a championship season. Can't you get them to wait a few weeks?"

"I've got to decide by tomorrow," the assistant said, "and be in Chicago by Monday, if I'm going."

"You've got a contract with us, you know."

"I know, and if you won't let me out of it, I've got no decision to make."

"Ah, Bo, you know we'll let you go, if that's what you want to do."

"I'll give you my answer tomorrow morning. Fair?"

Catfish nodded and moseyed back to his classroom, wondering what he would do if his assistant boarded that plane Monday morning.

Friday came and so did frigid temperatures, cold rain, and sleet.

Catfish was worried sick. He arrived at school early and paced the hallway until Bo Campbell showed up.

"Well, are you deserting us?" Cat asked, chuckling halfheartedly.

"No, this is home, and I like it here. I'm staying."

Catfish wanted to hug his assistant, but settled for a firm handshake.

Putting aside his worries, the coach focused on his students until mid-afternoon when he turned his full attention to the upcoming game. Talco had a good team, having lost only to Winnsboro when they allowed the winning touchdown on a punt return in the last minute of the game. Against the Trojans, he would have three backups starting, one snapping the ball on every down, on a cold, wet night. Would Dudley bobble it a couple of times? Dewey was a strong linebacker. How would the slender Meek perform in his place? Without Hunnicutt, he had no power runner. Speedy backs on a slippery field often tackle themselves. The district title that had looked secure two weeks ago was now teetering on a shaky beam, and he felt like someone was twisting a knife in his stomach.

"Boys," Catfish said, addressing his team just before kickoff, "this is for the district championship. You're the best team I've ever coached, and it'd break my heart to see you let a little adversity or a little nasty weather end your season prematurely. It'd be unfair to yourselves, to your school, to your parents, but most of all, it'd be unfair to one of your teammates. Stickfinger would love to line up with you tonight and help win the title, but he can't. He's a senior, so if you let down out there, he'll never get that chance.

"It reminds me of Billy Radican. When he saw his fellow soldier go down beside a burning German ammunition truck, he didn't hunker down to protect himself from the explosion or enemy gunfire. He risked his life to give his friend another chance. So, go out there and win this game and give your injured teammate a chance to get well and join you for the playoffs."

Mount Vernon won the toss and chose to receive the kickoff. The first play of a key ballgame often sets the tone for what follows, and the coach had a plan.

"Dale," Catfish said to his quarterback before he sent him onto the field. "First play is stingaree right."

The cold ball and damp air made for a short kickoff. Cunningham tucked it in and tiptoed on the frozen field for fifteen yards, out to the forty. After a brief huddle, the Tigers lined up, and Dale barked signals.

305

Dudley Miller snapped the ball flawlessly, and the quarterback spun to his left, deftly slipped the ball into the hands of his left guard, and then followed his blockers around left end.

Meanwhile, Zim tucked the football under his arm and headed around right end, where he saw nothing but open space. The opposition finally caught up to him on their eighteen.

Back in the huddle, Fleming said, "They don't know what hit 'em, so let's do it again."

Zim worked down to the two-yard line. From there, Cunningham took the ball and followed Lowry and Zimmerman into the end zone. Fleming missed the point-after, but the Tigers had that all-important first score.

For the remainder of the quarter, the Tiger defense was like an iron gate, shut and locked, and every time the Trojans came looking for the key, they got slapped back. However, the advantage went for naught as Mount Vernon's offense sputtered with their lightweight runners slipping down with every attempt to cut upfield. The period wasted away with neither team gaining significant advantage in the resulting kicking contest.

In the second period, the Tigers received a punt at midfield. With Meredith, Meek and Cunningham pounding into the line between their tackles, they avoided slippery cutbacks and pushed down to the thirty-five. With the defense sucked into the middle, Fleming again called the trick play to Zim.

It had never worked better. Totally fooled, the Talco defense did not see the big guard until he was within ten yards of the end zone. The point-after made the score 13-0.

Fleming kicked the ball to Talco, and Harry Dixon gathered it in at the three-yard line. The meteoric runner dashed, cut, and faked, totally disregarding the slippery conditions, and sailed ninety-seven yards for a touchdown, the most sensational run of the season. Suddenly, the Trojans were within a touchdown of the Tigers, and on an icy field, anything could happen.

Receiving the kickoff on their fifteen, the Tigers methodically fought their way to the Talco forty-four, utilizing their backup runners most of the way. Then Meredith slithered through a hole at left tackle, broke past the logjam at the line of scrimmage, and headed for the end zone. The fullback's odds of scoring did not look good when the swift Dixon took a dead-aim bead on him and pinned Meredith against the sideline. But the freshman made a veteran-like stop-and-spin move that left the fleet defensive man sprawled on the wet turf. Meredith scored untouched, and Fleming added the point-after with less than a minute remaining in the first half, building the score to 20-6.

Starting the second half, the Trojans gained three quick first downs before the Tiger defense stiffened just short of midfield. However, a dandy punt pinned Catfish's boys back inside their ten.

While the coach worried about a bad snap by Dudley Miller, a flubbed handoff, or a hard hit jarring the ball lose, his new center and rookie backfield played like pros. Meek, Meredith, Cunningham, and occasionally Moore, bulled their way down the field, chewing up yard-stripes and running the clock. The ninety-plus-yard drive culminated in a two-yard dive by Cunningham into the end zone. Fleming booted the point-after, and the Tigers knew they had their eighth straight win and fourth district victory.

The Tigers racked up one more score in the final stanza, and when the game-ending gun sounded, Talco had managed only four first downs and sixty-four yards of offense. Of their three passes, the Tigers had intercepted one and taken it back thirty-five yards. Dixon had covered more yards on that touchdown run than his entire team had gained from the line of scrimmage. Meanwhile, Mount Vernon had just ten first downs, but had ground out two hundred thirty-five yards.

Savoring the 34-6 win, Catfish lavished praise on his boys. They had stood up and faced down their critics. They had overcome about the worst imaginable adversity. They had proven they were much more than a two-man show, and they had done it all against a title contender on an icy field. But the celebration had to be cut short.

The Tigers had one more conference contest, and it was against Gilmer, a perennial district-title challenger. With only one loss, the Buckeyes were still in the race. If they could beat the Tigers, then whip Mount Pleasant and Winnsboro, they would once again take up residence on the district throne.

Devall of the *Optic-Herald* joined the coach in applauding the Tigers' valiant effort against the Trojans. "The entire team should be All-District," he declared. Piling up a season total of three hundred twenty points while allowing only twenty, they had played head and shoulders above their opposition all season. Reaching back to the 1946 team, the Tigers had a thirteen-game winning streak going. Their closest challenger had come up short by nineteen points, and Mount Vernon had the best coach in East Texas, maybe in the state.

What Devall did not know, and neither did the fans or the Tigers, another problem lurked that could jeopardize the district title and their season.

The stress of the past two weeks had taken its toll on their coach. While winning on the gridiron, he was losing yet another battle with ulcers.

28

November 8, 1947

Catfish rested, drank fresh milk, and ate bland foods throughout the weekend. He must fight off this attack. Friday night's game against Gilmer was for the district championship. He had fought through late-season ulcer attacks before, and he would do it again. Being laid up at this juncture could be disastrous.

Dorothy Nell urged him to let her call a doctor, but the coach did not want such news to reach his team. His boys had responded well to every challenge, but he could not bear being the cause of them having to handle another one right now.

Forty-eight hours of rest, proper diet, and care brought some relief, and he showed up at school Monday, and then at practice that afternoon. So did a fretful Dewey Moore.

"Stickfinger," Catfish said, "Dudley did a fine job Friday night. You keep circling the field and sweat that ice cream out of your system. Maybe you'll be back in shape for the playoffs."

"Coach," Dewey responded. "I think I can play."

The center had made up his mind that weekend. He would do anything to avoid that incessant running. If his finger was going to throb anyway, then let it hurt while doing something he liked to do.

"What?" Catfish asked, turning on Dewey. "Can you grip the ball?"

"I practiced with Dale this weekend. I can do it."

"And your doctor's orders?"

"I won't tell him if you won't," Dewey replied, with a sheepish grin.

"Let's see you snap the ball," Catfish said, winking at his assistant.

Three snaps convinced the coach, and the pardoned center joined his teammates in the huddle, with the understanding that Miller would replace him for extra points and punts. The Tigers' wounded soldier would have his chance to help win the championship.

On paper the Tigers appeared to have the Buckeyes outclassed. Gilmer's only loss had been to Talco, but by a whopping twenty-nine points, while Catfish's boys had bested the Trojans by twenty-eight. The Buckeyes had skimped by Pittsburg by seven, and the Tigers had demolished the Pirates by forty-four. But as Catfish had told his team many times, "there are no paper victories."

Catfish took it easy and practice went well, but as the game approached, the coach could not fight off the worries. Thursday, he dropped by Superintendent Fleming's office and asked for the afternoon off.

"Your ulcers," Fleming said, noticing Catfish was hunched forward and grimacing. "I'll drive you to the hospital."

"No," Catfish said. "Just get me home, and don't tell anybody."

When Dorothy Nell saw her husband, she took charge. "Get in the car," she said immediately. "I'm taking you to a doctor."

"Let's just take him to the hospital," Fleming suggested.

After one look, the doctor had the coach assigned to a room in the month-old hospital.

"Can I get out tomorrow?" Catfish asked.

"No!" the doctor replied bluntly.

The coach turned toward his superintendent, his tired eyes pleading for help.

"Catfish," Fleming said, "Coach Campbell and I will take care of the team."

"I can't let them down now," the coach said with watery eyes. "Those boys have done everything I've ever asked of them. Dewey has practiced all week with a broken finger. Zim has played with a broken hand. Dale has played three games with his ankle swollen double its normal size. I have to be there for my boys."

"Coach," Fleming said, "your boys know you'd be there if you could. Why, they'd jump off the top of the Empire State Building for you. You've always found a way to motivate them, but this time I'm taking that assignment. Those boys are going to win this final game for their sick coach."

The players were shocked at the news, but responded exactly as Superintendent Fleming hoped they would. With fierce determination, they prepared to do battle Friday night for their coach. No cause could have inspired them more.

On a cold, muddy field, the Tigers unleashed their pent-up emotions on the Buckeyes, 40-0, while Catfish listened to a special play-by-play of the game on a phone hookup to the press box, arranged by local businessmen.

The scoring started when Dale Moore tossed a pass to Pat Loyd who galloped thirty-five yards down to the four-yard line. Meek then plunged into the end zone. Fleming missed the point-after, and Catfish sat up in bed and scribbled a note.

Early in the second period, Meek continued his heroics. He ripped off runs of twenty-eight, fifteen, and thirteen yards. At the beginning of the longest of those, Gene Fleming had delivered a crushing block on a Buckeye that echoed throughout the stadium. Meredith then got the touchdown, giving his team a two-touchdown lead, but the big tackle again missed the extra point, prompting Catfish to make another note.

Zimmerman, Lowry, Fleming, Tinsley, and "Stickfinger" Moore led a stalwart defense. Dudley Miller substituted for Dewey for most of the offensive plays, including snapping for punts and extra points, but the hard-hitting Dewey insisted on filling his linebacker slot. Cunningham showed both speed and power, well beyond expectations, while Campbell and Loyd snatched every pass thrown their way.

The second half started with Gene Fleming picking off a Gilmer aerial and lugging it back to the thirty-two-yard line. The elusive Meek then circled left end for a touchdown. Fleming converted the point-after, bringing a smile to Catfish's face.

Following the kickoff to Gilmer, Zim belted an enemy ball carrier on the first play, vibrating loose the pigskin on the twenty-three where the Tiger guard fell on it. From there, Dale sailed an aerial to Cunningham for another score. Fleming converted and Mount Vernon then led 26-0.

The first play after kicking the ball to Gilmer was a Buckeye attempt to skirt their left end. When the runner found himself trapped, he pitched the ball toward a trailing teammate. Pat Loyd picked it off on the Buckeye twenty-two, and if he had not slipped on the muddy field, he would have scored. Instead, the Tigers rammed Cunningham into the line twice, then quarterback Moore dropped back and hurled a pass to Bud Campbell who raced into the end zone. Again, Fleming's toe was accurate, making the score 33-0.

Freshman fullback Meredith accounted for the final tally, culminating a long drive with a two-yard dive across the double stripe.

The Tigers were undefeated District 19-A champs and ready for their coach to return and prepare them for their long-time nemesis, the Edgewood Bulldogs. While the Bulldogs finished their regular schedule with a game against Mount Pleasant, the Tigers had an off week, giving Catfish precious time to mend.

With Catfish still recovering, Superintendent Fleming and Bo Campbell drove to Mount Pleasant on Friday, November 21, to watch their next opponent tie the Titus County Tigers, 13-13.

"We can beat that bunch," the assistant said while driving to a restaurant to meet with Edgewood school officials to discuss the details of their upcoming bi-district contest.

"Don't make too much of tonight's game," Fleming advised. "Edgewood already had their district title sewed up and were just playing around with Mount Pleasant until time to meet us in the one that really matters to them."

At the meeting of the two schools, Bulldog officials insisted on deciding the game site by a coin flip, rather than negotiating a neutral stadium. The coin settled in the Bulldogs' favor, giving them home-field advantage for the contest scheduled at seven-thirty on Friday, November 28.

Meanwhile, the new eight-bed Franklin County Hospital was busy. Saturday night Hoffman Moore, school board member and father of Dewey, Dale, and Johnny, made an emergency entrance with a cerebral hemorrhage. The Moore family suddenly forgot about their other afflictions: Dewey's broken finger, Dale's sprained ankle, and Johnny's broken foot. Their father's condition was critical.

Wednesday, Catfish left his hospital bed, checked with his friend Hoffman, who was improving steadily, and returned to his team. That afternoon, he took over preparations for the bi-district tilt, with his number one concern being a letdown by his boys after the highly emotional final two district games. Next he worried about the long layoff prior to the contest. The open date three weeks earlier had resulted in the loss of three key players. First, the lack of urgency of a regular Friday night game likely contributed to the horsing around that broke Dewey Moore's finger. And a Friday night game would just as likely have prevented the resignations of Condrey and Hunnicutt from the team. Finally, he fretted over the Bulldogs' playoff-winning tradition. Two consecutive regional championships undoubtedly had the Edgewood team confident of a third, while creating doubts in the minds of Catfish's players, doubts that could balloon if things went badly early in the game. The last worry bore the dual names of Judd Ramsey and Billy Ray Norris. The first was a hard-nosed fullback, and the second was a steady, accurate-throwing quarterback.

A couple of things worked in Catfish's favor. Ample preparation and healing time ranked number one. Second, Edgewood knew about the loss of Condrey and Hunnicutt, and probably guessed that Dewey Moore would be hampered. They might not know that Meredith, Meek, Parchman, and Cunningham were proven performers, especially behind an offensive line that took a backseat to no one. Less tangible was the coach's firm belief that he had a team with on-field leaders, smart kids, and players who refused to lose. Destiny was too vague a term, but his boys had a spirit about them that was undeniable, and between two evenly matched teams, that alone could swing the outcome to his boys.

Game day arrived without a catastrophe. Even Hoffman Moore was back home, though still unable to work. L. D. Lowry, Jr., arranged to have radio station KSST in Sulphur Springs broadcast the game, his furniture store sponsoring the program, and Hoffman listened to the game, "resting" with his ear never far from his radio.

A spirited Edgewood team took the field as regional champs for the past two years, and victors over Mount Vernon in their two prior meetings. Adding to their home-field advantage, the Bulldogs won the coin toss and took the ball, bringing a smile to Catfish's face. He liked the idea of his stalwart defense starting the game.

On the kickoff, Fleming hit a good one that flipped end-over-end down to the five-yard line. Norris returned it to the Edgewood twenty. Three running plays later, the Bulldogs lacked twelve yards for a first down. Catfish loved it.

The Bulldogs' punter stepped forward, dropped the ball to his foot, and felt a solid hit. Then he heard a second thud. Zim had broken through the line and extended his stout arms, reversing the flight of the ball. The big guard then cradled around the pigskin on the nine-yard line: Mount Vernon's ball.

Parchman pounded the line behind Lowry and Zimmerman for eight yards, one step from the goal line. Dale Moore, his ankle mended, followed Dewey and Zim into the end zone on a quarterback sneak. With Miller snapping the ball, the point-after was good. The Tigers had that all-important lead, 7-0. Catfish could not have scripted a better start.

Fleming's next kickoff went to Judd Ramsey who brought it back to the thirty. Again the Bulldogs could not crack the formidable Tiger forward wall. They punted successfully this time, down to the Tigers' forty. Cunningham gathered in the ball and romped back to the Bulldogs' forty-two. The Tigers were looking good. Might as well hit those 'dogs again while they were on their heels.

Dale Moore dropped back and lofted a pass to the flat to a wide-open Pat Loyd, but the ball never arrived. Judd Ramsey darted in front of Loyd and grabbed the ball. He did not slow down until sixty yards later. The point-after failed, and the Tigers held a one-point lead.

The two teams then battled back and forth in the middle of the field until the midpoint of the second quarter when the Bulldogs' Norris hit Covin with a pass for a forty-seven-yard gain, down to the Tigers' one-yard line. Williams got the final step for the touchdown. Another failed point-after left the Bulldogs with the lead, 12-7.

Again the Edgewood defense held the Tigers, and with the aid of a penalty, pushed Catfish's boys back to their own five, forcing a desperate punt. Miller came in and made a perfect snap back to Meredith who sailed a beautiful spiral out to the forty-five, but Ramsey fought his way back to the thirty. Norris wasted no time, drilling a pass to teammate James in the end zone. The quarterback then skirted right end for the extra point and a 19-7 advantage.

The Tigers had now given up as many touchdowns in half a game as they had in the entire season. It was one of those moments that could make or break a team. How would Catfish's boys respond?

The answer came in a hurry.

The Tigers received the kickoff and brought it out to their own twenty-three. The offense hurried to the line of scrimmage where Fleming and Tinsley promptly opened a gaping hole in the right side, and Cunningham romped for ten yards. The Tiger fans took note and hoped for a sustained drive, like they had come to expect from this team. If it was to happen, their All-District line had to take control of the line of scrimmage. Undoubtedly, the Bulldogs knew their opponent's tendency and braced for the assault.

Instead, disregarding the earlier interception, Dale Moore dropped back and spiraled a bullet to Loyd who raced forty-nine yards before being corralled by a determined Bulldog tackler. Three running plays drove the ball to the three, from where Meek knifed into the end zone. With a perfect snap from Dudley Miller, Fleming made the point-after, closing the score to 19-14. A stadium full of fans then knew there were no quitters wearing purple and white.

The Tigers received the kickoff to start the second half, but their offense was unable to sustain a drive. However, the Tiger's defense dominated the quarter and slowly pushed the Bulldogs deeper into their territory. When the third quarter expired, Catfish's boys faced fourth down near midfield.

Starting the final quarter, the most accurate punter in District 19-A booted a high spiral to Edgewood's fifteen. Desperate to move the ball out, one of the Bulldog linemen was flagged for holding Fleming, pushing Edgewood back inside the ten. Fearful of a disastrous mistake, Edgewood punted. On a dazzling run, Cunningham returned the ball to the Bulldog twenty-four. After Zim picked up seven yards on his trick play, Meredith and Meek drove the ball to the four-yard line where they faced fourth down and a golden opportunity to erase that five-point deficit.

Finding themselves well into the final quarter against a quality team like the Bulldogs, the Tigers knew they might not get another chance to score. They had to find a way to get that final four yards and regain the lead. Otherwise, their season was over.

Fleming searched the eyes of his teammates in the huddle. Maybe he recalled Catfish's humor regarding "the Rambler." "You need four yards, he'll get you four yards. You need eight, he'll get you four yards." Or maybe he saw something in Kenneth Meek's eyes.

With the season on the line, the Rambler got the ball, and summoning what seemed like superhuman strength, he ripped his slight frame out of the grasp of two tacklers before lunging into the end zone. Fleming's kick was true, and the Tigers led, 21-19.

While the two teams prepared for the ensuing kickoff, Catfish cornered his assistant, Bo Campbell.

"We need to pin them deep and make a strong defensive stand right now," he said, sensing the game had reached it pivotal point. "I'd like to offer a reward to fire these boys up. How about you and I promise a silver football to the player who makes the tackle on the kickoff?"

Campbell agreed, and while Catfish relayed the message to his players, his assistant called Fleming over.

"Son, this is the most important kick you've made all year," he said, and then reminded him of the techniques they had practiced endlessly.

In the Tigers' huddle on the field, Zimmerman hushed his teammates. "Boys, you can all run down there, but the ball carrier is mine. I'm gonna win that silver football."

Fleming swung a heavy foot into the ball, and it sailed deep into Bulldog territory. As Williams caught the ball and headed upfield, cutting to his left, he was suddenly blotted out by a shiny white uniform tattooed with the single purple digit, six. The ferocious hit left both Williams and Zimmerman slow in getting to their feet.

Two thousand fans knew that if the Bulldogs were to regain the lead, they had to do it now. Likewise, if the Tigers were to advance to the regional championship game, they had to make a stand now.

The Bulldogs tried an end sweep, but lost five yards to a relentless Bud Campbell. Norris dropped back to throw a pass but was smothered by Fleming, Campbell, and Loyd for a ten-yard loss. Another run failed when Lowry slammed the runner to the turf, and the Bulldogs had to punt from the shadow of their own goalpost.

The kicker never had a chance. Zim tore through the Bulldog line and smothered the kick. Tinsley outfought two Bulldogs for the ball, and the Tigers were in business on Edgewood's fifteen, with the clock ticking down. A score would ice the game.

Meek and Meredith gained six and eight respectively, placing the pigskin on the one, from where Meredith finished the job. The failed point-after seemed unimportant. The Tigers had an eight-point lead, and the clock was now their ally.

Before Fleming kicked the ball to the Bulldogs, he called his teammates together.

"We haven't allowed them across midfield in the second half. If we can stop them one more time, we're bi-district champs."

Fleming boomed another kick to the Bulldogs who brought it out to the twenty-four. After failing to gain a single yard on three plays and facing another fourth-down-and-long situation, an exasperated Edgewood team watched the game clock tick to zeroes. The Tigers had their first victory over the Bulldogs, 27-19, and 1947 would see a new regional champion.

The Tigers had not dominated the Bulldogs, but the statistics were reflective of the score. Mount Vernon rushed for one hundred ninety-two yards, while being pushed back only two. They ground out nine first downs and completed one pass for forty-nine yards. The Bulldogs managed only four first downs, all in the first half. They ran for one hundred yards, but were shoved back fifty-three in losses, netting only forty-seven, Norris completed four passes for one hundred eight yards.

Now the Tigers would have to wait a week to learn whether their opponent for the regional title would be Clarksville or Athens. The coach still preferred to play every Friday night, but he accepted the benefits of the extended time off and tried to push aside his worries.

The coming Wednesday would change that.

29

December 3, 1947

On Wednesday afternoon in a routine head-on tackling drill, Zim lined up against Pat Loyd. Both were known as hard hitters, and maybe each felt a need to protect his reputation. In any case, they collided like a couple of young rams. Zim stepped away with a limp left arm, clutching his clavicle and shoulder area. Everyone stared, hoping for something minor, a stinger maybe.

Bo Campbell checked the big guard and quickly shot a glance toward Catfish.

"I think something's broken," the assistant said.

"What's broken?" Catfish asked, and then ran his fingers along Zim's collarbone. He winced, and his face drained pale.

Within an hour a doctor confirmed their fears: a broken collarbone. Zim, who had blocked two punts in the Edgewood game, had made countless game-saving tackles and game-winning blocks throughout the season, would miss the biggest game of the year.

"Zim is the best guard I've ever coached," Catfish said, shaking his head. "We don't have a backup that can do what he does, offensively and defensively, but fortunately we have a couple of good boys who can step in for him."

"We've had some bad breaks this year," Devall reported in the December 5 *Optic-Herald*. "Dale has had that bad ankle, Dewey the broken finger, and we've lost a couple of outstanding backs, but this may be the worst setback yet."

The official All-District team had been announced that week, and Devall's earlier prediction of the selections missed the mark, but not by much. Every starter on the Tigers' team appeared on one of three lists.

Pat Loyd	LE	First Team
Charles Lowry	LT	Second Team
Herb Zimmerman	LG	First Team
Dewey Moore	C	Second Team
Gayle Tinsley	RG	Second Team
Gene Fleming	RT	First Team
Bud Campbell	RE	Second Team
Dale Moore	QB	Second Team
Roy Cunningham	LH	Honorable Mention
Billy Jack Meredith	FB	Second Team
Kenneth Meek	RH	First Team
Buck Parchman	RH	Honorable Mention
Dudley Miller	C	Honorable Mention

While the Tigers were finishing a successful football season, the other district schools were preparing for the upcoming basketball schedule. Deport had been barred from competition due to the melee and verbal outburst following the district championship game in Talco the prior year, so the league was pared down to eight teams. Nine players currently in football uniforms would make up the heart of Catfish's basketball squad that could not swap uniforms until December 15, only two weeks before the start of district play.

Friday night, December 5, Athens defeated Clarksville, 20-7, a team the Tigers had outscored 24-0. But that had been back in September when Catfish's team had been at full strength. Since that game in which Stiles had been shut down, the big Clarksville fullback had run wild, vastly improving his team's performance.

The Dallas newspapers picked Athens as the region's favorite. A town four times the population of Mount Vernon, Athens had been in Class AA until recently, and two of their nine victories this season had been over AA teams, Palestine and Jacksonville. Their two losses had been to New London, 26-20, and to Mexia, 26-6.

The Hornets' big gun was a back named Jimmy Hawn, a one-hundred-seventy-pounder. The most recent in a long line of famous athletic brothers, this one was being forecasted as a "can't miss" college prospect. Additionally, the Hornets claimed Sonny Mitchell, the coach's son, a fine runner, hurdler, and high-jumper.

Catfish gave his boys some unique advice regarding Mitchell.

"Don't tackle him low. He'll leap right over you. Aim for his chest, right between the numbers."

After considerable haggling over the location of the game, whether Commerce, Sulphur Springs, or Greenville, a coin flip on December 9 brought the contest to Mount Vernon, at two-thirty on Friday afternoon, December 12.

On game day, Devall's newspaper carried the Tigers' team picture on the front page, and the headline, in inch-tall letters, proclaimed, "HORNETS, TIGERS IN TITLE CLASH HERE TODAY." Inside, a full-page ad reiterated the event, along with a half-page-sized cheerleader overshadowing a Cotton Bowl-like stadium while screaming into her megaphone, "YEA, TIGERS—LET'S WIN THE REGIONAL TITLE TODAY." Crammed at the bottom of the page was a list of forty-nine proud sponsors who supported the ad. Locals would have been hard-pressed to name that many local businesses. They included all those surrounding the town square, eleven grocery stores, seven service station operators, a couple of barbershops, a lady's shop, and a dairy operation.

By game time, the temperature had dipped to fifteen degrees, yet over thirty-five hundred fans packed into Tiger Field, which was designed to hold twenty-five hundred. Superintendent Fleming, though spending long hours at his wife's bedside in a Dallas hospital, had warned the Tiger faithful to arrive early. The east stands were reserved for Athens' fans, and by kickoff, the locals should anticipate a standing-room-only crowd. Even early arrivers would be fortunate to get a bleacher seat, while stragglers would be lucky to just grab a fence-line position with an open view. This would be Mount Vernon's largest sports event ever, and the only one to attract reporters from both Dallas newspapers. The only people in Mount Vernon who did not know about the event had long since taken up residency in the local cemetery.

The game started to the yells and whistles of a boisterous crowd, stomping their cold feet to retain blood circulation. After an exchange of punts, pushing the Hornets back to their eighteen, Sonny Mitchell skirted right end and galloped sixty-three yards before Billy Jack Meredith corralled him. From the nineteen, Hawn made a bruising run to the eight, then drove for three more to the five. From there Mitchell swept around right end into the end zone, and the visitors, after Gatlin's point-after, had an early seven-point lead.

Unable to sustain a retaliatory drive, the Tigers had to punt again, giving Athens the ball just beyond midfield. Then Mount Vernon got a break.

As Lee Mitchell's son, Sonny, rounded his left end, Pat Loyd remembered Catfish's advice: "He'll hurdle you if you try to tackle him low. Hit him right between the one and two on his chest." As he had done in the Mount Pleasant game, Loyd nailed the runner and drove him to the frozen turf. The jarring lick separated Mitchell from the football, and Billy Jack Carter, replacing the injured Zimmerman, recovered on the Tigers' forty-nine.

Meek and Meredith alternated lugging the ball until the Tigers had advanced to their opponent's five-yard line. On fourth down and three yards needed, the Hornets bunched up along the line of scrimmage, obviously keying on the two runners. Instead, Dale tossed a pass to Loyd for an easy score. Fleming's kick split the uprights, tying the game at 7-7.

After stalling Athens' offense, the Tigers regained the ball at their own thirty-three. Fleming noticed that the Hornets were still ganging up along the line of scrimmage, and made his play selection accordingly.

The Tiger quarterback faked a handoff to Meredith and then sent a spiral to Meek for thirty yards. First and ten on the Hornets' thirty-seven, Dale again dropped back and arched a pass toward Bud Campbell who had raced down to the fifteen where defenders Sonny Mitchell and Randy Wesson closed rapidly on the Tiger receiver. As they jumped to intercept the pass, Campbell, resorting to his basketball instincts, shielded the would-be thieves from the football, leaped to his maximum height, and tipped the ball up and forward. As the defenders collided, the pigskin floated harmlessly toward the cold ground, but Campbell twisted away from the tangle of bodies, reached out with his left hand and tapped the ball with his fingertips, momentarily stopping its descent. Regaining his balance, the lanky end got a hand on the ball and cradled it against his chest. The defenders scrambled to their feet, too late to catch up with the tall Tiger, and helplessly watched Campbell sail into the end zone. Fleming's kick made it 14-7 at halftime.

The second half began with Athens kicking to the Tigers. Meek returned the kick but fumbled on the twenty-six, where the Hornets' Carl Andress recovered the loose football. On first down Mitchell swept right to the eleven-yard line. Two more Mitchell carries reached the one. From there the one-hundred-seventy-pound Hawn powered the ball into the end zone, and Gatlin tied the score, 14-14.

After the Tigers failed to sustain their next drive, Meredith punted the ball out of bounds on the Hornets' thirty-yard line. On first down, Mitchell clicked off seventeen yards, followed by Hawn stepping off eighteen to the Tigers' thirty-five. Another gallop by Mitchell carried to the Tigers' twenty-five, and Athens appeared to be on their way to the go-ahead score. However, on the next carry by Hawn, Charles Lowry's crunching tackle stopped the power runner dead in his tracks, and separated him from the football. A hustling Gayle Tinsley recovered.

The remainder of the third quarter became a defensive battle, neither offense finding much success. Meredith repeatedly pushed the Hornets back with pinpoint punts that skipped out of bounds, eliminating a return.

The final period began with Athens trying to recover from one of Billy Jack's well-placed kicks. After a couple of failed runs, Jimmy Hawn dropped back to pass. As he released the ball, Gene Fleming rammed his right shoulder into the passer's ribs, and the ball fluttered short where Charles Lowry grabbed it on the Hornets' thirty-three, giving the Tigers the chance they needed to break the tie in a game that would likely be decided by a touchdown or less.

With the Hornets' defensive front supported closely by linebackers Butch Bledsoe, Claud Ramsey, Ken Morgan, and Jimmy Hawn, Tiger quarterback Moore went back to the air, completing a pass to Bud Campbell to the twenty-two. In a game where the difference might be penetrations, the Tigers needed only three yards to take a three-to-two lead. However, after four unsuccessful passes, Athens took over, and Mount Vernon had squandered its opportunity to gain a decisive advantage.

As they had done so many times throughout the year, the Tiger defense held the Hornets without a first down and regained the ball on a wobbly punt. Mixing passes and runs, Mount Vernon moved the ball steadily while the game clock ticked away valuable seconds.

Throughout the contest, the Hornets had crowded the line of scrimmage with nine defenders, determined to stop the Tigers' already weakened running attack. With the ball on Athens' forty-yard line and time running out, Fleming decided it was time to make them pay.

Dale Moore faked a handoff to Meek, and dropped back thee steps, his strong right arm cocked. With Athens' linemen fighting to reach him, the sophomore released a sensational pass that found Pat Loyd down on the enemy's nineteen. The clock showed a little over forty seconds remaining in the game, enough time for two more plays.

The Tiger quarterback hurried a pass that sailed over Campbell's head, eliminating any chance of an interception. With the clock dropping below thirty-five seconds, Mount Vernon rushed back into its huddle.

With wide eyes, everyone looked at Fleming, anxious for one last pass to try to win the game.

Meanwhile, on the sideline Catfish asked Bo Campbell what he thought about the X-pass where the two ends cross in the middle of the opponents' backfield, designed to confuse the two defensive safeties. Dale was having a great game throwing the ball, and if either Pat Loyd or Bud Campbell should break free, the Tiger quarterback could hit the open receiver with a pass for the winning score.

"If Zim were in there, Stingaree right might get us a touchdown," the assistant replied. "Without him, I'd go for the field goal."

It was a crazy idea. Mount Vernon had never kicked a field goal, not even a short one under ideal conditions. The temperature had dropped to ten degrees, the rock-hard ball rested on the left hash mark near the Tiger's side of the field. It was a nasty angle, narrowing the window between the uprights to half its natural width. Catfish looked out at his big tackle. He had never had a headier or steadier player.

"Guthrie," the coach called out, "get in there for Meek. Lineup at right tackle and tell Fleming to kick a field goal."

While the words echoed in Catfish's head as if from some alien voice, Billy Jack Guthrie scampered onto the field and whispered the coach's decision to the big tackle.

"Field goal," Fleming said to his teammates. "We've got time, so everybody be deliberate and think about your assignment. Linemen, close your spacing and make sure nobody gets through. We're gonna win this thing right now."

The coaches froze in their tracks. Though Fleming had never kicked a field goal under game conditions, Bo had worked daily with his big tackle on kickoffs, and had often demonstrated the field goal technique, showing why he had been considered the premier kicker in the Southwest when he had handled those chores for Southern Methodist University.

A sharp angle on a frozen field with only seconds left in a championship game, the assistant thought. I'd sure hate to have to go out there and kick it under these circumstances.

"I don't know what to do," Billy Jack Carter said frantically, breaking from the huddle.

Carter had replaced Zim on defense, with Guthrie playing the offensive guard slot. But Guthrie was now lined up as Fleming's replacement at right tackle. Carter had never even lined up for an extra point.

"Anchor your right foot behind Dewey's left," Lowry said, "and loop your left in front of my right. When the ball is snapped, turn and grab the center, forming a wall. I won't let anybody squeeze between us."

The crowd rose to its feet, counting the yard markers from where Billy Jack Meredith kneeled to set the ball on the frozen ground: twenty-nine yards from the goalposts to the line of scrimmage, and about six more from where Meredith waited for the snap. Some Mount Vernon fans recalled how Bo Campbell had booted two kickoffs against Texas Christian University some sixty-five to seventy yards, splitting the uprights. A few recalled Gene Fleming blasting a kickoff beyond the back of the end zone in an earlier Tiger game. Here the big tackle needed about a forty-yarder to safely reach the goalposts with enough height to clear the crossbar. If Fleming hit it solidly, he had the range.

As the Tigers lined up along the line of scrimmage, Catfish noticed the splint on the middle finger of Dewey's right hand. Dudley Miller had been snapping on punts and extra points because the stiff finger hindered Moore's gripping of the ball. In their haste, the coaches had forgotten to substitute Miller for Dewey, and now there was no time to make the change.

From his wing position, Dale Moore looked up and down the line, then glanced back at Fleming and Billy Jack. The linemen were still tightening their spacing, and the clock was ticking down. The quarterback started the cadence, hoping everyone would get set before the ball was snapped.

Catfish held his breath as Dewey tried to grip the ball with his splinted right hand.

"Hut," the quarterback barked.

The coach's eyes widened as he watched the ball sail back toward Meredith, a perfect spiral at just the right height.

The Hornets crashed into the Tigers' forward wall with all the force they could muster as Meredith nimbly picked the ball out of the air, calmly placed it on the frozen turf, and Fleming stepped forward. The kicker's right toe swung into the ball, sending it on its dramatic flight. Some of the Hornets leaped high, arms stretched toward the heavens, hoping to deflect the pigskin.

Thirty-eight hundred spectators went silent, their eyes glued to the end-over-end kick, watching the ball clear the desperate fingertips of the Hornet defenders and arch toward the goalposts. It seemed an eternity.

"He hit it good," Bo Campbell muttered, his eyes glued to the flipping ball.

"It's between the uprights," Catfish said, having stepped onto the field and aligned himself with the pigskin's line of flight.

"He did it!" Bo Campbell yelled, leaping into the air as the ball dropped over the crossbar.

The referee raised his arms, confirming the kicking teacher's judgment and sealing a 17-14 Tiger victory.

In an unbelievable and impractical turn of events, the Mount Vernon Tigers had won the Region 5 championship. Not only that, but they had completed an untied, undefeated season, winning their fifteenth consecutive game over two seasons.

Tiger fans leaped into the air and hugged everybody within reach, while laughing, screaming, and crying. Many vaulted the fence and stormed onto the field, searching for their particular hero, or for anybody wearing a purple-and-white uniform. The Mount Vernon players collapsed into a hugging, leaping, backslapping cluster around their kicker. Zim's teammates yanked him into the celebration pile. The big guard ignored the pain along his left clavicle, as well as the tears in his eyes.

Athens' fans sat stunned. Cold, shocked, and unbelieving, they were at a loss for action or word. They had prepared themselves for a tie, co-champions, or maybe settlement based on penetrations or first downs, but not for what they had just witnessed. Actually, the last drive to the nineteen-yard line had given the Tigers a 3-2 penetrations advantage, along with twelve first downs to ten for their opponent. But the miracle field goal made all that irrelevant.

Regardless of the statistical advantage, Mount Vernon's coaches had decided to take one last shot at winning on the scoreboard rather than the stat sheet, and it had paid off.

Sonny Mitchell led all rushers with one hundred thirty-nine yards, but Dale Moore's six completed passes in thirteen attempts for one hundred seventeen yards more than compensated. Both touchdowns came off his strong arm, as well as the play that set up the winning field goal.

"Our boys won this year in spite of every imaginable obstacle being thrown at them," Catfish would say later.

"A storybook ending to a fairytale season for the Tigers," Devall wrote. "The heroics and heroes witnessed today will be remembered as long as Tiger fans gather to talk about their teams of old."

324

"Boys," Catfish said to his team in the field house, "you are champions today, and you deserve to enjoy it to the ultimate." He allowed them their victory yell. "But, Monday afternoon we start a new journey in pursuit of another championship. I'll see you on the basketball court."

In eighteen days, the Tigers would play the Talco Trojans on Tuesday, December 30, their first of fourteen district basketball contests. While his basketball players shed their football uniforms, that sobering thought tempered Catfish's celebration with new worries.

While the coach looked ahead, Devall looked back. In five seasons at Mount Vernon, Catfish's gridiron teams had won forty-two games while losing six and tying two, an eighty-four percent winning percentage. Catfish's Tigers had captured three district titles, three bi-district crowns, and a pair of regional championships. His 1944 and 1947 teams had won eleven contests each, without a single loss. His teams had averaged over twenty-seven points per game while allowing only five.

Along with the newspaperman, Tiger fans wondered if Coach Milburn "Catfish" Smith had anything more to prove at the High School Class A level. Even if a prophet had told them what lay ahead, they would not have believed it.

1947 Football Team
Undefeated Regional Champions

Front Row (left to right): Mgr. Jack Perrin, Louis Agee, Paul Gilbert, Stanley Jaggers, Drue Hightower, Donald Yates, Coach Catfish Smith, Ronnie Smith (son), Roy Cunningham, Billy Frank Groom, Dale Brakebill, Glen Slaughter

Second Row: Johnny Moore (standing), Dudley Miller, Buster Simms, George Wims, Billy Jack Carter, Frank Carr, Kenneth Meek, Gayle Tinsley, Buck Parchman, Dale Moore, Billy Jack Meredith, Mgr. Mack Mahaffey

Back Row: Assistant Coach Bo Campbell, Maurice "Bud" Campbell, Gerald Skidmore, Pat King, Charles Lowry, Gene Fleming, Pat Loyd, Herb Zimmerman, Dewey Moore, Charles Stretcher, Billy Jack Guthrie, Supt. Millard Fleming

1948 Basketball Team
Undefeated State Champions

Front Row: Dewey Moore, Pat Loyd, Gene Fleming, Gerald Skidmore, Maurice "Bud" Campbell, Herb Zimmerman, Robert "Slats" Banks

Second Row: Mgr. Robbie Cannaday, Mgr. Dudley Miller, Billy Jack Meredith, Dale Moore, Kenneth Meek, Billy Burton

326

30

December 20, 1947

One hundred fifty people showed up for the Mount Vernon football banquet held in the high school gymnasium in late December 1947. On the stage stood a beautifully decorated Christmas tree, along with a white banner with purple lettering that spelled, "REGIONAL CHAMPS."

Dough Rollins, assistant coach at Texas A&M University and Catfish's college mentor, was the guest speaker.

"I've been privileged to attend several of your games this year," Rollins said, "and I've been mightily impressed with your players, the loyal fans, and your school spirit.

"Now, I'd like to point out my part in all this. You see, I've coached five men who have been instrumental in the winning tradition you presently enjoy. Marvin Coffey, Johnnie Hammer, Bob Killingsworth, Herman "Sleepy" Morgan, and finally Milburn "Catfish" Smith. All except Hammer played on my nineteen thirty-three East Texas State championship team. The following year that squad won again, going undefeated, scoring one hundred and sixteen points while giving up only six on a desperation pass in the last seconds of the last game. I'll never get over watching that ball get tipped, tipped again, and finally settling into the hands of Milton Jowers of Southwest Texas. That nineteen thirty-three team started a winning tradition that lasted fifteen years, and those boys have maintained that winning spirit ever since.

"'Sleepy' brought it here, then moved on to coach the Highland Park Scots, who lost out to Breckenridge of San Antonio for the state AA championship this year. Lendon 'Skinny' Davis is Morgan's backfield coach. You'll remember that he played for 'Sleepy' on your 1938 regional championship team. Then when Morgan left Mount Vernon, he made room for your current coach, who has had a little success of his own."

Again the crowd applauded.

"A few years back I had an outstanding end down at College Station. The kid's name was Herbie Smith, and at one hundred fifty-eight pounds, he was as tough as they come. After Herbie had just had an exceptional game in our Sugar Bowl victory, I told some folks at a banquet that this Smith kid was the best end I'd ever coached.

"Well, a couple of days went by, and I'd forgotten about the comment. Then I received this telegram, charges reversed. It said, 'Coach, you must have your Smith boys mixed up. You know I'm the best end you ever coached.' It was signed, 'Catfish.'

"Well, he was right, of course," Rollins continued, " but I'm beginning to think he's an even better coach than he was a player."

The Mount Vernon faithful rose to their feet and applauded a full three minutes without interruption.

Afterwards, Catfish presented silver footballs to all the players who had not qualified for a letter jacket. With that done, he reached into his coat pocket and hesitated.

"I've got one more silver football to present," Catfish said, and then cleared his throat. "Herb Zimmerman, would you please come up here?"

The big guard made his way to the head table and stood beside his coach. Catfish looped his long arm around Zim's broad shoulders.

"Back in the Edgewood game, I shot off my mouth and promised a silver football to the player who made the tackle on a crucial, fourth-quarter kickoff. If that Bulldog return man had known about it, he might have refused to run that one back. Number six here," Catfish said, squeezing Zimmerman's shoulders, "just about ruined that boy's day with a bone-rattling tackle."

The assembly applauded, and Catfish waited for silence.

"And we know about bone-rattling tackles, don't we Zim?" Catfish said, referring to the big guard's mending collarbone.

"Standing here beside me," Catfish went on, "is the best guard I've ever coached, the best I've ever seen." After hesitating a moment, Catfish handed over a silver football with a raised purple M. The coach hesitated as if to say more, but while he struggled with his emotions, the audience stood and applauded.

*   *   *

With the district opener only three days away, Catfish arranged a basketball scrimmage for his squad against the Winfield Bearcats on

Saturday night, December 27. Other than Joe Zane Condrey, the coach had back his entire 1947 team, with the addition of Bud Campbell, the sensational guard from the junior varsity, and freshman Billy Jack Meredith. His boys were a little rusty due to lack of practice time, but they handily defeated the Bearcats, 34-14.

The starting lineup varied. Robert "Slats" Banks, a six-foot-three senior, occupied the center or post position, relieved by six-foot-two senior, Gene Fleming, who doubled at forward as well. Pat Loyd and Gerald Skidmore, six-two and six-feet tall respectively, filled the forward slots. Herb Zimmerman and Bud Campbell, a couple of six-footers, played guard, but got ample backup support from leather-tough Kenneth Meek, the Moore brothers, and Billy Jack Meredith. Billy Burton, at five-six, was an excellent ball-handler from the prior year's junior varsity.

After only one warm-up game to prepare for district play, Mount Vernon took on Talco in the Tiger's lair on December 30. Catfish's boys breezed by the Trojans for a 33-14 district win, with all reserves getting into the contest. Bud Campbell gave notice to the league, swishing in eighteen points, while freshman Meredith added five.

On Friday, January 2, Pickton came to town and received a similar welcome, 34-18. Then on Monday night, the Tigers challenged Saltillo in what was the most lopsided victory of the young season, 35-9. Continuing to warm up for a series of district games, the Tigers bused to Detroit and claimed another victory, 38-24, and then mauled Bogata, 74-12.

Clarksville was next, coming in after a surprising three-point win over a stout Winnsboro team. The Tigers jumped to a quick lead and held an 18-5 advantage at halftime. They increased their lead in the second half, using mostly backup players, and claimed another victory, 31-15. Earlier Dale Moore and Billy Jack Meredith had led the junior varsity with eighteen and sixteen points respectively, trouncing Clarksville's B squad, 43-7.

Next came the Winnsboro Red Raiders, projected to be the stiffest competition in the district. With Acie Cannaday coaching them, they had come within a point of downing the Tigers the prior season. With a hot start this year, the Red Raiders had defeated AA Sulphur Springs before slumping against Clarksville. Bud Campbell anxiously looked forward to playing his old team. He and Robert Banks had consistently led the Tigers in scoring, Bud with fifty-eight points through six games and "Slats" with fifty-two.

As expected, Cannaday's boys gave the Tigers their first real test. Bud Campbell got off to a slow start, but came on strong to toss in nine points. Gerald Skidmore matched Bud's total while Zimmerman pitched in six, Fleming five, and Banks four. The Tigers prevailed in their fourth district contest, 34-26.

Meanwhile in town, Charles Mahaffey had left his feed business to his brother Walter and purchased both the Crescent and Rutherford drug stores. Earlier Mal Moore had bought the old Mercer's Drug Store building to expand his "Toyland" business, so as of January 1, Mahaffey became the sole owner of the local drug business. A native of Mount Vernon, he was coming back to a profession he originally entered in 1914 as an intern at Crescent Drugs.

Of more concern in town was an outbreak of polio. Both Bobbie Strickland and Clovis Lawrence had been stricken with the deadly disease, and townspeople, led by L. D. Lowry, Jr., raised three thousand dollars to go along with eight hundred donated by the local American Legion to purchase an iron lung, along with other essential equipment. Lowry accepted the chairmanship of the local March of Dimes drive, aided by Mahaffey and Superintendent Fleming who solicited Catfish's help in raising money.

On the brighter side, Charles Bruce returned to town and accepted a teaching job and became the sportswriter for the *Optic-Herald*. Bruce had spent his war years serving as gunner and information officer aboard the U.S.S. *Tuscaloosa* during the Normandy invasion and later as liaison officer on the British carrier, *Victorious*. Bruce, a master's degree graduate of Texas Tech in Lubbock, taught history and civics classes.

Next on the Tigers' schedule were the Buckeyes. An ill Bud Campbell missed the game, but feeling at home in their gym, Catfish's boys walloped their guests by a tally of 52-11. High scorer was young Billy Jack Meredith with fifteen points, but everybody got into the scoring column with Banks, Loyd, and Dale Moore each contributing seven.

During the last week in January, the basketball schedule came to a halt for a week due to blizzard-like weather. A layer of sleet covered the ground, topped by a couple inches of snow. The temperature dropped to thirteen and reached a high of only twenty-two for the week. Schools and most businesses closed their doors as travel became impossible.

With improved weather, the Tigers resumed their season by

defeating the Pittsburg Pirates, 44-9. This was another game where all but one Tiger made at least one bucket. Fleming and Banks each had seven while Bud Campbell and Dale Moore contributed six each. With non-starters getting the majority of the playing time, backups scored four more points than the starting lineup.

Following that blowout, the Tigers treated Mount Pleasant almost as "unpleasantly." Campbell had eleven, Banks ten, and Loyd seven as Catfish's boys tossed in thirty-eight, allowing the Titus County boys only thirteen.

Taking on little-known Cunningham, the Tigers found themselves in a fight. Though they prevailed 37-30, it was their narrowest escape so far. Bud Campbell assured victory for the Tigers with fourteen points, while Banks and Skidmore added seven each and Pat Loyd six.

With the first half of the season completed, the undefeated Tigers had racked up twelve wins, eight of those being district victories. In the conference, only Winnsboro had come close to challenging Catfish's roundballers. Fan expectations soared, predicting a district championship and maybe another run for the state title, though few, if anyone, could have imagined what was in store for Catfish and his boys.

The Tigers began the second half of the season with a rematch against Talco. The Trojans were a different team this time around, challenging the Tigers, who were without Robert Banks, for most of the game, but ultimately succumbing to Catfish's boys, 36-28. Campbell and Zimmerman led the Tigers with nine each, while Loyd added six.

Pittsburg proved no more of a challenge the second time around, with the Tigers winning 58-18. Campbell pitched in sixteen with Loyd (14) and Banks (13) close behind. Prior to the varsity game, the Tigers' reserves had sunk their Pirate counterparts, 42-13.

The return match with Bogata gave Catfish's reserves ample playing time as the Tigers waltzed to a 61-18 victory. "Slats" Banks had his best game with eighteen points, followed by Fleming's ten. Like the big boys, the junior Tigers claimed an easy win, 30-12.

The Tigers then ventured into class AA basketball territory by tackling Sulphur Springs, a team Acie Cannaday's Red Raiders had trimmed earlier. Catfish's boys were more than equal to the test, winning by twenty, 41-21. Banks led the way with thirteen, backed up by Campbell's ten.

The rematch with Clarksville was no match. The Tigers stampeded their opponent, 62-14. Catfish used his reserves liberally, and they responded by again outscoring the regulars, 35-23. Fleming led the scoring with eleven, but Dale Moore came off the bench with ten and freshman Meredith contributed five.

*　　*　　*

While Catfish's basketball boys were winning fifteen consecutive games, the world received a shocking revelation. Two hundred sixty secret Nazi documents captured in Berlin at the end of the war revealed that Germany and Russia had earlier concocted a plot to carve up Europe, Asia, and Africa. Signed by Soviet Foreign Minister Molotov and by Ribbentrop for Hitler, the key document, dated September 28, 1939, revealed that the two powers had agreed to divide Poland between them, while Russia would get Finland and the Baltic States, with the exception of Lithuania.

In spite of these documents, as well as a non-aggression pact signed with Stalin in 1939, Hitler had invaded Russia on June 22, 1941. Realizing *der Fuhrer* had used the pact to trick him into staying out of the war during Germany's *blitzkrieg* of Western Europe, Stalin became an ally of the United States; however, the documents put at question Stalin's ambitions and intentions. With America's relationship with the Soviets already tenuous over occupation of Berlin, the United States and much of the free world eyed the Russians with grave suspicions. With World War II barely over and much of Western Europe in a shambles, was there a new enemy lurking on the horizon? Would we be drawn into another world war?

Several of Catfish's seniors had potential for university-level athletics, and he had hoped his boys would graduate in May with nothing more serious than college on their minds. However, with this latest news, he wondered if yet another class of his boys would soon find themselves on a battlefield rather than an athletic field.

*　　*　　*

In mid-February the season was winding down to the final three district contests. If the Tigers could beat Gilmer, Winnsboro, and Mount Pleasant, they would be undefeated district champs. Of the three, Winnsboro had proven the toughest in the first half of the season, but Catfish was leery of the upcoming opponent, the Gilmer Buckeyes.

With Bud Campbell ailing, the Tigers journeyed to Gilmer. "Slats"

Banks poured in twenty-two points, leading his team to a runaway victory, 58-19. The reserves played the entire second half, Billy Burton pitching in six points and Dale Moore four. Also, the junior varsity whipped the Buckeyes, 24-16, to remain undefeated in district play.

The upcoming rematch with Winnsboro was considered crucial to the Tigers' chances for a district title. An earlier eight-point defeat of the Red Raiders provided no sense of guaranteed success the second time around. The game lived up to its billing through the first half, at which point Mount Vernon led 17-16. In the second half, Bud Campbell caught fire and accounted for sixteen points against his old mates. Banks contributed fourteen points, and Fleming eight on the way to a lopsided final of 47-22.

That left the Tigers needing only a victory over Mount Pleasant to complete an undefeated District 16-A championship. In their past thirteen conference tilts, Mount Vernon had averaged forty-eight points per game, while holding their opponents to sixteen, a remarkable thirty-two-point margin of victory. Also, they had easily handled the Titus County boys in their prior meeting, winning 38-13.

If this final game ever held any suspense, it was gone by halftime with Catfish's boys leading 24-2. Again Bud Campbell led all scorers with fourteen, but the sizeable early lead allowed the reserves to play extended minutes and outpoint the regulars for the third time. Backup Dale Moore pitched in eight while the Tigers closed out their district run with a 46-15 win. Remarkably, the score was almost identical to their average district score, which was 48-16.

Catfish's boys completed the regular season with twenty-one wins, fourteen of those being district contests, and no defeats. His team had qualified for the regional playoffs for the fifth consecutive year.

Rather than sit idle waiting for their bi-district opponent, Catfish managed a couple of warm-up games. First, his boys met Sulphur Springs, a Class AA opponent. The Wildcats did not provide much competition as the Tigers devoured them, 55-24. Banks led with eighteen, followed by Bud Campbell's thirteen.

Next, Catfish surprised some fans, and drew criticism from others who did not want to take unnecessary chances with the Tigers' perfect record. The coach scheduled Blossom, a perennial playoff team, and one Catfish's prior squads had never defeated. The Tiger fans need not have worried. Blossom's domination of Mount Vernon came to an abrupt end, 41-16, with this version of Tigers. Campbell stuck in eleven points, Banks ten, and Zimmerman nine.

Still not satisfied, Catfish again put his boys' perfect record on the table. With fifteen consecutive football wins and twenty-three basketball victories without a defeat, Catfish risked it all against the defending Class A state champions, East Mountain, coached by Jack "Lash" Woodruff. Furthermore, he agreed to enter the enemy's den for the ultimate test of his team.

Some loyal Tiger fans boldly questioned Catfish's judgment this time, but the coach had learned a hard lesson in 1945. His team had coasted into the playoffs where they had faced a great Quitman quintet. His players were not prepared for the level of competition they met and responded poorly when faced with adversity. The coach blamed himself for that, and had vowed to not make that mistake again.

In a hard-fought game that saw Catfish slapped with three technical fouls, his Tigers proved their mettle, winning 35-32. Banks was the big scorer with fifteen, while Loyd pitched in seven. Bud Campbell fell below his average with only five points, something he would not forget.

While Tiger fans breathed a collective sigh of relief, Catfish's boys prepared for the Hooks Hornets, another old nemesis, in a two-of-three series to qualify for the regional tournament.

Evidently, it was a year of redemption for Catfish's boys. They blistered the Hooks team, 40-20, with the most balanced scoring attack of the season. Every starter contributed at least five points.

In the second game of the series, the Tigers struggled and went into halftime leading by only two, 20-18. The second half showed a much more aggressive Tiger defense, and Catfish's boys again prevailed, 41-28. This time Gerald Skidmore and Herb Zimmerman provided the punch with ten points each, while Banks added nine.

The Tigers now had won twenty-six games without a loss and were headed for the regional tournament. Amazingly, their opponent would be the same team they had vied with for the regional championship in football and had defeated on Fleming's miraculous field goal: the Athens Hornets, coached by Lee Mitchell. Without a doubt, revenge would be an emotional factor in this contest.

The regional tournament was held in Greenville, and the game opposite the Tigers-versus-Hornets contest was Garland against Plano. The winners of these two games would meet for the regional championship and the right to go to Austin for the state meet.

The Tigers met the Hornets at two o'clock on Saturday afternoon. Athens brought a respectable, but not great, 16-4 record, however

Catfish knew the quality of Coach Mitchell's quintet and the tough schedule they had played, including several Class AA teams.

Even with Pat Loyd out sick, Catfish's squad once again rose to the challenge, taking the contest by a score of 38-29. The Tigers jumped into an early lead that they never relinquished, sporting a sixteen-point advantage at one juncture. At halftime their lead was 22-13. Catfish's big scorers came through once again. Banks threw in fourteen and Campbell thirteen. Zimmerman, a defensive whiz, provided seven, also.

Following the Tigers' contest, the Plano Wildcats defeated Gordon "Chief" Smith's Garland Owls by a single point, 30-29, to set up the regional championship game at eight o'clock that night, pitting the undefeated Tigers against the 1947 regional-champion Wildcats who had only two losses for the season.

The championship game was hotly contested. Though the Tigers built a twelve-point lead at one juncture, they let it slip away and even fell behind. At halftime Catfish's boys clung to a fragile 14-10 margin. When the competition became unusually physical in the second half, the seasoned Tigers kept their heads, and prevailed, 37-27.

"Mount Vernon's boys won the fans over by sticking to good clean play when the Plano boys got a little nasty," a Greenville fan commented.

With fifteen points, "Slats" Banks led his team. Bud Campbell managed only four, but three of his teammates contributed five each. Still ailing, Pat Loyd was one of those sticking in five points.

Catfish's team had maintained their undefeated season with their twenty-seventh consecutive victory. Since all his players except Robert Banks had played football as well, these boys had now competed in forty-two consecutive sporting contests without a loss. Now they were bound for the state tournament to play Texas City at three-ten the following Thursday, March 4th. Other Class A teams in the tournament were Dimmitt, Sinton, Nocona, Brenham, Throckmorton, and defending champion, East Mountain. In Class B, the little West Texas town of Carey, where Catfish had made his coaching debut, would be in Austin vying for the title exactly a decade after Catfish had led them to their first state championship.

So this trip to Gregory Gym in Austin would be Catfish's fourth. He had led the Carey Cardinals there twice, and he had also taken his 1944 Tigers there, losing the championship to Nocona by one point in overtime. Further, he swore the 1945 Tigers should have been there, and in his heart, he believed that squad would have won the state title.

With that background, the Tiger coach was not in awe of the event or the opponents. His players sensed their coach's confidence, trusted his judgment, and knew no one they would rather have lead them into this battle, the ultimate of high school sports.

31

March 4, 1948

The Tigers traveled to Austin to meet the Texas City Stingarees in the first round of the Texas State High School Basketball Tournament. Catfish's boys wasted no time proving they belonged. Bud Campbell poured in fifteen points as the Tigers built a 25-10 halftime lead. The Stingarees got tougher in the third quarter and closed the gap to 32-28. With six minutes remaining, the difference was a mere three points, but then Campbell iced the game with three quick buckets. Catfish's boys prevailed, 38-30, led by Bud Campbell's twenty-two points, an individual season high. Banks added five, and all six Tigers that participated in the game contributed points.

Texas City's forward, Chuoke, led the Stingarees with twelve points, getting help from Mosher with seven and Hughes with six. The Tigers' aggressive style of play resulted in Sutton and Chuoke being called for four fouls each, and their team committing a surprisingly high fifteen.

Meanwhile, the Dimmitt Bobcats slipped by Sinton, 45-44, in a game billed as the meeting of two stars, Harvey Fromme of Sinton and Carl Jowell of Dimmitt. The much-ballyhooed contest provided all the anticipated dramatics, including a last-second free throw by Jowell for the win. The six-foot-two forward led his Panhandle team with seventeen points while center Lewis Martin pitched in sixteen in the victory that elevated them to Class A tournament favorite. Fromme sank eighteen in Sinton's loss, while classy James Knox tossed in thirteen. The win bracketed the Bobcats against Mount Vernon in a semi-final match at eleven-thirty Friday morning.

In other games, the defending state champion, East Mountain, trailed Nocona most of the contest, but skipped ahead near the end and held on for a 37-33 win to advance against Throckmorton, whose impressive fifty-three points overwhelmed Brenham by seventeen.

Coach T. B. Little's Throckmorton team was led by six-foot-seven center, Mart Halbert, who scored twenty points against Brenham, placing him right behind Bud Campbell as the first-day point leader.

At eleven-thirty Friday morning, Catfish's Tigers met the Dimmitt Bobcats who jumped into a quick 9-7 lead, which they extended to 15-11 by halftime. But the third quarter belonged to the Tigers, scoring nineteen while the Bobcats managed only nine. Early in the final stanza, Catfish's boys clung to a 34-30 lead, but Dimmitt then showed why they were highly regarded, and with less than a minute remaining, the Bobcats pushed ahead for a two-point lead, 39-37. With the Tigers unable to score the tying bucket, the game clock ticked down until it showed only six seconds. The Bobcats owned the ball out of bounds, and if they could just execute the inbound pass and dribble for six counts, they would win the game and qualify for the state championship contest.

With a few unimaginative fans heading for the exits, Mount Vernon huddled.

"When they inbound the ball," Bud Campbell said to Pat Loyd, "streak for our goal. I'm going to steal the pass and get the ball to you."

As improbable as the plan may have sounded to everyone else, when the Dimmitt player raised the ball over his head and heaved it toward a teammate, Loyd broke toward Mount Vernon's goal. Meanwhile, Bud Campbell leaped into the air and made a point-blank snare of the pass. Before Bud's feet reached the floor, he whipped the ball toward the fleeing Pat Loyd who turned and looked back just as the ball arrived. Catching the Dimmitt boys by surprise, Loyd had a relatively easy layup to tie the score at 39-39.

With only two seconds remaining on the clock, the Bobcats had no chance to make a comeback, forcing an overtime period to determine the outcome. However, in fighting to hold off the Bobcats in the final quarter, Gene Fleming and Gerald Skidmore had fouled out of the game, leaving the Tigers shorthanded for the additional three-minutes of play.

In the extended time both teams struggled to score, but Dimmitt finally managed a foul shot that gave them a one-point lead, 40-39. With time running out, again the Tigers' backs were against the wall.

With just enough time for one last attempt, Bud Campbell tried a corner shot, but the ball caught the rim and caromed off. However, Robert "Slats" Banks leaped and stretched his right hand slightly above that of the taller Lewis Martin, just getting his fingertips on the ball.

That was all it took. The ball glanced up over the rim and trickled through the net. The Tigers had won, 41-40.

The Tigers' hero, Robert Banks, not only accounted for thirteen of his team's points, but he also helped Gene Fleming hold Dimmitt's Martin to only two. In the Bobcat's prior game against Sinton, the tall center had pitched in sixteen. Bud Campbell, the leading Tiger scorer in their prior game against Texas City, added ten, in addition to the miracle steal and pass that gave Catfish's team the opportunity to beat Dimmitt in overtime. Pat Loyd contributed nine points, the two at the end of regulation being his most important of the season.

Jowell led Dimmitt's valiant effort with fifteen points, while Rice added ten and Fulfer contributed nine.

The stunning victory over the tournament's Class A favorite not only qualified Catfish's team for the state championship Saturday afternoon, but also validated his logic in earlier challenging Blossom and East Mountain. His Tigers showed the mental and physical toughness he had insisted they must develop.

Now, who would oppose them for the state title?

Immediately after Mount Vernon's victory over Dimmitt, East Mountain faced the high-scoring Throckmorton quintet that had earlier thrashed Brenham, 53-36. The expected thriller pitted East Mountain's Jimmy Fountain against Throckmorton's six-foot-seven Mart Halbert.

Fountain and his teammates struggled early, but ultimately reminded the fans that they were the reigning state champions by defeating their West Texas opponent, 45-35. The win required an impressive comeback by the Mountaineers, led by Fountain's seventeen points and Eugene Hill's ten. Now, in an ironic twist of fate, East Mountain would face Catfish's Tigers at three thirty-five Saturday afternoon for the championship.

Those Mount Vernon fans, who had earlier questioned the wisdom of Catfish's decision to challenge this Upshur County team, had long since forgotten their second-guessing. They now pointed to the prior victory, and predicted a repeat performance. However, the Mountaineers were led by Jack "Lash" Woodruff, one of the few coaches in Texas with a winning record comparable to Catfish's. As it should be in championship contests, two outstanding teams, led by two of the state's most successful coaches, would square off for the highest schoolboy basketball title in the land.

Suddenly, the previously little-known Mount Vernon team became the press's favorite to win the state championship, based on their prior win over Coach Woodruff's East Mountain club and the Tigers' clutch victory over Dimmitt. However, Catfish once again reminded his players, "there are no paper victories."

For Bud Campbell, he relished the chance to show the Mountaineers that they had not seen his best effort when they had held him to five points earlier in the season. Having an all-star tournament, he was primed to cap it off with his best game of the year.

With time to kill, Catfish took a break from the gym Friday afternoon and watched the Texas Longhorns' football team in an Orange-versus-White intra-squad contest. The Longhorns ran the T-formation, and Catfish was always looking for a new wrinkle or two to use with his Tigers. From the fullback position on the White team, Tom Landry rumbled for four touchdowns, one a fifty-three yarder. Displaying power, speed, and finesse, Landry led his squad to victory, 57-7. Catfish smiled and thought of the Swede.

Saturday afternoon, Catfish led his basketball squad onto the hardwood of Gregory Gym. With over five thousand screaming fans and the Texas sports world looking on, the Tigers grabbed a 7-1 lead in the first two and a half minutes, capitalizing on their familiarity with Fountain and his pals. With no letup by the Tigers, the first period ended with Catfish's boys leading, 13-3. In the second quarter, Mount Vernon further shocked the attending sports pundits by running their advantage to 19-3. For a nine-minute span of time, the last five of the first quarter and first four of the second, the Tigers totally shut down the high-flying Mountaineers, not allowing them a single point. When halftime arrived, the Tigers led 21-8, and the defending state champions looked defeated.

Held to one first-half point, Jimmy Fountain, the outstanding but lame guard of the Mountaineers, had another plan. In the third period, in one of the most courageous efforts ever, he overcame his leg injury and brought his team back, closing the gap to six points, 30-24.

Accepting the challenge, Bud Campbell responded in the final quarter with six quick points, rebuilding the Tigers' lead to 36-24. Then Hargraves, a stalwart Mountaineer, re-injured an ankle and was helped off the court, dooming his team's chances at a miracle comeback. From there, Catfish's boys coasted to a 44-33 victory and captured the state championship, convincingly.

With sixteen points and help from Eugene Hill, the ailing Fountain had made a valiant effort to retain the title for his team, but Bud Campbell matched him, plus a point, with seventeen. Both were named to the All-Tournament Team, along with Carl Jowell of Dimmitt, Mart Halbert of Throckmorton, and Harvey Fromme of Sinton.

Bud Campbell, Mount Vernon's junior varsity standout of the prior season, had scored forty-nine points in the three games to lead all scorers and was clearly the tournament's most valuable player. Additionally, he was one of only three unanimous choices across all classes of teams, B, A, and AA, for All-State honors. With tears in his eyes, he proudly lofted the state championship trophy overhead. Two years earlier, he had left New Hope and joined Catfish's team for this moment.

In the awards ceremony, famed University of Texas athletic director, D. X. Bible, presented the huge silver state championship trophy to Catfish, who immediately turned and kissed Dorothy Nell. When the crowd applauded, the coach thought they wanted an encore and obliged them, embarrassing his gleeful wife.

Catfish's teams had just done something never accomplished before in the recorded history of Texas high school athletics. His football team had gone undefeated, winning eleven consecutive games and the regional crown. His basketball team had then completed thirty games without a loss, capturing the state title. In the same academic year, his teams had won forty-one athletic contests without a single defeat, not counting the junior varsity's string of victories. Additionally, his football team was in the midst of a fifteen-game winning streak, and his basketball team would surely extend its thirty-game streak the coming season. Those sages, who had watched Texas high school athletics for a quarter of a century or more, literally stood in awe.

"Perhaps there's a certain amount of luck that goes with winning the close ones," a reporter wrote, "but there is much skill involved also. Coach Smith's boys have had the ability to come through when the chips are down all year. Grid fans who witnessed the regional championship battle between the Tigers and the Athens Hornets can never forget the dramatic, game-winning field goal by Gene Fleming . . . now to add to those memories will be the crip shot fired by forward Pat Loyd to throw the Dimmitt game into a tie and send the contest into overtime where Robert 'Slats' Banks tipped in the winning points. The classy performances of Maurice 'Bud' Campbell and all the other Mount Vernon athletes can't be overlooked."

"Stars and standouts were many," another wrote. "The Tigers have the best balanced team in the tournament. Herb Zimmerman and Pat Loyd's hustle and fight were outstanding. Gene Fleming's control of the backboards, Gerald Skidmore's deadeye accuracy, Robert Banks' cool precision, and Bud Campbell's floor play, speed, and deadly shooting were applauded by the thousands attending the games in Austin."

Sportswriter Morris Williams wrote that Mount Vernon would likely pass an ordinance that prohibited their coach from allowing the sun to set on him outside the city's boundaries. "Should he transfer his coaching affections, Mount Vernon citizens will probably hang him from the nearest pine tree." And other sportswriters were asking the question Mount Vernon fans dreaded to hear.

Why would Catfish continue at Mount Vernon when he could have his choice of Class AA schools? Indeed, would he? After all, Catfish had left Carey after winning the state basketball title there.

Mount Vernon fans, numbering approximately one thousand, turned out Sunday afternoon to welcome home their state champions. They gathered on the downtown square at three with a huge banner that spanned the width of Main Street, bearing the words, "WELCOME CHAMPS," in resplendent purple and white. The Tiger band in full uniform serenaded their heroes. The townsfolk could not recall a bigger celebration.

Standing there, tall and straight and soaking up the thrill of the moment, Catfish reflected back to August 1943, when Superintendent Fleming had promised just this kind of celebration on the town plaza. Neither could ever have imagined it being this good.

On Monday, March 8, Catfish presented the state championship trophy to the school in a special ceremony. Also, the regional championship football trophy, provided courtesy of the American Life Insurance Company, had arrived and was presented to the school, the first of its kind ever received by Mount Vernon.

Tuesday night the basketball team, along with their guests, were entertained with a wiener roast on the Cherry Hill farm owned by Patsy Bogue's family. The youngsters, numbering almost thirty, warmed by the fire and ate hotdogs and marshmallows, while listening to Gayle Tinsley strum his guitar and sing.

The celebration would continue on March 26 when Mr. and Mrs. Bill Meek held a party in honor of the champs at their home. The mothers of the Moore boys and Billy Jack Meredith assisted Mrs. Meek as co-hosts. After a delicious meal, the aggregation moved to Moore Motors showroom where a throng of high school students joined the team for more fun and entertainment.

342

On Thursday following the wiener roast, a cold front swept across East Texas, slamming its fair-weather citizens into a ten-degree deep-freeze. Snow and sleet covered the roads and decorated the landscapes and trees as only Mother Nature can. Most stayed inside, trying to keep warm, but Mr. and Mrs. Louie Raney had to leave their hearth and brave the cold when baby Jauquita Lou chose that time to make her entry into the world.

The *Optic-Herald* managed to get its paper out, and local readers lazed by the fire and read, especially an elaborate advertisement that incorrectly listed a popular cold medication at a ridiculously low price. Charles Mahaffey, new owner of Rutherford's Drug Store, read it also, and winced. If all the wheezers and sneezers in town should turn out, he would be in trouble. As luck would have it, the weather broke, and the popular drug store sold one hundred forty-five bottles of the medicine the first day, clearing Mahaffey's shelves.

"Most were perfectly healthy customers," Mahaffey explained with a laugh.

"If you don't want to sell it," columnist Olin Hardy advised good-naturedly in his popular "Pop's Corner," "don't advertise it here!"

Things were getting back to normal in Mount Vernon.

Meanwhile, colleges in the Southwest were pursuing Catfish's senior athletes, offering athletic scholarships. Charles Lowry committed to play football for Coach "Dutch" Meyer of Texas Christian University in Fort Worth. Herb Zimmerman and Gene Fleming visited that school also, however, they were still considering similar offers from Southern Methodist University, as were Bud Campbell and Robert Banks.

Then Fleming received an invitation to play in the state high school All-Star game, which concluded the annual Texas Coaches School held in August. Catfish congratulated his star lineman, kicker, and rebounder, calling him the best all-round athlete and student he has coached.

Then on Wednesday, March 17, Superintendent Fleming arranged to have President Harry Truman's speech to Congress aired over the school's public address system. The president urged speedy passage of legislation supporting his European Recovery Plan. Further, he asked for renewal of the Selective Service Act's drafting of young men eighteen and older. The draft had been discontinued the prior year; however, with the threat of war in Korea, the Commander in Chief wanted to maintain a standing army numbering in excess of one half million soldiers.

Such a buildup of servicemen left in doubt plans for college, job, and marriage for many of the graduating seniors. Interviews with some of the boys held by the staff of *The Tiger's Tale* got mixed reactions. "It looks like I'll be in the army instead of college," Charles Lowry lamented. "I'd like to finish my education first," said Dewey Moore. "Compulsory military training is the right thing, if we need it," replied George Wims. Maybe Gerald Skidmore's response was the most unique. "I'm already telling all the girls what to send me for Christmas while I'm in the army."

For Catfish, it was no laughing matter. Preparing young men for the real world, for a hard and challenging world, was his life's work. His boys had learned how to win on the gridiron and the hardwood, always persevering and always finding a way, but had he prepared them to win when and where it counted most? If not, all the wins, all the championships, and all the trophies counted for nothing.

*   *   *

With the hoopla of the basketball season over, Catfish decided to enter a team in the Mount Pleasant Relays, which were held on Friday, March 26, though Mount Vernon had no track and no track team.

"The band is going," he explained to some of the boys prior to school on Monday, "and Fay Eula Gilbert just might win the Queen of the Relays contest. So, come up to the field this afternoon, and we'll start preparing."

Jogging around in basketball uniforms, a few boys made an effort to prepare for some of the running events. Catfish selected Gayle Tinsley to run the quarter-mile race, so the youngster estimated the distance and began training.

Friday morning, Gayle, along with Pat King and Wallace Hunnicutt, decided to skip classes and go to Mount Pleasant to see the parades, the bands, and enjoy all the fanfare. While standing around the square after lunch, someone told Gayle that Catfish was looking for him.

Gayle headed for the track and found his frantic coach.

"Where have you been?" Catfish demanded to know.

"Watching the parades," Gayle admitted.

"Played hooky, didn't you?"

Gayle nodded.

"We'll settle that on Monday. Get dressed. You're running in the quarter-mile."

Gayle donned a basketball uniform and sneakers and came back onto the track where Catfish was visiting with the Gladewater coach.

"He can't run on this cinder track in tennis shoes," the Gladewater mentor said to Catfish.

"All we've got," Catfish replied.

"Well, he can borrow a pair of spikes from one of my boys."

Gayle found a pair that fit and was assigned the outermost lane on the oval track. Since the outside lanes were a greater distance, the starting positions were moved forward in a staggered alignment, each a few yards ahead of the runner in the lane to its inside. This positioned Tinsley well ahead of the other runners at the beginning of the race.

The gun sounded and Gayle took off, sailing along ahead of everybody and thinking it was a piece of cake. As he rounded the first curve and headed down the backside, he glanced back, and out of the corner of his eye, he saw a few of the inside runners. He kicked it into a higher gear and huffed on, but he noticed the others somehow had overcome most of the lead he had enjoyed from the start. He then turned into the far curve and noticed the inside runners were catching up like a hare chasing a tortoise, some gliding right on by him. Though his legs were a little rubbery, he pushed harder and hit the homestretch with only three runners ahead of him. Hurting now, he focused on the finish line and dug deep.

Suddenly, Gayle noticed a fence ahead. Though his eyes were a bit blurry, he could see that the fence crossed his lane. Either he had to cut inside to one of the inner lanes or run off the track. He guessed that dipping into another runner's lane would disqualify him, so he abandoned the track and continued toward the finish line the best he could. Needless to say, Gayle did not win the race.

"Son," Catfish said, grabbing his exhausted runner by the shoulders, "why didn't you move to the inside?"

"Didn't know I could," Tinsley gasped.

"Sure," the coach explained. "Once you reached the straightaway, you were supposed to slide down into one of the inside lanes."

It seemed to Tinsley that knowing that bit of information would have been much more valuable a bit earlier. The great football and basketball coach needs to hone his track coaching skills, the youngster thought to himself.

On Monday morning, Gayle was standing around in front of the school with the other students, waiting for the bell to signal their first period class, when Catfish walked up.

"Follow me," he said to Tinsley, and headed for Clovis Lawrence, a polio victim who stood near the entrance, braced on his crutches.

"Let me borrow one of your crutches, please," the coach said to Lawrence.

With Gayle bent over, Catfish swatted him five times with the crutch, and then handed it back to Clovis.

"You play hooky again," Catfish warned, "and I'll give you twice as many licks with my paddle."

The crutch was a poor substitute for a paddle, so Gayle felt he had gotten off rather light, but just as he settled into his desk in his first period class, Principal Bolger announced on the speaker that Gayle was to report to his office immediately.

"When do you have study hall?" Bolger asked.

"Fourth period," Tinsley replied.

"Come back to my office then."

Gayle obediently reported back at eleven o'clock.

"Go to each room, gather up the trashcans, and empty them in the dumpster out back," the principal said. "When you've done that, come back here."

When Tinsley returned to Principal Bolger's office, he was led to a small empty room and locked inside. When noon arrived, no one came to release him. Since his mother would be expecting him for lunch, he crawled out the window and hurried home.

When Gayle returned to school, he expected to be re-incarcerated, but Principal Bolger said nothing about it. Neither did Gayle, and the incident was over.

About this time, late March, Catfish and Bo Campbell announced they would form a high school baseball team, the first for Mount Vernon in over a decade. Twenty-five boys showed up for the first practice, each competing for one of fifteen uniforms provided by local businessmen. In addition to most of the football and basketball boys, players such as J. R. Lax, Newman Gilbert, Drue Hightower, Mac Anderson, Larkin Drummond, Jack Perrin, Stanley Jaggers, J. W. Burgin, and Robert Chambers took their turns with the bat and glove.

Following a few days of conditioning, Catfish divided them into two teams and held a couple of practice games. Dale Moore captained one team, and Gayle Tinsley the other. Moore's team won both contests, one 9-8 and the other 13-9. The pitching staff included Herb Zimmerman, J. R. Lax, and Newman Gilbert.

A schedule of games was soon worked out.

April 2	Gilmer	home
April 9	Pittsburg	away
April 16	Talco	home
April 23	Mount Pleasant	away
April 30	Winnsboro	away
May 7	Gilmer	away
May 14	Pittsburg	home
May 21	Talco	away
May 28	Mount Pleasant	home
June 1	Winnsboro	home

Seven-inning games were the standard, and three o'clock each Friday afternoon was game time.

One of the first things a baseball coach looks for is a pitcher.

"Larkin Drummond," one of the boys recommended to their coach.

"Why Larkin?" Catfish asked.

"He can stand behind the high school and throw an orange over the building and across the street in front of the school."

Catfish was suspicious, but after catching a few throws from Drummond, his doubts faded. Larkin could throw with remarkable velocity, but there was a problem. He was more likely to kill a batter than strike him out. Maybe young Drummond would develop into a pitcher, but the coach had to find someone who could throw strikes.

Herb Zimmerman wore glasses to correct a significant vision problem. The tale was told that he had once covered a referee's flag thinking it was a fumbled football. Yet, even without his spectacles, Zim proved spectacular. Though not the best eye on the team, he could throw a fastball that would challenge the best of hitters.

After three weeks of practice, the Tigers took on Gilmer at the local field, the one used by the semi-pro Lions.

"Fireballer" Zimmerman strode to the mound and mowed down the Buckeyes without allowing a hit until the sixth inning when Knight, Buckeye second baseman, managed a single. Meanwhile the Tiger batters banged out fourteen hits, including triples by Meredith and Banks and doubles by Brakebill (2), Loyd, and Meek. Fourteen Tigers went to bat and everyone with two or more at-bats got a hit while piling up eighteen runs, allowing only one on a combination of walks and a Buckeye single. The big pitcher helped his own cause with two hits and three runs.

J. R. Lax started on the hill in the game against Pittsburg. Through three innings, he allowed only two hits, but gave up five runs. With his team behind by a run, Zimmerman came in to relieve Lax, but gave up two more runs on four hits, one a home run by Clements, the Pirate leftfielder. While the Pittsburg hitters were roughing up Tiger pitchers, the Mount Vernon batsmen came to life in the fourth inning and destroyed opposing pitchers. With fourteen hits, Catfish's boys crossed home plate thirty times, shortstop Meredith getting six of those and centerfielder Pat Loyd five. Though the Tiger hitters contributed their part, Pirate pitching gave up twenty-one walks while Lax and Zimmerman gave free passes to only five of the Pittsburg boys. Tigers with three hits included Meredith, leftfielder Brakebill, and centerfielder Loyd. Third baseman Burton collected a couple, as did catcher Dale Moore. Every Tiger player contributed to the 30-7 runaway.

On April 16 Catfish's baseball squad won again, defeating Talco in a rather close affair. Zimmerman again proved to be "king of the hill" while striking out thirteen batters, blazing away until the final inning. Having given up five runs on five walks and three hits, with four errors committed behind him, Zim left the mound for Lax to strike out the last two batters of the game.

Meanwhile, the Mount Vernon hitters were beating out nine runs on seven hits and the Tigers had their third win, 9-5, with Zimmerman the winning pitcher in each case.

A week later Catfish's boys traveled to Mount Pleasant and squeaked out another win, 8-7. Again Zimmerman prowled the mound until the fourth inning, having given up two hits and two runs. Lax came on and gave up four runs on eight hits in two innings. Newman Gilbert relieved Lax in the sixth and finished the game allowing one hit and one run.

Though the Tiger batters had fewer hits than their opponent, six to eleven, Catfish's boys made theirs count the most. Billy Burton, the little third baseman, rapped out two hits, as did shortstop Meredith. Leftfielder Brakebill and catcher Dale Moore each stroked a single.

Then, Mount Vernon's string of forty-nine consecutive victories in athletic contests came to an end in Winnsboro, though the baseball Tigers had come up short a week earlier against Saltillo in a couple of scrimmages, 3-2 and 5-0, where Catfish featured his reserves.

The Red Raiders rapped out eight hits to four for Catfish's boys, who committed over a handful of errors. Zimmerman pitched into the sixth inning, allowing six hits and seven runs, then got relief from Lax and Gilbert. Acie Cannaday's boys handed the Tigers their first district defeat by a 10-2 score. However, the loss was not what had everyone talking.

Catfish had announced he would make a visit to Lamar Junior College in Beaumont, in response to that school's interest in his coaching services. He had consistently shunned invitations by other high schools for two years, but now the opportunity to move up to the college level intrigued the coach. Players and sports fans in Mount Vernon had known it would happen sometime, yet they were not prepared when the news came.

Mount Vernon fans, seized by dread, worried and waited.

32

March 31, 1948

When Catfish got back from South Texas, he called Superintendent Fleming.

"Lamar is a fine school, and its officials made a flattering offer, but my family and I want to stay right here. Coach Campbell and I are looking forward to another championship season with the Mount Vernon Tigers."

Fleming wasted no time notifying Devall at the *Optic-Herald* where Friday's front-page headline read, "CATFISH TURNS DOWN FLATTERING OFFER; WILL REMAIN HERE AS MT. VERNON COACH." The related article then summarized his five-year coaching record at Mount Vernon: eight district titles, five bi-district, four regional crowns, a state finalist team, and a state championship.

To say the citizens of Mount Vernon welcomed the news would be like saying, "Methuselah lived a full life." If the diehard Tiger fans should live nine hundred sixty-nine years, they would insist that Catfish be their coach to the last day.

With their coach's future settled, the Tiger baseball squad took on the Gilmer Buckeyes in what became a pitchers' duel between Zimmerman and the Buckeyes' Hurt.

After the Tigers came up with consecutive hits by Meredith and Banks in the first inning, the Gilmer hurler tried a pickoff throw to second that ended up in centerfield, allowing two runs to score. The game then settled down to a defensive struggle. In the sixth inning, Zim gave up a single, walked a couple of batters, and then an error allowed the Buckeyes to knot the score, 2-2.

Newman Gilbert came on to relieve Zimmerman, who had allowed only two hits in six innings. Gilbert shut down the Buckeyes, leaving two runners stranded. Now, if the Tigers could generate a run in their last at-bat and hold Gilmer in the bottom of the inning, the Tigers would have another win.

In the top of the seventh, Meredith drew a walk, followed by Dudley Miller's single, and then Robert Chambers slapped what proved to be the game-winning hit, driving in Meredith. Gilbert again blanked the Buckeyes in the bottom half of the seventh, and the Tigers celebrated the return of their coach with a 3-2 victory.

The following Friday, the Tigers defeated Pittsburg and followed that victory with another over Talco on May 21. With graduation at hand, the Tigers' baseball won-loss record stood at 6-1 with two remaining games, one against Mount Pleasant on May 28, and then they would face the undefeated district leaders from Winnsboro on June 1.

On the evening of May 21, graduation took center stage. Charles Lowry was declared valedictorian and Rosemary Carroll salutatorian. Aline Parchman placed third while Gayle Tinsley ranked fourth. Gene Fleming's grade average placed him among the top students, but his father disqualified him from being recognized because he had opted for a fourth year of high school, where others had completed their credits in three years.

Forty-six seniors from this remarkable class received diplomas, yet this celebratory occasion had one particularly sad footnote. Notably absent from the list of graduates was Joe Zane Condrey, the senior running back with college-level athletic skills.

The graduates of 1947-48, and especially the athletes, left the May 21 commencement ceremony to go their separate ways. With the renewal of the military draft, many of these young men were unsure of what was next for them.

With an uncertain summer ahead, the Tigers finished up their baseball schedule by losing a heartbreaker to Mount Pleasant on a blustery day, but then bounced back to give Winnsboro their only defeat of the season. Catfish's boys completed their initial baseball season with a 6-2 record, second to the Red Raiders in the district race.

Catfish spent the summer of 1948 playing semi-pro baseball for the Mount Vernon Lions. With the season winding down, he carried a .307 batting average, while Assistant Bo Campbell had murdered opposing pitching at a .364 clip. Catfish played catcher, his battery mate on the mound usually being Pop Griffin. Campbell was the leftfielder and power hitter for the team.

In early August Catfish attended the Texas Coaches School held on the Hardin Simmons University campus in Abilene. His fellow coaches honored him for both his regional championship in football and his quintet's state title in basketball. As a memento, they gave him a leather billfold with his name embossed on it. The week ended with Gene Fleming, headed to the University of Texas on a football scholarship, playing his last contest of high school football in the annual All-Star Game.

Several other players from that great class of 1947-48 were headed off to college on athletic scholarships. Most notable were Charles Lowry and Herb Zimmerman who would play for "Dutch" Meyer at Texas Christian University and Maurice "Bud" Campbell who signed to play basketball for "Buster" Brannon at the same school. Campbell would join Harvey Fromme and James Knox of Sinton, a pair of players he had met at the state tournament.

Back in Mount Vernon, preseason football practices began August 16, two weeks earlier than usual to accommodate a rule change that provided for a state football championship playoff system for Class A. With the graduation of Catfish's entire forward wall, along with backs Kenneth Meek and Buck Parchman, the coach had a rebuilding challenge like he had never known. Yet, he forsook his normal two practices per day due to the sweltering summer heat, and set daily drills for seven-thirty in the evening.

When Wallace Hunnicutt failed to show up for practice, Dale Moore sought him out, explaining that his former teammates wanted him back. "What about the coach?" Wallace asked. Dale set up a meeting. After Catfish stressed the necessity for following team rules, he shared a warm handshake with his smiling running back.

For the first time since his 1944 team, Catfish's returning experience was in the backfield with junior Dale Moore, sophomore Billy Jack Meredith, Roy Cunningham, and Wallace Hunnicutt. If Catfish could piece together a forward wall, his Tigers could have another good season. However, realistically, his boys could not be expected to take advantage of the new rule and compete for a state title.

As practice continued, the coach began to see several bright spots. Dudley Miller was a flawless performer at center and a reliable place-kicker. Dale Brakebill at end and Johnny Moore at guard proved they could play hard-nosed football with anybody, the kind of players every coach loved to have. Billy Clinton and Buster Simms had the muscle and agility to fill the tackle slots, and Billy Jack Carter was a steady lineman with size. Charles "Birddog" Stretcher and young Donald Yates were among the district's best ends, and Kenneth "Bruno" Kimbrell showed the same fire as Brakebill and Johnny Moore. This projected forward wall averaged one hundred fifty-five pounds, fifteen less than the 1947 line. These lads were undersized and unproven, but they had the same Tiger spirit as their forerunners, and in time, who could know?

The opponents on the 1948 schedule would answer those questions, hopefully before district competition kicked off with the Red Raiders.

September 10	Clarksville	away
September 18	Paris Reserves	home
September 24	Edgewood	away
October 1	Texarkana Reserves	home
October 8	Winnsboro	home
October 15	Mount Pleasant	home
October 22	Pittsburg	away
October 29	Open	
November 5	Mineola	home
November 12	Gilmer	away

"Boys," Catfish told his team as they prepared for their first game, "all your opponents are out there just dying to get even. They're thinking this is going to be a weak year for us, so you've got to prove to them that the names have changed, but you're still the Mount Vernon Tigers."

Catfish worked those boys often and late, determined to prepare them for the onslaught just ahead, but his players never questioned his demands.

"The beginning of every ballgame is crucial," he said on Thursday, the day before the first contest. "For this game, it's doubly important. From the first play, you've got to prove to Clarksville that you're the Tigers, and nothing has changed. If you'll put a lickin' on them, the other teams will take notice."

The Tigers traveled to the Clarksville game with Billy Jack Carter sidelined with an injured leg, but otherwise Catfish's boys were physically ready to play.

Mount Vernon won the toss and elected to receive the ball. After a modest return to the twenty-four, the Tigers gave the fans their first look at Catfish's 1948 offense. They liked what they saw.

After gaining twelve yards on a couple of running plays to Billy

Jack Meredith and Roy Cunningham, Dale Moore sent a long aerial downfield to Cunningham who hauled it in and romped to the eighteen of Clarksville. The Tigers went back to the running game for eight yards, and then Moore flipped a short pass to Dale Brakebill to the four. On the next play, Meredith rounded left end for the first touchdown of the new season. He then converted the point-after.

After the Tiger defense proved surprisingly stingy, Clarksville punted back to Mount Vernon. On the first play, Dale Moore followed his blockers around right end for eight yards before he met a Clarksville tackler helmet-to-helmet.

Back in the huddle, Dale gave his teammates a blank stare for about ten seconds before Meredith realized his quarterback was off in never-never land. Billy Jack called timeout and walked Dale to the sideline.

Robert Chambers came into the game at quarterback and fed the ball to Meredith, Cunningham, and Wallace Hunnicutt until the Tigers reached the thirty-five-yard line of Clarksville on the last play of the first quarter.

On the first play of the second period, the replacement quarterback spun clockwise, ready to hand the ball to Cunningham on a slant off right tackle. Unfortunately, his backfield was headed the other way. Chambers did just what he should have done in that situation; he tucked the ball under his arm and followed his backfield to the left side of the line where he found a huge hole. Breaking clear, he cut between the two defensive backs and sprinted into the end zone. A blocked extra point left the Tigers with a two-touchdown lead, 13-0.

On the sideline, Catfish was ecstatic. It was exactly the kind of start he had hoped for.

Midway in the second quarter, the Clarksville offense began moving the ball. Having started on their thirty-yard line, they drove the ball to the Tigers' fifteen before a fourth-down pass failed to get the yardage needed for a first down.

By now Dale Moore knew his name, could identify most of his teammates, and knew where he was. Back in the game he called a couple of running plays, then went back to the air with a beautiful pass to Meredith who turned a twenty-five yard pass into a sixty-yard touchdown, upping the score to 19-0. A pass attempt for the point-after failed.

Beginning the second half, Clarksville received the kickoff and played more like advertised. Emery, their premier runner, suddenly

354

seemed unstoppable, and indeed the Tigers' defense, consisting of six linemen, two linebackers, two cornerbacks and a safety, did not stop him until he had racked up two touchdowns, closing the scoring differential to 19-12.

The final quarter arrived without further scoring, but Clarksville continued to be potent offensively until Dale Moore intervened with an interception on the enemy's twenty-five.

A series of Mount Vernon line plays rammed the ball down to the five-yard line, when again Dale returned to the huddle a bit starry-eyed. Knowing the game had reached a critical point, Meredith again called timeout and ushered Dale to the sideline. Chambers reentered the game, and as before, promptly put the ball in the end zone. A successful point-after boosted the score to 26-12 and settled the outcome.

The Tigers had their first win of 1948, the sixteenth consecutive victory by the Mount Vernon footballers, spanning three seasons. Though not a dominating performance, Catfish's boys played better than most expected, considering their inexperience and the usual jitters and mistakes of first outings.

Catfish would have been happy except for the two touchdowns allowed. Other than in playoff games, his 1944, 1945, and 1947 teams, over a span of twenty-eight games, had only once allowed more than one touchdown in a contest. His first Mount Vernon team, the 1943 squad, had allowed two touchdowns once, and the 1946 team gave up two or more scores four times. Neither of the latter teams had won a title. Anyone who knew the coach could have predicted the focus and intensity level of the coming week's practices, even the local drug store owner.

Charles Mahaffey offered another bargain. Each member of the Tiger team was invited to drop by either of his stores after practice and have a free milkshake. Was Mahaffey serious? Did he not know about Catfish's rigid training rules? The Tigers did not deplete Mahaffey's supply of milkshakes. Not one player ever admitted to having claimed their prize, possibly because the drug store was closed prior to the end of the lengthy practices that week. Every night as Mount Vernon families gathered around their dinner tables, the stadium lights beamed down on Tiger Field, and no one guessed that the band was marching late.

Saturday, September 18, Catfish's tired team made their season's debut at home against the Paris reserves. In three prior meetings the

Tigers had tromped the junior Wildcats by scores of 34-0, 31-0, and 40-0. This year would be no different, with Mount Vernon winning 32-0.

While the Tiger defense no longer had the "seven stones of granite," they held Paris to only three first downs, all in the second half against Tiger reserves. While the 1947 regional champs had refused to allow Edgewood past midfield in the crucial second half of their playoff game, these Tigers drew the line at their own thirty for the entire game. Defensive end Donald Yates and lineman Johnny Moore, both lacking overpowering size, fought and scratched like Tasmanian devils, highlighting the defensive front.

Meanwhile, Dale Moore and his crew scored at least once every quarter. Meredith and Hunnicutt, now a one-hundred-sixty pounder, chewed up yardage as if the opposition were going half-speed. Sophomore Meredith captured two touchdowns, the first of the game, a fifteen yarder that capped a seventy-five yard drive, and the second being the final score of the game from eight yards out. Hunnicutt bulled his way for a five yarder, and Dale Brakebill snared a pass for a tally.

With reserves getting ample playing time, some new stars popped up on Catfish's horizon. Larkin Drummond broke through and blocked a Paris punt. His teammate, Kenneth Kimbrell, bulldogged the batted ball on the ten-yard line of Paris. J. R. Lax then romped into the end zone for the second Tiger score.

The downside was three missed extra points in five attempts. All anyone had to do was look back to the prior season to see how crucial the kicking game could be in close ballgames. Assistant Bo Campbell needed to create another golden-toed hero.

"Boys," Catfish said to his team the following Monday afternoon, "you'll be facing your first real test Friday night. Edgewood has retained most of their personnel from last year's district champs, and they are a proud team with a winning tradition that makes them better than most clubs the minute they step on the field. For us, this game is pivotal. If we are to be a championship team, it is absolutely vital that we defeat teams like the Bulldogs."

The 1948 Tigers were hearing the essence of their coach's philosophy: "If you want to be the best, you must beat the best." And one could add, "Anybody can come in second. Champions are never satisfied with less than first."

Another thing Catfish did not mention, but his players undoubtedly were aware of, was Edgewood's recent defeat of Winnsboro by a score of 34-0. If anyone questioned the potency of the current Bulldog outfit, that one game provided the answer.

When the Mount Vernon boys walked onto Edgewood's Granden Field, the atmosphere was different from anything they had known. Though only a non-conference contest, it had the feel of a playoff game. Dale Moore and Billy Jack Meredith felt the eyes of their teammates on them. These two veterans, though one was a sophomore and the other a junior, represented past Tigers who had withstood championship tests. For the 1948 squad to be successful, this duo had to show the way.

A crowd of two thousand Bulldog fans, with their hearts set on avenging last year's season-ending bi-district loss to the Tigers, yelled and screamed as Billy Ray Norris, their star quarterback, led his team onto the field. Like Meredith and Dale Moore, the Bulldogs' proven man-under-center was expected to lead the locals to victory.

The first quarter was a seesaw affair, neither team able to sustain a drive and take a lead. Meredith and Hunnicutt pounded away with gains of eleven and fourteen yards and Dale Moore tossed a few passes, but none broke loose to grab the momentum. Fumbles ended each Tiger drive prematurely, the most damaging being a loose ball on the enemy's fifteen. Norris and J. P. Covin led the Bulldogs, moving the ball up and down the field, but stalling each time prior to reaching the end zone.

The second period started much the same, with an Edgewood drive that balanced passing and running to carry the Bulldogs to the Tiger ten-yard line and a first down. With Covin out with an injury, his backup took off on a sweep around right end, but Cunningham charged across the line and dumped the ball carrier a yard behind the line of scrimmage. Norris then went to the air, but the Tigers' safeties rose to the challenge and batted three consecutive passes to the turf, handing the ball to Mount Vernon's offense.

Cunningham burst over right guard behind Frank Carr for five, placing the ball on the sixteen. Meredith plowed up the middle for fifteen, giving the Tigers ample breathing room. Cunningham got four more before Meredith blistered the defense for twenty yards across midfield and down to the Edgewood forty-five. From there, Dale Moore sneaked through the line, broke loose in the secondary, and with a rare combination of shiftiness and power, raced into the end zone. The quarterback then toed the point-after through the uprights, and the

Tigers had that all-important first score as time ran out in the first half.

The third quarter started much like the first: lots of offense but no points. But with the help of Meredith's splendid punting, the Tigers gradually improved their field position and again found a way to get more yards out of their offense.

With the Tigers taking over on their forty after a punt, Hunnicutt ran over two tacklers, bounced off another, and rammed ahead for thirty-eight yards. Meredith and his backfield mates pushed the ball on down to the four-yard line, where an untimely fumble gave the ball away only steps from the goal line. However, despair turned to delight when Clinton and Yates pried the ball loose from a Bulldog, and the big tackle pounced on it.

Three plays later, the determined Tigers had shoved the Bulldog defense back to the two-yard line. Then Robert Chambers trotted onto the field, a quarterback substitution on a critical fourth down that surprised both teams. Catfish desperately wanted a touchdown, and chose a surprise play he hoped would catch the Bulldogs off guard.

The Tigers broke from their huddle and lined up in their standard T-formation. With the defense waiting for Chambers to begin his cadence, Miller suddenly snapped the ball and surged forward. The Tiger quarterback followed his center right into the end zone with a stunned Bulldogs' forward wall wondering what had happened. The upstart Tigers had a fourteen-point lead late in the third quarter, and Catfish smiled.

Norris, the Bulldogs' quarterback, began the final stanza flinging the football all over the field. The flurry of passes caught Mount Vernon flatfooted, and the Bulldogs marched down to the Tigers' fourteen. With Catfish's boys geared up for another aerial, Norris pulled the ball down on a naked bootleg, and romped into the end zone. When the point-after sailed below the crossbar, the Tigers led, 14-6.

Then the Tigers responded with what Catfish would later call "a character statement." Taking the kickoff, the Tigers pounded away, grinding out yardage head-to-head and shoulder-to-shoulder. While the clock ticked away, the Tigers marched on relentlessly. When they reached the enemy's thirty, only seconds remained on the game clock. Dale handed the ball to Meredith one last time, expecting to grind the remaining seconds away. But when the sophomore fullback broke through a gaping hole in the line, he sped past two secondary defenders and breezed into the end zone. Moore booted the point-after, and

Catfish's new crop of boys had won, 21-6, a victory that told everybody that the 1948 Tigers were thoroughbreds ready to start the race for the district title.

The Tiger backs, led by Dale Moore and Billy Jack Meredith, had rushed for two hundred seventy-five yards against a playoff-caliber defense, while the Tiger defenders had held the Bulldogs to one hundred nineteen. Norris's one hundred ten passing yards offset that figure somewhat, but still came up fifty-five yards short of the Tiger offense's showing. More important to Catfish, the running game of Meredith, Hunnicutt, Cunningham, and Moore had, at a crucial point in the contest, pushed the Bulldog defense into their own end zone. But most impressive to the coach was watching his defense limit a potent Edgewood squad to a single touchdown.

While the young Tigers celebrated, Lyndon B. Johnson, a Texan seeking a seat in the United States Senate, was having his problems. Certified as the Democratic candidate in September, charges of voting fraud had been brought against his campaign. The counties involved were Jim Wells, Zapata, and Duval. Federal Judge T. Whitfield Davidson refused to allow Johnson's name on the ballot for the upcoming general election, pending investigation and resolution of the charges.

"Unless this matter is resolved by September twenty-seventh, the State of Texas for the first time will be deprived of a Democratic candidate for the United States Senate," said Dudley Tarleton, Johnson's legal representative.

This huge political issue was resolved when President Truman's Secretary of State ordered Johnson's name be put on the ballot, following a favorable decision on the case by the United States Supreme Court. Justice Hugo Black, ruling for Johnson, overrode Judge Davidson's decision; however, the review of ballots in the three counties was to continue, leaving some hope for Coke Stevenson, Johnson's challenger.

Locally, Charles Mahaffey sold his two drug stores, the Crescent to Roy and Lester Smith and their partner L. R. Bell. The Rutherford store was purchased by Mr. and Mrs. Clarence Maness, he a druggist from Arkansas. The enterprising Mahaffey was now out of the drugstore business, and possibly the locals had seen the last of free milkshakes and under-priced cold medicine.

Texarkana's reserves came to town on Saturday night as Mount Vernon's next opponent. Significantly outweighed on the line of scrimmage, the Tigers' hopes for a win seemed to rest on their speedy backfield and their highly respected kicking game.

In a strange contest, Catfish's undersized boys triumphed, 27-6, leaving many wondering how they did it.

Receiving the initial kickoff, the Texarkana boys tried three runs and had little to show for it, so they punted the ball away. Since linemen of the kicking team could not cross the line of scrimmage until the ball was kicked, return men had ample opportunity to catch the ball and even get a fair shot at picking up a few yards. Catfish always required two men back to receive kicks, and he usually had the two return men to crisscross, allowing for an exchange of the ball and forcing the defenders to divide their attention. In this case, Dale Moore caught the ball, faked a handoff to Hunnicutt, and raced sixty yards for a touchdown. The point-after gave the Tigers a seven-point lead.

Instant replays were still several years into the future, but some fans who witnessed the start of the game might have argued that point.

After the Tigers limited their opponent to three plays and a punt, Dale Moore again received the kick on his forty. If anything was different, it was Dale Brakebill's wipeout block of a Texarkana player, the key to setting Moore free on another sixty-yard scoring scamper. The extra point was good, and Catfish's boys had a fourteen-point lead less than five minutes into the game.

Breaking the trend, the visitors finally kept the ball and moved down the field to the Tigers' forty. There, their quarterback, named Fowler, chunked a pass to his teammate Clem who gained thirty-eight yards to the Tigers' two-yard stripe. Catfish's smaller defenders held for two downs, but then they were fooled by a Fowler-to-Clem toss into the end zone. The missed point-after left the Tigers with an eight-point lead, 14-6.

While Catfish's boys prepared for the second half, Glyndean Hall was crowned as Mount Vernon High School's football queen. Escorted onto the field by Drue Hightower, while the band played its rendition of "Let Me Call You Sweetheart," the popular queen flashed a winning smile to her proud classmates.

In the third stanza, a Meredith punt pinned the visitors back on their five-yard line. Struggling to push an extra yard away from their goal line, their runner fumbled the ball, and the Tigers captured it. Dale Moore then picked up three yards on a quarterback sneak. From there, Hunnicutt slammed into the end zone. Another successful point-after gave the Tigers twenty-one points.

In the final period, the Tigers worked the ball down to the Texarkana thirty-two. After a run by Hunnicutt, Moore hurled a pass to Meredith who fought his way to the eleven and a first down. After Hunnicutt picked up two more tough yards, Moore peeled out around right end behind a caravan of blockers and pranced into the end zone. The point-after was low, the first miss of the game for Catfish's boys. Score: 27-6.

With time running out and Texarkana desperate for a respectable showing, Fowler trotted onto the field with his teammates waiting for him back on their own seven-yard line. He came out firing the ball and did not stop until he had thrown seventeen consecutive aerials and had moved his team to the Mount Vernon fifteen. The visitors had finally found a way to attack the Tigers' defense, but it was too late. The final gun sounded with Texarkana plotting another pass play.

Catfish's boys had chalked up another win, their fourth of the year and Mount Vernon's nineteenth consecutive victory, spanning three seasons.

"Matched up against much larger players," the *Optic-Herald* article said, "Catfish's boys proved that their coach's favorite axiom still rings true. 'It's not the size of the dog in the fight, but the size of the fight in the dog.'"

The lengthy preseason was now over, and Catfish's boys would face Winnsboro to start district play. Thus far, the Red Raiders had not shown to be a district title contender, however, Catfish knew past games were irrelevant when these two old rivals suited up.

Also, the "old mentor" would rather croak than lose to his past protégé, Acie Cannaday.

33

October 5, 1948

Catfish's inexperienced linemen, the largest question mark of his team, had held the previous four opponents to an average of six points a game while opening holes for Tiger runners who had racked up an average of twenty-six points. Still the coach fretted while soothing his ulcers with a pint of milk.

"Forget the stats," Catfish said to Charles Bruce, sportswriter and fellow teacher, when presented with this evidence. "We're not a dominant team. We have a lot to prove, first to ourselves, and then to our opponents."

The start of the Winnsboro game appeared to bear out the coach's concerns when, on the Red Raiders' first play from scrimmage, Rhea Coppedge, their swift left halfback, romped down to the Tigers' ten-yard line. Now the suspect Tiger defensive front was on its heels and desperately needed to make a stand.

A repeat of the initial play lost two yards when Yates and Clinton broke through and trapped Coppedge, bolstering the young Tigers' sagging confidence. Three plays later, the stymied Red Raiders turned the ball over to Catfish's offense on the seven-yard line.

Meredith, Cunningham, Hunnicutt, and Dale Moore pounded the Winnsboro front wall until they reached the Red Raiders' thirty-four.

"Stingaree right," quarterback Moore called out in the huddle, glancing at his younger brother.

While the entire backfield stormed around left end, pulling the defense to them, left guard Johnny Moore sneaked along behind the right side of his offensive line and then turned upfield. Twenty-three yards later, a defensive safety brought him down on the eleven. Meredith then fought his way to the one-yard line from where one-hundred-sixty-pound Wallace Hunnicutt barreled into the end zone. Following the extra point, the Tigers led, 7-0.

After the Tiger defense forced the Red Raiders to punt, the Tigers' offense ran two plays that took them to their own thirty-eight. There, Dale Moore dropped back and hurled a strike to Hunnicutt who split the safeties at midfield and surprised many of the fans by outrunning everybody to the end zone for the Tigers' second score.

Just before halftime, the Tigers once again took over the ball and marched to the opponent's twenty-five. A pitch from Moore to Hunnicutt around left end closed out the first half with Mount Vernon's third touchdown. At intermission, the Tigers led, 21-0.

For Winnsboro, the second half only got worse. Early in the third quarter Dale Moore intercepted a Red Raider pass at midfield and galloped fifty yards to the end zone. Robert Chambers, Tiger reserve quarterback, scored twice, and Billy Jack Meredith closed out the touchdown parade, making the final score 48-0.

The Tigers had accumulated sixteen first downs while allowing Winnsboro only seven. Catfish's stable of runners had galloped for two hundred ninety-three yards, and Dale Moore had thrown for eighty-three more, a total of three hundred seventy-six yards of offense to only one hundred five for the Red Raiders.

With their first district victory under their belts and twenty consecutive wins on the board, these Tigers indeed had proven that only the names had changed. Any hopes upcoming opponents may have harbored for a weak Tiger team were shattered.

On Sunday, October 10, at the stately First Methodist Church, Dewey Moore, Catfish's "Stickfinger" center on his 1947 team, wed Martha Hill, daughter of Mr. and Mrs. Merle Hill, with Reverend C. S. Wilhite officiating. Dewey, son of Mr. and Mrs. Hoffman Moore and brother to Dale and Johnny, quarterback and guard on the Tigers' football team, had joined the United States Air Force and would soon be on his way to the Air Force's Technical Training school in Fort Warren, Wyoming where he would tackle a typewriter in a clerk typist course. An appropriate wedding gift for Martha, someone suggested, would have been a baton to replace her splintered old broom handle.

Catfish had little time to congratulate the newlyweds. Just ahead for him and his young Tigers stood Mount Pleasant, led by a new coach, Winnie Bays. The Titus County boys had defeated Clarksville, 14-6, Jefferson, 26-0, and Talco, 13-0, while losing only one, a 28-6 defeat at the hands of the Atlanta Rabbits. One-hundred-ninety-pound Milton Marshall, Bays's much-heralded fullback, was the most important gear in the opposition's engine, and for Catfish's boys to win, they must find a way to stop the opposing Tigers' bruising runner. No doubt, Mount Vernon's most bitter rival would be revved up to derail Catfish's title-bound locomotive.

With Tiger Field packed to its twenty-five-hundred-seat capacity, the two Tiger lineups battled to a standstill through the first quarter. Ending the first period, the visiting Tigers punted to Catfish's boys, the ball settling on the sixteen.

With eighty-four yard stripes between his team and pay-dirt, Dale Moore brought his offense to the line of scrimmage. Two running plays moved the ball eight yards, leaving Mount Vernon lacking two for a much-needed first down. For this key play, Catfish sent Robert Chambers onto the field, but not as a substitute for the quarterback. Oblivious to the sub, the defense focused its attention on Meredith and Hunnicutt, the two bread-and-butter backs for Mount Vernon.

Dale Moore bent under center and barked the cadence. Taking the snap from Miller, Moore turned and stuck the ball in Hunnicutt's gut over left tackle, and the black-clad defense converged on the hard-charging fullback.

Meanwhile, Chambers had swung toward the right sideline and cut upfield. As the quarterback drifted back a few steps, he kept his eyes on the struggling Hunnicutt. Then, Moore suddenly pulled the ball from behind his back and shot a bullet to Chambers who ran alone near the twenty-five. Gathering in the pigskin, Chambers sprinted seventy-six yards to the end zone. A stunned Mount Pleasant squad watched Dale Moore kick the point-after that gave Catfish's boys a stinging 7-0 lead.

Though Mount Pleasant's big fullback managed to grind out yardage, each drive eventually broke down, and Mount Vernon's one-touchdown lead stood until midway of the second period when Meredith and Chambers crashed in on fourth down and blocked a Mount Pleasant punt. The ball settled only twenty-three yards from the enemy's goal line.

On the first play from scrimmage, Meredith stepped off twelve yards to the eleven. With the defense braced for another line charge, Dale Moore faked a handoff to Hunnicutt, and tossed to Cunningham in the end zone. Moore toed the point-after between the uprights, upping the score to 14-0.

After Catfish's defense stopped the Titus County boys short of midfield, Dale Moore dropped back and received a punt that pushed him back to his own seventeen. Corralling the ball, the versatile quarterback headed upfield, broke two tackles, and then cut to the right sideline where a wall of blockers sealed off a lane for him. Eighty-three yards later, Dale pulled up with Mount Vernon's third score and a 21-0 intermission lead.

The second half became a slugfest in the middle of the field, neither offense able to land a knockout punch. With a comfortable lead, Mount Vernon chose a conservative running game. Likewise, their opponent showed little inclination to throw the ball, creating a back-and-forth tussle that lasted two minutes into the final quarter.

Facing fourth down, Mount Pleasant booted its sixth punt of the game. Dale Moore received the high floater and was promptly downed on Mount Vernon's thirty-five.

Lining up in a straight T-formation, the Tigers ran Meredith into the line for four yards. While everyone expected another clock-consuming line thrust, Moore dropped back and tossed a pass to young Donald Yates who raced forty-four yards to the enemy's sixteen. From there, Catfish's talented quarterback rolled out around right end and followed his blockers down to the one-yard line where Milton Marshall stopped him with a thunderous hit. The ball popped loose and tumbled into the end zone. A Mount Pleasant recovery would give their team the ball out on the twenty, but the determined Tiger quarterback, scrambling on hands and knees, snared the ball just as Marshall dove for it. The point-after upped the score to 28-0.

After Mount Pleasant returned the kickoff to their forty-five, they proceeded to march down the field until big Milton Marshall bulled into the end zone, and a spark of hope flared among the visitors. It would be short-lived.

Mount Vernon received the kickoff, and Dale used his stable of thoroughbred runners to pound the ball down the field to Mount Pleasant's thirty. The quarterback then crossed up the defense with a strike to Charles "Birddog" Stretcher for the final and fatal dagger.

Catfish's boys had a 34-7 win, their second district victory and twenty-first in a row. Four Mount Pleasant turnovers, two interceptions and a pair of lost fumbles, damaged the visitors' otherwise valiant effort. Mount Vernon's defense never allowed their opponent past their thirty-eight yard line, except for the touchdown drive. And once again, Catfish's defense had allowed only one score, the maximum the coach would tolerate without roaring and growling for a week.

Pittsburg was next on Mount Vernon's schedule, and according to the *Optic-Herald*, the "dope bucket" was full to the brim with predictions of a third district win for Catfish and his boys.

While the Tigers practiced to prove the prophecy true, Devall and his newspaper business celebrated their seventy-fourth anniversary. "Since the paper's beginning in 1874, it has witnessed a small, struggling hamlet grow to the current prosperous community of two thousand two hundred fifty souls. With pride the *Optic-Herald* joins the citizens and businessmen of this town in pledging a continuance of its best efforts in the future, keeping in mind our duty to our homes, our country, and our God."

Meanwhile, A. J. Petty, husband of high school instructor, Winnie Petty, must have wondered if his recently opened Magnolia service station would last even one year. Located just off the square on the south side of West Main, about six-thirty Tuesday morning, October 19, a gas explosion at his new business left Petty with serious injuries. The force of the eruption, set off by a struck match, hurled the proprietor from inside a storage room, through the doorway, and fifteen feet onto the drive, breaking his leg and slashing a long gash in his head, in addition to injuring four others. From his hospital bed in the new medical facility, Petty realized it could have been worse. His underground gasoline tank was being filled at the time of the explosion, which ignited the fill-pipe. Easily the fuel truck and the storage tank could have exploded and killed the four workers in the area.

The service station explosion was followed three days later by another boom when Catfish's boys blasted Pittsburg, 26-0. The win was their third in the conference race and twenty-second consecutive victory.

The Tigers received the opening kickoff and marched eighty-two yards for a score. Chambers finished the drive with a fifteen-yard scamper. In the second quarter, Meredith finished off a forty-five-yard drive with a twelve-yard sprint for a touchdown. The third period provided the third tally, which followed a seventy-five-yard march, capped by Dale Moore's plunge into the end zone. In the final stanza, Moore hurled a long pass to Chambers down on the ten-yard line. The quarterback then swept around left end for the game-ending score.

The Pirates' offense managed only six first downs, while garnering one hundred ten yards rushing on determined efforts by Gandy, Groce, Clements, and Reed. In contrast, the Tigers' explosive offense never faced a punting situation.

Following an open date, Catfish's team would face Mineola.

Dorothy Nell wondered if her husband worried more about the next opponent or some catastrophe that might befall his players with an idle weekend on their hands. When the coach started calling his players early Saturday evening, his wife threatened to cut the telephone cord.

"Leave those poor boys alone," she said. "They deserve some time away from their coach, and I deserve some time with my husband."

"I'm here with you," he said, glancing over at her.

"You know," she said with a grin, "I can't remember the last time you took me out, just you and me."

"It's not like it used to be," he said. "There's Ronnie to be taken care of."

"I bet my mother would watch him tonight. She's always asking me to bring him by."

Catfish leaned back from the phone and threw up his hands.

"Do you remember," she continued, sidling over close, "that first time you took me to the Joy Theatre?"

"Uh-huh."

"Do you remember the movie?"

He hesitated, rubbing the back of his neck.

"I didn't think so," she said, poking him in the ribs. "You were too busy trying to get your arm around me."

"Give me a second. I'll remember."

She waited.

"Give me a hint," he said.

"Nope. If it was the score of a football game, you'd remember."

Dorothy Nell picked up the phone and dialed her parents. Catfish could hear his mother-in-law's excited voice.

"We'd love to keep little Ronnie. In fact, we'd like for him to spend the night with us."

Catfish stood up and headed to the closet for a fresh shirt.

The theatre marquee read, "*The Fuller Brush Man* with Red Skelton and Janet Blair." Catfish sighed heavily as he stepped out of the car.

"Maybe you'll watch the movie this time," Dorothy Nell said as Catfish paid for the tickets. "A few laughs will be good for you."

A boy with a dim flashlight walked them to their seats. As soon as they sat down, Catfish put his arm around his wife and reached for her hand.

"No use wasting time," he said, kissing her on the cheek.

"Shhh," came from someone right behind them.

He started to turn around, but Dorothy Nell quickly leaned her head against his cheek and patted his hand.

Throughout the movie, the coach laughed, hugged his wife, whispered into her ear, and generally enjoyed himself. When it ended, Catfish stood and stepped into the aisle, glad to stretch his long legs.

"And you said you'd changed," the woman sitting by behind him said stiffly. "I'll swear you're the same character you were fifteen years ago."

"Ma'am, do I know . . ."

The theatre lights came on as Catfish turned to confront the heckler.

"Miss Binnion," Dorothy Nell said, looking back. "It's good to see you. I hope you enjoyed the show."

"Both shows, my dear. I don't know who's the bigger clown, Mr. Skelton or that husband of yours. I can't imagine why people around here take him so seriously."

"Irene, you're gonna ruin my reputation," Catfish said, his neck a little red.

"Oh, no," she said, "but don't ever forget. I know all about your college days."

Miss Binnion then winked at Dorothy Nell and headed for the door.

Standing in the aisle, Catfish waited for his wife, and together they eased toward the exit.

"I need to stop by the ladies' room," Dorothy Nell said in the foyer.

Irene Binnion had got there ahead of her, and was checking her hair in the mirror.

"Honey," Irene said to Dorothy Nell, "don't you worry about what I said in there. He's always pulling something on somebody, and I've learned the only way to deal with him is to put him on the defensive. He's only really loved two things in his whole life. One is sports, and the other is you."

"I know that," Dorothy Nell said, "though I'd have to add his family and his boys to that list."

"Now don't you let on that I've cleared him," Irene said as Dorothy Nell turned to the mirror.

Dorothy Nell smiled, patted Irene on the arm, and left.

Catfish was pacing the lobby. A nervous smile crossed his face when he saw her, and they stepped out onto the sidewalk.

"I hate these open dates. I wonder where Dale is, and Billy Jack,"

Catfish said glancing at his watch. "Let's drive by and make sure they're home."

Dorothy Nell shook her head as they headed for the car. Inside, she slid across the seat next to Catfish and leaned her head against his shoulder.

"It wasn't as good as the first movie you took me to," she whispered, "but I really enjoyed just being with you."

He took a quick glance down at her. Her eyes were closed, and she was smiling, and maybe remembering.

"Ginger Rogers and Cary Grant," he mumbled.

"What?"

"That first movie we went to," he said. "It was *Once Upon a Honeymoon.*"

She hesitated, pretending she could not recall.

"I think you're right," she replied, snuggling closer.

"Let's go home," he said. "It's too late to check on the boys."

34

November 1, 1948

On Monday morning, the community received terrible news. Mary Grace Arthur, longtime schoolteacher and wife of former school principal Paul Arthur, died at six-twenty that morning in the Franklin County Hospital after a month-long illness. A native of the area and a Mount Vernon High School graduate, she had taught English and speech at her alma mater and was a lifetime member of the First Baptist Church. As her pastor and friends knew, she had a favorite poem, *Crossing the Bar* by Tennyson. On Tuesday at two-thirty, Catfish and his fellow teachers sat damp-eyed and listened as Reverend Whitt recited it at her funeral.

> *Sunset and evening star,*
> *And one clear call for me,*
> *And may there be no mourning at the bar,*
> *When I put out to sea.*

Regardless, the school faculty did mourn the loss of their friend. Also, the Sunday school class that she had taught until her illness, Dorcas Matrons, pledged to install a stained glass window in the new First Baptist Church in her memory.

As Mount Vernon grieved, the country was electing a president. Harry S. Truman had served all except eighty-three days of Franklin Roosevelt's fourth term. Pre-election polls indicated voters were not pleased with the Missourian's wartime job or after-war policies and that Thomas Dewey would defeat Truman in a landslide. The early edition of the November 3 *Chicago Daily Tribune* prematurely announced, "DEWEY DEFEATS TRUMAN," but when the votes were all tallied, the gritty Truman and his running mate, Alben Barkley of Kentucky, had won with twenty-eight states and three hundred three

370

electoral votes to Dewey's sixteen states and one hundred eighty-nine electoral votes. Strom Thurmond carried the other four states on the Dixiecrat ticket, pulling a good chunk of Democrat votes from Truman.

Then on Wednesday, the Smith's telephone rang. Dorothy Nell's uncle, Grady Gist of Marshall, was deathly ill. She drove to the school, picked up Catfish, and they hurried to the bedside of the brother of Dorothy's mother.

Amid all these happenings, Catfish missed two practices, but Bo Campbell led team preparations for the Mineola contest. Always the motivator, Catfish searched desperately for a spark to inspire his boys for the upcoming battle with the Yellow Jackets.

"This is the last football game our seniors will play at Tiger Field," he said at Friday's pep rally. "So we're dedicating this game to them. I especially want to recognize Robert Chambers. He missed last season and the regional championship due to a knee injury. He has worked harder than anyone else, and has come back and done a fabulous job for us. I know his teammates will give a supreme effort tonight, as Robert has done, and reward him with a victory."

With a win the Yellow Jackets could stay in contention for the district title. They had recently defeated Winnsboro, 27-0, but had one conference loss, a 7-0 shutout by Gilmer. Annually, Mineola had been a formidable opponent for the Tigers, and regardless of Mount Vernon's gaudy winning record, the coach fretted. Maybe it was the open date, two weeks without a game, that worried him most. Seldom did it work to his advantage.

Regardless of the cold, blustery weather, sixteen hundred fans showed up to cheer on their Tigers, and they were quickly rewarded.

Mount Vernon kicked the ball to Mineola to start the contest, and immediately shut down the Yellow Jackets' offense. After receiving the ensuing punt, the Tigers marched relentlessly down the field as their faithful followers had come to expect. However, at the eleven-yard line of the Yellow Jackets, a fumble cut the drive short.

After the Tigers' defense held again, the Mineola punter dropped back to boot the football away. Dale Brakebill knifed through and deflected the kick, giving the Tigers a fresh opportunity from their opponent's twenty. Amazingly, penalties and a stout defense handcuffed the Tigers who managed only a two-yard advance before running out of downs.

Once again Catfish's defense stifled the Yellow Jackets' offense, walling them inside their own thirty-four throughout the first quarter,

371

and yielding only to the forty-two in the second. The first half ended with the score deadlocked, 0-0.

Receiving the kickoff to start the second half, the Tigers marched eighty yards, all rushing, and Meredith rammed the ball into the end zone from the five, giving Catfish's boys a 7-0 lead. Suddenly, the frustrated Tiger fans' confidence returned, but the celebration was short-lived.

Two possessions later, the Tigers failed to get a first down and lined up to punt. When the ball was snapped to the kicker, he bobbled it forward, and as he attempted to pick up the loose ball, the blocker immediately in front of him drifted backwards and they collided. Meanwhile, onrushing Yellow Jackets arrived, and one fell on the ball at the twenty-three. In a defense-dominated game, everybody in the stadium and on the gridiron understood the potential severity of the miscue.

The jubilant Yellow Jackets pounded away at the Tigers, but Catfish's stubborn defense yielded only five yards in three plays. The quarter ended, and the teams swapped ends of the field with the Mineola boys needing five yards to keep their district title hopes alive.

The ball rested on the eighteen-yard line when the Yellow Jackets approached the line of scrimmage for their final attempt at maintaining the drive. No one gave much notice to a halfback named Kelley who entered the game during the quarter change.

The Mineola quarterback pitched the ball to John Kelley who headed around right end. The Tiger defense had him cut off, and appeared to have him trapped for a loss that would turn over the ball to the Tigers. However, Kelley suddenly stopped, sidestepped a hard-charging defender, and sailed the ball toward the end zone. The Yellow Jackets' Browning snared the pigskin at the five and darted across the goal line. With only the point-after needed to knot the score at 7-7, Dokey lined up and toed the ball through the uprights.

The remainder of the final quarter was dominated by the two defenses, and the game ended in a deadlock. And just like that, the Tigers' commanding lead for the district title was in jeopardy, and their fabulous winning streak had ended at twenty-two games.

"I think Mount Vernon must be as surprised as Dewey was in losing to Truman," someone said, reflecting the general sentiment that the fans had indeed witnessed a major upset in district 15-A.

The Tigers' offense had gained almost two hundred yards to Mineola's one hundred twenty-seven. They had two more first downs and led in penetrations, but the two fumbles negated all other advantages, along with a halfback named John Kelley, a name the Tigers would not forget. Emotionally, Catfish's boys had lost, and it was a bitter pill for the seniors.

"Next year," the coach said, "we'll play ourselves rather than have an open date."

Gilmer, lurking on the horizon, suddenly had the district championship within their grasp. The Buckeyes had always been tough on the Tigers, and this year's squad, unbeaten and untied, promised to be one of their best. The district championship would be decided Friday night, November 12, on Gilmer's home turf.

A quick check of Catfish's record against the Buckeyes showed a 3-1-1 advantage for the Tigers, however, only the undefeated 1947 team had bested Gilmer by more than twelve points. Even the great 1944 Tiger regional champions had squeaked by with a last-second touchdown, 7-0. No undefeated Tiger team had ever entered a crucial game with more doubters.

*   *   *

Narvel Lawrence steered the bus cautiously through the heavy fog as Catfish fretted in his seat behind the driver. Facing another night game in dismal weather on a muddy Buckeye Field, he knew that passing the ball would be almost impossible. What last minute plan, what surprise could he pull out of his box of tricks to make the difference in what promised to be a close game?

Though expectations back in September had been relatively low for this team, the mere thought of letting the championship slip away now galled the coach. I've never played for second place, and I'm not about to start now, he told himself. Either I've got to count on my boys to go out there and whip the Buckeyes in an old-fashioned slugfest, or I've got to think of some scheme to give us a big boost. Never an indecisive man, why was he struggling with this decision?

His boys sat quietly on the wooden benches in the locker room decked out in their white uniforms with purple numerals. Without a word, their tall, lean coach paced back and forth before them, sipping on a bottle of milk. Never before at a loss for words, this was not like him.

"Boys," he finally said, "for the last hour I've racked my brain for a special play, a strategy to surprise the Buckeyes tonight, and get a quick, easy touchdown. I've thought of a few, and they just might work."

Then he scanned the faces of each of his players, his eyes searching for a clue to their state of preparedness. Was it there—that rigid determination, a smoldering anger, the battle attitude? The intense quiet was almost eerie.

"However," he continued, "from the start of this season, I've harped on fundamentals, conditioning, and playing with heart. A champion does not use a sucker punch to win. A champion squares his shoulders, grits his teeth, and takes his opponent straight on, best man win.

"I brought my 1944 team here when Gilmer wore the district crown. We had to kick the door down and take that title from them. Well, now you wear the crown, and tonight the Buckeyes stand at the door of your throne."

Catfish hesitated, gulped down some of his white elixir, and then a wide smile broke across his face.

"Hold your heads high when you go out there tonight. The nineteen forty-seven team passed their title to you, and left you a legacy to defend. Now, it's up to you to play like the champions you are. You do that, and the victory will be yours."

The Tigers practically exploded out of the dressing room. The disappointing tie with Mineola was a weeklong burden they were ready to jettison from their minds. They burst onto the field as proud, reigning regional champions, undefeated in twenty-three straight games, with an unstoppable offense and an unyielding defense.

Receiving the kickoff, Cunningham returned the ball to the Tigers' forty. Meredith sliced through the Buckeye defense past midfield. Hunnicutt followed that with an eight-yard gain. Meredith slashed for another first down, with four yards to spare. Cunningham skirted left end to the fifteen. Meredith then plowed down to the one-yard line, where Dale Moore sneaked across. After the failed point-after, the Tigers led 6-0.

Following the kickoff, Catfish's defense put up a stone wall, and three plays later the Buckeyes punted back to the Tigers, the wet ball splashing down at the Gilmer forty.

Again, with dangerous Dale Moore orchestrating the offense, Catfish's stable of runners followed their forward wall of Clinton, Johnny Moore, Miller, Carr, and Simms down to the eight, where Cunningham broke free for the second touchdown. The point-after made the score 13-0.

Late in the second quarter, with Gilmer owning the ball on their twenty-eight-yard line, the Buckeyes sent two players, including George Owens, toward their bench on the east side of the field and trotted two apparent replacements onto the field. Then, the offense came to the line of scrimmage, splitting a flanker to the west sideline. A Tiger defender followed the flanker, but then became confused when he lined up a foot out of bounds. When the ball was snapped, quarterback Hurt dropped back and spiraled a beauty to a streaking George Owens along the east sideline. Thinking Owens had left the game, the Tigers had not covered him, and he sailed untouched for seventy-two yards and a score. The point-after failed, and the score tightened to 13-6.

During halftime, the Tigers discussed the play, and realized they had been duped. The right flanker, standing just off the field, was actually out of the game. Owens, who appeared to have gone to the bench, had stopped a foot in bounds and stood nonchalantly but remained in the game. The "hideout" play, Catfish called it.

Smarting from the deception, the Tigers shut down the Buckeye offense starting the third quarter, and then rammed home another touchdown on a fifteen-yard pass from Moore to Brakebill. Suddenly, Catfish's boys had regained their two-touchdown lead, 19-6, and maintained it until the fourth quarter.

In the final stanza, the Buckeyes failed to sustain their first drive, and again punted to Mount Vernon. The Tigers drove the ball steadily to the enemy's five-yard line where Moore tossed a scoring pass to Charles "Birddog" Stretcher, building a 26-6 lead.

The Gilmer offense, smothered again after two first downs, punted to the Tigers who promptly fumbled the slick ball, which Dale Moore pounced on. A penalty then brought Mount Vernon to a fourth down back on their eighteen. The wet ball slipped as Dudley Miller passed it back to Meredith, the punter, and it arrived around his knees. The sure-handed kicker caught it, but then appeared indecisive. Seeing a charging defender coming from the left, the blocking-back slid across in front of Meredith to prevent a blocked kick and collided with the punter, sending the ball spinning on the muddy turf. The best Meredith could do was fall on the pigskin, which gave Gilmer possession only eight yards from the Tigers' goal line. The third Buckeye pass attempt to Owens put the ball into the end zone, and closed the scoring gap to 26-13.

The Tigers took the kickoff and drove down the field, reaching Gilmer's three-yard line. From there Moore pitched the ball to Hunnicutt who bowled his way into the end zone. The missed point-after finalized the score at 32-13.

The Tigers were once again district champs and undefeated in twenty-four consecutive games. They had dominated their opponent, fifteen first downs to four, and two hundred ninety-five yards to two hundred twenty-seven, seventy-two of the Buckeye yards coming on the "hideout" play.

"Coach," Bruce of the *Optic-Herald* said to Catfish after the game, "how did you repeat as champions in an obvious rebuilding year?"

"Well," the coach said, smiling, "I'd say we've got some rather special lumber and nails among this bunch of boys. All I did was swing the hammer."

Winning the district championship then pitted Catfish's team against New London in a bi-district contest in Gladewater. The game was set for Friday night, November 26.

The coach was worried. His team was facing another weekend without a game.

35

November 19, 1948

Friday night of the off weekend, Catfish paced his living room floor. He had told his boys that the nine o'clock curfew, normally applicable to weeknights only, was to be followed this weekend as well. As the deadline approached, he began making phone calls. Finally satisfied that his boys were accounted for, he picked up the paper and tried to concentrate.

The first article that got his attention praised Congressman Wright Patman for his role in getting the Lone Star Steel plant located just forty miles from Mount Vernon. Employing eight hundred workers and producing almost a thousand tons of iron daily, it had been established a year earlier and quickly became the largest industry in East Texas. The town on the outskirts of the plant even shared its name: Lone Star. The article then explained that Mount Vernon once had borne that name.

Established in 1848, the current Mount Vernon community had originally been called Keith, named after Postmaster W. S. Keith. Then in November 1850, W. C. Wright had become Postmaster and changed the name to Lone Star.

For the next twenty-five years the community bore that name, but in 1875 Franklin County was carved out of Titus County, the town was elected as the county seat, and soon its name became Mount Vernon in honor of President George Washington's famous home. The name stuck, and since then, the only attempt to rename the town had occurred in late spring of 1948, according to rumors, when some sports fans suggested Tigerland. Others wanted Smithville, but neither proposition ever got past light conversation.

Catfish enjoyed the bit of local history and saved the article for his history class, but his attention quickly settled on his football team's next opponent, New London.

A small article announced that the Waits Bus Line would run a charter bus from Mount Vernon to Bears Stadium in Gladewater for the seven-thirty game. Tickets for the luxury transit could be purchased at Rutledge Café for a dollar each.

Also, the *Optic-Herald* reported that Coach Willis's New London team consisted of seasoned veterans with marked advantages over the "Bantam Tigers" in age, weight, and experience. Still, Devall's paper predicted that Catfish's scrappy "little kid" team would give a good account of itself.

By then Catfish had memorized the numbers. His forward wall averaged one hundred forty-seven pounds; at one hundred seventy, New London's line outweighed the Tigers by twenty-three pounds per player. With only two seniors among Catfish's starters, underclassmen dominated the lineup with four juniors, four sophomores, and a freshman; New London's starting lineup listed all seniors. New London's dazzling fullback, Connie Majouirk, outweighed Catfish's heaviest player, Buster Simms, by twelve pounds and at one hundred eighty-five, carried a thirty-eight pound advantage over the average Tiger defender. However, this would not be the first time the undersized and inexperienced Tigers had faced such apparent disadvantages, and their record spoke well of their chances.

Throughout the next week of practices, Catfish played down all the handicaps his team appeared to have. He was adept at turning smaller players into bulldogs on the gridiron, and with boys like Johnny Moore, Dale Brakebill, Donald Yates, and Kenneth Kimbrell, the job was a snap.

Early in the first quarter, New London's curly-headed Majouirk capitalized on his superior physical size when he took a toss from his quarterback at the forty-yard line, headed around right end, and steamrolled his way into the end zone. Later in the same quarter, finishing off a fifty-five-yard drive, he pounded his way across the goal line from five paces out. Then midway of the second quarter, following a teammate's interception, the impressive running back broke loose on a seventy-eight-yard gallop for his third touchdown of the half.

The overpowered Tigers struggled from the start. Though they twice moved the ball inside the opponent's twenty, each time they failed to cross the goal line, and the intermission score stood at 21-0, New London.

Majouirk returned for the second half and picked up where he had left off. Ripping off large chunks of yardage, he carried his team down to the Tigers' eight, where he scored his fourth touchdown of the game.

The scrappy play of the "Bantam" Tigers continued until the final gun, but they were simply unable to match the physical play of their opponent. Billy Jack Meredith put his punting skills to frequent and impressive use, averaging thirty-six yards per try, and added a fifty-yard quick-kick. Though the Tigers blocked the only two punt attempts by New London, neither opportunity resulted in Mount Vernon points, and those failures settled the outcome, a 27-0 loss.

This score represented the most points ever given up by a team coached by Catfish Smith and by far the worst defeat. It also ended the Tigers' string of unbeaten games at twenty-four. Still the coach praised his overachievers and pointed to next year.

"We'll have solid performers returning at every position," he said. "Five juniors, a dozen sophomores, and a handful of freshman, most of whom played heavy minutes this season, will all be back. They'll be larger, more confident, and experienced."

The key speaker for the December 3 football banquet was Dr. James Gee, president of East Texas State Teachers College. Gee had been an All-America football player at Cornell University under Gil Dobie, had coached the sport at the University of Florida, and had come to East Texas State in 1947 from Sam Houston State. Master of Ceremonies was journalism teacher and sportswriter, Charles Bruce. One hundred fifty family members, fans, and guests coughed up a dollar to attend the gala event.

Dr. Gee spoke of the importance of developing character and how the field of athletics lends itself to that high purpose. A sports enthusiast, the stocky, strong-jawed university leader echoed many of the axioms the players had heard from their coach, though delivered with a bit more eloquence by Gee.

Catfish gave the privilege of introducing each player to his assistant, Bo Campbell, and the boys received a standing ovation at the conclusion. Then came the shocker.

L. D. Lowry, Jr., stepped to the podium. On behalf of fans and businessmen, he commended the achievement of the 1948 Tigers and the athletic department. After summarizing Catfish's outstanding six-year won-loss record in football, 50-7-3, and five-year basketball record, 124-16, he rattled off all the championships and crowns Catfish's teams had won. Then Lowry asked Catfish and Bo Campbell to step forward.

"Fellows," Lowry said, "we citizens of this community want to

379

express our appreciation for the swell jobs you have done." He then reached into his coat pocket and pulled out two sets of car keys.

"Coach," he said to Catfish, "I believe you're partial to Fords." He handed over a set of keys to a new 1948 black Ford sedan.

"Coach Campbell," Lowry continued, "I hear Pontiac is your preference."

Initially, the two coaches were stunned to silence, but finally Catfish dabbed at the corners of his eyes and voiced his thanks.

"Words cannot express our feelings of appreciation for these wonderful gifts," he said, glancing at his assistant. "We have the best and most loyal fans in the state of Texas." Coach Campbell followed with like sentiments.

Similar gratitude was expressed in a letter from the two coaches published by the *Optic-Herald* the following Friday. According to Catfish, the pair were particularly surprised since " . . . the team didn't go farther than the district title. . . ."

"Coach," Miss Binnion called to Catfish in the hallway the following Monday. "I see you have stepped up in the world."

"What gave you that idea?" the wary coach asked.

"Why just a few years back the president of East Texas State was determined to kick you out of the school, but now his successor has come here and honored you and your boys."

Catfish smiled. "Now, if I could just capture your respect, I believe I'd be in high cotton."

"Oh, but you've always had that," she replied, poking a finger into his chest. "However, amid so much praise, I see it as my duty to remind you of the wisdom of humility."

"Irene," Catfish said, "you have done your job well."

Smiling, he nodded to her and headed for the gymnasium. With his gridiron team out of the playoffs, he had more time than usual between the end of the football season and the beginning of basketball. He spent the week storing football equipment, laundering uniforms, and airing up basketballs, yet one more event had to occur before football could be completely set aside.

The All-District Teams were announced in the December 17 edition of the paper. The Tigers did not dominate as in past years, but were well represented.

First Team	Second Team	Honorable Mention
Dale Moore	Billy Jack Meredith	Wallace Hunnicutt
Charles Stretcher	Dale Brakebill	Robert Chambers
Johnny Moore	Buster Simms	Billy Clinton
		Frank Carr

With the recognition of Billy Clinton, a one-hundred-seventy-pound tackle, Mount Vernon had placed a freshman on the honored team three years in a row. Dale Moore had done so in 1946 and Billy Jack Meredith in 1947.

After introducing and applauding the honored players in a school assembly, Catfish filed away the bittersweet season and turned his attention to his basketball squad. Before the first district contest, he hoped to arrange an unusual challenge: his young Tigers against Mount Vernon's undefeated state champions of the prior season. What better test for his upstart team?

The three-game challenge was planned for December 28, 30, and would end with a New Year's Eve game followed by a midnight celebration. The town was abuzz with the prospect of again seeing their state champions in action.

Old Tigers still speculate the outcome of such a challenge, but since so few of the 1948 squad were available, Catfish had to make do with intra-squad contests.

On Tuesday evening, January 4, Catfish took his young Tigers to Mount Pleasant to meet their archrival. One advantage to a shortened football season was an early start to basketball practice, and the fruit of that blossomed quickly. Billy Rex Lawrence and Mac Anderson led the way with fourteen and eleven points respectively, as Catfish's boys won, 35-29.

Friday night brought on Talco, and the Trojans grabbed the early lead and held a surprising 6-1 advantage at the quarter's end. With a tenacious defense that yielded only two points in the second period, and with a mild scoring burst, the Tigers reversed the advantage and went into halftime leading, 9-8. The game bounced back and forth throughout the third stanza, but in the final period, Mac Anderson poured in six of his eight points, and along with Lawrence's eight, the Tigers captured their second district victory, 22-17.

On Tuesday, January 11, the Tigers traveled to Gilmer and claimed their third win, 36-26. At halftime, Catfish's young team led 24-8, and coasted through the second half with steady floor play by Meredith and Dale Moore, while Lawrence and Mac Anderson rang up fourteen and ten points respectively.

Reaching back to the 1948 season, Catfish's boys had now won thirty-three consecutive basketball contests, however, next would be the undefeated Winnsboro squad.

A tall quintet of Red Raiders got sweet revenge, having defeated Mount Vernon only twice in any sport in the past eight years. With hot shooting, Winnsboro dominated, 41-16. If the Tigers got any satisfaction in the land of the Raiders, it was through a double-overtime win by the junior varsity. Tied at seventeen apiece at the end of regulation time, Dudley Miller sank the winning bucket in a second overtime under "sudden death" rules.

On the following Tuesday, with sleet and a cold wind that cut like ice, the Tigers traveled again, this time to Mineola where they returned to their winning ways, 29-19. Leading all the way, the Tigers sank fifteen of twenty-four free throws to ensure their victory. Meredith led with ten points, while Sinclair pitched in six for the struggling Yellow Jackets.

The next morning when Catfish arrived at his classroom, Jack Henry stood waiting for him.

"Good morning, Coach," the grade school principal said.

"What can I do for you, Jack?" Catfish replied with a nod.

"Got lunch plans?"

"Nothing special."

"Maybe you could come over to our new cafeteria. I'd like to update you on our little basketball team."

"Sure. I'd like that. Things running smoothly with the cafeteria?"

"I don't know how we ever managed without it. Using two shifts, we serve over four hundred kids daily. The grade school classes are served eleven-thirty to twelve, and the high school the next thirty minutes. Lester Armstrong donated the woodwork in the kitchen, and it turned out really nice. Forrest Johnson had his agriculture boys build twenty-five tables for us so we can seat two hundred and fifty students. With all the additional help from the PTA and school board, I'd guess we saved a couple thousand dollars."

"Sounds good. I'll see you at noon."

At the end of his last morning class, Catfish headed across the vacant lot where the old Franklin Institute once stood, crossed Kaufman Street and climbed the steps and long walkway to the grade school. At the south end of the building, he climbed the stairs and followed the hallway to the center of the building. Jack Henry stood beside the entrance to the left and ushered Catfish inside where they joined the end of the waiting line.

Catfish, at six feet four inches, towered over the students around him, as did six-foot-two Henry. While the coach was lean and long, Henry was a big, solidly built man, head to foot, probably weighing two hundred twenty pounds.

"Tell me about this basketball team you and Wayne have this year," Catfish said when they were seated at one of the tables.

Wayne Pierce, playing basketball for Coach Tully at East Texas State, helped Henry when he could. A former two-sport star at Mount Vernon, Pierce was especially popular with the young basketball players.

"Coach Pierce is doing a fine job," Henry said, smiling. "This could be our best team ever. We've got five boys that range from five-nine to six feet: Donald Jumper, Dalton Banks, Clarence Jones, Charles Pierce, and Allen Dyer. These boys are going to be fine basketball players. But that's not all. I've got a couple of smaller boys with good ball-handling skills: Billy Jack Meredith's little brother, Don, and George Turner. That little Meredith kid has extraordinary peripheral vision, handles the ball well with either hand, and has an uncanny way of getting the ball through the hoop.

"I'd sure like you to drop by and see them play a game or two. I know the boys would be excited to see you there."

"I'll do that," Catfish replied. "If Don is anything like his brother, he'll be an outstanding athlete."

Thursday, after putting his high school boys through practice, Catfish rushed home, had dinner, and returned to the gym to watch the grade school team play Hagansport. He was shocked at what he saw.

Clarence Jones, a tall, lanky kid, showed excellent skills and poured in shot after shot. When he was not scoring, Charles Pierce was. The halftime score was 23-7, the Tigers leading. Catfish knew his high school team was averaging less than thirty points per game. These sixth, seventh, and eight graders were going to outdo that easily.

In the second half, when Mount Vernon reached thirty points, Coaches Henry and Pierce began frequent substitutions. The scoring pace dropped off very little with Dalton Banks and little Don Meredith maintaining the offensive barrage. Don, only a fifth grader, managed to get inside the lane twice, and though he was among taller boys, he got off shots with relative ease. On each occasion, with his back to the defender, he faked one way, then spun and shot a half hook-shot that landed softly on the backboard and dropped through. The final score read 43-17.

Catfish walked down to the gym floor after the game, shaking his head. Henry met him smiling.

"I'm not sure they couldn't beat my boys," Catfish said, pumping Henry's hand. "What's their record so far?"

"Seven wins, one loss," Henry said. "Early in the season we played Sulphur Bluff when we had three starters out sick. They whipped us fifteen to five. But since then, we've gotten our revenge, twenty to six and thirty-two to twenty-four."

"I'm shocked at the number of points your boys score. Can they do that against stiff competition?"

"We'll find out next week," Henry said. "We'll be playing Sulphur Springs' junior high club."

"Against ninth graders?"

Jack Henry nodded, smiling.

"I'll be here to see that," Catfish said, giving Henry a pat on the shoulder as he left.

Friday, Catfish and his boys traveled to Talco to challenge the Trojans in a district contest. The game stayed even throughout, with Talco leading most of the time. With one quarter to go, the Trojans held an 18-15 advantage, but then the Tigers stepped up their defensive intensity and made a few buckets to pull the game out, 22-21, capturing their seventh conference win against the one loss to Winnsboro.

On Saturday night, the Tigers hosted the Greenville Lions, a much larger school. Early on, the Tigers played poorly and got down twelve points, but in the second half, they came storming back. With only five seconds on the clock, they trailed 27-25 with the ball out of bounds. On a last ditch try, Mac Anderson put up a long shot that swished through the net, apparently tying the score. But the referees huddled and decided the shot came too late. The Tigers had their second loss of the season, though not to a district opponent.

The following Tuesday, Catfish's boys took on Mount Pleasant, and won a barnburner, 36-34. The score wavered back and forth, was tied seven times, and the largest lead was three points, but the Tigers had their eighth district victory.

On Thursday night Catfish returned to the gym to see the grade school team play Sulphur Springs. Though Jones, Pierce, Dyer, and their teammates did not score as freely as against Hagansport, they defeated the Wildcats' squad, which included a couple of ninth graders. The final score was a lopsided 29-14. Again, the reserves played in the final quarter, when young Don Meredith scored four points.

Talking to Jack Henry and Wayne Pierce after the game, Catfish learned that Sulphur Springs had not brought their top lineup.

"I recommend you get them to come back and bring their best," Catfish said. "I'd like to see your boys perform in a tight game."

The grade school coaches took the advice, and the Sulphur Springs coach was more than happy to bring his "A" team back for redemption the following week.

Meanwhile, Catfish's Tigers took on the Gilmer Buckeyes. Though the opposing players were noticeably taller than the Tigers, Catfish's boys used their quickness to take an early lead and held a 21-13 advantage at halftime. The Buckeyes closed the gap to 31-25 in the third quarter, but with key buckets from Billy Jack Meredith and Mac Anderson, the Tigers pulled away in the final stanza, winning 42-33.

Then on Monday night, Catfish's boys squared off with a good Mineola team. The Tigers grabbed the lead early and never relented. They led 14-11 at halftime, and finished going away, 30-22.

That set up a return match between the two league leaders, the Tigers and Red Raiders of Winnsboro. The Red Raiders had won easily in the first half of the round-robin schedule, and both teams were undefeated in the second half. If Winnsboro could beat Mount Vernon, they would capture the district title. If Mount Vernon should win, the two would have a playoff to determine the champion. It could not have come at a worse time for Catfish.

36

February 4, 1949

Billy Jack Meredith had sprained an ankle in Thursday's practice, while Dale Moore was in bed with the flu, and it appeared both would miss the all-important Winnsboro game Friday night. Since Catfish's arrival at Mount Vernon, his teams had won the district title five years in a row, but he knew a sixth was in doubt.

With neither team playing well, the lame Tigers hung even with Winnsboro through the first quarter, 5-5. The tall, seasoned Red Raiders flexed their muscles in the second period and burst out to a 19-12 lead.

During halftime, Catfish paced. It was a do-or-die game, and the coach was not ready to relinquish the district crown.

"Billy Jack," he called to his injured sophomore.

"Yes, sir," the youngster said, easing over to his coach.

"How's that ankle feel?"

"It's better," Meredith said, though it was swollen so badly it had torn the edges of the double layer of tape encasing it.

"That Rhea Coppedge is killing us. Think you can handle him?"

"Yes, sir."

"Then I want you in the lineup for the second half," Catfish said, patting Meredith on the back.

Young Meredith played an unforgettable half of basketball, faking Coppedge out of position repeatedly and scoring fourteen points. He pulled his Tigers close, but ultimately the Red Raiders and Coppedge were too good. They prevailed 38-27, though Catfish's gifted sophomore outscored his adversary by two points.

Acie Cannaday's Winnsboro Red Raiders were the new District Champions, and his old mentor was the first to congratulate him.

"Ace," Catfish said, draping an arm across the young coach's shoulders, "I hope you win state, but next year we'll be back to take the district crown away from you."

Though Catfish was disappointed with the 19-6 record and runner-up in the district race, back in January he could hardly have expected more. From his 1948 state championship team, he had lost all five starters and had rebuilt his 1949 squad around only two players from that undefeated unit: Billy Jack Meredith and Dale Moore.

Likely, the remainder of the district rejoiced to see the Red Raiders break Mount Vernon's stranglehold on the league. Over six basketball seasons, Catfish's teams had a 78-3 record in regular district contests, all three losses coming at the hands of the Red Raiders, coached by Catfish's former assistant. In district playoff games, the Tigers' record was 14-1, the lone defeat by Deport in the opening game of a two-of-three series in 1947, though Catfish's boys rebounded and won the following two contests and the title. So, a district opponent's odds of beating the Tigers were one in twenty-three.

The Tigers' season was essentially over, but they still had a finale against the Omaha Indians. With Billy Rex Lawrence and Mac Anderson ill, Catfish inserted freshmen Billy Hunt and Wayne Foster into the lineup.

Billy Jack Meredith poured in fifteen points, and the Tigers squeaked out a 35-34 victory to end their season, but Catfish was not ready to forget basketball.

Three nights later the coach went to see Wayne Pierce and Jack Henry lead their grade school team in their finale of the season against a reinforced Sulphur Springs Wildcat team. In an offensive battle the "Little Tigers" lost 38-36, but Catfish considered it an impressive showing by his future players. He stepped into their dressing room following the contest and shook the hand of every boy, congratulating them on an outstanding 8-2 season, including that night's thriller against the junior high Wildcats.

A quick scan of the score book showed that Clarence Jones had scored sixty-eight points in ten games to lead the team, and Charles Pierce had added fifty-seven. Catfish did not add up young Don Meredith's, but noted that the fifth grader had contributed a few points in almost every contest.

In the first week of March, Catfish and Bo Campbell drove to Austin and attended the state basketball tournament, where they watched Texas City, the team they had defeated the prior season, win the championship in Class AA.

"Sure glad we caught them last year," Catfish commented. "Not sure we could beat this bunch."

"Catfish," Bo said, "that nineteen forty-eight team of ours could beat every team down here."

"You're probably right," Catfish said, smiling. "By one point."

The two coaches then hung around and watched the University of Texas during their spring football drills. The Longhorns' ran the T-formation, using a few wrinkles that Catfish wanted to evaluate and possibly implement during his own upcoming spring practices.

It was mid-March now, a couple of weeks before the start of football drills, and Catfish dropped by Superintendent Fleming's office after classes one afternoon. Fleming had a couple of guests, so Catfish headed for a chair next to the secretary's desk.

"Come on in, Coach," the superintendent called out.

The coach ambled in as a young man and woman rose to their feet, as did Fleming. The young man looked somewhat familiar, but Catfish was terrible with names, unless he had assigned a nickname, and he drew a blank.

"I'd like you to meet this fine couple," the superintendent said. "They're preparing to be student teachers in the Commerce school system, to complete the requirements for their teacher's certificates.

"This is Carolyn Majors," Fleming said. "Oh, I'm sorry Carolyn. She's Carolyn Zimmerman now."

"And you must be H. B., Herb's older brother," Catfish said to the man.

After the coach shook hands with both, Fleming explained that they were graduates of Mount Vernon High and were completing their degrees at East Texas State Teachers College. In the fall they expected to become teachers at Falfurrias. From his thirty-two years of experience in education, Fleming was offering a few tips.

"I feel like I know you, Sergeant Zimmerman," Catfish said. "I've read about your military exploits. I believe you were awarded the Combat Infantry Badge, the Asiatic-Pacific Ribbon, the Philippine Liberation bar, and the Bronze Star. We discussed it in my history class a few years back."

"That's been a while," H. B. said, somewhat embarrassed, "and much of it, I'd like to forget."

"I understand," Catfish said, "but I wanted my students to see the reality of war, as well as the glory and honor. Your story showed both sides."

The coach turned to leave, feeling he had interrupted the meeting.

"What do you need, Catfish?" Fleming called after him.

"I came by to get your advice on something," the coach said. "I've been asked to help the seniors with their play, *Tattletale*, and I know nothing about such things."

"Who'll be helping you?" the superintendent asked, enjoying seeing his coach squirm a bit.

"Irene Binnion and Mrs. St. Clair," Catfish replied. "I think I'll just have to decline."

"Catfish," Fleming said, placing a hand on the coach's shoulder, "I think you'd better give it a try. These kids have chosen you as their class sponsor, and you'd sure be letting them down if you ducked out."

"But, sir," Catfish complained, "I don't know the first thing . . ."

"No matter. Miss Binnion and Mrs. St. Clair are old pros at this. All you've got to do is ask how you can assist them."

"You're asking me to be Irene Binnion's assistant?"

"I expect you'll learn a lot from her," Fleming said, patting Catfish on the back and dismissing him while doing his best to stifle a laugh.

Catfish accepted his "role," helping arrange props, furniture, and backdrops for the scenes. He offered a few suggestions, which prompted an array of responses from Miss Binnion.

"Catfish," she once replied, "we're going to need a music stand for the next scene. Be a good boy and run over to the band hall and get one for us."

"Why are you antagonizing him?" Mrs. St. Clair asked when the coach was gone.

"Oh, I think it's good for him to be on the receiving end of orders for a change," Miss Binnion said, laughing.

Catfish soon got some relief. He was invited to speak at a citywide picnic honoring ninety-one-year-old Dr. Fleming who was finally hanging up his medicine bag. The doctor had been a physician for sixty-seven years, all but seven of those in Mount Vernon, and he was considered to be the oldest practicing doctor in the state of Texas. The affair was held May 1st on the town plaza, and brought out hundreds of the doctor's patients, former patients, and friends.

Catfish delighted the crowd when he spoke. "I asked Dr. Fleming how many patients he's cared for. He said, 'Oh, four or five thousand at least.' I said, 'Why, that's more people than we have in town.' He said, 'Not if you count those in the cemetery.'"

When the laughter died down, Catfish smiled as only he could and said, "Now I understand why we're celebrating his retirement."

Then the coach proceeded to heap upon the fine gentleman the praise he so richly deserved. "Every community that lasts and flourishes must have a bedrock of citizens. Dr. Fleming ranks among a highly select few in our town."

Present at the ceremony were other long-term, stalwart citizens of Mount Vernon such as M. L. Edwards, local merchant for forty-nine years, Joe Parchman, a sixty-year businessman, and Dr. H. E. Chandler, pioneer physician and surgeon.

Next, Mount Vernon's forty-one graduating high school seniors received their diplomas, with Patsy Bogue as valedictorian and Mary Hays salutatorian. With school dismissed, Catfish looked forward to playing a little semi-pro baseball.

Breaking away from the ball diamond on June 24, Catfish and Dorothy Nell attended the grand opening of Mount Vernon's first self-serve grocery store, a Piggly Wiggly on West Main. Operators Robert Peterson and Leon Bridges housed their new business in the building where they had run a grocery store for years. Some of the attractions included an open twenty-two-foot refrigeration unit for produce, an eight-foot unit for frozen foods, and an eight-foot double-decker unit for dairy and packaged meat products.

Then in July the town had another fire. Of all places, it happened on the second floor of the fire station, which housed City Hall. Fortunately, no official records were damaged, and J. D. Maples, local carpenter and contractor, quickly made the necessary repairs. The cause was determined to be a lightning strike during a storm.

The next momentous occasion was the announcement that signs would be erected on all streets corners, identifying them, and all dwellings would receive assigned numbers, which were to be conspicuously displayed on the front of each house or building. The project was sponsored and funded by the local Rotary Club and its president, Charlie Brown, along with the Chamber of Commerce. According to Postmaster W. L. Nelson, the postal system required assignment and implementation of the addresses for free mail delivery to homes and businesses. Charles Alton Shurtleff offered to post the numbers on the homes to ensure visibility and consistency.

In early August Catfish attended the Texas Coaches School in Beaumont. Earlier he had agreed to select ten players from the best in North Texas to compete in the North-South All-Star Game scheduled for the end of the coaches' meeting. Back in March, he had chosen six from teams participating in the state basketball tournament in Austin, and four more from those competing in the city-conference playoffs in Houston.

Back from Beaumont, Catfish completed and announced the Tigers' football schedule for 1949.

September	9	Clarksville	here
September	16	New Boston	there
September	23	Edgewood	here
October	1	Paris	here
October	7	Winnsboro	there *
October	14	Mount Pleasant	there *
October	21	Pittsburg	here *
October	28	DeKalb	here
November	4	Mineola	there *
November	11	Gilmer	here *

* District opponent

New Boston replaced Texarkana from the prior year's schedule, and DeKalb filled the open date that Catfish detested. The Tigers had last played New Boston in 1937 and records as far back as 1919 showed no prior contest with the DeKalb Bears. However, the Bears had advanced to the semi-finals in the Class A playoffs the previous season. As was his habit, Catfish had scheduled DeKalb under his philosophy that "to be the best, you have to beat the best," and a playoff team should give Catfish's boys a strong test.

The coach called his 1949 team together at nine o'clock Monday morning, August 15. Practice for the first fifteen days would be at seven-thirty in the evening to avoid the peak heat of the day.

The *Optic-Herald* wrote, ". . . the 1949 Mount Vernon Tigers will don their uniforms to start the greatest grid season in the history of the school." Considering the 1938, 1944, and 1947 teams, hopes were indeed high.

Eleven lettermen were returning, including five of the seven 1948 starting linemen and three of the four running backs. Thirty-eight boys showed up for uniforms, and in spite of a predominantly veteran crew, Catfish put the linemen through a strenuous conditioning program and drilled them on fundamentals, while Bo Campbell did the same with the backfield. Newcomers were shocked that the coach did not attempt a single offensive play or defensive set until the second week.

Eight days prior to the Clarksville game, Catfish told Charles Bruce, reporter for the *Optic-Herald*, "They're looking better than we expected at this point." Bruce went on to write that newcomers Joe Long, Keith Drummond, Jerry Mills, Billy "Red" Rouse, John DeBusk, Buddy Knight, and the Simons boys, Nix and Max, had impressed the "railbirds." Knight was a first-year transfer, and thus ineligible until the following season.

Letterman Donald Yates, at one hundred forty-five pounds, quickly earned the right end position, vacated by the graduation of Charles Stretcher, while one-hundred-sixty-pound Larkin Drummond replaced Frank Carr at guard. Johnny Moore, 1948 left guard, moved to the backfield, the type of move that had proven successful for Catfish several times in past years. Kenneth Kimbrell, at one hundred fifty pounds, moved into Johnny's vacated guard slot, and one-hundred-forty-pound Louis Agee lined up at left halfback, the only open backfield position.

On his way home from practice one afternoon, Catfish noticed the old Crutcher Hospital was being torn down. He pulled over and learned that Teague & Son Chevrolet had purchased the property and was clearing space for a modern six-thousand-square-foot showroom and six-bay auto-repair shop. "It'll have a solid plate-glass front so folks driving by can see the newest cars," contractor F. E. Berry explained. To make room for the new business, a fifty-year icon had to be sacrificed.

The Friday morning issue of the *Optic-Herald* announced that Robby Campbell, one of Catfish's 1944 stars and now a halfback for the University of Houston Cougars, could be seen on television throughout the fall. KLEE-TV would be carrying the Cougars' five home games, the first airing on September 17. The coach thought back to that afternoon in 1943 when Campbell had been the first player to show up for his initial practice, sporting a buzz haircut and weighing no more than one hundred thirty pounds.

Classes started on September 6, the day following Labor Day, and the coach had three days left to prepare his team for Clarksville. With a growth of thirty students and four new teachers, the school enrollment was five hundred ninety. One of the teachers, the homemaking instructor, was new in name only. Mrs. Rufus Bolger was the former Miss Viola Gillespie. The others were Miss Virgie Beth

Hughes, history instructor, Mrs. Essie Stanley as librarian, and Mrs. Frank Burns in music.

Catfish's lineup Friday night listed his forward wall at an average of one hundred fifty-nine pounds and a backfield averaging one hundred forty-six. Clarksville's line came in at one hundred fifty-four per man and one hundred forty-eight in the backfield. Up and down the line, the only size advantage appeared to be one-hundred-seventy-five-pound right tackle, Buster Simms, against Clarksville's Sommerlin who was listed at one hundred sixty-four. Regardless, the Tigers found advantages up and down the line and throughout the backfield in a 47-0 romp.

Starting the game by kicking to their opponent, the Tigers' defense held and forced Clarksville to punt. Billy Clinton broke through and blocked the kick, sending the pigskin tumbling into the end zone where Donald Yates fell on it, marking the first score of the game and of the season.

Midway through the first period, Clarksville again punted to Mount Vernon. Dale Moore received the spiraling football on his own thirty-five, and dashed and danced his way sixty-five yards for the Tigers' second score.

Late in that same stanza, the Tigers ground out a long drive, culminating with Louis Agee bursting through for a thirteen-yard touchdown. Later still, the Tigers blocked another Clarksville punt, sending the ball bounding into the end zone where Clarksville's Washington fell on it for a two-point safety. The first period ended with the Tigers leading, 21-0.

The second quarter was Meredith time. Concluding a sixty-yard drive, Billy Jack raced ten yards for his first score, the fourth for his team. Only minutes later, the fullback streaked for nineteen yards to the one-yard line, and then finished the drive for his second score of the period and the final of the first half. Score: 34-0.

The third period was relatively quiet until near its end when Dale Moore tossed a ten-yard touchdown pass to Roy Cunningham. Only minutes later, Clarksville punted down to Mount Vernon's twenty, where Dale Moore gobbled up the ball and headed across the field. Known for his long kick returns, the defense was drawn to him like metal filings to a magnet, ignoring Dale Brakebill who was crossing the field from the opposite direction. When the two Tigers met, Moore slipped the ball to the fleet end, who sailed eighty yards for the final score.

Tiger reserves played the final quarter and protected the 47-0 shutout.

Regardless, Catfish saw some problems. His offense had played sporadically, accounting for only seven first downs. His quarterback had completed only two of eight passes against a rather weak defense, and the Tigers had failed on four of six extra points. Otherwise, Catfish's boys had racked up two hundred yards of offense while allowing one hundred nine, not a bad first game.

While Catfish made sure his boys understood they were not world-beaters, Mount Vernon had bigger concerns.

L. D. Lowry, Jr., urged local citizens to contribute to the National Foundation for Infantile Paralysis. Franklin County had seven cases of polio while the nation was experiencing an eighty-three percent rise in such occurrences. During the first eight months of the year, over seventeen thousand cases had been reported, compared to ninety-seven hundred during the same period the prior year, the worst national epidemic in thirty years.

Franklin County victims had received over twelve thousand dollars of support from the national organization, the money received by Postmaster Nelson at the local headquarters in the post office where contributions were being collected.

Temporarily setting aside these health worries, on Friday the Tigers traveled to New Boston to take on the Lions who had lost their first game to Honey Grove, 25-7.

Catfish's boys hit town like a runaway locomotive.

On the sixth play of the game, Roy Cunningham scored the first six of twenty points the Tigers would rack up in the initial quarter. Louis Agee accounted for the second score on a five-yard run, and Dale Moore passed ten yards to Donald Yates for the third touchdown. Moore converted on two of three point-after tries.

In the third period Billy Jack Meredith romped fifteen yards on a pitchout for a score, and then only a few plays later, he repeated the performance from the twenty-six-yard line. Dale Moore swept around left end for the third score of the second half, and in the final stanza, Kenneth Jaggers, quarterbacking the reserve team, scored from the three. The final was a duplicate of the first game, 47-0.

The statistics were gaudy: eighteen first downs to only one for New Boston, three hundred ninety-one yards of offense to thirty-seven, four completed passes with no interceptions to zero of three throws for the opponent with two intercepted.

394

The stingy Tiger defense featured Johnny Moore, Larkin Drummond, Donald Yates, and Billy Clinton.

Catfish cut the celebrating short by reminding his boys they would face the Edgewood Bulldogs next. A perennial playoff team, the Bulldogs thrived on a winning tradition that rivaled that of Mount Vernon. Catfish had to find a way to bring his boys down from the clouds and back to reality. His proven method was a week of tough practices and wind-sprint after wind-sprint.

The front page of Friday morning's paper read, "EDGEWOOD ELEVEN HERE FOR GRID CLASSIC; TIGER SWEETHEART TO BE CROWNED." In the past, the article pointed out, Catfish's teams had defeated the Bulldogs twice and had lost to them twice, thus the upcoming game would decide whether it would be "top dog" or "top cat." Beside that story was a picture of Catfish and Bo Campbell standing in front of their new Ford and Pontiac with L. D. Lowry, Jr., handing over titles to the vehicles. Catfish, even taller in cowboy boots, wore his familiar smile and a tiny football dangling from a long gold chain hanging from the watch-pocket of his slacks.

The coach wondered about the timing of the picture. He knew how excited Mount Vernon fans always got for an Edgewood game. He assumed this was a subtle reminder that the locals had amply rewarded him and his assistant, and now he was expected to produce an all-important win against an archrival that had defeated Hillcrest of Dallas by an impressive 33-12 score the prior week.

With veterans like Dudley Miller, Billy Clinton, and Buster Simms in the line, along with outstanding performers Donald Yates, Dale Brakebill, Kenneth Kimbrell, and Larkin Drummond, Catfish knew he had a powerful forward wall. Behind this lineup, he had veterans Dale Moore, Billy Jack Meredith, and Roy Cunningham, along with newcomer Louis Agee.

Could this be his best team ever?

Most everyone in town believed the Edgewood game would answer that question.

37

September 23, 1949

Douglas Phillips, a one-hundred-sixty-five-pound back who ran with power and speed, was Edgewood's field general and leader. Against Hillcrest, he had accounted for half of his team's touchdowns, running for one and throwing for the other. To win, the Tigers would have to find a way to corral him, or at least slow him down.

In the game billed as the ultimate test of the 1949 Tigers, the *Optic-Herald* described the result as, ". . . the only thing tested was the scorekeeper's ability. . . ." Like a sickle swung by a giant farmer, the Tigers cut swath after swath through the Bulldogs' defense, chalking up eleven touchdowns and a 72-24 victory. The previous high score for a Tiger team had been fifty-eight points against lowly Bogata. Scoring so easily and so often against their once-feared nemesis, Catfish's team looked as good as the great '38, '44, and '47 Tiger teams, maybe better.

Dale Moore and Billy Jack Meredith, the team leaders who had risen to the task in the 1948 Tiger meeting with the Bulldogs, accounted for seven touchdowns, four for the quarterback and three for the fullback. Roy Cunningham added another, as did Glen Slaughter, Louis Agee, and Johnny Moore.

The Tigers rolled for fourteen first downs and three hundred sixty-nine yards rushing. With their running success, passes were unnecessary. As evidenced by the list of scorers, almost every reserve entered the contest, and several played extended minutes. The Tigers scored three touchdowns in every quarter except the second where they managed two. All Edgewood points came in the final stanza against Tiger reserves.

Catfish's leaders on defense were Dale Brakebill, Kenneth Kimbrell, Dudley Miller, Johnny Moore, Billy Clinton, Donald Yates, and Larkin Drummond. Tiger reserves Joe Long, Stanley Jaggers, Neal Suggs, Eddie Turner, and John DeBusk gave the Bulldogs little relief.

Douglas Phillips was the bright spot in the Bulldogs' darkest hour, accounting for three of his team's four touchdowns with outstanding throws, two to Henry Humphries. The Edgewood quarterback rushed for most of his team's yardage and completed ten of nineteen passes for one hundred seventy-three yards.

Now, what would the Tigers do for an encore?

The next opponent, the Paris reserves, had never scored a touchdown against a Tiger team, while Catfish's boys had averaged thirty-five points a game against them. The upcoming contest promised to be another rout.

Surprisingly, the Paris boys broke their scoring drought with one touchdown, but they also gave up seven to the blistering Tiger offense in a lopsided contest, 48-7.

The Tigers scored three times in the first quarter on a sixty-five-yard punt return by Dale Moore, a six-yard scamper by Glen Slaughter, and a fifteen-yard end sweep by John DeBusk. Dale Moore tossed three touchdown aerials, one to Dale Brakebill, another to Billy Jack Meredith, and the third to Donald Yates who later left the game with a back injury. The seventh tally came when backup quarterback, Kenneth Jaggers, threw to Roy Cunningham.

In one of his best outings, Dale Moore completed seven of eleven passes for one hundred sixty-four yards, while his backs stepped off two hundred five paces rushing.

Jimmy King and Walter Warner accounted for Paris' lone score on a nifty fake-pass where the speed-merchant Warner circled behind King and took the ball from his cocked passing hand, the Statue of Liberty play.

The Tigers had scored fifty-three points per contest during preseason, and the question in Mount Vernon was, "Can Catfish's boys win the state title?" Beginning the prior season, Class A, previously limited to a regional championship, would play two more games and determine a state champion, a realistic goal for this team.

Catfish warned his boys that such talk was premature. They had to prepare to meet the Winnsboro Red Raiders who had just dismantled a highly regarded Atlanta Rabbits team, 40-13. But how could Catfish convince his boys to lower their eyes from the distant mountain peak and focus on the dangerous boulder directly in their path? After all, a Catfish-coached football team had never lost to Winnsboro. Over six contests, his teams had won by an average score of 31-1. In twenty-four quarters of play, the Red Raiders had scored only one touchdown against Mount Vernon.

Overconfident or not, the 1949 Tigers won easily, 58-7, and increased their fifty-three-points-per-game scoring average while extending their unbeaten streak over the Red Raiders to seven years.

Scoring nine touchdowns, despite one hundred fifteen yards in penalties, the Tiger offense amassed four hundred sixty-two yards on fifteen first downs. Dale Moore scored three times, both Meredith and Cunningham scored twice, while Louis Agee and Stanley Jaggers each added one. Meredith had the longest run, a fifty-six-yard touchdown gallop.

The Tiger defense allowed the Red Raiders only five first downs on one hundred twenty-six yards of offense, while intercepting four Red Raider passes and giving up only one completion. Dale Brakebill, Kenneth Kimbrell, Johnny Moore, and Larkin Drummond led the defensive charge.

James McRea, one-hundred-seventy-pound fullback for Winnsboro, and Joe Grady Tibbs, left halfback, carried the workload for the Red Raiders, though Tibbs sustained a leg injury and missed the second half. McRea scored the lone Winnsboro touchdown on a brilliant forty-five-yard run.

The next week the Tiger juggernaut humbled Mount Pleasant, 39-0, improving Catfish's seven-year record against his alma mater to five wins against two losses, each loss by a single touchdown. The win came at a heavy price, however, when Billy Clinton had to be helped off the field due to a leg injury that would likely keep him out of the lineup for several weeks.

The Pittsburg Pirates were next on the Tigers' schedule, but Mother Nature took priority over man's plans and glazed the roads with a winter blast that put Northeast Texas into a snow and ice shrouded deep freeze. With travel impossible, the game was delayed until November 18, a week after completion of the regular schedule.

As the weather warmed and the roads cleared, the Tigers began preparations for the DeKalb game, a non-conference affair. Cecil Pirkey, former East Texas State standout, coached the Bears who had come within one win of playing for the Class A state championship the prior season. Were the Tigers finally going to face a real test?

Before a sellout home crowd of twenty-five hundred, Catfish's boys met the unbeaten, untied DeKalb team, and regardless of the opponent's record, most Tiger fans expected another thundering victory.

And they were right. The Tigers whipped their seventh opponent by a score of 48-0, signaling to the football world that Catfish's 1949 squad was set to challenge the best the state had to offer.

The first quarter started slowly with the Tigers getting a lone touchdown, but the second period saw them spin the scoring wheel for twenty-seven points and a 34-0 halftime lead.

Billy Jack Meredith, Dale Moore, Donald Yates, Dale Brakebill, and Roy Cunningham each scored in the first half, and then retired from the contest. Glen Slaughter and Stanley Jaggers added a pair in the second half, while Elvie Sinclair added his name to the list of scorers. Kenneth Jaggers converted six of seven extra points.

Catfish's crew racked up fifteen first downs while stepping off two hundred seventy-five yards of offense, including eighty-four through the air on four-of-eleven passing by Moore and Kenneth Jaggers. Meanwhile, the Tiger's stingy defense gave up only ninety-one yards and four first downs.

Through seven games, Mount Vernon's high-powered offense had scored three hundred fifty-nine points while their defense had allowed only thirty-eight, all against Tiger reserves. Mount Vernon had the team and the coach to legitimately be thinking, "State Championship." But first, they had to take care of Mineola.

While the Tigers had been clawing to shreds everything in their path, the Yellow Jackets had been quietly stinging into submission each of their opponents. After the date with Mineola, only a weak Gilmer squad and a floundering Pittsburg team remained on Catfish's schedule, so the Yellow Jackets represented the only plausible obstacle to what the *Optic-Herald* had earlier predicted as ". . . the greatest grid season in the history of the school."

The previous year the Yellow Jackets had befuddled the Tigers to a 7-7 tie, the only mar on Mount Vernon's 1948 regular season record. But no one doubted that Catfish's 1949 squad showed dramatic improvement over the prior one. Amid all the fanfare, undefeated Mineola waited quietly for the arrival of Catfish's record-setting Tigers.

Mount Vernon won the toss and, anxious to get its scoring machine on the field, chose to receive the initial kickoff. When the Tigers' return man slipped down, Catfish's boys had to start from their own twelve-yard line. As they had done in the previous eight games, they began a steady march with their powerful ground game; however, when they reached the Yellow Jackets' forty-seven, their offense fizzled.

With Billy Jack Meredith's deadly accurate punting, they figured to pin Mineola deep, hold them there, and get the ball back around midfield. As expected, the Tiger punter angled the ball toward the sideline where it came floating down on the Yellow Jackets' ten. However, John Kelley drifted over near the boundary line, reached out, made the catch, and headed upfield. With exceptional broken-field running, he slipped through the Tiger wall and outran everyone to the end zone. The conversion failed, and Mineola held a slim 6-0 lead over a team averaging fifty-one points per game.

The two teams spent the remainder of the first quarter and half of the second in a midfield fight that saw neither threaten to score. Tiger fans waited impatiently for their vaunted offense to burst loose and grab the lead, but without steady Billy Clinton at his left tackle position, Mount Vernon's running game just did not have its usual punch.

By varying play selection, the Tigers got their offense rolling and drove the ball across midfield. Unable to get his ball carriers to the outside, Dale Moore pounded the ball inside, along with a few passes. The Tigers kept hammering away until they reached Mineola's twelve-yard line where the Yellow Jackets' defense stiffened. On third down, Moore tried an end sweep, but was swarmed at the ten-yard line, two yards short of a first down. Dale struggled to his feet and hobbled to the huddle. On fourth down, he dropped back to pass, but his knee collapsed as he sailed the ball over Donald Yates' head.

Mineola took over and slowly pushed out from their goal, picking up two first downs before they punted back to Mount Vernon. With Dale Moore unable to play, Catfish sent Kenneth "Butch" Jaggers in to receive the punt and to play quarterback.

With the freshman leading the team, the Tigers reverted to basic, conservative plays, trying to avoid a disastrous mistake deep in their territory. The Yellow Jackets sensed Mount Vernon's tentativeness, and loaded up on the line of scrimmage. On fourth down, Meredith punted the ball back to Mineola, and Catfish's defense held the Yellow Jackets until halftime with the Tigers trailing, 6-0.

Throughout intermission, Catfish had Billy Jack Meredith practice at quarterback, knowing the Yellow Jackets would have to respect the versatile Tiger's ability to run, pass, or kick. Meredith had never played the position, but adapted quickly.

Mount Vernon returned for the second half, frustrated but determined. Meredith led the Tigers on a methodical drive, feeding the ball to Louis Agee and Roy Cunningham, along with a few quarterback sweeps. When Agee had to leave the game with a knee injury, the drive sputtered near midfield.

Meredith punted out of bounds on Mineola's twenty-five, avoiding a Kelley runback. The Tiger defense had not allowed the Yellow Jackets past their thirty-six-yard line since that initial punt return, and now they desperately needed to hold the Yellow Jackets, get the ball back near midfield, and complete the drive to the end zone. They were just a touchdown and extra point away from the lead.

The Yellow Jackets plugged away with their running game, getting one first down, and then another. Just past midfield, they reached a critical third down, needing five for a first down. The Tiger defense pulled up tight to the line of scrimmage. A stop here, and they would get the ball back.

Initially it looked like an off-tackle play, and the Tigers' defense held its ground, but then the Mineola quarterback set his feet and sailed a pass to Benny Sinclair. Dale Brakebill hit the tall end just as he latched onto the ball and brought him down. Everybody looked to the first down marker. It was close.

The referees brought out the chains and measured: a first down by half the length of the ball. Mineola's only pass of the game had proved big.

The Yellow Jackets breathed a sigh of relief, while the Tigers' shoulders slumped. The emotional swing was probably worth another Mineola first down, and then somehow the Yellow Jackets had reached the Tiger fifteen. But, it was fourth down again, and this time Mineola needed eight yards against the district's top-rated defense.

Disregarding that one Mineola pass play, the Tiger defenders crept close to the line of scrimmage. Another Yellow Jacket score could put the game out of reach of a wounded Tiger offense.

On a quick count, the Yellow Jacket quarterback pitched the ball to Bobby Walker who headed around left end. The Tigers pursued and appeared to have him trapped at the ten, but the power-packed runner bounced off two tacklers, and sped into the end zone. Kenneth Rhodes toed the point-after through the uprights, and Mineola led 13-0.

The Tigers were down, but in other contests they had scored three touchdowns in less time than showed on the clock, and they just needed two with accompanying extra points.

Cunningham received the end-over-end kickoff on his ten-yard line and dodged, darted, and spun his way to the forty. Dale Moore hobbled back onto the field and hurried his team to the line of scrimmage. Limping badly, he dropped back three awkward steps and zipped a pass to Donald Yates, who crossed midfield before being stopped. Moore then threw a quick slant-in pass to Brakebill who scrambled to the thirty-five.

"Donald," the quarterback asked in the huddle, "can you split those defensive backs and get open?"

Yates nodded his head.

Moore stumbled as he dropped back, but reaching his left hand to the ground, he regained his balance. Meanwhile, Yates drove toward the defensive back, and then planted his right foot and cut sharply inside, heading for the goalpost. With Benny Sinclair bearing down on him, Dale waited just a split second longer, and then zinged the pass toward the gritty little end. Yates reached up, pulled the missile down, and streaked into the end zone. Moore had to be helped up and assisted off the field, while "Butch" Jaggers came on and kicked the point-after. Now, the Tigers needed one more score.

After the kickoff, the fired-up Tigers stymied everything the Yellow Jackets tried, forcing them to punt. Receiving the ball on their own thirty, Mount Vernon had plenty time for one last push and the winning touchdown.

On the prior drive the Tigers had scored on three pass plays, but the hit Dale Moore had taken as he threw the touchdown pass had him on the sideline. Meredith lined up at quarterback, knowing he must throw the ball to have any chance. After two completions, he winged a third toward Yates, but a Mineola linebacker leaped up and tipped the ball. Kelley was playing deep safety, and alertly cradled the ball at his own forty.

The Yellow Jackets made one first down, crossing into Tiger territory, but then Mount Vernon jammed the line of scrimmage and stopped two running plays. The Mineola quarterback tried his second pass of the game, but Meredith was ready. He picked off the aerial and returned the ball to midfield.

Knowing this was the Tigers' last chance to score, Dale Moore limped back onto the field. Handing the ball to Meredith, Cunningham, and a hobbled Agee, the Tigers drove slowly but steadily down to the Yellow Jacket sixteen. With time running short and needing five yards for a first down, Dale dropped back to pass. When he pushed off his right leg to throw the ball to Brakebill, his knee gave way. The pass sailed high and out the back of the end zone. The ball went over to Mineola.

The Yellow Jackets took their time and ran out the game clock. Their perfect record remained, and the Tigers' heretofore-glorious season was in a shambles.

The Tigers led in penetrations, first downs, and in yards gained, but they also led in penalty yards, fifty to twenty. But the most important statistic did not appear on the stat sheet: the ninety-yard punt return by John Kelley, Tiger nemesis of 1948 as well. Also, Catfish accepted blame. "I didn't have a backup quarterback ready; it cost us the game."

With the district race lost, the Tigers' motivation against 1-7 Gilmer would be pride. With Catfish's quarterback and left halfback out with injuries, along with standout tackle, Billy Clinton, he challenged his players to prove their mental toughness.

"If you lose to Gilmer, you'll destroy all you've accomplished this year," Catfish warned. "If we're really the best team in this district, we've got to prove it tonight."

Eighteen hundred loyal fans turned out on Armistice Day, hoping to see their Tigers rebound from the loss to the Yellow Jackets. They got their wish in the first quarter.

Billy Jack Meredith, taking handoffs from "Butch" Jaggers, was unstoppable on the opening drive, and finished it off with a three-yard plunge into the end zone. Jaggers toed the extra point through the uprights for a 7-0 lead.

After shutting down the Buckeye offense, the Tigers took off on another drive. This time Donald Yates snared an aerial from Jaggers for a twenty-five yard score. Again, the freshman quarterback's toe was true, and the Tigers had a 14-0 advantage.

Miscues stopped Catfish's offense through the second quarter, but his rugged defense never faltered and kept zeroes on the scoreboard for Gilmer until the third period when Meredith took over again and burst free for a fifteen-yard score. By then the Tigers were in charge, and their fans delighted in their patched-up but powerful offense.

The stubborn Tiger defense repeatedly handed the ball back to its offense which, in the fourth quarter, produced two more touchdowns: a thirty-yard scoring pass to Donald Yates followed by Meredith's third tally of the game on an eight-yard run.

Taking a 35-0 win, the Tigers celebrated, half-heartedly. And then a cold downpour swamped the field, parking lot, and streets, sending players and fans scurrying for shelter.

Against Gilmer, the Tigers had matched some of their earlier efforts. With fourteen first downs on three hundred thirty-five yards of offense, including four-for-eight passing by young "Butch" Jaggers, the Tigers had been impressive.

While the offense got most of the attention, Catfish's defense had held the Buckeyes to seven first downs and only forty-eight yards rushing. When Gilmer had thrown the ball, the Tigers had picked off three aerials, handing the ball back to Jaggers and company. Mount Vernon's stiff defense had forced the Buckeyes to punt seven times, while the potent Tiger offense had never faced that dilemma.

After the game, Catfish hurriedly checked on the Yellow Jackets' contest. As he feared, they had defeated Pittsburg, making them the undefeated district champs.

Due to inclement weather back on November 4, the Tigers now had to play a makeup contest against Pittsburg. With Dale Moore improved and ready to play and Louis Agee mending, the Tigers would be missing only Billy Clinton. The question was incentive. Did the Tigers have enough left?

Billy Jack Meredith answered that question on the first drive of the game. Running like a man possessed, the fullback fought his way for hefty chunks of yards, and finally capped the march with a thirty-two yard scamper up the middle of the field. Unfortunately for the Pirates, he was just getting started. When the first quarter expired, Meredith had three touchdowns and an interception to his credit, and the Tigers led 20-0.

In the second quarter, Dale Moore hurled a twenty-yard pass to his brother, Johnny, and little brother sped into the end zone with the Tigers' fourth score. Dale followed that with a thirty-six-yard toss to the pass-catching sensation, Donald Yates, setting up a four-yard score by Cunningham. Then with Jaggers subbing for Dale Moore, Yates grabbed a twenty-two-yard pass for the third touchdown of the quarter and sixth of the game. The first half ended with the Tigers leading 40-0.

Tiger substitutes played the second half, yet in the final quarter, an ailing but determined Louis Agee plunged over from four yards out to end Tiger scoring.

Pittsburg finally showed some spark, mostly from Billy Groce who finished a solid drive with a four-yard touchdown in the fourth quarter, setting the final score at 46-6.

Catfish's offense had churned out seven touchdowns and four hundred fifty-one yards, while racking up fourteen first downs. His quarterbacks had completed eleven of twenty-two passes for two hundred sixty yards. Meanwhile his defense had shut out Pittsburg until the reserves took over in the final quarter.

The 1949 Tigers' bittersweet season was over. Possibly the most potent offense ever to wear the purple and white, it had stumbled only once. The Mineola game would be replayed in the minds of Tigers for years to come, wondering what happened and dreaming of what might have been. Were they good enough to have won the state title?

The Mineola Yellow Jackets had provided their answer when on Friday night, November 4, they had humbled the mighty Tigers, 13-7.

Catfish had to forget what might have been, and look ahead. He announced that basketball practice would start Monday afternoon. His Tigers' season would kick off December 9 against Greenville, beginning the chase for another championship.

38

December 2, 1949

As Catfish put his basketball squad through their paces, the All-District football teams were announced for conference 15-A. Tigers filled nine of the twenty-two slots.

Dale Brakebill	End
Kenneth Kimbrell	Guard
Dudley Miller	Center
Buster Simms	Tackle
Dale Moore	Quarterback
Billy Jack Meredith	Fullback
Larkin Drummond	Guard
Donald Yates	End
Roy Cunningham	Halfback

Honorable Mention: Billy Clinton, Johnny Moore

Had Billy Clinton not missed half the season with a leg injury, he likely would have joined his teammates on the first team, and thus the Tigers would have placed every one of their offensive players, other than one halfback, on the honored team. Even the 1947 team did not dominate the all-star lineup to that extent. Ironically, this fabulous team was only the second Catfish squad to not win the district title in the past six years.

December 9 was set for the annual football banquet, and Catfish had lured the former University of Texas football great, Peppy Blount, to be the guest speaker. With record ticket sales to the event, it had to be postponed when Catfish entered the Franklin County Hospital with bleeding stomach ulcers.

For the past month the coach had been having problems with his stomach, drinking milk constantly, taking medication, and maintaining a bland diet. Thinking that if he could just hang on until the end of the football season, the pressure would be off, and he could relax and heal. It was an every-season problem, and his plan seldom worked out.

While Catfish lay in bed, Assistant Bo Campbell worked the basketball team and prepared the players for their opening game against the Greenville Lions, a Class AA school. A dozen years earlier Campbell had been an outstanding athlete in Mount Vernon, and friends and fans had welcomed him home after his kicking career at Southern Methodist University and a stint in the army. Now, they were especially glad to have him around.

From the 1949 team, the Tigers had veterans Billy Jack Meredith, Dale Moore, Mac Anderson, Billy Rex Lawrence, and Dale Brakebill to form a solid nucleus for their team. These would get ample help from Billy Hunt, "Butch" Jaggers, Donald Yates, Wayne Foster, and Newman Gilbert. Though this team lacked a highly skilled tall player, clearly it had the talent and experience to make a run for the district title.

With Catfish tossing and turning in his bed, Greenville proved bigger and better, and handed the Tigers an opening season loss, 44-37. Mac Anderson pitched in a dozen points while Billy Rex Lawrence added seven in the losing cause. Ray (17) and Green (13) combined for thirty of the Lions' total.

From his hospital room, Catfish fretted over the loss. Dorothy Nell reminded him that the more he riled himself, the longer he would be away from the team. He took her hand and squeezed it, acknowledging that she was right. Slowly, he turned and stared out the window. He hated losing, but he hated it most when he felt he had let his boys down.

In a rematch the Tigers defeated the Lions, 30-18, obviously playing much better defense. Billy Rex Lawrence sank twenty-one points with a terrific shooting exhibition. Before fouling out of the game, Dale Moore shut down the Lions' Ray, who managed only six points after having racked up seventeen in the first encounter.

Two days before Christmas, the Tigers took on the Quitman Bulldogs and lost their second contest of the young season, 45-30. Lawrence slumped to only six points, but Dale Brakebill contributed eight. Bright of Quitman killed the Tigers with twenty-three, while Gilbreath controlled the backboards.

On December 29, Catfish was back to lead his team against

Atlanta, and the frustrated Tigers got going early and rolled like a snowball downhill. The score ballooned to a 47-18 blowout with Dale Brakebill pouring in twenty points to go with Mac Anderson's nine to pace the Tigers. Cruse had eight in a hapless effort by the long-legged Jack Rabbits.

A return match with Quitman produced considerably different results. The Tigers won 42-33 with Meredith (13), Lawrence (9), and Dale Moore (8) providing the offensive punch. Bright was held to eleven, but Gilbreath pitched in ten for the Bulldogs.

The Tigers then traveled to Mount Pleasant and played their first district contest. Lawrence (18), Meredith (10), and Anderson (10) carried the Tigers to a 45-33 victory. Brown (11) and Garrett (9) provided the scoring punch for the Titus County boys.

Catfish's boys then overpowered the Talco Trojans, 50-23. Billy Rex Lawrence performed like a scoring machine and rang up thirty-one points, more than the entire Trojan team. The high-point man for Talco had only eight, typifying their scrappy, yet futile effort.

The Gilmer Buckeyes were next, and with balanced scoring, the Tigers won rather easily, 40-24. Mac Anderson threw in eleven points, while Lawrence and Meredith each had ten. Waller of the Buckeyes countered with ten.

Against Winnsboro, the reigning district champs who had defeated the Tigers twice the prior season, the Tigers struggled and trailed 14-13 at halftime. Turning up the defensive pressure, Catfish's boys held the Red Raiders to only seven in the second half while scoring fifteen. The 28-21 win was their eighth of the season and fourth district victory without a loss. Lawrence carried the Tiger scoring burden with eleven.

Catfish had kept the first half of his promise to Acie Cannaday. After losing the district title to the Red Raiders in 1949, Catfish had congratulated Cannaday, wished him success in the playoffs, and promised to be back for the title in the '50 season.

The Tigers then traveled to Mineola, determined to make up for their football loss to the Yellow Jackets. Mac Anderson pitched in sixteen, carrying the team in the first half. Billy Rex Lawrence and Newman Gilbert added eight and ten respectively in the second half to ensure a Tiger 37-23 win. Benny Sinclair, the end who had bottled up the Tiger footballers and caught a key first-down pass, led the Yellow Jackets with eleven.

With their offense hitting on all cylinders, the Tigers entertained the Pittsburg Pirates on January 20. With eighteen points from both

Lawrence and Anderson and thirteen from Meredith, the Tigers walloped the Pirates, 72-24. Catfish cleared his bench, letting players like Donald Yates (5), Billy Hunt (8), "Butch" Jaggers (3), and Wayne Foster (6) take the floor. Graves from Pittsburg contributed half of his team's points before being disqualified on fouls. On the end of the bench, he joined teammate Wilkens who had committed five fouls in the first half. Then Franklin was the third Pirate sent to the bench with excessive fouls. The Pirates committed twenty-two fouls in a desperate effort to slow down the Tigers' barrage of baskets.

With this win the Tigers finished the first half of the round-robin district format undefeated; therefore, Catfish was assured that his Tigers would at least compete for the conference title at the season's end.

Before beginning the second half of district play, Catfish took his team to Clarksville for a non-conference affair. His boys won easily, 43-15. Surprisingly, Billy Hunt led the Tigers with sixteen points. Every player Catfish put into the contest scored, while limiting Clarksville's scoring leader to four points.

Mount Pleasant was the first district opponent on the Tigers' second half of round-robin play. Playing at home, Catfish's boys struggled against a fierce attack by Mount Pleasant, highlighted when Dale Moore dove for a loose ball and collided with the visitor's Hightower. The referees stopped play, and the crowd fell silent as Dale lay unmoving on the hardwood. As the guard regained feeling in his legs, his teammates assisted him off the court and to a waiting car that rushed him to the local hospital.

Meanwhile, the game continued, and at halftime Mount Vernon trailed 9-7. The Tigers' prolific scorer, Billy Rex Lawrence, was scoreless. Meredith had three points, Brakebill two, and Dale Moore had added two prior to his exit.

Lawrence's shooting woes continued after intermission, and Billy Hunt replaced him. The sub promptly fired in eight points. Meanwhile, Meredith added six, Anderson and Newman Gilbert contributed five each, and the Tigers pulled it out, 31-23, maintaining their undefeated league record.

After the game, which saw thirty-four personal fouls committed, Catfish hurried to the hospital. Dale Moore had broken a vertebra in his back and would wear a cast around his abdomen for several weeks, likely for the remainder of the season.

Thursday, January 26, was a dismal day. A cold front hit East Texas, and the temperature dropped to thirty-seven degrees within a couple of hours. As the thermometer plummeted and the continuous drizzle turned to sleet, the Tigers headed to Talco for a rematch. Catfish's boys romped, 55-37, collecting their seventh conference win against no losses. With balanced scoring, Anderson led with fourteen, but got plenty of help from Lawrence (13), Meredith (10), and Gilbert (10). In a heated contest, Brakebill, Hunt, and Meredith fouled out of the game, while Lawrence, Anderson, and Gilbert lacked only one foul being disqualified. The Tigers, with a total of twenty-nine fouls, came excruciatingly close to lacking five qualified players to finish the contest.

Frye for Talco pitched in seventeen points while Warren added nine in a frustrating loss to the Tigers, a team they were tired of losing to.

In the dressing room after his players had showered and dressed, Catfish gathered his players around him. Many of the boys had played for him for three years, and had heard dozens of his motivational speeches. They expected another one.

With all his boys seated, the coach stood before them. He was pale, his bottom lip quivered, and tears welled up in his eyes. Something was different. Normally, the tears did not come until well into his speeches.

"Boys, I've just made the hardest decision of my life," he said, his voice shaking. "At the end of this season, I'll be leaving to coach basketball at East Texas State."

The room fell as silent as an Egyptian tomb. Catfish tried to continue, but his emotions were out of control. Pulling out his handkerchief, he dabbed at his eyes. Some of the players had handkerchiefs, but most used their shirtsleeves.

"My seven years with you at Mount Vernon High School have been my happiest in fifteen years of coaching. Your spirit has been an inspiration to me. I will always be pulling for you, for all future Tigers, to carry on as the Tigers of the past.

"Boys, I'll never forget a single one of you. Each of you . . ." he said, unable to throttle his emotions. "You'll always be my boys, and forever champions."

Whether he had more to say will never be known. His boys rose, gathered around their coach, hugging him, their long arms reaching for his shoulder, his head, his arm, just to touch him at this overwhelmingly emotional moment.

On Friday, January 27, the *Optic-Herald* headlines shocked Tiger fans with the news. "CATFISH SMITH RESIGNS POST AS HEAD COACH

OF MT. VERNON TIGERS," it read. As had been conjectured so many times, their coach was leaving. He had accepted a position at his college alma mater. He would be head basketball coach and first assistant football coach for the East Texas State Lions.

The announcement ". . . comes as a shock to local sports fans, but they are unanimous in congratulating him upon advancement in the coaching profession. . . ." said the news article. The report went on to list Catfish's accomplishments at Mount Vernon. His football teams had won four district titles, three bi-district crowns, two regional championships, and competed for a third, while winning fifty-nine games and losing only eight. His basketball record was five district championships, missing only once, and his boys appeared positioned for a sixth. He had won two regional crowns, taking those teams to the state tournament where they had lost the title by a single point in 1944 and won it all in 1948. His roundballers had won one hundred fifty-eight games, while losing twenty-four. His current basketball team was leading in the race for the district title with seven consecutive wins, and sported an overall record of thirteen wins and two defeats.

"Though we will feel a great loss in the going of Coach Smith," Superintendent Fleming said, "we are fortunate in having . . . Assistant Coach Wayne Bo Campbell. We expect to rebuild and continue the splendid tradition of the past seasons."

But Catfish Smith was synonymous with Mount Vernon athletics. For seven years he had inspired young men to perform beyond their apparent capabilities. In addition to the tactics, strategy, and motivational speeches, there was something intangible about the man, something that made his players believe they would win, always.

With the current basketball season not yet finished, what would happen to this group of boys who knew their coach would soon be leaving? Could they maintain their competitive spirit and capture one more district crown? Then, could Mount Vernon ". . . rebuild and continue the splendid tradition . . ." as the superintendent hoped?

39

January 27, 1950

For Catfish it was a bittersweet weekend. He dearly loved Mount Vernon, the school, the fans, and his boys. He could not quite picture himself anywhere else, but also he looked forward to the challenge at a higher level, leading even more gifted athletes. He had good memories of East Texas State, and he had friends there.

On Saturday morning he scanned the *Optic-Herald*, beyond the headlines, his picture, the accolades, his won-lost record. A memory from his 1947 team jumped out at him.

Gerald Skidmore had enrolled in the department of journalism at North Texas State. Catfish remembered the boy's first attempt at news writing, *The Tiger's Tale*, and the memory brought a smile to his face. And Catfish remembered Gerald on the basketball court. "Drive, Skidmore, drive!" the coach heard his own voice echo in his mind. Gerald was still driving, and it pleased his old coach.

And Abe Martin of Texas Christian University had accepted an invitation to speak at the Tigers' delayed football banquet, the paper said. Ex-Tigers Herb Zimmerman and Charles Lowry played football for the Horned Frogs, as did Bud Campbell for their basketball team. Zimmerman was being considered for All-Southwest Conference honors, and seemed destined to be an All-American. Coach Martin promised to bring the film of his team's game with the University of Texas where Gene Fleming, another former Tiger great, was a Longhorn.

Catfish felt fortunate to have coached so many boys, so many outstanding young men. Where were they now? The coach hoped he had prepared them well. Otherwise, all the wins, all the championships, and all the titles were useless, like dead leaves fallen from a stately oak they had once adorned.

Monday came, and then Tuesday night when the Tigers played the Mineola Yellow Jackets, the last home game of the season, possibly the last for Catfish in the gymnasium he had come to love. His Tigers came out afire and swept away the Yellow Jackets, 68-31, like a prairie fire before the wind. Catfish's boys rang up their second highest point total of the season, with Billy Rex Lawrence pouring in sixteen, Meredith thirteen, Brakebill ten, Anderson twelve, and Gilbert eight. Benny Sinclair, a highly respected Tiger nemesis, fought spiritedly for ten in a losing cause.

The Tigers then beat Gilmer 49-28 with Billy Jack Meredith hitting twenty, his highpoint for the season. True to his character, Meredith had fourteen in the second half, which, along with Donald Yates' five and Anderson's seven, brought the Tigers back from a 17-16 halftime deficit.

That brought the Tigers back to Winnsboro and the second half of Catfish's promise to his protégé, Acie Cannaday. The Red Raiders hoped to avenge their five-point defeat by Catfish's boys in the first half of the season, and the Tigers could not afford a loss. Mount Pleasant was right on their heels, within reach of winning the second half of the round-robin and forcing the Tigers into a playoff for the district championship.

The Tiger shooters could not find the range, and Dale Moore's absence weakened their defense. In the first half, Catfish's squad struggled to score nine points, six by Lawrence. However, the Red Raiders managed a mere eleven, so the game was there to be won in the second half, and how many times had Catfish's boys made dramatic comebacks? Tiger fans were primed for another.

In the second half Billy Jack Meredith scored six, Gilbert and Anderson four each, and the Tigers racked up nineteen, but Joe Grady Tibbs of Winnsboro went on a rampage, scoring fifteen while his teammates added four more. The Red Raiders matched the Tigers point-for-point, and the buzzer sounded with Winnsboro ahead, 30-28.

The loss was costly for the Tigers, throwing them into a three-way tie with Winnsboro and Mount Pleasant for the second half of the round-robin season. Catfish's boys must win their final two regular season games and hope both their adversaries dropped a game, a very unlikely occurrence. Otherwise, the Tigers would face a one-game playoff to determine the second-half winner. If they should lose that game, then they would face a two-of-three series for the district championship. This one loss could result in four extra contests for the Tigers to capture the district crown.

On February 6, the Tigers traveled to Mineola in a must-win

situation, and they did, 68-29. Billy Jack Meredith and Dale Brakebill carried the Tigers in the first half with seven points each, and then in the second half, Billy Rex Lawrence poured in sixteen. Mac Anderson added a dozen points and Newman Gilbert eight as the Tigers breezed to victory. Benny Sinclair fought back with ten points and Castillo added eight for the over-matched Yellow Jackets.

With Dale Moore still sidelined with a back injury, the Tigers entered the Pirates' den and trounced them, 64-30. Meredith tossed in sixteen, Lawrence seventeen, Brakebill nine, and Anderson seven. The game was never in doubt, and the Tigers had completed their regular season schedule with eleven district wins and one loss. Their overall record was 16-3, with the losses coming at the hands of Quitman, Class AA Greenville, and the two-pointer to the Red Raiders.

Now the Tigers had to sit and wait for the outcome of a crucial game between Winnsboro and Mount Pleasant. Catfish's boys would face the winner in a single game playoff for the second half of the round-robin.

Meanwhile, the fabulous junior varsity had claimed their district title with an overall 16-2 record, losing only to Greenville and by one point to non-conference Quitman. Donald Yates, Eddie Turner, Ken Knotts, "Butch" Jaggers, Glen Slaughter, Dudley Miller, Billy Clinton, Stanley Jaggers, Wayne Foster, and Dale Mills comprised this team, many of whom would join Billy Jack Meredith, Mac Anderson, Dale Brakebill, and Billy Hunt to form the heart of next year's Tiger team.

In their final game of the regular season on Tuesday, February 10, the Mount Pleasant Tigers defeated Acie Cannaday's Red Raiders, thus tying Mount Vernon for the second half of the season. The tie would be resolved Thursday, February 12, in Whitley Gym in Commerce. Should Mount Vernon win, Catfish's boys would own the district title; otherwise, they must play Mount Pleasant in a two-of-three series.

In a bizarre game that saw Mount Vernon's leading scorer, Billy Rex Lawrence, totally shut out, the Tigers struggled, yet still led 4-3 after the first quarter. In the second period, the offenses improved, and at halftime the score stood knotted at 13-13.

In the third period, Mount Pleasant's Garrett (14) and Beal (8) caught fire and thrust the Titus County boys ahead, 25-14. With Lawrence as cold as an iceberg, Meredith and Anderson held to three points each, and Dale Moore out for the season, Catfish made a bold move. He inserted his reserves for the final stanza.

In a remarkable comeback, Billy Hunt (6), Wayne Foster (5),

"Butch" Jaggers (2), and Eddie Turner (2) helped Dale Brakebill (6) pull ever closer to Mount Pleasant. By outscoring their opponent 16-3, the young Tigers claimed the lead, 30-28 with a minute to go in the game. But Garrett and Hightower scored five unanswered points at the end, and Mount Pleasant captured a 33-30 win, forcing a two-of-three series for the district championship.

To eliminate home court advantage, the first game was scheduled to be played in Mount Pleasant, the second in Mount Vernon, and if required, the third in Whitley Gym in Commerce. Regardless, Catfish faced a dilemma. Should he go back to his regular starters or should he send his fiery reserves onto the hardwood?

If the championship were to be determined by one game, Catfish might have gone with his backups, but he believed he was facing a marathon, not a sprint, and he did not want to shatter the confidence of his starters at the beginning of the race.

The Tigers looked like a different team in the first contest of the series, winning 41-36. Lawrence (9), Anderson (8), Meredith (7), and Turner (6) carried the Tigers' scoring load, while Garrett fought back with eleven but got little help from his mates.

With his team's confidence intact and playing on their home court, Catfish's squad faced Mount Pleasant needing to win one of the next two contests. The pressure was on Mount Pleasant, and they responded like champions. With balanced scoring, the Titus County boys came back to capture the second game, 37-31, forcing a third and deciding contest.

Lawrence (14) and Meredith (11) had led the Tigers, but could not overcome Mount Pleasant's combination of Garrett (11), Hightower, (12), and Smith (8). Catfish's boys had played well, but had lost to a better team that night. The next night, Saturday, February 18, he had to somehow make sure his Tigers were the better team.

On Saturday morning the Tigers traveled to Whitley Gym in Commerce for the showdown. In a bitterly fought game, the lead bounced back and forth. Catfish's boys led 11-9 at halftime. Then in the all-important second half, the Tigers got some clutch shooting from Meredith (7), Hunt (9), Gilbert (5), and Mac Anderson (4) to pull the game out, 29-27. For Mount Pleasant, Garrett, who had scored an average of a dozen points in the three prior games, was held to five, but ultimately free throws, Catfish's pet peeve, made the difference. Meredith sank three at the end, along with Hunt's three and Gilbert's two, while Mount Pleasant managed only one of eight.

Catfish's boys had won another district title, their sixth in seven years. On February 25th they would travel once more to Whitley Gym and play the Commerce quintet in the first round of the regional tournament.

In a rather easy victory, Catfish's boys defeated Commerce, 49-28. Ten Tigers got into the scoring act. Lawrence's fourteen led the way, but he received ample support from Hunt (9), Anderson (6), and Meredith (5). Leading 36-19 after three quarters, Catfish's reserves played out the final stanza, outscoring the Commerce boys 13-9. The victory bracketed Mount Vernon against the much taller Gaston Red Devils that night for the regional title. The Red Devils had qualified for the championship game by defeating Hooks, 51-45.

If Mount Vernon could win just one more game, their twentieth of the season, Catfish would make his fifth trip to the state tournament in Austin, his third with a Tiger team. But his team had been erratic, and when one loss means elimination, inconsistent play can send you home.

The Tigers struggled but led 17-15 at halftime. Lawrence and Hunt had pitched in six each, but Meredith had managed only one and Anderson two. The Red Devils would have been in trouble except they had tossed in seven free throws in the first half, while the Tigers countered with only three.

In the second half, the Tigers turned cold, while Gaston warmed up, outscoring the Tigers 22-7, and captured the regional championship, 37-24. Lawrence (9) and Hunt (6) received little help in keeping up with Leverett (11), Poland (10), and Bradshaw (6) of Gaston, and the Tigers missed eight of twelve free throws while the Red Devils cashed in six of ten.

The loss finalized the Tigers' 1950 season with a 19-6 record, one win short of the state tournament, and thus ended Catfish Smith's seven-year era at Mount Vernon. However, the man everyone called "Catfish" had placed Mount Vernon High School among the top echelon of athletic programs in the state of Texas, and he had firmly established a winning tradition that would carry over for years to come.

At the delayed football banquet, twenty championship trophies covered a long table decorated in purple-and-white, all won by Catfish's teams. One hundred ninety-five fans gathered for a final party honoring their departing coach and his last Tiger team. His loyal fans presented the coach with a gift certificate entitling him to a tailor-made suit, along with many other gifts. After Catfish made a short, emotional speech, he introduced the 1949 football captains, Dale Moore, Dudley Miller, and Billy Jack Meredith. Meredith, elected 1950 co-captain with Donald Yates, then introduced each member of the Tigers' squad. Bernard Stringer, local representative of the Southwestern Life Insurance Company, presented a Most Valuable Player trophy to Dale Moore.

Wayne "Bo" Campbell, the Tigers' new head coach, made a stirring speech, dedicating himself to upholding the high standards and winning tradition set by his friend and fellow coach.

Some in Mount Vernon predicted Catfish would last no more than one season at the college level. "His demanding tactics, relentless conditioning drills, and strict training rules were accepted by our high school boys, but those college fellows won't stand for it." Others predicted the coach would win at the next level, as consistently as he had at Carey and Mount Vernon. A fellow coach had a unique way of summing up the coach who had dominated his district for seven years. "What kind of coach is Catfish? He's the kind that can take his boys and beat yours, or he can take yours and beat his."

Harless "Crow" Wade, writing in East Texas State's *East Texan*, announced that Milburn "Catfish" Smith would replace Darrell Tully as the Lions' cage coach. "Smith, who is a former All-Lone Star Conference forward in basketball and All-LSC end in football, will return to his Alma Mater with one of the most impressive and successful high school coaching careers in the state." Wade went on to say, "Smith's coaching career hit its peak in the 1947-48 season when he had the eminent distinction of guiding undefeated teams throughout an entire school year, keeping a clean record in both football and basketball."

Five former Catfish nemeses, Dick Gilbreath of Quitman, Jimmy Fountain and R. C. Moore of East Mountain, Charles Whitten of Blossom, and Bob Fuller of Clarksville, would now be playing for him on the East Texas State basketball team that had just completed its season by reaching the semi-finals in the national NAIB tournament in Kansas City.

Regardless what the future held for Catfish and Dorothy Nell, they would leave Mount Vernon with a lifetime of memories, more than most coaches could ever hope to have. And they would be leaving a town that she had called home for thirty-eight years, a town filled with friends and well-wishers.

For an emotional Coach "Catfish" Smith, the hardest part was leaving "his boys."

417

EPILOGUE

Many of Catfish's "boys" accepted athletic scholarships and excelled at the next level of competition, the most notable being Herb Zimmerman who became an All-American at TCU and was inducted into that university's Hall of Fame. Other prominent college-level players include J. C. Cannaday, Charles Shurtleff, Charles Lowry, Billy Jack Meredith, Dale Moore, Gene Fleming, Robby Campbell, Maurice "Bud" Campbell, Dale Brakebill, and Keith Drummond. Also, Donald Yates and Kenneth Kimbrell played on Catfish's undefeated East Texas State championship teams.

Predictably, several of his players served in the military, with Donald Yates and Dale Brakebill reaching the rank of colonel. The players who served in World War II or the Korean War are too many to list here, but their records testify to their preparedness. Likewise, an astounding number of his players became leaders in the business world: presidents of banks, founders and CEOs of companies, journalists, lawyers, financial analysts, owners of automobile dealerships, ranchers, motivational speakers, oil company executives, home builders, and community leaders.

Kenneth Kimbrell and Herb Zimmerman pursued coaching careers, while Dudley Miller became a college professor, as did Catfish's son Jimmy Smith and his wife Francie Larrieu, a five-time United States Olympic Team member who established 36 national records and a dozen world records. Also, Stanley Jaggers, Larkin Drummond, and Maurice "Bud" Campbell excelled in the education profession.

As for Catfish, a second book is in progress that will cover his years as a college coach at East Texas State and Baylor University. While at East Texas State he led his teams to a 29-game winning streak, including two Tangerine Bowl appearances, and in 1953 he was voted College Coach of the Year by the Texas Sports Writers Association. Since his coaching years, he has been enshrined in four halls of fame, honored by the Texas House of Representatives in House Concurrent

Resolution 161 for his unique contribution to Texas athletics, but possibly the greatest honor of all is the continuing work of the Catfish Winners organization, a collection of approximately one hundred of his "boys" who share their success by awarding scholarships to deserving Mount Vernon graduates each year.

To learn more about the Catfish Winners Scholarship Fund, write to Catfish Winners, P. O. Box 7, Mount Vernon, TX 75457.

MOUNT VERNON Won/Loss Record

Year	Football	Titles	Basketball	Titles
1943-44	4-2	2nd in Dist.	28-3	State Finalist
1944-45	11-0	Reg. Title	24-1	Reg. Finalist
1945-46	9-2-1	Bi-dist. Titl	22-5	District Title
1946-47	7-2-1	2nd in Dist.	21-7	Bi-dist. Title
1947-48	11-0	Reg. Title	30-0	State Title
1948-49	8-1-1	Dist. Title	19-6	2nd in Dist.
1949-50	9-1	2nd in Dist.	19-6	Bi-dist. Title
Totals	59-8-3		163-28	

Dist. Title	District Championship
Bi-Dist. Title	Bi-District Championship
Reg. Finalist	2nd in Regional Tournament
Reg. Title	Regional Championship
State Finalist	2nd in State Tournament
State Title	State Championship

INDEX

Abilene, Texas, 188, 189, 352
Adams, Russell, 172, 198, 199, 200, 201, 207, 209, 214, 216, 217, 218, 223, 231
Adams, Virginia Grace, 70
Adkins, Herby, 10
Agee, Louis, 273, 326, 392, 393, 394, 395, 396, 398, 400, 401, 402, 404
Anderson, Mac, 346, 381, 382, 384, 385, 387, 407, 408, 409, 410, 413, 414, 415, 416
Anderson, Sara, 271
Armstrong, Lester, 382
Army Air Forces, 18, 22, 34, 36, 42, 83, 100, 129, 134, 135, 157, 166, 167, 176, 231
Arp, Texas, 253
Arthur, Mary Grace, 69, 370
Arthur, Paul, 69, 70, 76, 77, 83, 370
Athens, Texas, 316, 318, 319, 320, 321, 324, 334, 341
Atlanta, Texas, 214, 215, 216, 217, 363, 397, 408
Attaway, Eldon (Winfield), 29, 30, 31, 32, 33
Austin Statesman, 15, 117
Austin, Texas, 15, 28, 76, 94, 113, 116, 117, 171, 177, 245, 268, 334, 335, 337, 416
Avinger, Texas, 175

Banks, Dalton, 383
Banks, Harvey (Winfield), 30
Banks, Robert, 174, 223, 249, 251, 252, 254, 255, 256, 257, 258, 259, 260, 264, 265, 268, 326, 329, 330, 331, 333, 334, 335, 337, 338, 339, 341, 342, 343, 347, 350
Banks, Travis, 142
Bankston, Harold, 136
Bankston, Roy, 136
Bartley, Robbie, 132
Baugh, Sammy (TCU), 138

Bays, Coach Winnie (Mt. Pleasant), 363
Bean, Margaret, 286
Bell, L. R., 359
Bell, Matty (SMU), 10, 266, 267
Berry, Coach Bob (ET), 169
Berry, F. E., 392
Bible, Coach D. X. (UT), 341
Binnion, Irene, 69, 70, 71, 91, 262, 263, 264, 368, 380, 389
Birdsong, Betty, 271
Birdsong, Evelyn, 271
Black, Louis, 98
Black, Mildred, 30
Blossom, Texas, 104, 106, 107, 123, 175, 226, 333, 339
Bogata, Texas, 227, 229, 233, 235, 243, 249, 254, 329, 331, 396
Bogue, C. J., 127, 172, 232
Bogue, Patsy, 286, 342, 390
Bolger, Dave, 41, 188, 219, 228, 229
Bolger, Jr. David, 229
Bolger, Rufus, 41, 70, 107, 151, 219, 261, 346
Bolger, Snow, 229, 230
Borger, Texas, 42
Bougainville Island, 14, 115, 186
Bounds, Roger, 211
Boyd, Sam, 8
Boze, Silvia (ET), 27
Brakebill, Austin, 268
Brakebill, Dale, 233, 273, 297, 326, 347, 348, 352, 353, 354, 356, 360, 371, 375, 378, 381, 393, 395, 396, 397, 398, 399, 401, 402, 406, 407, 408, 409, 410, 413, 414, 415
Brannon, Coach Buster (TCU), 352
Brenham, Texas, 335, 337, 339
Brewer, Anita, 264
Brewer, Olan Ray, 72, 85, 172, 222, 249, 271
Brewer, Weldon, 235, 236, 251, 252, 263, 264

Bridgers, John, 8, 11
Bridges, Leon, 390
Brookshire, William (Commerce), 169, 170, 171
Brown, Abbie, 148
Brown, Charlie, 148, 225, 244, 268, 286, 390
Bruce, Charles, 330, 362, 376, 379, 392
Bruce, W. H., 225, 245
Buckner High School, 113
Bull, Ronnie, 10
Burgin, J. W., 346
Burton, Billy, 251, 326, 329, 333, 348
Burton, Sammie, 40, 110
Bynum, Sam, 204

C. W. Brown (Carey), 22, 27
Campbell, Bill, 42, 46
Campbell, D. H., 290
Campbell, Maurice, 251, 252, 258, 265, 273, 278, 279, 280, 281, 282, 283, 284, 285, 288, 290, 293, 297, 311, 316, 318, 320, 321, 322, 326, 329, 330, 331, 332, 333, 334, 335, 337, 338, 339, 340, 341, 342, 343, 352, 412
Campbell, Robby, 49, 54, 63, 72, 90, 127, 143, 144, 145, 146, 150, 151, 152, 154, 155, 158, 159, 161, 164, 165, 166, 170, 172, 179, 271, 392
Campbell, Wayne Bo, 40, 127, 172, 240, 266, 271, 272, 280, 282, 283, 284, 285, 287, 304, 305, 310, 312, 315, 317, 322, 323, 324, 326, 346, 350, 351, 356, 371, 379, 380, 387, 388, 391, 395, 407, 411, 417
Cannaday, Acie, 81, 87, 172, 174, 204, 219, 223, 228, 235, 236, 240, 242, 243, 254, 258, 266, 279, 289, 329, 330, 331, 349, 361, 386, 408, 413, 414
Cannaday, J. C., 40, 94, 102, 103, 104, 105, 106, 108, 109, 110, 113, 117, 121, 122, 124, 172, 174, 223, 266
Cannaday, Robbie, 232
Carey Cardinals, 27, 28, 335
Carey, Texas, 9, 21, 22, 27, 28, 35, 39, 42, 43, 47, 100, 116, 129, 139, 267, 335, 342, 417
Cargile, Beth, 70

Cargile, Dan, 49, 64, 65, 72, 73, 79, 84, 87, 89, 91, 93, 94, 126, 143, 147, 150, 155, 159, 166, 172, 269
Carr, Frank, 232, 297, 326, 357, 374, 381, 392
Carroll, Rosemary, 351
Carter, Billy Jack, 268, 283, 297, 320, 322, 326, 352, 353
Caudle, James, 49, 53, 56, 72, 77, 84, 94, 126, 143, 159, 166, 172, 174, 178, 179, 193, 194, 195, 196, 199, 200, 201, 202, 203, 204, 205, 206, 207, 208, 209, 213, 214, 215, 216, 217, 218, 231, 232
Cebu, Philippines, 14, 186
Chambers, Robert, 232, 346, 351, 354, 355, 358, 363, 364, 366, 371, 381
Chandler, Charles, 167
Chandler, Doris Jean, 167
Chandler, Dr. Eddie, 42, 65, 144, 145, 166, 167, 178, 219, 390
Chandler, Faye, 145
Chandler, J. T., 167
Chandler, Jr., Leon, 167
Chandler, Leon, 166, 167
Chandler, Mamie, 178
Chandler, Rebecca Ann, 166
Chandler, Truett, 167
Chastain (Mt. Pleasant), 255
Cherry, Coach Blair (UT), 138
Cherry, James, 143, 172, 179, 195, 198, 199, 200, 201, 202, 204, 205, 206, 207, 208, 209, 213, 214, 215, 216, 217, 218, 223, 227, 231, 232
Chessire, Faye, 70
Chicago Cardinals, 304
Churchill, Winston, 179, 181
Clark, Joe, 50, 63, 66, 72, 84, 90
Clark, Ray, 269
Clark, Robert, 142, 148
Clarksville, Texas, 44, 57, 77, 78, 79, 82, 131, 138, 161, 188, 200, 208, 213, 214, 226, 227, 240, 243, 255, 257, 258, 273, 284, 285, 291, 316, 318, 329, 331, 353, 354, 355, 363, 391, 392, 393, 409, 417
Clinton, Argeree, 65
Clinton, Billy, 233, 352, 358, 362, 374, 381, 393, 395, 396, 398, 400, 403, 404, 406, 414
Closs, J. R., 8

Cody, Andrew (Winfield), 98
Cody, Billy Rex, 172, 179, 193, 194, 195, 196, 198, 199, 200, 201, 202, 203, 204, 205, 206, 207, 209, 213, 214, 215, 216, 217, 218, 223, 226, 231, 232, 269
Cody, Edmond (Winfield), 98
Cody, Howard (Winfield), 211
Cody, Jr., H. S. (Winfield), 98
Coffey, Marvin (ET), 327
Combs, J. W., 287
Commerce, Texas, 108, 109, 110, 165, 166, 168, 169, 170, 171, 217, 225, 319, 415, 416
Condrey, Joe Zane, 200, 204, 213, 214, 231, 236, 237, 239, 241, 242, 245, 248, 249, 250, 251, 254, 257, 258, 260, 268, 269, 270, 273, 275, 276, 277, 279, 284, 285, 287, 288, 290, 291, 292, 293, 294, 295, 297, 300, 301, 302, 312, 313, 329, 351
Connley, J. M., 94, 172
Coody, Coach (Mt. Pleasant), 291
Cooper, Texas, 211
Coppedge, Rhea (Winnsboro), 258, 362, 386
Corregidor, Philippines, 156, 160
Cotton Belt Railroad, 65
Covin, J. P. (Edgewood), 314, 357
Cowan, C. E., 244
Cowan, Frances, 91, 124
Cowser (Winnsboro), 242
Craveth, Coach Jeff (USC), 139
Crescent Drug Store, 42, 43, 106, 125, 224, 230, 233, 303, 330, 359
Crowston, Clarence, 56, 58, 59, 60, 61, 62, 66, 68, 72, 78, 79, 84, 89, 90, 92, 93, 94, 98, 100, 102, 103, 104, 109, 113, 116, 118, 126, 143, 144, 145, 147, 149, 150, 152, 153, 154, 155, 158, 159, 161, 163, 164, 165, 166, 170, 171, 172, 174, 177, 178, 179, 191, 195, 205, 207, 223, 231, 266, 267, 269, 270, 271, 340
Crozier Tech, 22, 28
Crutcher Hospital, 42, 212, 220, 233, 247, 392
Cunningham, Roy, 231, 249, 250, 268, 269, 276, 292, 293, 305, 306, 307, 311, 313, 314, 315, 318, 326, 352, 354, 357, 359, 362, 364, 374, 394, 395, 396, 397, 398, 399, 400, 401, 402, 404, 406
Cunningham, Texas, 331

Daingerfield, Texas, 240, 242
Dallas News, 237
Daubs, Dr. W. H., 230, 233, 247
Davis, Bobbie Jean, 149
Davis, Cecil, 202
Davis, Lendon, 40, 86, 266, 327
D-Day, 135, 142, 148, 182
DeBusk, John, 392, 396, 397
DeKalb, Texas, 253, 391, 398
Dennis, Coach Tom (Rice), 188
Deport, Texas, 106, 108, 109, 118, 175, 187, 188, 197, 198, 199, 200, 226, 255, 256, 259, 260, 318, 387
Detroit, Texas, 329
Devall, Charles, 42, 43, 45, 46, 84, 90, 93, 128, 131, 146, 155, 166, 177, 178, 191, 192, 196, 203, 205, 217, 219, 224, 235, 237, 240, 242, 245, 247, 251, 256, 265, 297, 307, 317, 319, 324, 325, 350, 366, 378
Dewey, Thomas, 370, 371, 372
Dickerson, George, 143, 147, 155, 159, 166, 172, 178, 179, 194, 195, 196, 198, 199, 200, 202, 203, 204, 209, 214, 216, 217, 222, 231, 232, 236, 240, 241, 242, 246, 248, 250, 268, 269
Dimmitt, Texas, 337, 338, 339, 340, 341
Dixon, Harry (Talco), 248, 302, 306, 307
Dodd, Bobby (Georgia Tech), 138
Doenitz, Admiral Karl, 182
Dooley (Mt. Pleasant), 243
Doris Candy Kids, 26, 211
Drummond, James Musick, 75, 114
Drummond, Keith, 392, 418
Drummond, Larkin, 346, 347, 356, 392, 395, 396, 398, 406
Dyer, Allen, 383, 384

East Mountain, Texas, 177, 265, 334, 335, 337, 339, 340, 417
East Texas State, 9, 26, 27, 42, 70, 109, 110, 112, 166, 169, 234, 327, 379, 380, 383, 388, 398, 410, 411, 412, 417
Eastus (Nocona), 122
Edgewood, Texas, 217, 218, 219, 235, 237, 238, 239, 240, 241, 250, 251, 273, 289, 311, 312, 313, 314, 315, 316, 317, 328, 353, 356, 357, 358, 359, 391, 395, 396, 397
Edwards, Larry, 224

Edwards, M. L., 43, 45, 101, 136, 185, 219, 224, 229, 247, 390
Eisenhower, General Dwight D., 114, 133, 182, 227
Emery (Clarksville), 285, 354
Enola Gay, 189
Escobedo (Sidney Lanier), 118, 119
Eubanks, L. J., 142

Faithful Five Majorettes, 123, 124
Fleming, Dr. J. M., 219, 233, 389, 390
Fleming, Gene, 108, 126, 143, 147, 154, 172, 174, 178, 179, 194, 195, 196, 198, 200, 203, 207, 213, 214, 217, 218, 223, 231, 235, 236, 237, 239, 240, 241, 242, 244, 245, 246, 247, 248, 249, 250, 251, 252, 253, 254, 255, 256, 257, 258, 259, 260, 267, 268, 276, 278, 279, 280, 281, 282, 283, 284, 285, 286, 287, 288, 292, 293, 295, 296, 297, 300, 306, 307, 311, 313, 314, 315, 316, 318, 320, 321, 322, 323, 326, 329, 330, 331, 332, 333, 334, 338, 339, 341, 343, 351, 352, 412
Fleming, Millard F., 38, 39, 40, 41, 42, 43, 44, 45, 46, 47, 51, 56, 60, 69, 70, 76, 77, 83, 95, 96, 97, 98, 99, 102, 103, 108, 113, 116, 120, 123, 124, 168, 172, 246, 259, 260, 261, 262, 263, 269, 300, 304, 310, 312, 319, 326, 330, 342, 343, 350, 388, 389, 411
Ford, Billie, 268
Fort Worth Poly, 22
Foster, Wayne, 387, 407, 409, 414
Fountain, Jimmy (East Mountain), 339, 340, 417
Foust (Carey), 28, 129
Fox, Coach (Winfield), 33
Franklin Institute, 382
Fromme, Harvey (Sinton), 337, 341, 352
Fry, Hayden, 10
Fuller, Bob (Clarksville), 417
Fuquay, Dr. Zack, 219, 225

Garner, Laura, 70
Gaston, Texas, 243, 416
Gee, Dr. James, 379
Gibson, W. G., 69, 70
Gilbert, Dorothy Lynn, 180, 271
Gilbert, Fay Eula, 344

Gilbert, Mack, 200, 217, 218, 223, 226, 227, 231, 267, 269
Gilbert, Maxine, 271
Gilbert, Newman, 346, 347, 348, 349, 350, 351, 407, 408, 409, 410, 413, 414, 415
Gilbert, Paul Dean, 249, 326
Gilbert, Reggie (Edgewood), 217, 218, 239
Gilbreath, Dick (Quitman), 110, 113, 407, 408, 417
Gillespie, Viola, 69, 116, 392
Gilmer, Texas, 40, 44, 77, 91, 92, 93, 107, 131, 138, 155, 157, 158, 159, 188, 200, 205, 206, 207, 208, 214, 225, 226, 227, 235, 240, 246, 247, 249, 250, 256, 258, 272, 273, 288, 297, 298, 307, 309, 310, 311, 330, 332, 333, 347, 348, 350, 351, 353, 371, 373, 374, 375, 381, 385, 391, 399, 403, 404, 408, 413
Godwin, June, 91, 124
Goering, Marshal Hermann, 132, 227, 245
Goodwin, Ronnie, 10
Goolsby, Coach Jim (Quitman), 112, 176
Grady, Charley (Winfield), 33, 34, 35, 36, 71, 98, 99
Grand Prairie, Texas, 176
Grand Saline, Texas, 235, 240, 273, 285, 287, 288, 291
Grau, Billy, 143, 172, 202, 203, 217, 218
Greenville Evening Banner, 176
Greenville, Texas, 176, 260, 319, 334, 335, 384, 405, 407, 414
Gregory Gym, 113, 117, 335, 340
Gresham (Carey), 28, 129
Griffin, Pop, 271, 272, 351
Guthrie, Billy Jack, 185, 232, 237, 268, 269, 297, 322, 326

Hagansport, Texas, 56, 58, 383, 385
Halbert, Mart (Throckmorton), 338, 339, 341
Hall, Glyndean, 360
Hardin Simmons University, 352
Hardy, Olin, 191, 343
Harvey, C. E., 225
Hasty Courts, 42, 44, 46, 113, 133
Hawn, Jimmy (Athens), 318, 320, 321
Hayes, Coach Doc (SMU), 28

Henry, Jack, 41, 172, 224, 225, 233, 241, 265, 382, 383, 384, 385, 387
Hess, Rudolf, 227
Highland Park Scots, 38, 327
Hightower, Dorothy, 271
Hightower, Drue, 326, 346, 360
Hightower, Wayne, 155, 172
Hill, Eugene (East Mountain), 339, 340
Hill, Joyce, 91, 124
Hill, Martha, 124, 180, 271, 363
Hirohito, Emperor, 190
Hitler, Adolf, 74, 75, 101, 132, 134, 142, 179, 181, 182, 183, 245, 332
Ho-229, 183
Hogan, Charles, 40, 94, 103, 104, 105, 106, 109, 110, 113, 118, 119, 121, 122, 124, 127, 140, 143, 144, 145, 146, 147, 150, 151, 153, 154, 155, 158, 159, 161, 163, 164, 165, 166, 170, 172, 174, 179, 223, 269
Holcombe, Marion, 69
Holmes, Leonard, 114
Holton, Ed, 233, 268
Homma, General Masaharu, 226
Honey Grove, Texas, 169, 394
Hooks, Robert (Edgewood), 218, 239
Hooks, Texas, 175, 228, 252, 254, 255, 256, 257, 259, 334, 416
Hopewell, Texas, 30, 75, 114, 178, 185, 186, 219, 223, 237, 260
Horne, Jack, 90, 126, 140, 143, 147, 150, 152, 154, 159, 164, 166, 170, 172
Huckeba, William, 148
Hughes Springs, 240
Hughes, Rex (Mineola), 147, 241
Hughes, Virgie Beth, 393
Humphries, Henry (Edgewood), 397
Hunnicutt, Wallace, 199, 200, 204, 231, 237, 242, 244, 245, 247, 248, 268, 269, 277, 279, 284, 288, 290, 291, 292, 293, 297, 300, 301, 302, 305, 312, 313, 344, 352, 354, 356, 357, 358, 359, 360, 361, 362, 363, 364, 374, 381
Hunt (Carey), 28, 129
Hunt, Billy, 233, 387, 407, 409, 410, 414, 415, 416

Ingram, Billy, 94, 172, 174
Ingram, T. (Van), 264
Irby, Patsy, 91, 180, 225, 236
Irby, Tom, 50, 52, 56, 66, 72, 79, 84, 93, 126

Jacobs, Carson, 185
Jaggers, Butch, 394, 397, 399, 400, 402, 403, 404, 407, 409, 415
Jaggers, Stanley, 224, 297, 326, 346, 396, 398, 399
James, Coach Bill (A&M), 188
Jodl, General Alfred, 182
Johnson, Archie, 271
Johnson, Boody, 8
Johnson, Forrest, 382
Johnson, Lyndon B., 359
Jones, Clarence, 383, 384, 387
Jones, Glyn, 40, 188
Jones, Joy, 286
Jones, Ruby Jo, 70
Jowell, Carl (Dimmitt), 337, 339, 341
Joy Theatre, 43, 101, 224, 230, 367
Jumper, Donald, 383

Katy Park, 7
Keith, W. S., 377
Kelley, John (Mineola), 372, 373, 400, 401, 402, 403
Kennamer, Coulter (Atlanta), 216, 217
Kidwell, Myrtle, 219
Killingsworth, Bob, 38, 327
Killingsworth, Mabel (Winfield), 30
Kimbrell, Kenneth, 273, 353, 356, 378, 392, 395, 396, 398, 406
King, General Edward, 160
King, Mrs. A. P., 124
King, Pat, 268, 297, 326, 344
Kingston, Texas, 176
Kirby, Ollie (Greenville), 182
Knight, Buddy, 392
Knotts, Robbie, 94, 103, 172, 174
Knox, James (Sinton), 337, 352

Ladonia, Texas, 169
Landry, Tom, 340
Lawrence, Billy Rex, 381, 382, 387, 407, 408, 409, 410, 413, 414, 415, 416
Lawrence, Clovis, 330, 346
Lawrence, Harlan, 268, 271
Lawrence, Narvel, 84, 373
Lax, J. R., 346, 347, 348, 349, 356
Legendre, Sidney, 160
Lewis, Bob, 189
Lilenstern, D. R. (Winfield), 211
Linden, Texas, 255
Little, Coach T. B. (Throckmorton), 338
Lone Oak, Texas, 75

Lone Star Conference, 27, 43, 417
Lone Star Steel Company, 377
Lone Star, Texas, 27, 43, 377
Long, Joe, 233, 392, 396
Loveless, Alvis O., 157, 183, 227
Lowry, Charles, 126, 143, 144, 147,
    154, 172, 178, 179, 200, 202, 218,
    231, 236, 237, 242, 250, 267, 268,
    278, 279, 280, 281, 283, 284, 288,
    293, 294, 306, 311, 313, 316, 318,
    321, 323, 326, 343, 344, 351, 352,
    412
Lowry, Jr., L. D., 45, 47, 48, 105, 107,
    124, 135, 137, 192, 219, 234, 268,
    284, 313, 330, 379, 394, 395
Loyd, Coach Roland (Hooks), 228, 254,
    255, 257, 259
Loyd, Lollis, 40, 94, 102, 103, 108,
    110, 117, 118, 121, 124, 125, 172,
    174, 223
Loyd, Pat, 174, 185, 209, 223, 225,
    226, 227, 228, 231, 236, 237, 242,
    250, 251, 252, 253, 254, 255, 256,
    257, 259, 260, 264, 265, 268, 278,
    279, 280, 281, 283, 284, 285, 288,
    290, 291, 293, 294, 296, 302, 311,
    314, 316, 317, 318, 319, 320, 321,
    322, 326, 329, 330, 331, 334, 335,
    338, 339, 341, 347, 348

M. L. Edwards Store, 43, 45, 185, 224
MacArthur, General Douglas, 156,
    157, 160, 161, 183, 190, 191, 227
Mahaffey, Charles, 330, 343, 355, 359
Majors, Carolyn, 230, 388
Majouirk, Connie (New London), 378
Malinta Hill, Philippines, 160
Maness, Clarence, 359
Manhattan Project, 184, 189
Mann, Reverend J. C., 192, 219
Maples, J. D., 390
Maples, Leon, 224
Marshall, Milton (Mt. Pleasant), 292,
    293, 296, 363, 365
Martin, Coach Abe (TCU), 412
Martin, Lester, 98, 124
Martin, Mrs. Lester, 124
Mattingly, Raymond, 27
McBrayer, Erlena, 69, 70, 71
McCaw General, 19
McDonough, Tom, 41
McDowra (Deport), 106, 109, 198
McLeod, Texas, 161, 162, 163, 164,
    165, 166, 169, 170

McRea (Mount Pleasant), 255
McRea, James (Winnsboro), 398
Meek, Bill, 220, 342
Meek, Kenneth, 127, 155, 172, 174,
    195, 199, 200, 204, 222, 231, 232,
    236, 237, 239, 242, 245, 248, 249,
    250, 251, 255, 260, 265, 268, 269,
    277, 278, 279, 283, 284, 285, 286,
    288, 290, 291, 292, 294, 295, 296,
    305, 306, 307, 311, 313, 314, 315,
    316, 318, 320, 321, 322, 326, 329,
    347, 352
Mercer, Fred, 64
Mercer's Drug Store, 42, 43, 64, 65,
    77, 85, 330
Meredith, Billy Jack, 224, 225, 233,
    241, 242, 249, 265, 268, 269, 271,
    284, 287, 288, 291, 292, 293, 294,
    295, 296, 297, 302, 306, 307, 311,
    313, 315, 316, 318, 319, 320, 321,
    323, 326, 329, 330, 332, 342, 347,
    348, 350, 351, 352, 354, 355, 356,
    357, 358, 359, 360, 361, 362, 363,
    364, 365, 366, 368, 372, 374, 375,
    379, 381, 382, 383, 385, 386, 387,
    393, 394, 395, 396, 397, 398, 399,
    400, 401, 402, 403, 404, 406, 407,
    408, 409, 410, 413, 414, 415, 416,
    417
Meredith, Don, 225, 233, 383, 385,
    387
Meredith, Jeff, 47, 48, 91, 219, 225,
    284
Meyer, Coach Dutch (TCU), 188, 343,
    352
Middleton, Jim (Carey), 28, 129
Mikeska, Mike, 271
Miller Hotel, 42, 60, 84, 87, 166, 203,
    252, 269, 273, 276
Miller, Bessie, 60, 72
Miller, Dr. A. C., 19, 20, 21, 25
Miller, Dudley, 242, 268, 278, 279,
    280, 297, 299, 302, 304, 305, 306,
    307, 309, 311, 314, 318, 323, 326,
    351, 352, 358, 364, 374, 375, 382,
    395, 396, 406, 417
Miller, Mary, 211
Mills, Jerry, 392
Mineola, Texas, 131, 138, 146, 147,
    187, 188, 195, 196, 199, 200, 214,
    235, 240, 241, 242, 273, 288, 289,
    353, 366, 371, 372, 373, 374, 382,
    385, 391, 399, 400, 401, 402, 403,
    405, 408, 412, 413, 414

Minick (Mineola), 241

Minshew, Glynn, 172, 174, 223, 226, 269

Mitchell, Coach Lee (Athens), 319, 334, 335

Mitchell, Sonny (Athens), 318, 319, 320, 324

Mitchell, Vera, 123, 180, 287

Moffett, Charles, 180, 287

Moffett, Judge A. C., 224

Moore, Dale, 173, 174, 225, 232, 236, 239, 241, 242, 246, 248, 250, 253, 265, 268, 269, 270, 274, 275, 276, 278, 279, 280, 284, 285, 288, 290, 291, 292, 293, 294, 295, 296, 299, 302, 303, 305, 307, 309, 310, 311, 312, 313, 314, 317, 318, 320, 321, 322, 323, 324, 326, 329, 330, 331, 332, 333, 342, 346, 348, 352, 354, 355, 356, 357, 358, 359, 360, 361, 362, 363, 364, 365, 366, 368, 374, 375, 381, 382, 386, 387, 393, 394, 395, 396, 397, 398, 399, 400, 401, 402, 404, 406, 407, 408, 409, 413, 414, 417

Moore, Dewey, 173, 174, 178, 225, 232, 236, 239, 240, 242, 250, 265, 268, 278, 280, 281, 282, 283, 284, 285, 290, 292, 293, 295, 299, 302, 303, 304, 305, 309, 310, 311, 312, 313, 317, 318, 323, 326, 342, 344, 363

Moore, Finley, 220

Moore, Hoffman, 173, 220, 224, 234, 268, 272, 284, 312, 313, 363

Moore, Jinkins, 172, 174

Moore, Joe, 268

Moore, Johnny, 173, 174, 224, 225, 233, 268, 312, 326, 342, 352, 353, 356, 362, 363, 374, 378, 381, 392, 395, 396, 398, 404, 406

Moore, Mal, 212, 330

Moore, R. C. (East Mountain), 417

Morgan, Herman, 38, 39, 327

Morgan, J. C., 94, 172, 174

Morris, Lacy (Mt. Pleasant), 294, 302

Moulton, Cynthia, 286

Mount Pleasant, Texas, 41, 42, 44, 52, 85, 87, 88, 89, 97, 105, 107, 108, 131, 138, 150, 151, 152, 161, 165, 175, 188, 200, 202, 203, 211, 213, 215, 227, 232, 233, 235, 240, 243, 244, 246, 247, 248, 249, 250, 251, 253, 255, 272, 273, 277, 291, 292, 293, 294, 295, 296, 302, 307, 312, 320, 331, 332, 333, 344, 347, 348, 351, 353, 363, 364, 365, 381, 384, 391, 398, 408, 409, 413, 414, 415

Murphy, Audie, 176

Mussolini, Benito, 75, 133, 134, 179

Myrick, Coach Ed (Commerce), 169

Naples Buffaloes, 175, 297

Naples, Texas, 175, 297

Narramore (Winfield), 253

Nash, W. A., 268

Nelson, W. L., 45, 390, 394

New Boston, Texas, 391, 394

New Hope, Texas, 45, 251, 273, 341

New London, Texas, 318, 376, 377, 378, 379

New York Herald Tribune, 264

Newberry, Martha, 136

Newsom, Curly, 56, 57, 58, 275, 276

Newsom, Evelyn, 70

Newsom, Tom, 88, 268

Newsome, Cecil, 185

Newsome, Nell, 124

Neyland, General Robert, 22, 23, 27

Nimitz, Admiral Chester W., 142

Nocona, Texas, 119, 120, 121, 122, 123, 139, 193, 335, 337

Norris, Billy Ray (Edgewood), 312, 313, 314, 316, 357, 358, 359

Norris, Robbie Nell, 271

Olsen, Merlin, 10

Omaha, Texas, 387

Optic-Herald, 42, 45, 46, 84, 88, 90, 97, 105, 127, 128, 131, 144, 154, 160, 167, 191, 192, 200, 205, 210, 219, 224, 225, 230, 233, 235, 236, 240, 242, 245, 249, 251, 256, 265, 307, 317, 330, 343, 350, 361, 366, 376, 378, 380, 391, 392, 396, 399, 410, 412

Orren, Gwendolyne, 65, 72, 91, 124, 234

Owens, George (Gilmer), 375

Padget, Billie, 148

Padget, C. L., 148

Padget, Eunice, 148

Padget, Rex, 148

Palmer House, 42

Pampa, Texas, 21, 32

Papen, Franz von, 227
Parchman & Meredith, 43, 47, 224, 233
Parchman, Aline, 351
Parchman, Buck, 127, 142, 143, 172, 231, 232, 249, 268, 269, 279, 280, 285, 290, 293, 295, 297, 302, 313, 318, 326, 352
Parchman, C. J., 142, 143
Parchman, Frank, 126, 140, 142, 143, 147, 159, 166, 172, 178, 179, 193, 194, 195, 196, 200, 203, 215, 217, 231, 269
Parchman, Jack, 142
Paris, France, 142
Paris, Texas, 131, 138, 139, 142, 143, 144, 145, 234, 235, 236, 237, 238, 273, 285, 353, 355, 356, 391, 397
Parrish, Bessie, 178
Parrish, Lela, 160
Parrish, W. H., 178
Patman, Congressman Wright, 220, 377
Patton, General George, 142, 227
Penn, Alfred, 234
Penn, Clara, 234
Penn, Frank, 87, 108, 128, 229
Penn, Glenn, 85, 86, 87, 98, 100, 101, 108, 271, 299, 300
Penn, Lizzie, 87, 128, 228
Perrin, Jack, 326, 346
Peterson, Robert, 390
Petty, A. J., 366
Petty, Winnie, 366
Phillips, Douglas (Edgewood), 396, 397
Pickton, Texas, 252, 255, 329
Pierce (Van), 264
Pierce, Charles, 383, 384, 387
Pierce, Dewey (Grand Saline), 288
Pierce, Glenn, 40, 50, 51, 52, 53, 56, 63, 64, 65, 66, 68, 72, 77, 78, 79, 80, 81, 82, 89, 90, 93, 94, 97, 102, 103, 104, 105, 108, 110, 116, 117, 118, 121, 122, 124, 127, 143, 144, 147, 150, 151, 152, 154, 155, 157, 158, 159, 161, 163, 164, 165, 166, 170, 172, 174, 223, 234, 235, 246
Pierce, James, 72, 79, 84, 90, 125, 132
Pierce, Wayne, 40, 50, 51, 52, 80, 82, 83, 110, 234, 383, 385, 387
Pittman, James, 126, 143, 172, 179, 194, 195, 200, 201, 202, 203, 208, 218, 231, 236, 237, 242, 248, 250

Pittsburg, Texas, 41, 44, 77, 88, 90, 131, 138, 153, 154, 157, 188, 200, 203, 204, 205, 226, 235, 240, 245, 256, 257, 271, 273, 297, 310, 331, 347, 348, 351, 353, 365, 366, 391, 398, 399, 404, 405, 408, 409
Plano, Texas, 40, 109, 110, 113, 335
Ply, Bobby, 10
Pope, Charles, 132
Pugh, Harry Jack, 40, 49, 52, 53, 56, 65, 72, 73, 84, 89, 90, 93, 94, 100, 102, 103, 104, 106, 108, 109, 113, 124, 126, 143, 147, 152, 159, 164, 165, 166, 170, 172, 174, 223, 267, 269

Quitman, Texas, 110, 112, 113, 177, 252, 256, 257, 260, 334, 407, 408, 414, 417

Radican, Billy R., 129, 130, 305
Ramsay, Landon, 220
Ramsay, Lucky, 268
Ramsey, Judd (Edgewood), 217, 218, 219, 312, 313, 314
Raney, Jauquita Lou, 343
Raney, Louie, 343
Redwine, Bill (Carey), 28, 129
Reed, Bunyon (Winfield), 211
Reeves, Weldon, 135
Rhodes, Kenneth (Mineola), 401
Rogers, Howard, 172, 179, 196, 200, 203, 208, 217, 269
Rollings, Leonard, 40, 110
Rollins, Coach Dough, 111, 327, 328
Rommel, General Erwin, 132
Roosevelt, Franklin D., 156, 179, 180, 181, 370
Roper, Quince, 98
Rouse, Billy, 392
Rouse, Dr., 220, 221, 223
Royal, Darrell, 9, 11
Royse City, Texas, 40
Rudder, James Earl, 135, 136
Russell, Coach Red (Pittsburg), 297
Rutherford Drug Store, 42, 43, 101, 125, 144, 210, 290, 330, 343, 359
Rutherford, G. W., 107, 124, 210, 219
Rutherford, Mrs. G. W., 107

Salters, Ed (Deport), 256, 259, 260
Saltillo, Texas, 65, 167, 175, 224, 234, 329, 348
Sanders (Mount Pleasant), 296

Santo Tomas, Philippines, 160
Schenider, Captain George, 167
Scott, Hal, 133
Scott, Loraine, 223
Scott, Pat, 223
Scovell, Field, 245
Seay, Allen, 188
Seay, Donald, 188
Seay, Edward, 188
Seay, James, 188
Seay, Jimmie, 188
Seay, L. E., 133
Self, Peggy, 180
Sheirman, Mildred, 271
Sheppard Air Base, 34, 36
Shields, A. J., 34
Shurtleff, Alton, 268, 390
Shurtleff, Charles, 49, 50, 53, 54, 55,
    57, 61, 62, 64, 66, 72, 73, 79, 84,
    89, 94, 103, 126, 143, 147, 150,
    151, 155, 159, 161, 163, 166, 172,
    174, 188, 189, 190
Sidney Lanier, San Antonio, 116, 118,
    177
Simms, Buster, 233, 326, 352, 374,
    378, 381, 393, 395, 406
Simons, Max, 392
Simons, Nix, 392
Sims, Coy, 172, 231, 236, 242, 250,
    268, 269
Sinclair, Benny (Mineola), 382, 401,
    402, 408, 413, 414
Sinclair, Elvie, 399
Sinton, Texas, 335, 337, 339, 341, 352
Skidmore, Gerald, 174, 251, 252, 253,
    254, 255, 256, 257, 258, 259, 260,
    261, 262, 263, 264, 273, 284, 285,
    326, 329, 330, 331, 334, 338, 342,
    344, 412
Slaughter, Glen, 233, 273, 326, 396,
    397, 399
Smith, Alfred, 96, 98
Smith, Dorothy Nell, 9, 86, 87, 98,
    100, 101, 102, 107, 108, 111, 112,
    125, 126, 128, 130, 133, 134, 138,
    139, 140, 141, 167, 168, 177, 210,
    211, 212, 220, 221, 222, 223, 224,
    228, 233, 234, 236, 245, 267, 272,
    309, 310, 341, 367, 368, 369, 371,
    390, 407, 417
Smith, Gertrude, 70
Smith, Herbie (A&M), 328
Smith, Ida, 24, 81, 96, 97, 98, 124
Smith, Jimmy, 11

Smith, Lester, 219, 233, 359
Smith, Minnie, 98
Smith, Morris, 97
Smith, Ronnie, 234, 245, 272, 326,
    367
Smith, Roy, 125, 219, 225, 233, 359
Smith, Russell, 211
Smith, Sam, 24, 25, 29, 30, 37, 38,
    80, 81, 96, 97, 98, 99, 112
Smith, Vernon (Georgia), 26
Snell, Dan, 212, 213
South, Loyd, 185
Southern Methodist University, 28, 40,
    86, 174, 266, 322, 343, 407
Soward (Mt. Pleasant), 292, 294
Sowell, Jim, 88
Sparks, Deryl Jean, 271
Speaker, Tris, 9
St. Clair, Irene, 69, 70, 71, 72, 389
Stalin, Joseph, 181, 332
Stanley, Mrs. Essie, 393
Stanley, Ronnie, 10
Steed, Milton, 183
Stevenson, Coke, 359
Stiles, Jess (Clarksville), 284, 285, 318
Stingaree Play, 305, 322, 362
Stinson, Billy, 94, 172, 192, 193, 236
Stinson, Frank, 30
Stinson, Jim Mac, 286
Stone, Chief Justice, 227
Streicher, Julius, 227
Stretcher, Charles, 268, 297, 326,
    353, 365, 375, 381, 392
Strickland, Bobbie, 330
Stringer, Bernard, 417
Stringer, Mary Lou, 70
Stroman, C. L., 232, 237, 240, 242
Suggs, Bob, 56, 61, 81, 83, 84, 88, 89,
    90, 91, 94, 96, 98, 102, 116, 117,
    153, 154, 172, 245
Sulphur Springs, Texas, 131, 138,
    145, 168, 169, 170, 175, 187, 195,
    234, 235, 249, 272, 313, 319, 329,
    331, 333, 384, 385, 387

Talco, Texas, 44, 93, 94, 107, 131,
    138, 143, 153, 161, 175, 188, 200,
    208, 209, 213, 227, 235, 240, 242,
    243, 247, 248, 254, 259, 273, 289,
    291, 297, 298, 301, 302, 304, 305,
    306, 307, 310, 318, 325, 329, 331,
    347, 348, 351, 363, 381, 384, 408,
    410
Taylor, C. S. (Winfield), 211

Taylor, Dr. (Winfield), 211
Taylor, G. A. (Winfield), 211
Teague, Charles, 219, 220, 230
Teague, Grady, 219
Teague, Hiram, 219, 230, 247
Teague, Lonnie, 142
Tell, Texas, 27
Terrell, Texas, 251
Tetter, R. A. (Winfield), 211
Texarkana, Texas, 353, 359, 360, 361
Texas City, Texas, 335, 337, 339, 387
Texas A&M University, 51, 135, 166, 188, 327
Texas Christian University, 138, 188, 323, 343, 352, 412
Texas Coaches School, 188, 272, 351, 390
Texas Tech University, 138, 330
T-formation, 45, 50, 51, 52, 63, 66, 127, 144, 155, 179, 293, 297, 340, 358, 365, 388
The Tiger's Tale, 260, 344, 412
Thomas, Tobe (Winfield), 211
Thompson, Duncan, 216
Throckmorton, Texas, 113, 114, 115, 116, 117, 335, 337, 338, 339, 341
Tibbets, Jr., Colonel Paul, 189
Tibbs, Joe Grady, 398, 413
Tinsley, Bea, 269
Tinsley, Gayle, 126, 143, 155, 172, 205, 222, 234, 249, 268, 269, 270, 278, 279, 282, 283, 284, 286, 287, 288, 292, 293, 295, 296, 302, 303, 311, 314, 316, 318, 321, 326, 342, 344, 345, 346, 351
Tinsley, Pep, 269, 270
Tinsley, Tommy, 269
Tittle, Leacho, 143, 145, 171, 172, 179, 193, 201, 202, 206, 208, 218, 222, 231, 269
Tojo, Hideki, 101, 134, 142
Trull, Don, 10
Truman, Harry S., 180, 190, 191, 227, 343, 359, 370, 371, 372
Tucker, Jinx, 8
Tully, Coach Darrell (ET), 383, 417
Turner, Eddie, 233, 396, 415
Tyler Yannigans, 187, 188, 191, 193, 194

Ultra Secret, 182
University of Texas, 9, 138, 341, 352, 388, 406, 412

Van, Texas, 165, 166, 168, 169, 260, 264, 265
Vaughn, Joe L., 145
Vinzant, Coach (ET), 110
Vogle, Vance (Winnsboro), 201

Wade, Harless, 417
Wagstaff, Coach (Tyler), 267
Walker, Stanley, 264
Wallace, Coach Jewel (San Angelo), 139
Watson, Ann, 75
Welch, I. J., 247
Whitley Gym, 109, 414, 415, 416
Whitley, Dr. S. H., 70, 71
Whitt, Doyle, 30
Whitt, Reverend John, 97, 98, 125, 221, 223, 370
Whitten, Charles (Blossom), 417
Wichita Falls, Texas, 138, 139, 188
Wichita Henrys, 22, 37
Wilhite, Rev. C. S., 363
Williams, Clarence, 41
Williams, Reverend S. M., 128
Willis, Coach (New London), 378
Wims, George, 172, 268, 297, 326, 344
Winfield, Texas, 24, 28, 30, 33, 36, 42, 44, 70, 80, 96, 97, 106, 155, 178, 211, 223, 253, 255, 267, 328
Winnsboro, Texas, 44, 55, 80, 81, 82, 84, 105, 106, 108, 131, 138, 147, 149, 150, 175, 188, 199, 200, 201, 235, 237, 238, 240, 242, 243, 247, 248, 249, 250, 251, 254, 258, 271, 273, 277, 278, 279, 288, 289, 290, 291, 293, 302, 305, 307, 329, 331, 332, 333, 347, 348, 349, 351, 353, 356, 361, 362, 363, 371, 382, 384, 385, 386, 391, 397, 398, 408, 413, 414
Woodruff, Coach Jack (East Mountain), 334, 339, 340
Worley Hospital, 33
Wright, Jack (Commerce), 169, 170, 171
Wright, W. C., 377

Yamashita, General Tomoyuki, 226
Yantis Owls, 253
Yantis, Texas, 252, 253, 255

Yates, Donald, 233, 273, 326, 353, 356, 358, 362, 365, 378, 392, 393, 394, 395, 396, 397, 399, 400, 402, 403, 404, 406, 407, 409, 413, 417
Yocum, Jerry, 50, 52, 53, 54, 55, 56, 61, 66, 72, 78, 79, 89, 90, 92, 126, 143, 147, 155, 166, 172

Zercher, Kemper, 69, 70, 71
Zimmerman, Bob, 186, 187
Zimmerman, H. B., 114, 115, 186, 189, 230, 388
Zimmerman, Herb, 114, 178, 179, 185, 191, 196, 199, 200, 207, 218, 230, 231, 236, 237, 242, 243, 244, 245, 249, 250, 251, 253, 254, 255, 256, 260, 267, 268, 269, 270, 273, 278, 279, 280, 281, 282, 283, 284, 285, 288, 290, 291, 292, 293, 294, 295, 299, 302, 306, 310, 311, 313, 315, 316, 317, 318, 320, 322, 324, 326, 328, 329, 330, 331, 333, 334, 335, 341, 343, 347, 348, 349, 350, 352, 388, 412

Printed in the United States
20287LVS00001B/100-117